DISCARD

SISTERS
OF THE
LOST
NATION

SISTERS
OF THE
LOST
NATION

NICK MEDINA

BERKLEY

NEW YORK

BERKLEY
An imprint of Penguin Random House LLC
penguinrandomhouse.com

Copyright © 2023 by Nicholas Medina
Penguin Random House supports copyright. Copyright fuels creativity, encourages diverse voices,
promotes free speech, and creates a vibrant culture. Thank you for buying an authorized edition
of this book and for complying with copyright laws by not reproducing, scanning, or distributing
any part of it in any form without permission. You are supporting writers and allowing
Penguin Random House to continue to publish books for every reader.

BERKLEY and the BERKLEY & B colophon are registered trademarks of
Penguin Random House LLC.

Library of Congress Cataloging-in-Publication Data

Names: Medina, Nick, author.
Title: Sisters of the lost nation / Nick Medina.
Description: New York : Berkley, [2023]
Identifiers: LCCN 2022031860 (print) | LCCN 2022031861 (ebook) |
ISBN 9780593546857 (hardcover) | ISBN 9780593546871 (ebook)
Subjects: LCGFT: Thrillers (Fiction) | Novels.
Classification: LCC PS3613.E314 S57 2023 (print) | LCC PS3613.E314 (ebook) |
DDC 813/.6—dc23/eng/20220811
LC record available at https://lccn.loc.gov/2022031860
LC ebook record available at https://lccn.loc.gov/2022031861

Printed in the United States of America
1st Printing

Book design by Nancy Resnick

To
Nan
&
Gram

Content Warning

Sisters of the Lost Nation includes content that addresses issues of addiction, drug abuse, murder and death (off-page), physical assault and battery, sex trafficking (off-page), sexual abuse of a minor (off-page), self-harm, and racism. Please read with your well-being and best interest in mind.

SISTERS
OF THE
LOST
NATION

PROLOGUE

"Do you hear that?" her uncle whispered.

"Hear what?" she said, refraining from taking a big bite of the caramel apple she'd made.

"The rustling. Over there. In the bushes."

Her ears strained. The fire burning in the pit between their lawn chairs popped, sending up orange embers that failed to alleviate the encompassing darkness. She shook her head and lifted the apple to the corner of her mouth where she still had teeth capable of piercing the hard flesh; adult incisors had yet to fill the holes in her smile.

"Listen," he hissed, once more stopping her from taking a bite.

"I don't hear any—" The rustle of leaves sounded from far off in the yard, back where the manicured lawn merged with the untamed field that bordered the house. "Is someone there?" she asked, tongue lisping against her gums.

"Not someone . . . not really." Her uncle's spindly body shifted, making his leather jacket—black as the night, his feathered hair, and the shiny motorcycle he'd rode in on—creak.

She questioned him with her eyes.

"I shouldn't tell you," he said.

"Tell me what?"

Twinkling in the orange and yellow light, his eyes, usually brown and warm, looked black now too. "About what I found at work a few months ago," he said.

She grew silent, thinking about where her uncle worked. The cemetery. "What'd you find?"

"Do you really wanna know?" he asked, pulling on the scraggly beard he'd barely been able to grow.

She nodded. She guessed so.

He slowly leaned forward in his chair.

"I found three unearthed graves," he said. "Someone dug them up."

The wind blew, making the fire thrash.

"Why would someone do that?"

"I don't know, but it wasn't very smart." He poked the fire with a stick, casting more embers into the autumn air. "A man, a woman, and Hilaire Broussard—the last official chief of our tribe, our nation— were the three dug up. . . . Do you know what becomes of a body after it's spent years in the ground?"

She didn't gamble a guess, she just looked toward the house, wishing her parents would come back out. It'd taken them both to wrangle her tantrum-throwing three-year-old brother to bed.

"The bodies turn to bone," he said. "Skeletons. They still look like bodies, only without all the skin." The flames cast shadows that leapt about his face. "That's what I expected to see when I looked into the open graves," he said, "skeletons that resembled bodies, a bone for every head, arm, leg, finger, and tiny toe."

She cast an uncertain gaze at the ground where her little sister sat atop a sleeping bag, legs crisscross applesauce, oblivious to everything their uncle was saying. Her busy tongue licked the caramel from the fruit she wouldn't eat. It was past her bedtime, but she'd stay up as long as Mom and Dad were busy with their brother; only five, she already knew how to go unnoticed.

"Bones were missing," their uncle carried on. "Taken."

The older girl redirected her gaze from her little sister to her uncle, who showed no sign of jest.

"The woman's fingers were gone," he said. "Her toes too . . . every

2

little piggy. And the two big bones from her left arm, below the elbow. The man's skeleton didn't look like it was missing anything at all, but someone—*something*—had gnawed on his ribs. There were gashes in the bones. And the chief"—he looked her dead in the eyes—"was without a head."

She jumped in her seat, causing a glob of warm caramel to drip onto her dress. She wiped it with her free hand, smearing it, getting her fingers sticky.

"The skull was gone, but it wasn't taken. It, as a matter of fact, took something itself."

She pulled at the braid hanging along the left side of her face, getting caramel in her hair. "What'd it take?" she asked, wondering how it could take anything at all.

He leaned closer to the fire, inches from the flames.

"A life. More than one. The spirit of a chief, you see, is a powerful thing. The skull became a head again when it was lifted from the grave . . . resurrected."

"Resurrected?" she echoed.

"Alive again," he said, his voice measured and grievously low, prolonging every word. "But not like it was before. Not like the old chief. It's angry now that it's been ripped from its rest. And ravenous. Hungry for revenge. It'll eat anyone it encounters. It'll tear flesh from bone."

"How?" she said.

"It rolls, gathering mud and moss on its decaying flesh."

The wind blew again, chillier than before.

"But how do you know what it eats?"

"Because it devoured the person who dug it up." His expression morphed from serious to sad. "And I'm pretty sure it ate Miss Shelby, too."

A lump formed in her throat when she thought about Miss Shelby, the only adult she'd ever considered a friend. Miss Shelby had gone missing that summer, followed by whispers that she wasn't coming back. The girl's eyes prodded her uncle for more even though she wasn't sure she wanted to hear it.

"There were footprints in the mud leading *to* the chief's grave, but none leading away."

She pondered what that meant, not hearing everything he said. "You swear?" she asked.

"The head is out there and it's hungrier than ever," he went on whispering, nodding. He looked to his left, to his right, behind his back. "Spine-chilling is what it is. If you see it, you'll know what I mean."

"Have you?"

He nodded slowly. "Remember when we went fishing in June?"

"Yes," she squeaked.

"And you remember what the fish looked like when we reeled them in from the water?"

She recalled the catfish her father and uncle had caught for supper. She'd watched with curiosity, which had quickly turned to sadness, then dismay as the fish gills gradually stopped gasping at the bottom of the catch bucket, loaded with ice.

"The head has the same eyes as the fish, beady and unblinking, only they're cloudy and flat, sunken deep into its skull. Its hair grows wild, tangled with beetles, twigs, and burs, and it trails the head like a tail. The flesh itself is rotten and foul, dead as the Heaven and Hell tree, once the tallest old oak on the reservation—its branches stretching for the stars, its roots reaching for the abyss below—and as ragged around its missing neck as the hem of my jeans." The chain he wore on his wallet rattled as he lifted a foot over the fire, showing off the frayed cuff of his pant leg, streaked with mud. "The mouth"—he paused, clenching his jaw to steel himself—"that's the worst part of it. It can stretch as wide as it wants . . . wide enough to suck you between its wormy lips." She thought of the catfish again, their mouths gaping and wide, flanked by whiskers that had curled and turned black after her father had hacked off the fish heads and tossed them into the fire he'd stoked to cook the fish fillets. "It's got a tongue of old leather and teeth like shattered glass, jagged and sharp. If it sees you, it'll roll after you, which means you'd better run. And fast! Just one nibble on the back of your heel means you'll never escape."

"Never?" Her voice barely made it over the crackle of the fire. She thought of Miss Shelby again. Gone forever. "Can't it be stopped?"

He shrugged. "Can't kill something that's already dead. I don't have any idea how to stop it. All I know is it's a good thing you're not out here alone."

She suddenly had to pee but didn't want to walk the fifty feet from the firepit to the back door. Never had home seemed so far away. Never had she been so afraid in the dark.

The leaves rustled in the yard again, closer than before.

"Better not let it get you," he said.

She sprang up from her seat and grabbed her little sister by the arm, dragging her to safety. The caramel apple she'd been so eager to eat fell to the ground, a gift to the ants. Abandoned, it rolled through the grass, picking up dirt and bits of black ash.

PART I

Day 36
7:21 p.m.
70 Hours Gone

Guided by fear and the muted moonlight, Anna stepped toward the trees, and then she was passing through them, leaving her old reality behind for the one unraveling before her. Black bark to her sides and ash beneath her feet, she smelled the earthy odors of dirt, mud, burnt wood, and something so vile her stomach turned. It was the same smell the wind had wafted her way on the nights she'd been chased. Only the odor was stronger now. Inescapable.

Anna's lowered gaze slowly passed over the ground to the brush surrounding her. The tall grass bore brown-red stains, streaked from the rain. The bushes did too.

Her little brother's voice sounded in the distance, moving farther away. It faded until it was gone, reinforcing that Anna was alone. And though she didn't feel safe pressing forth, she knew she wouldn't feel any better if she turned back.

She couldn't. Not until she knew.

Eyes closed, she coaxed her legs to carry her deeper into the field. The few steps they took might as well have been arduous miles. Reluctant as her legs had been, her eyelids were far more inflexible.

When Anna eventually lifted them again, her eyes were like strangers to the darkness, unable to make sense of what was before them, but maybe they just didn't want to. A moment passed and then the horror set in.

Distressing sounds floated toward Anna from a few feet away. A lifeless eye observed her. A dead girl lay rotting on the ground.

Day 1
4:18 p.m.

Her classmates had bowed before her in the cafeteria, shouting, *All hail the king!*

"King" was marginally kinder than the assumptive and vile labels Anna was used to, but the smirks on her classmates' faces had stripped it of any majesty the title might have possessed. Anna had wanted to say something biting in return, but she knew an ireful "fuck off" wouldn't slay them all, so she clenched her cinnamon gum between her teeth and said nothing instead, which was precisely what they wanted. For her to shut up and take it so they could laugh and laugh.

She dragged her feet through the dirt after the dismissal bell and told herself not to think about it. Or them. They weren't worth it. Eight months stood between her and commencement day, after which she'd never have to see her bullies again. Maybe then she wouldn't be so silent.

The steady beep of a reversing truck and the grumble of heavy machinery carried on the air from across the Takoda Indian Reservation. The noxious scent of hot asphalt came with it. The road beneath Anna's feet was hard-packed dirt, but it wouldn't be for long. A construction crew contracted by the Takoda Tribe, to which Anna belonged, had

11

begun paving over the reservation's dirt roads a month earlier. Soon the reservation would be linked by smooth, black streets like the ones in town, and gone would be the days when shoes got covered in dust from trampling over uneven dirt roads. It was just one more change made possible by the Grand Nacre Casino and Resort on the rez, which had triumphantly opened its doors two years earlier.

Anna stalled where the dirt road met one of the black streets. She recognized the need for change and the pride that came with being able to afford it, but the dark-green-and-purple smear on the asphalt ahead gave her pause. It was the second such smear she'd seen that week; the thirteenth since the construction crew started paving the dirt roads. There'd been plenty of roadkill—opossums, raccoons, armadillos—over the years, but never had there been so many small purple smears.

It wasn't just the asphalt's fault. The cooling weather, as summer turned to fall, drove frogs to search for spots where they could keep their little bodies warm. The black streets retained heat after the sun set far better than the dirt roads ever had.

The purple smear grew as Anna approached until it was wider than the bottom of her boot. It was the largest casualty yet, a bullfrog easily a pound and a half in size. Hind legs and webbed feet jutted out from the smear, indicating that the poor thing had been run down mid-hop. Anna's insides quivered at the sight—sick and sad, though she knew those very legs would be deemed good eatin' if they were battered and fried in any kitchen throughout the state, from Shreveport down to New Orleans. This king of frogs had thrived and survived through the most dangerous stages of its life—egg, tadpole, young adult—escaping threats posed by insects, fish, crayfish, birds, snakes, raccoons, and the froggers who hunted in the bayous and swamps. It'd beaten the odds over and over, only to end up as a wasted smear. Had it hopped a few inches to the left or a few to the right, it would still be the king of frogs, but by some twist of fate, it'd aligned itself for death.

Anna raised her gaze as an old car slowed and swerved around her. It rattled away through the trees on the far east side of the reservation where few went and even fewer resided. She could see her destination in the distance, set within an overgrown field that encompassed it and its lone neighbor nearly a football field away. She carried forth to the mouth of the dirt driveway that led to the abandoned trailer. Despite having been inside a dozen times or more, the sight of it made her feel like she'd just swallowed something slippery and swampy, something like the dead frog, especially when the sun was sinking. Her stomach churned. She always took a deep breath before running down the drive and up the trailer's rickety steps. And she always looked over both shoulders before going inside.

The door was gone. The trailer was dim. Just over ten years had passed since electricity powered the lamps. It was, in fact, ten years to the day that Anna had sat across the fire from her uncle, listening with horror and fascination as he voiced his theory about what might have happened to the trailer's owner. A sick anniversary only Anna bothered to remember.

Ten years to the day since her fear had been born.

Failing sunlight filtered through the filthy windows and disheveled blinds, casting a dull brown glow on the deflated couch. Anna never sat on it. Never would. She only came for the books. Two large bookcases lined the far wall, each loaded with a collection that had taken the trailer's owner a lifetime to amass. Anna had only begun browsing the collection a few months earlier, back in July after Erica Landry and Amber Bloom—best friends, both nineteen—had vanished into thin air, leaving their families wondering and worrying on the rez. She hadn't been daring enough to enter the trailer before then. The sensation of eyes upon her put her on edge within the trailer's walls, making her suspect that she'd be punished if she got caught. But the books and the wisdom they held, wisdom that might just make her feel safer at night, were worth the risk. The books were everything.

Anna lowered the bag from her back and unzipped it. She pulled three moldy books from within and reinserted them on the top shelf of the bookcase from which they came, proceeding to grab the next three in line, each equally moldy and topped with a layer of dust that turned into a sticky paste when she tried to brush it away. Anna crammed the books into her bag, zipped it, and headed back to the doorway to return to the road where she could pretend she hadn't invaded the trailer at all. A flash of movement through the window made her pause. She squinted through the filth, then jumped back, startled, when a ladybug fluttered past her face and crash-landed against her chest. Its translucent wings folded beneath its red-and-black shell as Anna ushered the bug onto her palm, wondering what made such small insects so bold.

The movement outside the window continued, and Anna realized it was only a cloud passing over the trailer, casting a shadow that crawled across the windowpane. When her gaze moved up, she saw herself reflected in the dirtiest part of the glass. The rusted metal of the window frame created the illusion of a ragged crown upon her head.

She hadn't done anything wrong in the cafeteria earlier, yet it was she who ended up feeling sorry. And it was her whom Principal Markham had called to his office, where she sat across from the balding man, staring into his expectant eyes, refusing to say anything more than, *They did this.*

Anna slung the backpack onto her shoulders and stepped away from the window and the rusted crown. Outside, she blew the ladybug from her palm and dashed down the dirt drive to the slick, new street. The purple smear added to the slimy sensation in her stomach. She stepped over it, coaxing her eyes to remain on the horizon, but the memory of what she'd seen when she inspected the smear earlier brought her to a stop. The frog had certainly been run over, but Anna couldn't recall seeing tread marks stamped into the remains. She only assumed a tire had done the damage because the frog was in the road.

Reluctantly turning, she bent to inspect the former king of frogs once more. No marks. Something other than a tire had apparently squashed it. Something softer. Something smoother. Anna shivered. She tried to cast the thought aside, but suppressing it wasn't any easier than casting aside the incident at school.

All hail the king!

Her eyes darted back toward the condemned trailer, seeking a place to hide.

"Shit," she said, when she spotted something dark and round, slightly larger than a bowling ball, shifting from side to side beneath the trailer's rotting steps. It was the very thing she feared, the very thing that must have flattened the frog, the thing that might have made Amber and Erica disappear.

Anna turned toward home, only for her head to reel around on her neck. The round form was gone from beneath the trailer's steps. Vanished. Her flesh prickled as though swarmed by biting mites. Something moved in the overgrown grass along the edge of the dirt drive. The tall brown blades shimmied. Whatever had slipped inside the undergrowth was moving in her direction, picking up speed the closer it got.

Anna gasped and ran. The books in her bag thumped against her back all the way home.

Day 1
5:04 p.m.

The house shook from the force of the slammed door. Grace, upside down on the sofa, one foot over the headrest and her head hanging over the edge of the middle cushion, stopped babbling into the phone and moved the receiver from her ear.

"Saw it again?" she said, and smiled at her big sister in a way that some might have found mocking, but which Anna interpreted more affectionately, as though the smile were part of an inside joke they'd shared for years.

"It was a raccoon," Anna said, panting, trying to believe her own words instead of the nagging doubt at the back of her mind telling her that what she'd seen was much more human than that.

"You only come home this sweaty when you think you've seen it."

"It was a raccoon," Anna insisted. "Maybe an armadillo."

Grace flicked her eyebrows and went back to babbling into the phone, speaking in a dialect of breakneck gibberish called "Idig." Anna knew how the language worked. The infix "idig" was inserted at certain points within each word to disguise it. "Ball" became "bidigall." "What" became "whidigat." "Hello" became "hidigellidigo." Grace and her best friend, Emily, had become fluent in the ridiculous language. Anna could interpret a word or two when she listened hard, but she wasn't quick enough to completely decode her sister's conversations. Their parents were even worse. They hadn't a clue what Grace was saying.

Grace had started speaking "Idig" a year before Anna first entered the condemned trailer. Anna loathed the sound of the cumbrous language. Partly because Grace chose to share it with Emily instead of her, and partly because it was so fake. It turned Grace into something fake as well, eliciting phony expressions, gestures, and laughs.

More upsetting was that Grace had started sneaking out through their shared bedroom window, coming and going through the night, sometimes staying out until dawn, never telling Anna where she was going or when she'd return. And Anna, hoping to win Grace back, never snitched, despite knowing deep down that she should.

"Dinner in ten. Grace, hang up the phone. Anna, check on your grandmother," Dorothy, Anna's mother, said from the stove.

Anna tossed her bookbag onto her bed. She could hear her father making a racket in the yard, the thin walls no match against his resonant voice. Her brother, Robbie, was out there with him, aiming at things in the trees.

Anna pushed aside the old bedsheet tacked up in the entryway between the former dining room and the kitchen where her mother was spooning Hamburger Helper onto plates. "Everything all right?" she asked.

Grandma Joan's eyes snapped open, and her head sprang forward. A glistening tongue slid over dry lips as bony shoulders hitched up to earlobes. "I fell asleep again. Don't even know what time it is," she said, her voice ragged in her throat.

Anna let the sheet fall behind her, thinly closing off the former dining room, cramped with a bed, an armchair, a small table, a slew of boxes, and a wheelchair in the corner. "You closed them again?" Though the day would only remain lit for a little longer, Anna moved the curtains aside to welcome a bit of life into the drab room.

"What's it matter?" Gran said. Her words, slow and slurred, leaked through the gap between her lips on the right side of her mouth, which drooped a half inch lower than the left side. Anna was almost used to her grandmother's new way of speech, but though it'd been six months since the stroke, she still wasn't used to that saggy piece of lip. Sometimes the droop made her angry. Sometimes she was just glad Gran could still speak.

"Sunlight helps you feel better," Anna said.

"Did you read that?"

"It's a fact." Anna swept bread crumbs from the table next to Gran's chair, then dropped onto the edge of the bed just a foot away. "Good day or bad?" she asked.

"Hard to tell anymore. How was school?"

Anna sighed. "Eight more months."

The left side of Gran's mouth curled up in a show of support. Her left hand, wavering, reached for the top of Anna's head while the right one, marginally withered, remained still atop the armrest. Anna lowered her head. Gran's hand absently brushed through Anna's hair as it had so many times when Anna was small. Knotty knuckles and crooked fingers swept well below Anna's shoulders, like always before, only now Anna's hair ended at her ears, not the small of her back. Still, Gran's hand brushed through the air in search of the braids that once hung there.

The clang of a spoon against a bowl pulled Anna from the trance of her grandmother's touch. She rose from the bed and pushed the wheelchair from the corner. Gran refused to get in it. She grabbed the chair's handles and limped on imbalanced legs instead. Anna swept the curtain aside, following Gran to the living room where the dining table now obstructed part of the TV screen.

Dorothy brought plates to the table. Anna helped Gran get seated. Grace righted herself on the couch, persistently jabbering into the phone, twirling its cord around her finger.

"Robbie!" Dorothy called over her shoulder toward the backyard. "Go get your father," she said to Anna.

Anna raised the window in the kitchen that looked out onto the yard. Her father, hands on his hips, stood watching Robbie strike various shooting stances. "Dinner," Anna said. Her father waved in her direction. His eyes stayed on Robbie.

Anna returned to the table. Dorothy banged her spoon against the bowl again. Grace's eyes rolled to the back of her head. She said something like "lidigatidiger" and hung up the phone.

"Joan?" Dorothy said, holding up a pitcher of sweet tea. Gran motioned for her to pour.

The screen door slammed. Chris's booming voice flooded the house. "Just listen to me and you'll be knocking them from the trees. Bam! Bam! Bam! Whooiee, boy, you'll be the next Davy Crockett!" He took his usual seat at the table and said, "I'm thirsty," his tone implying that his glass should already be full.

Dorothy set the pitcher down on her side of the table. Anna picked it up and held it out to her father, now drinking from the glass Dorothy had filled for Robbie. Robbie stood in the space between the kitchen and the living room. The muzzle of the rifle swung from side to side as he aimed it at a window, a picture on the wall, the front door.

"Put that thing down." Dorothy slapped a palm against the table. Chris laughed. Robbie slung the rifle across his back and hopped into his seat. A dirt-streaked hand burrowed into the bread bag and pulled out a slice.

"I'd appreciate it if you'd leave the gun outside," Dorothy said.

"Mom," Robbie whined, bread thick on his tongue. He pegged her with his pleading brown eyes and sucked his bottom lip between his teeth. Anna knew he'd get his way. He was the youngest, the only boy, and the prettiest of the Horn children. Anna couldn't care less that her baby brother's features were more appealing than hers, but Grace openly groused about how unfair it was that Robbie had longer

19

eyelashes, higher cheekbones, and fuller lips. She said it wasn't right for a sister to be uglier than her brother. It was obvious to Anna that Grace was just glad she wasn't the ugliest of the three.

A mix of steamed broccoli and cauliflower landed in a heap on Chris's plate. "Oof," he said, passing the spoon. "Smells worse than when we found George Saucier."

"Chris," Dorothy said, tone flat, eyes narrow.

"It's true. I'm not making it up. He was dead a whole week before someone found him." Anna's father tended to the dead on the reservation. Tight-lipped and respectful on the job, he amused himself by spilling the gory details at home. "Your broccoli smells like George Saucier."

"Eeewww," Grace said. She skipped the veggies and took a sniff of the strawberry lip balm she'd just smeared across her lips.

"Oh," Chris said, swallowing a mouthful of ground beef and cheese, "I talked to Eaton this morning." Chairman Eaton Ballard had been elected to lead the tribe after the previous chairman, Joseph Broussard, had died two years earlier. "Said he and the tribal council will hear you out at the next monthly meeting, Anna. They hold them on Wednesday mornings, so you'll have to miss some school, but it'll be worth it."

Anna's fork clanged against her plate. "I told you not to."

"Just give it a try. You're onto something."

"I'm not onto anything."

"You have an idea. You want to waste it?"

"No one's going to care," she said. "Everyone who goes to those meetings just wants to know how the tribe can make more money. I wouldn't know what to say."

"You tell them what you told me. About the stories. And the past."

"It's all about the future now. No one cares about the past."

"Our future is our past," Gran said.

"I don't want to do it."

"Too bad," Chris pressed. "I already told Eaton you'll be there. The meeting's at the end of the month. Plenty of time to get a plan together. That's all they want. To hear that you have a vision. No one expects you to know how to do everything on your own. You think anyone else knows what they're doing around here? The bottom line is that you have a good idea, and when there's a good idea, things get done."

Anna scraped her fork against her plate, creating three parallel paths through the Hamburger Helper. She regretted telling her father about the idea she'd had. It wasn't even an idea, really. It had started as a question.

Why doesn't the tribe have a preservation society? she'd asked, thinking a dedicated space for the tribe's old stories and artifacts would help future generations appreciate the tribe's unique history. Not to mention that she wouldn't have to creep into Miss Shelby's run-down trailer if there was somewhere official she could go. She hadn't expected her father to be so inspired by the question. The more she thought about it, the more trivial it seemed. A preservation society? Who'd give a shit about that? As far as she could tell, only she cared about Miss Shelby's old books and the history they held. She used to hear the tribal tales as a child, listening with undivided attention as Miss Shelby Mire, the last of the Takoda Tribe's official singers and Legend Keepers, passionately brought them to life. Miss Shelby always told the stories; she never read or recited them. They came from her mouth as effortlessly as the breath she exhaled. But Miss Shelby had disappeared ten years ago, when Anna was seven, a mystery that morphed into a murder so upsetting that hardly anyone spoke of it anymore for fear of keeping the horror alive. The stories stopped then, their remnants—a significant piece of the tribe's past—left to rot on Miss Shelby's shelves in her abandoned home.

"I don't want to speak at the meeting. I can't."

Chris grumbled, mouth full.

"Is everything all right, Anna?" Dorothy asked.

"Anna got voted to homecoming court at school," Grace blurted.

"Shut up," Anna said beneath her breath.

"That's great," Dorothy said, not really hearing. Her eyes twinkled with imagined confetti, a sparkling tiara, and endless flowers as she fantasized about a dream that couldn't come true for a girl like her when she'd been Anna's age. If she didn't love her daughter so much, she would have realized that Anna couldn't possibly be homecoming queen either.

"What is she, the court jester?" Robbie, more realistic than his mother, said.

Anna kicked him under the table.

"The girl who says she has no friends," Chris said in between licking cheese from his thumb.

"She was voted *king*," Grace revealed.

Anna's chest deflated like a burst balloon. She sneered at Grace's grin, teasing and toothy. Combined with the words still ringing in her ears—*All hail the king!*—the grin suggested that Grace wanted to humiliate her too.

"King?" Chris questioned.

"It was just a joke," Anna said, reluctant to acknowledge that it was much more than that.

"The entire senior class wrote Anna's name on the nomination ballot for homecoming king," Grace explained. "Normally the results wouldn't be announced until the pre–homecoming game pep rally on Friday, but Megan Bradley, who's head of student council, made the announcement today at lunch because she couldn't believe what had happened. She said there'd have to be a revote."

Megan Bradley had acted outraged when she made the announcement, condemning her classmates for the prank, but Anna suspected Megan wasn't as innocent as she made herself out to be. There'd been too many tells on her face: her brow had furrowed just a little too low, her lips couldn't keep a frown, her blue eyes had twinkled as if she'd just unwrapped a birthstone pendant on her birthday, the most important day of the year.

"That's awful, Anna. I'm sorry they did that to you," Dorothy said. The fantasy faded from her eyes.

"King?" Chris said again. "What the hell's wrong with them?"

"It's what they do," Anna muttered. She wanted to get away from the table as desperately as she'd wanted to flee from the cafeteria and Principal Markham's office when he'd called her in to explain what had happened, as though she had orchestrated the entire incident.

"And Megan?" Chris said. "You think she played a part in it?"

Anna shrugged. She nearly stabbed her plate with her fork.

"What's Megan's story?" Chris carried on. "She hasn't been around in a while."

"Like, forever," Grace said.

Anna gritted her teeth. "Megan Bradley's a bitch."

"Whoa!" Robbie laughed.

Dorothy huffed but didn't object to Anna's language. How could she after what Anna had been through? Gran's droopy lip twitched.

"What goes around, comes around. Remember that, Anna." Chris sighed. "If you want me to—"

"It's fine," Anna snapped. "Everything's fine." She didn't want to talk about it. She just wanted to see what stories she could find in the latest books she'd pulled from Miss Shelby's shelves.

"Fuck them all," Grace said. "Right, Anna?"

"Yeah," Anna agreed. The declaration restored some of her faith in Grace. Maybe they weren't as distant as she'd thought. "Fuck them all."

"*Whoa!*" Robbie hollered louder than before.

The plates rattled from Dorothy's palm hammering the tabletop.

"Anna," Chris said, a smile pulling at the corners of his lips. "Dinner language."

"Grace said it first."

Grace shrugged, knowing she could probably get away with saying it again.

"Things will get better," Dorothy promised.

"Things are better than they were," Gran said.

"*Screw* them," Grace went on. "You know what I think, Anna? You should claim your crown."

Anna dropped her fork into the mess on her plate. Sauce splattered the tabletop. "I'm done."

"You barely touched your food," Chris said.

"Speaking of homecoming. Can I get the dress?" Grace asked, turning to Chris.

"What dress?" he said.

"The one I've been asking about for weeks." Her eyes widened with disbelief. "The dance is Saturday."

"Didn't I buy you a dress last year?"

"I can't wear the same dress I wore to last year's homecoming. I already told you that."

"You only wore it once."

Grace groaned. "Fine. But if you won't get me a new dress, you can get me a cell phone. I don't have one yet."

"Forget the cell phone," Chris said. "You're not getting one."

Grace groaned again and pounded her fists against the table. "You're so unfair."

"I'm not spending hundreds of dollars on something you don't need."

"Mom?" Grace protested.

"It's a lot of money," Dorothy said.

"Of course," Grace huffed. "The one thing you two agree on."

"Watch it," Chris said.

"It's not about the money, and you know it. You could buy me the phone if you wanted to. The checks just came in the mail."

Tribal members eighteen years old and up had started receiving monthly per capita payments shortly after the casino opened in 1994. In just two years, the money had turned things around on the rez. Suddenly there were shiny cars parked where rusty ones used to sit on blocks in wait of repair; air conditioners hung from windows that used to be wide open in hopes of a breeze; satellite dishes sat atop mended roofs; designer names like Polo, Guess, and Ralph Lauren appeared on waistbands, tags, and lapels; and—in the ultimate sign of mid-1990s wealth—some cut the cord and made their calls from cell phones. With a grand dropped into their mailboxes each month, it felt like the sky had started to rain gold.

"When you turn eighteen—"

"Three years!" Grace shrieked. "Everyone will have a cell phone by then."

"You don't need it," Chris said.

"Robbie didn't *need* a gun, but you bought him one anyway."

"It's almost squirrel season!" Robbie said.

"You've never shot a squirrel in your life."

"That's because I didn't have a rifle."

"Fine," Grace said to her father. "I wanna shoot a squirrel too. Buy me a gun."

"The rifle's mine," Chris said. "I bought it for myself. Robbie's just using it."

"What?" Robbie's face fell. He hugged the rifle to his chest. "You told me—"

"See!" Grace said.

Chris pointed to the new couch, then the sparkling white oven, the refrigerator, and the newly installed dishwasher, which had required additional plumbing in the kitchen. "Are you forgetting about all this? I'm not made of money."

Grace slumped in her chair. "Maybe I'll just run away like Erica and Amber," she muttered.

"Off to L.A., are you?" Chris said with a smirk. Though no one had been able to track the teens down, some believed—too hopefully, perhaps—that they'd thrown caution to the wind and taken off for Tinseltown because of something Amber's dad had read in her diary, found crammed beneath her mattress. While Anna would have liked to believe that Amber and Erica were careless and carefree on the road to making their dreams come true, she didn't buy it. Not when they had per capita checks waiting at home. Still, she didn't dare voice what she feared had happened to them.

"It's just a phone," Grace said. "That's all I want."

"Sorry to break it to you, but we don't always get what we want," Chris said.

Anna knew that to be true. She dug her fork out of the mush and forced herself to eat so that she could leave the table, which, currently, was all she really wanted.

Day 33
5:01 p.m.

Her throat closed up as if an invisible hand had wrapped around her neck upon finding a chambermaid coat hanging from her card's slot in the timecard rack. It'd been ten days since she'd been up to the eighth floor, and she'd convinced herself that her new manager, Fox Ballard, wouldn't want her up there again, not after she'd confronted him about Missy Picote. She was starting to learn that Fox was all smiles when she kept her mouth shut, but a single question could quickly produce a frown.

She reluctantly slipped into the chambermaid coat and buttoned it shut. Nervous fingers left black smears on the fabric and the little nametag that read *Anna Horn*. She cursed and rushed to the sink to scrub her grimy hands. The filthy water that spiraled down the drain reminded her of when she used to give Robbie his bath. Wrangling him into the tub had helped prepare her for the demands of the hotel, she thought, as she ascended to the eighth floor, where she maneuvered one of the cumbersome housekeeping carts from its closet.

Suite 808 felt cold inside, as though the surly man she'd encountered in the road on her way to work had sauntered through. The thermostat, however, was set at seventy-eight degrees, the usual temperature for an unoccupied room. Anna lowered it in accordance with Fox's demands.

Luxurious as the suite was, it no longer dazzled Anna. It might as well have been a cave or something worse. She remembered when it seemed like a dream, so much better than home. Now it was like a cage, a cell.

She finished her duties fast and wheeled the housekeeping cart back to its closet. Though she no longer wanted to service suite 808, she felt a pressing need to uncover what went on behind its closed door, for Missy's sake. Which is why she left a wet rag on the vanity in the bathroom.

Hunkered down inside the housekeeping closet, her ear to the door, Anna vowed that she wouldn't fuck up this time. The emergency stairwell door clanged open down the hall. She tensed. It slammed shut. The lock of a room door snapped. The door opened. Then shut. Anna sucked in a deep breath and let it out slowly. Someone had entered suite 808, she was sure of it.

A few more minutes passed, then—fingers trembling—she grasped the handle and pulled the closet door open precisely as the stairwell door clanged again. Sudden sweat beaded on her forehead; her hand ached from squeezing the door handle too tight. She could've looked to see who was in the hall, but that's not what she wanted. She needed to see what was going on inside the suite, which meant she needed to wait.

A lock disengaged. A door opened and shut. The hall fell silent again, leaving Anna to assume that at least two people were now in suite 808. Loosening her hold on the handle, she counted to one hundred in her head, then again to ensure she'd allowed the occupants enough time to begin whatever they'd come to do.

There was no one in the hall when she peeked past the doorframe. Her moment was now. She gathered her nerve and crept from the closet. Her feet lost speed the closer they carried her to the suite.

Fingers slick with sweat, they slid over the keycard in her pocket. She removed it, careful not to drop it. Should she risk going in? Her head pivoted, eyes looking in every direction. She couldn't trust her ears to tell her if anyone was approaching. Fox had already snuck up on her too many times in the past.

Anna stepped to the side of the suite's door, dodging the peephole's line of sight. Fingers trembling, she wiped the sweaty keycard against her coat, then extended it toward the designated slot in the lock. Her eyelids shut as her hand plunged the card into the opening. The lock clicked. She grabbed the lever and pushed the door open, just a crack.

A voice from within froze her in place.

". . . nothing to worry about," it said. *"Laissez les bon temps rouler!"*— *Let the good times roll*, the same saying that glowed in neon lights above the roulette wheel in the casino attached to the hotel. It took Anna a second to register who the voice belonged to, but by then it was too late. The door's lever slipped from her hand as the door opened wide.

"Housekeeping," she blurted.

Face-to-face with Fox, her countenance mirrored his surprise, though they didn't wear matching expressions for long. His turned to fury as he bulldozed out of the suite, plowing Anna backward while pulling the door shut behind him. She'd been so stunned that she hadn't peered past him to see who else was inside.

"I left a rag on the vanity," she said. The sentence came out as an indistinguishable blur of sound.

"You know better," Fox growled. He latched on to her left bicep so tight she thought she felt his fingers beneath her skin. "Downstairs. *Now!*"

He dragged her down the hall toward the elevator. They'd only gone a handful of feet when the stairwell door clanged a third time. Fox's free hand struck the back of Anna's head, then closed around it.

He didn't get a firm enough grip, though, to stop her from glancing over her shoulder. A man, tall and thin, sporting a black baseball hat that shielded his eyes, emerged through the stairwell doorway. An overnight bag hung from one hand.

"I'm sorry. I'm sorry." Anna hated how easily she crumbled in Fox's tightening grasp. He'd gotten a handful of hair in addition to the back of her head. If she tried to look over her shoulder again, she'd surely end up with a bald spot and a broken neck. "I came for the rag," she said. "Let me go."

"Shut the fuck up."

Fox wrangled her to the elevator, where he slapped the down button just before pinning her arms behind her back. Pressing her against the wall, he held her captive while awaiting the elevator's arrival. His power over her filled her with fear, her weakness in the face of his strength turned the fear to terror.

The elevator dinged and the doors rolled open. "Downstairs," he said again. He removed one hand from her arms and took the elevator access card, necessary for reaching the eighth floor, from her coat's pocket, leaving her with the keycard that unlocked suite 808 still in her hand. "Not a word!" He shoved her into the glass box, then inserted the access card so that he could light up the button for the basement, off-limits to hotel guests. "Sheets need pressing," he said.

Anna cemented her back against the glass, maximizing the distance between herself and him. With the elevator doors rolling shut, he tucked the access card into his pocket and said, "Wait for my call."

The scream that'd been begging for release didn't break free until the elevator cleared the seventh floor. Anna pounded her fists against the glass, imagining it was Fox's face.

Her hands were at her sides and her jaw was set when the elevator doors slid open again. She'd only been in the bowels of the building a time or two before. Doing laundry had never been one of her tasks. The resort's basement was a concrete world that lacked the splendor of the floors above. Gray, its underground wings inherently cold, it smelled of dust, earth, bleach, and chlorine from the pool and spa on the hotel's ground level. Anna heard the laundry room before she came upon it. Workers dressed in blue from head to toe pushed large laundry carts along rows of industrial washers and dryers inside.

Anna ignored Fox's order about the sheets. The laundry room workers were fine on their own. She knew he'd only banished her to the basement to get her out of his way. Fuming, she threw her hands over her head and reeled about the space, drawing curious glances from the workers tirelessly loading and unloading machines. Even with eight floors separating her from Fox, she could still feel his hands upon her. The back of her head ached. Her arms stung.

With half a mind to get back on the elevator, Anna paced along the cavernous hall, her fury intensifying by the second. She was angry at herself for failing again. Angry for not defending herself the way she thought she should. Angry at Fox for treating her worse than he'd treat a snarling dog.

She pressed the button to call the elevator but couldn't get on when the doors opened. She had no way of gaining access to the eighth floor without the card Fox took, and right now all she wanted was to know what he was doing up there. She considered her options. She knew she could report Fox to hotel security for what he'd done—bruises were already turning her upper arm purple—but even if security tracked him down, the question was what would they do after that? Not only was Fox chummy with everyone around the casino and resort, he was also the tribal chairman's nephew, which meant he had pull on the reservation. Anna had seen how much other employees respected him. They moved out of his way when he strolled down the center of the hall, always with a smile and a nod. It would be her word against his if she reported him, and even if they believed that he'd caused the bruises, would they take her claim about suspicious activity on the eighth floor seriously? She didn't believe they'd just barge in and demand to know what was going on, especially if Fox cooked up some excuse. For all she knew, suite 808 could have been Chairman Ballard's private playground, off-limits to anyone other than family, friends, and the objects of his desire.

Alternatively, she could call Tribal Police Chief Luke Fisher and tell him what she suspected. Fox, though, had already denied involvement with Missy Picote's disappearance, and he'd undoubtedly deny it again, leaving Anna in no better of a situation than she was already in. And besides, Missy's father's remarks at the monthly tribal council meeting earlier that week had made his suspicion clear; he suspected that Missy had gone off on her own, driven by her vice, like the last time she'd run away. Everyone else believed that too.

Anna backed away from the elevator, opting to keep her mouth shut. Staying in the basement wouldn't do her much good, but Fox said he'd call upon her there, and, at the moment, refraining from angering him more than she already had seemed like the best bet. She'd stick to her story about the rag on the vanity. It wasn't a lie.

She located the phone on the laundry room wall, which is where she leaned, eyeing the enormous ironing machine and imagining what it would spit out if Fox were forced onto its conveyor. When his call finally came through, she answered on the first ring.

"Eight-oh-eight," Fox said.

"You took my elevator access card."

"Use the stairs."

"I don't have access—"

He hung up before she could get through to him. And then it hit her. The emergency stairwell. How could she have overlooked it? That's where she should have been all along, waiting and watching for the people who'd gone up to come back down. She didn't need access to the eighth floor for that. Of course, it was too late now. Fox wouldn't have called if the coast wasn't clear. Anna took the elevator up to the seventh floor, then went the rest of the way on foot. She expected Fox to be waiting for her by the eighth-floor stairwell door, but the door was shut and there wasn't a soul in sight.

Anna knocked, then yanked on the door's lever. It opened without resistance. Strange. She only had to look down to see that a coin had been taped over the lock plate, preventing the lock from engaging.

The eighth floor was quiet, the hall empty. Deflated, Anna pushed one of the housekeeping carts from the closet to suite 808 and stuck her keycard into the lock. The suite was dark. Glimmers of light shining in from the hall reflected off gold picture frames and glass tabletops.

The hairs on the back of Anna's neck bristled in response to the chill that coursed down her spine. She sensed a ghostly presence that made her think of mud, moss, and a rolling head, prompting a breathy "Hello?" from her lips.

Dismissing her unease, she turned on the light and entered the suite, letting the door swing shut. The state of the main room was as expected: the curtains were drawn, the throw pillows were fluffed, and the billiard balls were still racked and waiting atop the pool table's green felt. An open beer bottle dripped condensation onto the counter in the galley kitchen. Two more occupied the nightstand in the bedroom, an encompassing puddle beneath them.

The bed was messier than usual. Rumpled sheets hung from the mattress and the comforter had been kicked to the floor. The bathroom, too, had seen extra use. Two bath towels were soaked in the tub.

Anna restored the suite, but as she cast a last look over her shoulder and reached for the bedroom light switch on her way out, she noticed something beneath the bed, something the vacuum hadn't sucked up. It looked like a little green ball from her vantage point, no wider in diameter than a nickel.

Crossing the room, the foot of the bed obscured the object from Anna's sight, so she bent and fished beneath the box spring until she felt it in her hand. It wasn't a ball at all, she discovered, but a little plastic tube, red on one end and topped by a rounded green cap on the other.

Anna's fingers quivered upon pulling the green cap from the tube of strawberry lip balm. The pink wax's sweet and artificial scent wafted up to her nose, filling her with panic like none she'd ever known.

Day 4
6:00 a.m.

Grace was in her bed when Anna woke, though she hadn't been there in the early morning hours when Anna, wondering what time her sister would sneak in, succumbed to sleep. The old dress Grace hadn't wanted to wear to the dance was on the floor. Scuffed high heels lay near it, kicked off in the dark.

Anna ate, showered, and dressed, careful not to wake the rest of the house. Only she worked on weekends; everyone else slept in. It was a short walk across the reservation from the Horn house to the Grand Nacre Casino and Resort. Anna made it to the housekeeping office and punched her timecard with two minutes to spare. A slew of young women, slowly donning chambermaid coats, greeted her there. Once they shook off the grogginess of too little sleep following a Saturday night of who-knows-what, they'd giggle and spread the latest rumors on the rez. Most were older than Anna, early twenties and up. While Anna got along with them well enough, she never engaged in gossip. She'd smile and nod and forget what they'd said once she was back home with her nose in a book.

Anna cracked her knuckles, readying her hands for the yanking, tugging, and pulling they'd do to shake out the heavy duvets and replace the queen-size sheets. She'd tend to twelve or fifteen rooms on her shift, faster than any of the others.

It was the same dull routine every weekend at the hotel. Blankets, sheets, trash bins, toilets, carpets, soap, shampoo, shower caps. Sometimes she was repulsed by what she found clotted on the sheets. Sometimes she was surprised to find a tip on a nightstand. There wasn't one today.

As she yanked fluffy pillows from their cotton cases, Anna, having skipped the pre–homecoming game pep rally on Friday, wondered who'd replaced her as king and if the royal couple had been bowed to the way she'd been. Grace had gone to the dance last night with Miguel Leon, a chubby, mildly popular boy in his junior year. Grace had made it clear that they were going as friends. She had a crush on Kevin Mills, one of Miguel's buddies, which meant Grace got to be near Kevin all night even if she couldn't wrap her arms around him during the slow songs.

"Anna?"

She'd just started on the toilet when the unfamiliar voice crowded in behind her.

"Horn?"

She dropped the toilet brush into the bowl and exited the bathroom, her damp and gloved hands raised at her sides.

"There you are."

A man in his early twenties, wearing a black T-shirt and baggy jeans, stood just beyond the guestroom's entrance. His brick-colored skin confirmed that he was from the rez. If not for the bags under his eyes and the generic tribal tattoos zigzagging up his muscular arms, he'd have been exceptionally handsome; still, he was handsome enough. Anna recognized him. She'd seen him while replenishing the towels by the hotel pool, showing off his abs while flirting with cute girls from on and off the rez. Anna had seen him at the resort's arcade, too, the few times she'd taken Robbie to try his hand at Skee-Ball. She suspected if she spent any time at the hotel gym, she'd see him pumping iron as well. Familiar as he was, she didn't know his name.

"You know how many rooms I had to search to find you? Tanya wouldn't tell me where you were." Tanya was Anna's manager. "She says you're the best worker she's got."

Anna lowered her hands. Water dripped from the tips of her index fingers. She waited expectantly, her face masking the pride she felt upon hearing what Tanya had said.

"I'm Fox. I'm the housekeeping evening manager." He flashed an electric smile. Genuine, not fake—he liked his title.

"Fox?"

"Fox Ballard. I know your dad."

The name clicked. With Eaton Ballard holding the title of tribal chairman, the Ballards were a big deal on the rez. They were a big family too.

"Eaton's son?" Anna asked.

"Nephew."

"I see." The family connection explained why someone who was no more than twenty years old when the resort opened for business was already manager of one of the hotel's biggest departments. He couldn't have been qualified. Not in any exceptional way. But neither were many of the others running the resort. Dozens went from struggling to make ends meet before the casino to being gainfully employed, snagging whatever positions they could get at the resort. Productivity, as a result, was a game of wait and see. Anna recognized this, but the ones with luck on their side were too blinded by their sudden strokes of good fortune, especially if they came from families with power, to realize that the enterprise wasn't being run as efficiently as it could be. That's not to say that plenty of prudent and altruistic tribal members weren't putting their all into the endeavor, but the ne'er-do-wells were just a bit more noticeable to Anna. "What'd you need?" she said.

"You. I've seen you around the hotel. You're not like the other girls. You don't gossip. You get your work done. I have an opening on the evening shift, and seeing as though Tanya says you're the best she's got . . ."

"If I'm the best she's got, she won't want to let me go."

"It's not up to her. It's up to you." He flashed that smile again, and Anna could feel it working on her, making her want to smile in return. Maybe, she thought, he genuinely liked her.

"You said she wouldn't tell you where I was."

"That's only because she wanted me to stay and talk to her."

Anna wasn't so sure about that. Tanya had a boyfriend. "Tanya's been good to me," she said.

"I'll find her someone new."

"Thanks, but—"

"You haven't heard me out yet." Fox stepped deeper into the room and closed the door behind him. Big as he was, he knew how to make himself seem small. He leaned against the TV stand, shoulders slumped, hands in his pockets. "I need someone in the evenings. It might be three days a week. Maybe four or five. It depends on how busy we are. Either way, you'll have more hours than you have now, which means you'll make more money. And it's easier too. Being on a later shift means you won't have all these rooms to clean."

Anna could see that Fox didn't just have bags under his eyes. Red spiders dwelled in his sclera and drippy snot glistened in his nostrils, all of which stood in contrast to the magnificence of his physique, making Anna wonder if his muscles were as fake as the infix Grace used to disguise her conversations. Refraining from judging him just yet, she pulled the rubber glove from her right hand and fussed with the white cotton shawl collar of her chambermaid coat. She hated the uniform. Vanda green—the worst shade of green, if you asked Anna—the knee-length garment had a white apron around the waist, puffy sleeves that sat high on the shoulders, and big round buttons down the middle.

"You'd basically be tending to guests' needs," Fox said. "Bringing them towels when they bitch to reception. Making sure they don't run out of toilet paper. Providing toothpaste and razors and shaving cream to all the idiots who left theirs at home or lost their luggage. You might have to clean some of the common areas. Restock the housekeeping carts. Wipe down the ice machines, vacuum the halls. Shit like that."

Anna pulled at the shawl again, wishing she could tear it off. "Why not offer the position to Lindy or Etta? Etta has arthritis. She could use a break."

"It's not for them," Fox said, shaking his head. "Lindy has kids she needs to be with in the evening. And I already know that Etta doesn't want additional hours. Did I mention you'd be making more? Money, money, money, Anna."

The offer was tempting. Snacks, magazines, and gum were pretty much all Anna could afford earning minimum wage a few hours every Saturday and Sunday, and six months still stood between her and her first per capita check.

"Why do you keep pulling on your collar?" Fox said. "It makes you look nervous."

Anna thought a while longer. "Let me wear what you wear to work, and we'll have a deal."

He looked down at his shirt and jeans, forgetting he wasn't on the clock, then shrugged. "Deal!" He thrust out his right hand. Anna shook it, surprised to find his grip was neither strong nor weak. She still didn't know what to make of him. He seemed to like her. And he was the most attractive boy who had ever sought her out. The *only* boy who had ever sought her out. "Looks like you're done in here," he said, glancing about the room.

"I just have to finish . . ." She hitched a thumb over her shoulder toward the bathroom.

"Finish it later." Smiling, he jerked his head toward the door. "Come with me for a minute."

Fox exited the room, and Anna followed him through the hall to the elevator. He pressed the fifth-floor button, then wiped his nose against his wrist.

"I'll let Tanya know you're working for me now," he said. "What time do you get out of school?"

"I'm home by three thirty."

"Let's get you started on Wednesday. Be here by five?"

Anna nodded.

"Like I said, it's an easy job." He wiped his nose against his flesh again. "Restock the linen closets and carts with amenities. Scrub the crud from the elevator buttons. Keep the common areas clean." The elevator dinged. The doors slid open. "I've got a few other girls on evenings. They'll do the heavy lifting."

"Then why do you need me? It sounds like you have things covered."

Fox shook his head. "The others aren't working out the way I'd hoped. They talk too much. That's what I like about you, Anna. You don't talk much, do you?"

"When I want to," she said.

He chuckled and shook his head. "I could've given this position to anyone, you know? I chose you." Fox led her from the elevator, past the fifth-floor housekeeping closet, to the guestroom near the emergency stairwell at the end of the hall. A DO NOT DISTURB sign hung from the door's handle. Fox put a keycard in Anna's hand and motioned toward the room's lock. Anna keyed it open.

The odor that wafted out of the pitch-black room told Anna that things were amiss. Instead of the fresh aromas of clean linen and lavender fields–scented disinfectant, a mix of smoke—cigarette and otherwise—grease, a chemical smell not unlike burnt plastic, and something awfully animal assaulted Anna's nose.

"This is a non-smoking room," she said.

"Turn on the light."

Anna reached for the switch beyond the door. A lamp lying sideways on the floor cast light over upended chairs and a mattress propped against the drawn shades over the balcony doors. Discolored sheets, pillows, and duvets littered the floor. Anna wondered if the golden stains were from beer or something worse. An open pizza box sat atop the TV. Few of the slices had been eaten. Some were on the nightstands. Others were stuck to the wall, sauce smeared across the fleur-de-lis–patterned wallpaper.

The animal scent weakened once it was freed unto the hallway. Its origin was the bathroom. Fox nudged Anna forth. The bathroom light came on with a snap, illuminating an explosion of vomit dripping from the flooded sink. Anna jumped back to keep it from speckling her shoes the way it'd already speckled the mirror above and the tiles below.

"What happened here?" she said, retreating to the doorway.

"Do we ever really know what goes on in these rooms?" Fox shrugged and nudged her forth again. "The real question is, do we need to know?"

Anna's gaze moved slowly over the mess. She smelled sweat, then ammonia, and knew it meant meth. The drug had arrived on the reservation in early '95, spreading like wildfire across the Takoda Nation. It was as if the Takoda people had been a forest full of kindling, ill-equipped to battle the resultant blaze. No fault of their own, they'd been targeted by drug traffickers seizing the opportunity to circumvent federal drug laws by taking advantage of jurisdictional confusion on sovereign land. It was the same on countless reservations across the country.

"Take care of this for me," Fox said.

Anna's head sprang up, redirecting her eyes from cigarette ash mashed into the carpet to Fox's face. He was still smiling. "I thought you said—"

"I know what I said." His infectious grin turned awkward, as though he were embarrassed. "Just this once," he said. "To see if you're really as good as Tanya says."

"What exactly did Tanya say about—?"

Fox's awkward grin stretched farther across the right side of his face. "Don't ask questions," he said, cold words warmed by the way he laughed when he spoke them. "I'll see you Wednesday." He stepped over shattered glass on his way out.

Anna exhaled the breath that would have finished her question, ultimately heading to the housekeeping closet for disinfectant and rubber gloves.

Day 5
7:48 a.m.

Backpack pulled tight to her back, Anna went inside the building that often felt like a prison disguised as a high school. Her locker was on the second story in the senior hallway, and, as luck would have it, she was the only senior from the rez. It was as though she were aligned for loneliness just as the king of frogs had been aligned for death in the road.

Heads turned when Anna passed through the foyer. Impossible to ignore, she could only assume that all eyes were on her because of what had happened the previous week. She expected a chorus of *All hail the king!* to ring out.

Grace and Emily lagged behind her, having been driven to school in Emily's mother's smoke-filled car. The three of them were among only a handful of teens from the rez who attended the high school in town. Along with the more abundant Black kids and the few dozen Hispanics, they stood out like freckles on a white face.

Anna turned toward the girls when she reached the stairs. Guilt clouded Emily's eyes, as if she'd just stolen something. Grace's long black hair hung in front of her face; her arms hugged her chest. For a second, Anna thought her peers were staring at Grace, but that couldn't be. They never did.

"See you at lunch?" Anna asked, just to say something.

Grace parted the curtains of her hair. "Mystery-meat Monday," she said, forcing a laugh. "See ya."

Grace and Emily darted toward the sophomore wing, leaving Anna to take the stairs. None of them noticed Gary Cooper, the linebacker who'd hauled in an interception at the homecoming game to score the winning touchdown, jerking his fist in front of his mouth or repeatedly poking the inside of his left cheek with his tongue.

Anna quickened her pace at the top of the stairs, eager to get through the hall. The lockers of the football heroes, cheerleaders, and elected members of the homecoming court bore gold and silver stars. Anna strived to keep her eyes ahead, but she could feel the popular girls watching her through the mirrors affixed to their locker doors as they applied fresh coats of lipstick that would eventually end up on their boyfriends' cheeks.

Kelly Chapman—yearbook photographer, her point-and-shoot always at the ready—locked eyes with Anna through one of the mirrors. The encounter lasted less than a second, but it felt much longer than that. Anna read something in Kelly's eyes. What she read, however, was in a language like Idig, something Anna didn't understand.

Her locker, rusty around the hinges, bearing dents and patches of chipped paint, stood at the end of the hall. Thin pen and pencil lines meandered aimlessly across its surface like a map of roads to nowhere. Anna's heart fluttered at the sight of something taped to her locker door. A silver star as shiny as the ones that decorated the lockers of the cheerleaders and jocks. For a split second, Anna's heart fluttered with hope—longing for acceptance—but the flutter morphed into pulsing anxiety that made her hear gnashing, gnawing, and grinding when she read the word scrawled across the star.

DETHRONED!

Day 33
9:52 p.m.
23 Minutes Gone

Anna staggered from suite 808, head spinning, the strawberry lip balm locked in her fist.

"Fox!" she screamed. "*Grace!*"

Swirls of color dripped in her peripheral vision. The hotel, it seemed, was melting around her. Disoriented by her distress, she crashed into the wall, then whirled around and ran for the stairs, nearly taking a tumble down to the seventh story. Floor by floor, she searched for Fox; all she found were questioning stares from vacationers gearing up for a night with Lady Luck.

Fox wasn't in the Atrium Ice Bar. Neither was Grace. They weren't on the walkway over the gator pond, by the concessions in the movie theater, hanging by the pool, or in the arcade either. Minors' pathway be damned, Anna charged through the casino, checking each of the bars and the card tables, ignoring the flashing lights and dinging machines.

"Have you seen Fox?" she asked one of the security staff by the casino entrance.

"Me, I think he just left, *cher*," he said, sounding like a true Cajun.

Anna dropped the lip balm into her pocket and stormed out to the parking lot, looking for Fox's shiny new truck, listening for its "look at me" exhaust. With so many vehicles parked before her, it was hard to focus. She didn't see or hear the truck anywhere, not even in the distance beyond the lot. Anna reeled, torn between continuing her search for Grace inside or moving on to canvass the rest of the reservation.

"Shit," she huffed, and sprinted through the darkness, feet splashing through puddles left by rain that had fallen while she was working. She'd warned Grace to stay away from the eighth floor, and she'd foolishly thought her sister would listen. It suddenly felt like a thread was all that remained of their bond, and a fraying one at that.

The house quaked from the force of Anna leaping up the porch steps and barging through the door.

"What's with you?" Robbie, talking through a mouthful of peanut butter, said.

"Grace! Where is she?" Anna demanded.

Robbie shrugged and dipped his finger straight into the peanut butter jar for another scoop. Anna searched the house.

"Did she say where she was going?"

"Didn't ask," Robbie said. "Where does she ever go?"

Dorothy was on the phone in the corner. Anna overheard her cooking up an excuse to get out of Friday-night drinks with Autumn and Thomas Lavergne, which she and Chris used to regularly attend.

"Where's Dad?" Anna asked Robbie.

"At the Blue Gator Grill. Said he was going for free peanuts."

Unable to wait for Dorothy to hang up, Anna leaned in and whispered in her mother's free ear. "There's something going on with Grace."

Dorothy held up a finger, telling Anna to wait.

Anna growled and took a step back, staring at her mother like a dog yearning for scraps.

"Did Grace tell you where she was going tonight?" she demanded the instant Dorothy hung up. Her hand traveled over the lump of lip balm in her pocket.

"She's out with Emily."

"Where?"

"The arcade."

"I was just at the arcade." Her declaration made it clear that Grace wasn't there.

"I wanna go to the arcade," Robbie said.

Anna squeezed the tube in her pocket. "Grace didn't come home until morning the other day. It . . . it wasn't the first time. I should have said something, I know, but I. . . . And now she's gone again."

"Well, she'll be home tonight, that's for damn sure." Forehead furrowed, Dorothy went to the window and whipped the curtains aside. "She'll be home soon," she said, glancing at the clock. It was nearly eleven, Grace's curfew.

And if she's not? Anna thought.

Dorothy swatted one of the swaying curtains and retreated from the window. Anna's mind cycled through everything she'd been keeping inside herself for the past month: the lies, the secrets, the misgivings. She just didn't know where to begin or how to say it. Footsteps on the front porch filled her with relief, but then her father—sweaty and ruffled, the top few buttons of his shirt undone—walked in instead of Grace. Anna and her mother exchanged glances.

"I'll get to the bottom of this," Dorothy said.

"The bottom of what?" Chris asked. He tossed his keys on the table by the door.

Dorothy picked up the phone and dialed. "Karen? Hi, this is Dorothy Horn. Is Emily home?"

A brief pause ensued.

"Is Grace with her?" Another pause. "Can I talk to her?"

Anna exhaled the breath she'd been holding, thinking the *her* was in reference to Grace.

"Emily," Dorothy said, "where's Grace?" Her face grew stern. "Call me if you see her. Tell her to come home." Dorothy hung up. Anna and Chris inched closer, questioning with their eyes. "Grace lied," she said. "She wasn't with Emily tonight."

Anna's insides were like a balloon being filled to the brink of bursting. The pressure demanded that she do something to let it out or risk exploding into a million little pieces. Feet moving backward, she clutched the lip balm with one hand and nabbed Chris's keys from the table with the other. A split-second later, she was barreling out the door.

"Where the hell are you going?" her father cried.

Anna was down the porch steps and behind the wheel of her father's station wagon—jokingly called the "meat wagon" by Anna and her siblings because it doubled as a hearse—in no time at all. The old vehicle bounced when she threw it in reverse, then kicked up gravel as she peeled away, leaving Chris on the porch with his hands swinging over his head.

Enormous bald cypress trees, Spanish moss dangling from their branches, jutted up through the center of the hotel atrium. A shallow bayou surrounded the trees, and wooden walkways provided meandering paths over and across it. Giant flathead catfish, turtles, and alligators lurked within the water. The creatures were real. The bayou and bald cypress trees were not.

Dispirited gamblers dawdled along the walkways, perhaps persuading themselves they'd win back what they'd lost in the casino. Some pulled at their hair and dragged on cigarettes. Others gulped down gratis daquiris, hell-bent on getting their money's worth.

Anna stood on one of the walkways as well, just eight minutes before the start of her new shift. The pressure of the preservation society weighed on her shoulders. She'd been thinking about it on her walk to work. How could it compete with shiny lights, dinging machines, a man-made bayou, and per capita checks? How could she make others see its worth? Discouraged, she glared up at the guests peering down from their ornate indoor balconies above, eyeing her the way she'd eyed the alligators in the bayou below.

A five-foot gator slipped into the water from the imitation rock upon which it'd been baking beneath imitation sun. It floated to the edge of the make-believe bayou, its snout barely visible atop the water, and eyed a child making a doll dance along the wooden planks. The child, bored by the alligators, wasn't afraid. Metal rods prevented the animals from climbing out of the water. The alligators, known as tamahka in the native Takoda tongue, played a significant role in the Takoda's origin story: a pair of tamahka—one red, the other blue—had granted the Takoda people access to earth through a sacred hole in the ground because the Takoda were pure of heart and their souls were sincere. Once revered and feared, the tamahka were now nothing more than a draw, a tourist attraction for the Grand Nacre's guests to gawk at. The alligator's handlers put on a show every Saturday morning. They coaxed the beasts into lunging and snapping their jaws in exchange for strips of raw chicken. Boneless. Harmless.

Dispirited as the gamblers, Anna—still bothered by the star she'd found taped to her locker and challenged by the impending proposal she'd have to make—balanced her chin on the rail along the walkway. It was then that she spotted Fox, his hands busy with something she couldn't see, standing face-to-face with Chairman Ballard across the bayou by reception. Too far away to hear what they were saying, Anna was struck by how alike they were. Close in height and similar in stature—Fox the brawnier of the two—they looked more like father and son than uncle and nephew. They both stood with their spines straight, arms spearing the air when making a point. Wearing shiny watches and shiny shoes, the two men epitomized importance, though Anna had to wonder if Fox was just mirroring the man he wanted to be. Bored by them, like the child bored by the alligators, Anna's eyes drifted shut. Her stomach gurgled. She hadn't had an appetite all day. Even now she didn't feel hungry, just empty within.

"What are you wearing?"

Lifting her head with a start, Anna couldn't say if she'd closed her eyes for thirty seconds or thirty minutes. The casino and resort had a way of stealing time. She turned to find Fox standing next to her. His sleeves looked like they might split from the boulders of his biceps, and they were cuffed around his wrists, concealing his tattoos while on the job. A small gold coin rolled over his flexing knuckles—not a chip from the casino, but a token from the arcade.

Anna looked down at her apparel. Her pants—formerly her father's—were black like his, and she was wearing one of her mother's nearly white, billowy button-up blouses. With him wearing a purple button-up shirt and a dark green tie, she didn't think her clothes were a far cry from his.

"You're dressed like a waiter," he said, smiling. There was something different about his speech; his words ran together. The red spiders were still in his sclera—did one of the legs just twitch?—and the inner rims of his nostrils glistened again.

Anna ran a hand over the blouse. "Is it bad?"

He shook his head. "A dress wouldn't make a difference on you." He winked. Heat washed over Anna, making her blush. "You forgot your tag."

Anna pulled her nametag from her pocket and clipped it to the blouse. "I was about to clock in."

"You're early. I like that." Fox dropped the token into one of his pockets. "You know where the conference room is on two, right?"

Anna nodded.

"Good. I was just talking with my uncle. Short notice, but he needs the conference room tomorrow. Big business." He mimed turning a key over an invisible lock on his lips. "I need you to make the room shine. Literally. Polish the table. The coffee pots. Set out mugs and glasses and stock the fridge. Oh, and make sure there's real sugar in those little glass dishes. My uncle hates that saccharin shit. You impress him, you impress me. Understand?"

Anna nodded again.

"I knew you were the right choice," Fox said. He flipped the token in the air, then went on his way.

Anna looked down at her clothes again, her hands smoothing the blouse once more. *It's not bad,* she told herself. *Nothing like a waiter.* She hurried across the walkway on her way to clock in, her gaze drifting up as she cleared the small forest of man-made trees. The glass elevator to the right of reception was ascending. Fox stood inside, looking out in her direction. Given the distance between herself and the lift, Anna couldn't be sure, but it looked like Fox had zeroed in on her. The way he stared, his expression like a brick in a wall, seemed to set the world in slow motion.

The elevator inched up, sluggishly making its way past the fifth, then sixth floors. Anna was sure it would stop on the seventh because the elevator rarely went higher than that. The eighth floor was full of suites reserved for VIPs, like celebrities and Chairman Ballard. Regular guests didn't have access to the eighth floor. The elevator only went that high if triggered by an access card. Anna, like most of the staff, didn't have clearance to go up there. She'd only seen the suites once, back when the resort opened and everyone took a tour. She remembered how impressive the suites were and how disappointing it felt to go home after wandering through the spacious rooms containing king-size beds covered with luxurious spreads. Pool tables and big-screen TVs came included in the suites, not to mention fully stocked fridges, tables bedecked with artfully crafted desserts, and private chefs and bartenders permanently on call.

Anna had hoped to work in the suites when Tanya hired her at the hotel but quickly learned that girls like her weren't wanted among the bigwigs, high rollers, and performers who came to town. Anna didn't know the women who maintained the suites, but she did know they were pretty and white. The casino and resort had opened many doors for the Takoda people, but there were still some barriers in place. Pale complexions populated the spa and salon. They smiled in the gift shop and at the reception counter. It was unspoken, yet obvious. Darker faces belonged at the food stands, in the buffet, doing laundry, and selling tickets in the box office window.

The elevator completed its journey at the eighth floor. Fox turned and stepped through the parting doors, disappearing into the wonder-world of suites.

Day 7
10:03 p.m.

The sliding glass doors whispered shut behind her. Anna peered toward the pines beyond the resort's parking lot, knowing darkness would soon dominate her. She'd overlooked her aversion to walking alone at night upon accepting the evening shift. It was foolish fear, she told herself, that made her wary of the dark, but that didn't stop her arms from tightening around her chest the instant she left the lot's bright lights behind.

Streetlights didn't dot the rez, only power lines that hummed along the road. It was up to the moon and the starry sky spirits to light the way. A pair of brake lights cast a red glow upon the ground at the fork in the road ahead, one way leading into town, the other leading to the homes on the reservation, away from the casino and resort.

Anna trekked forth, expecting the vehicle to turn, but the brake lights continued to burn. Her pace slowed as she discerned that it was a pickup truck, shiny and red, like its lights, sitting high upon mudding tires. Apprehensive to pass it, Anna approached the truck with caution, her feet on the edge of the asphalt. Tinted windows prevented her from seeing who was inside. Just when she was about to pass the cab, the passenger window sank. A shadowy figure sat within the low glow of dashboard lights.

"Get in," he said.

"Fox?" Anna leaned close to the open window. Cool air and the commingled scent of cologne and new-car smell washed over her. "Where'd you go?" She hadn't been able to find him at the end of her shift.

"Get in," he said again. "I'll give you a ride."

Anna's hand stopped short of pulling the door open. A stone settled in the pit of her stomach. It was the same sensation she'd had when her peers had bowed to her in the cafeteria, like she was about to be the butt of a joke.

"I'm not in a hurry," she said, and that was true. Home had been feeling smaller than usual lately, suffocating at times. She often found herself wondering if the tiny house would fit the entire family much longer. And, little as she liked the idea of walking through the dark, being alone suited her better than being confined in the pickup's cab with Fox Ballard, someone she still had questions about.

"I used to walk, too, until I made something of myself." He ran his right hand over the dashboard, sporting a tortoiseshell design around the edges. "Eddie Bauer edition," he said.

"Eddie Bauer?" she questioned.

"Luxury trim. She's got a custom grille and an off-road bumper. I already lifted her four inches, but just wait 'til I'm done with all the mods. She'll be the baddest ride on the rez. Oh, she's got a twelve-disc CD changer and a subwoofer, too." He patted the passenger seat. "Hop in."

"I'll walk."

"Your loss." He shrugged and his eyes flicked to the rearview mirror. The street was dead behind him. "You did good tonight," he said.

Anna wondered if he'd been watching her. Had he inspected the conference room after she'd left? Had he seen his reflection shining atop the wood of the twelve-foot table she'd so meticulously polished?

"You did good the other morning, too. I meant to tell you that earlier. You made that guestroom look like new."

"Thanks," Anna said.

"Question is . . ." he went on, "can you keep it up?"

Anna was confused. He'd said she wouldn't have to do any heavy lifting, yet her new position didn't feel any easier than the old one. "What exactly—?"

A car slowed to a stop behind the truck. "Just keep it up and we'll be cool. Let me know when you get tired of walking." Fox slammed the gas, leaving Anna with a mouthful of exhaust at the side of the road. He turned toward the residential part of the reservation; the car behind him turned toward town.

The departed taillights left Anna among the moon's shadows. She could see the luminosity of the casino and resort through the screen of trees when she looked over her shoulder. The complex was so big and bright it made her think of the sun when it set on the horizon. Just a few years earlier, there'd been an expansive field where the resort now stood. It'd been a place for exploration, a place where a child's imagination could roam.

Anna used to run through the brush, rustling the flying grasshoppers lazily chomping on weeds and bark. There were far too many of the tiny creatures to count. Millions of them, maybe. They'd swarm overhead like a storm, their reedy wings clacking through the air, creating gray and green clouds before transforming into pounding rain as they came to rest around Anna again. She'd let them settle in the grass, then clap and run, becoming thunder, rousing the insects once more.

The memory called to mind a story she'd heard from Miss Shelby when she was small. Miss Shelby would sit with the tribal children among the grass beneath the shade of her favorite old oak. Its lowest branch served as a bench for her while its gnarled roots created little cubbies on the ground in which the kids sat. Perched upon the tree, Miss Shelby would look out into the field around her, allowing nature's elements to inspire the story that would spill from her mouth.

Fondness swelled in Miss Shelby's voice when she spoke of Grasshopper. She called him a lovable nuisance as much as an unlikely friend. She said he'd eat your crops clean, clearing an entire field of corn in no time at all. He'd chew and chomp and chew, then lie back in the sun, lethargic, while the rest of the world worked. His shortcomings aside, he was the embodiment of fun, hopping here, there, everywhere, and whenever he hopped by to say hello, the mouth was wanting to smile.

Anna remembered how she'd stay seated on the ground while the rest of the tribal children scattered. A single story was never enough. She always wanted more. Sometimes Miss Shelby would oblige, entertaining Anna with tales of Mother Wolf, Dragonfly, or Turtle. And then there were times when Miss Shelby would make Anna speak instead. And, unlike other adults, she'd listen, seemingly as interested in Anna's varied hobbies—climbing trees, catching toads, crafting paper dolls in the likenesses of Gran and Miss Shelby herself—as Anna was in Miss Shelby's tales.

Sometimes Miss Shelby would say things that perplexed her. *You don't live like one or the other. You live like both, and together they make you more,* she'd once said, then kindly smiled to erase the confusion on Anna's face. *One day you'll understand.*

Anna dismissed the memory. Rather, the memory was dismissed by the rustle beside her. Something moved through the shadowy brush. A cool gust of wind, carrying the scent of decomposition, ushered Anna to the middle of the road, where she was safest from the unknown hidden in the bushes and tall grasses. She carried on—eyes ahead, arms tight against her chest—telling herself there was nothing to the rustle keeping pace beside her.

The asphalt ended and Anna stepped onto the dirt road that would lead her home. It wasn't far now. Just a few more minutes. She could almost see the light of her front porch through the trees. But then something crunched in the gravel on the side of the road. The brush parted. Something small and round appeared. Something Anna didn't want to see.

She'd rarely been a fearful child. In fact, she'd been bolder than most, always exploring the fields alone, braving bugs, rodents, and snakes. She'd even wrangled a rattler once just to prove she could. While many, her siblings included, recoiled at the thought of a corpse, the dead never unnerved Anna. She had begged her father to let her watch him work when she was still too small to understand the enormity of death. When he'd offered to take her to a wake—not to gawk, though she'd done a bit of that—to witness the humbling affair of a spirit moving from this realm to the next, she'd gone eagerly along. Seldom had she found herself afraid as a child, but there was one thing that had inspired fear within her from the tender age of seven. And at seventeen, it still did.

She could still see the fire that had burned between them. She could smell it, too, the smoke and the smoldering wood. Uncle Ray, poking the flames, back when he was welcome in his brother's house, had told her what he'd seen while tending to the tribal cemetery grounds: three unearthed graves, a skeleton missing its skull.

Anna's heart kicked. She didn't like thinking about what Uncle Ray had said, especially when there was something emerging from the brush. Not wanting to look, her eyes betrayed her, dropping to the ground. Her vision narrowed, zeroing in on the small, round presence. Object? Animal? Monster?

The low light prevented her from making out its features. No dull eyes. No decaying nose. All she saw was a single glint of moonlight, twinkling upon a jagged tooth jutting out from the lower jaw of the nightmare at her feet.

Anna wheezed and skipped forward, nearly tripping. Her arms fell from her chest and pumped with all their might.

"Lord almighty," Gran said, slurred and slow, from her wheelchair beside the couch when Anna burst through the door and slammed it shut behind her. Grace and Robbie were sprawled upon the couch cushions, each with their eyes glued to the television set, unalarmed by Anna's abrupt entrance.

"Raccoon," they simultaneously said, diverting their eyes from the TV to smile and wink at each other.

Anna locked the door and took a deep breath to steady herself. "Shouldn't they be afraid of people?"

"Who or what would be afraid of you?" Robbie said.

"Who or what *wouldn't* be?" Grace giggled.

"It came pretty close," Anna said.

"A raccoon?" Gran questioned.

"Mom made you a plate." Grace dismissed Anna's apprehension like so many times before. "It's on the counter. Can we have nail time later?"

Anna quickly nodded. Grace hadn't asked for nail time in months. Having been her sister's beautician since they were small, the job as of late had passed to Emily, producing envy and resentment Anna kept caged inside. Heart rate returning to normal, she took refuge in the kitchen, where she rinsed fresh sweat from her face with cold water from the tap. She raked damp fingers through her hair, then filled a glass from the faucet. Cold chicken sat atop a pile of peas beneath aluminum foil on the plate her mother had made her. The chicken was dry. The peas were hard. Anna picked at the food, unable to swallow more than a few bites while recounting the tale Uncle Ray had told her, swearing it was true from his side of the flames.

It couldn't have been a ravenous human head at the side of the road, she thought. Impossible.

Day 33
10:49 p.m.
80 Minutes Gone

Anna sped across the reservation, traversing the river on her way, where the paved roads gave way to what remained of the dirt ones. Flying beetles and moths spiraled in the headlight beams; their yellow guts exploded on the windshield. It didn't matter that Anna didn't know the address of where she was headed. She only had to look for the red pickup truck parked out front, sitting in the shadows of the pow wow grounds and the vast fields beyond.

Anna barely put the station wagon in park before she was out the door and sprinting across the overgrown lawn. A light shone above the entry of the house in front of her. More moths flitted around her head. Heavy metal music seeped through the cracks, wounding the tranquil night. Anna whipped the screen door open and pounded on the wooden one behind it.

"Fox!" she shrieked. "It's Anna. Open up!"

A dog barked. The music blared. No one came to the door.

"Open the door, Fox!" Anna tried the knob. It turned, but the lock held steady. She resumed hitting the door so hard her fists turned numb. She threw her hip into it, then plowed her foot against the lock.

The wood creaked and cracked. Another side kick sent the door swinging.

The blaring music and the dog's booming barks intensified. The vibrations of sound tickled Anna's skin and rattled her teeth. The house was dim, and it only became darker when the dog, a German shepherd mix, leapt for her face.

Anna screamed, hands flying up in defense. A glint of teeth and penetrating, wild eyes filled her sight, and then it was on her, licking her, pawing her for attention.

"Get!" she yelled, startled.

The dog ran out. The screen door slammed shut behind it, leaving Anna with her heart thumping in her throat. The house was a wreck, reeking of rotten produce and sweat.

"Fox!"

Anna wound her way through the mess. Dirty clothes, including the button-up shirt and black slacks Fox had worn to work that day, hung from the kitchen counters, the cabinets, the chairs, the couch. His purple necktie was wrapped around the freezer's handle, its door open, dripping icy water onto the kitchen floor. Mold-speckled food sat on the table and lay strewn across the living room carpet, surrounded by a sea of empty beer bottles and putrid pizza boxes, alive with wriggly white maggots. The television—massive and new—was on, broadcasting a blank, blue screen as though Fox had been about to watch a movie but forgot to press play on the VCR.

The clutter on the coffee table perplexed Anna. She recognized the wad of balled-up cash and the cigarette lighters, but she couldn't make sense of the light bulbs with tubes coming out of them, coated with brown and black residue. Then she saw the little baggies full of tiny white crystals and she knew.

Anna recoiled. Reeling, she noticed the shadow on the wall in the hall. It made frantic, fast movements, projected through an open bedroom door.

Grace, she thought, and then, remembering Fox's strength, grabbed two of the empty beer bottles like clubs. She entered the hall and slunk toward the open door. Her body against the wall, she peeked into the room. Fox was alone inside. His back to her, she could see a sliver of his face via the mirror atop a nearby dresser, which also held the boombox blasting the formidable heavy metal. He stood shirtless, wearing nothing but a grimace on his strained face and a pair of boxers below. His hands held a pair of dumbbells, each the size of a small keg, which he manically lifted, one after the other.

Sweat streamed down his back. Through the mirror, Anna could see how his left bicep stretched the tattoos across it, making the tribal bands look like they were about to burst. His bulging veins were like nightcrawlers trying to break free from flesh. Each swing of his arms coaxed a grunt from his mouth. Anna watched for a small eternity, but he never tired. He was like a machine, only stoppable if someone hit a switch.

"Fox!" Anna screamed, coaxing her voice above the music, finally making herself heard.

The dumbbells fell from Fox's hands, sounding a frightening crash against the floor. It was a wonder they didn't go straight through it. Fox turned to Anna, his dilated pupils the size of olives in a jar of brine. The red streaks in his sclera were just as prominent as the swollen blue veins in his arms.

Anna's flesh crawled. She shook herself from his gaze, then brazenly crossed the room to kill the music. Resisting the urge to beat the boombox with the beer bottles, she momentarily set one aside so she could pull the plug instead.

Fox charged her like a bull, stopping short of where she stood, though Anna simultaneously jumped backward while raising the weapons in her hands. Her spine hit the wall, and she swung one of the bottles. It thumped against Fox's chest, doing little good; she might as well have taken a swing at a bald cypress. She was sure she felt the impact more in her wrist than he had against his pectoral. His face inches from hers, he panted stale breath past cracked lips. The intensity in his eyes wasn't produced by anger. He wasn't upset to see her in his house. He wasn't even curious as to why she was there or how she'd gotten in.

"Am I getting bigger?" he asked, excited and loud, like a reveler at a rock concert. He stepped back and flexed his biceps, nearly as big as his head. He made his pecs dance on his broad chest, then accentuated his winglike lats, which made him look like he was wearing a cape of flesh. "Bigger. Right?"

He fumbled with the boombox's plug. Unable to figure out where it was supposed to go, his thick fingers tossed it aside and wrapped around the dumbbells' handles again. He grunted and curled.

"Where's my sister?"

Fox curled harder, faster. Sweat trickled down the crevice of his chest.

"Fox, where's Grace?"

Each pump of his arms stretched his skin tighter. Not just around his biceps but around his neck and face. Anna swore the flesh would snap at any second.

"She was there at the hotel tonight. I know it. Now she hasn't come home." Anna freed herself from the wall. She faced him, leaving just enough space for the dumbbells to go up and down without hitting her. "Where is she, Fox?"

His arms were starting to slow. He was starting to strain. His bulging eyes verged on exploding straight out of his purple face. A roar, accompanied by a spray of spit, erupted from his throat. He squeezed out another rep. The veins in his arms practically promised to burst and spray blood all over the room.

Anna whacked the bottles against his hands with all her might. The dumbbells fell and so did the bottles, producing a crash more deafening than the one before. *Where the fuck is she?* Anna screamed.

"Who?" Fox rubbed his ears as though she'd hit him there instead of on his hands.

"Grace!"

"How would I know?"

"She was with you tonight."

"Bullshit." He started to scratch. His neck. His chest. His chin. Red marks appeared on his slick skin.

Anna whipped out the lip balm and held it in front of his face, hand quivering.

"What the fuck is that?" He tried to take it. Anna's hand shot back behind her head.

"It's hers. I found it in eight-oh-eight." Her voice dropped off when she said the suite number. "Why was it in eight-oh-eight?"

He bent to grab the dumbbells again. Anna kneed him in the chest. She knew he could take her down with hardly a thought, but she hardly cared.

"Why was Grace in suite eight-oh-eight?"

"She wasn't."

"No one knows where she is, Fox. *Please*."

"She wasn't," he said again, steadfast.

Anna thrust the lip balm in his face once more. "It was under the bed. Just tell me where she is. That's what I really want to know."

"She wasn't."

"What do you mean, she wasn't?"

"She wasn't."

"Where is she?"

"She wasn't. She wasn't!" The veins that had settled on his forehead popped out again, little centipedes wriggling down his brow. "She wasn't!" He bumped Anna with his chest, propelling her backward and out of the bedroom. He stalked forward, forcing Anna back through the hall and into the living room, all the while shouting, "She wasn't! She wasn't!"

When the front door, still open, came into sight, Fox plowed forth and heaved Anna straight through the closed screen door.

"She wasn't!"

Anna landed in pain on the porch. He slammed the door with the busted lock. The damaged screen door swung feebly. Anna went limp against the porch planks. She could hear the meat wagon humming beyond the grass, and she could feel the lip balm still clutched in her hand. She shut her eyes and nearly screamed when the dog licked the sweat from her face.

Day 7
10:42 p.m.

"Close the door," Grace said.

Anna obeyed and instinctively maneuvered the desk chair beneath their bedroom doorknob, the way they had when they were kids and wanted to keep Robbie out. "Everything all right?" Grace had lost her cool since being sprawled on the couch. Her eyes were wide, and her bottom lip was clamped between her teeth.

"I need some advice." She gave up on the butterfly clip she'd been trying to stick in her hair and flung it across the room. Her restless fingers opened a dresser drawer and pulled out a makeup bag, nail polish bottles clacking within. She hopped onto her bed and curled her legs up under her. Anna sat beside her.

"Everything all right?" she asked again.

Grace unzipped the bag and tipped it. Little bottles spilled out onto the bedspread, spinning toward the depression her weight made within the mattress. Anna picked one up and rolled it between her palms.

"We're going to sit at his lunch table tomorrow or Friday," Grace said.

The *his* was in reference to Kevin Mills, of course, the upperclassman Grace ogled any time he was near. Anna supposed he was cute in a weaselly sort of way. Awfully thin with pale skin, he had long, dark hair that intensified his bright green eyes. As far as Anna knew, Grace had never talked to the boy. Not in a serious way. She always took on the traits of a startled swamp rabbit whenever he was around: silent and still.

"You want me to sit at his table with you?" Anna questioned. "Won't that seem strange?"

"No, not *you*. Me and Emily."

The response might as well have been a bee sting. The nail polish bottle fell from Anna's hands. "Oh," she said, feeling foolish for thinking Grace might want her around.

"It was Emily's idea."

"Oh," Anna said again. "Well, it doesn't sound like a good one." She didn't like the thought of her sister making herself so vulnerable. More than that, she thought if Emily and Grace sat somewhere else, she'd be alone.

"You don't think I should?"

"What will you say?"

"I'm hoping he'll say something first."

"And if he doesn't?"

"I guess saying hi might work."

"Why not say hi before sitting at his table?"

Grace huffed and swung her hair over her shoulders. "You've never said hi to a boy. Ever."

"You asked for my advice."

"Not about this." Grace's jittery fingers moved over the nail polish bottles, nervously turning them.

"Then what?" Anna asked.

"You like chemistry, right? I mean, you're good at it."

"What?"

"Chemistry. You got an A in the class, didn't you?"

"It was easy."

"Then tell me how to make blue." Grace plucked a purple and a red bottle from the collection in front of her. "Can I do it with these?"

"Why do you want to make blue?"

"Miguel told me it's Kevin's favorite color."

"So the plan is to paint your nails blue, sit at his lunch table, and hope he notices you?"

"He'll notice me." She shook the two bottles in her hands. "Actually, he already has. . . . Emily said he flicked his eyebrows when I walked by at the dance."

"He . . . flicked his eyebrows?"

"Shut up, Anna." She groaned. "Will red and purple work?"

"Blue's a primary color."

"So?"

"I don't want you to become one of those girls."

"What girls?"

"The ones who rearrange themselves because they think a boy will like it."

"I'm not *rearranging* myself, Anna."

"You're trying to get noticed."

"What am I supposed to do? Listen, Anna, we all try to get noticed. All the time. Everywhere. That's life. Especially for people like us. If the others don't notice us, we disappear."

"If they notice us, they try to get rid of us," Anna argued.

Grace groaned again.

"Let him notice something other than your nails."

"Like what?"

"You. Just you."

Grace pressed the purple and red bottles together, picturing the ideal outcome. "So this won't work?" she asked.

"You can't make blue. Where were you in first grade?" Anna took the bottles away. "The fact that you don't already own blue tells me you don't really like it."

"I do now."

Anna dropped the two bottles among the rest. "Which will it be?"

Grace made her decision, and Anna carefully applied the polish the way she had so many times before. It was when she grasped Grace's right hand that she noticed the bead bracelet tied around Grace's wrist, poking out beneath her sleeve. The shiny glass seed beads—the white ones like little teeth—created a woven pattern of red hearts and colorful flowers. The sight led Anna to run the brush over one of Grace's cuticles, the bracelet being another reminder of how close Emily and Grace had grown. Miss Karen, Emily's mom, crafted and sold the bracelets to supplement her income, only the designs she sold depicted traditional geometric patterns and abstract representations of eagles and feathers. Emily must have had her mom make the bracelet special for Grace.

"There's something else I wanted to talk with you about," Grace said.

"Huh?" Anna focused on the nails once more.

"Fox Ballard called after you left for work this afternoon."

"Fox called here? What'd he want?"

"He wanted to know if I'd be able to clean rooms on weekend mornings."

"Why's he hiring for mornings? Shouldn't Tanya—?"

"He said he spoke to Tanya. She said if I'm anything like you . . ." Grace rolled her eyes.

"You'd have my old job." Anna put the brush back into the nail polish bottle and cracked a teasing smile. "Now you can stop begging Mom and Dad for money."

"I've never begged."

"Right. You've only demanded that they buy you things."

"Not even." Grace batted a cotton ball at Anna, careful not to ruin the polish. "It's not like they ever give in . . . or even hear me." She blew on her nails. "Tell me the truth. How bad's the job? Like, is it really gross cleaning up other peoples' messes?"

Anna shrugged. "Shitty toilets. Bloody sheets. Nothing a little soap and water can't fix."

"Eeewww. There's no cure for AIDS, Anna."

"We wear gloves. You'll be fine. Wet towels and dirty Q-tips on the bathroom floors are usually the worst of it." She didn't dare tell Grace about the vomit she'd cleaned last weekend. "You'll get a checklist of things to do in each room. Just follow the list, make sure everything's in order, and you'll be all right."

"Do people really leave shit in the toilet?"

"You're lucky if it's in the toilet." Anna couldn't resist.

"Anna!"

"Shit happens. You can handle it."

Grace sighed. "You think I should take the job?"

"A little hard work will do you good. But I have some bad news . . ."

"What?"

"The chambermaid coat is green, not blue."

Day 8
4:01 p.m.

Children around Anna's age were old enough to remember the tragedy when Miss Shelby Mire went missing and young enough to let it spawn eerie ideas in their imaginations. Anna supposed Miss Shelby's dearest friends—Miss Mary Forstall, Miss Paula Bishop, and Miss Vicky Peltier—kept Miss Shelby alive deep in their aging hearts, no doubt converging around her grave in the tribal cemetery on her birthday to remember her while silently wondering if they'd ever get the answers to the mystery surrounding her murder, namely the one that would give them a reason why.

For years, Anna had thought she knew what had happened to her only adult friend. She'd believed Uncle Ray when he told her that the head had probably made a meal of Miss Shelby. It was years later that she learned otherwise, when her father finally told her where and how Miss Shelby's body had been found, and how she'd died. The cause of her death didn't change the impact it'd had on Anna; Miss Shelby's death had devasted her spirit. Nor did the truth diminish the horror of Uncle Ray's story. Just because the rolling head hadn't eaten Miss Shelby, didn't mean that it hadn't—or couldn't—devour others, like Amber and Erica.

Ten years gone, the mystery of *why* remained, and Miss Shelby's name was rarely spoken on the rez, though there'd been a time when her memory was revered. Her likeness had been memorialized in a mural on the rear exterior wall of the Blue Gator Grill, capped by words—NEVER FORGOTTEN—that were so washed out now that they contradicted themselves. Equally faded was Miss Shelby's face, surrounded by distressed depictions of Frog, Grasshopper, Brother Eagle, and a slew of enlightening characters Miss Shelby once spoke about, their stories all forgotten, history lost. The excitement spawned by the construction of the casino had overshadowed just about everything, turning Miss Shelby into something as fleeting as her stories once she'd exhaled them. Anna knew her siblings and the other tribal teens were spooked by Miss Shelby's old trailer because that's where she was last alive. Few went near it. None went in it. The doorless entryway seemed to dare Anna to come inside. The deflated couch, long since infested by mice, gave rise to a sick and empty sensation in the pit of her stomach. Even so, she didn't fear the trailer. Nor did she want to see what it housed go to waste.

She knelt on the thin carpet, streaked with mud, and unzipped her backpack. The three books she'd helped herself to nearly one week earlier were inside. She placed them back upon their shelf, in their rightful spots. The books had been worthwhile, all relaying fascinating and sometimes heartbreaking accounts of Native American history, but none had given her what she really wanted, none contained the revelation she was searching for. That was okay. Many shelves remained. Hundreds of books awaited her. Thousands of pages that hadn't been turned in ten years or more.

Reaching for the next book in line, Anna wondered, too, about the songs Miss Shelby used to sing. The way the ancient melodies used to flow out of her was a singular experience, a gift, perhaps, given by the Great Spirit itself. With no known recordings, the songs, it seemed, had all been lost. The stories, she hoped, might still be found.

Anna deposited the next book into her bag. It was a bigger volume than those she'd just returned, nearly as big as the three of them combined. She considered grabbing another just as the echo of a slamming screen door reverberated off the trailer's walls.

Anna reflexively ducked, as if the ghost of Miss Shelby had returned home, putting her at risk of getting caught snooping through her old friend's things. Crawling to the window, she carefully avoided contact with the couch. Through the broken and disheveled blinds, she peeked out at the field that stretched before the trailer. Beyond the field was another boxy abode nearly identical to Miss Shelby's.

A 1995 Chevy Cavalier, black, sat parked in the dirt outside the distant trailer. A young woman, pinching a cigarette between her right thumb and forefinger, occupied the porch steps. Anna was sure she must have seen the young woman around. Her parents, no doubt, would have been able to identify the woman with ease, but Anna couldn't figure if the woman was a Langdon, Ballard, Broussard, Landry, Peltier, Picote, Deshautelle, Forstall, or Bloom.

There was something sad about the young woman. Maybe it was fatigue. The way she lifted her cigarette to her painted lips—slowly, without much desire—implied that she might nod off at any second. Reddish streaks ran through her big hair, which made her even more mysterious to Anna. Pretty, too, especially in contrast to the weathered porch and the trailer's dirt-streaked siding. She didn't seem to belong.

Anna's chin drifted to the windowsill and accidentally rattled the blinds against the glass. The young woman, mid-drag on her cigarette, sat straight and shot her gaze at the Mire trailer. It seemed like they'd locked eyes for an instant, but Anna told herself that that couldn't have happened, not with the distance, the dirty glass, and the disheveled blinds in the way. She dropped beneath the window, heart racing, and lay next to the mice-infested couch until the screen door slammed again.

Day 9
7:53 a.m.

Her mind a jumbled mess of thoughts about the pitch she'd yet to prepare for the preservation society, Miss Shelby's lost stories and songs, and Grace's lunchroom plan, Anna didn't need anything else added to the mix, but it was there waiting for her when she arrived at school. She could see it before she reached it. Not a silver star taped to her locker this time, but a small, pale figure affixed with a strip of clear packing tape across its middle.

Chest heaving, Anna glowered at the dollar store doll, naked and upside down on her locker door. Its amorphous nether region assaulted her eyes. She ripped the doll away and punched the locker, adding another dent to its dinged surface. The doll's hair had been chopped. Short bristles stuck out of its squishy head. The only thing that suggested a degree of femininity was its chest, marked by two nippleless mounds.

Anna gritted her teeth as she turned the doll over in her hands. She knew what to expect on its back. A large black question mark in permanent ink.

Anna held in her fury until the homeroom bell rang, then, timing it perfectly because the perpetrators of the prank were bound to be watching and she would afford them as little pleasure as possible, she buried her face in her locker and released her rage. The doll tight in her grasp, she slammed the locker door and stormed down the hall, ignoring the hall monitor's cries of "Get to class!" as she marched to the main office.

She heaved the office door open with such force that the inset glass rattled in its frame. The smiling doll's head squeaked the instant Anna slammed it onto the receptionist's desk, its rubber stomach crushed beneath the weight of her palm. The receptionist's flying fingers stopped upon her keyboard. Her eyes darted to Anna, and her lips folded into a frown.

"I'll let him know you were here," she said.

Anna didn't move. She just stared, her breath coming and going through her nostrils with such force that her belly might as well have been a bellows someone was squeezing.

"He can't see you right now," the receptionist said.

"I'll wait."

The lady pointed to a chair by the door. Anna shook her head. "It's Friday," the receptionist said, practically pleading for mercy. She found none in Anna's gaze. Exhaling slowly, she pressed the intercom button on her desk. "It's Anna Horn. She'd like to see you. Again."

Minutes passed. Anna didn't budge. The receptionist didn't type. She just sat there looking uncomfortable, wetting her lips every few seconds. When Principal Markham finally appeared, he looked tired and disheveled despite the early hour. His tie hung loose around his neck, its tip dangerously close to dipping into the mug of coffee he held low in his right hand. Glaring at Anna, he jerked his head toward his office.

Principal Markham dropped onto his chair behind his desk. The cushion of his seat sighed beneath his weight, sounding as exasperated as he looked. His eyes drifted from Anna's face to the doll in her hand to his coffee, cloudy with cream. He took a loud sip. "The doll?" he said. "Is that it?"

"You said it would stop."

"If you ignore it, it will."

"It's getting worse."

"If you don't know exactly who's doing it—"

"Everyone's doing it."

"Can you specifically name—?"

"You know I can't."

"And you know we can't monitor your locker all day, Anna."

"I'm not asking you to do that."

"And if they're not hurting you . . ."

But they were hurting her. More than Anna ever let on.

Principal Markham tightened his tie and leaned in closer across his desk. "I can see that you're bothered." His tone had lightened, sounding more understanding. "Will you take my advice this time? The school counselor. Mr. Taylor. Will you go see him? He has good ideas. He can help."

"I don't want to talk to Mr. Taylor. I just want this to stop. I want to be left alone. That's all I've ever wanted."

"Yes, but, Anna, did you ever think that all of this might start with you? If you want it to stop, you ought to ask yourself what you can do about it."

"I've come to you," she said. "More than once."

"I've offered you help. I've given you my recommendation. Sometimes in life, Anna, you have to change things for yourself."

Anna pulled her bottom lip between her teeth and nodded. "You're blaming me," she said.

"I'm not blaming you. I'm asking you, what can you do to change?"

Heat rose in Anna's cheeks. The doll squeaked again in her grasp. "This isn't fair."

"It could be easy," Principal Markham said. "Change."

Anna remained silent long enough for his assertion to become a firm part of the past. Nothing but the *tick tick tick* of the clock on the wall made any noise. "May I have a pass back to class?"

Mr. Markham, Anna thought, just wanted to continue sipping his coffee, tugging on his tie, and periodically strolling through the school to observe everyone he outranked, making himself feel like he'd done something great with his life. He'd never know what it was like to get bowed to the way she had, the years of mockery, alienation, and isolation.

Anna trudged back up the stairs to retrieve her notebook and texts. Giving the doll a final squeeze, she tossed it atop the heap of bodies that'd already amassed at the bottom of her locker.

A two-tone blue-and-white pickup truck idled in the spot where Chris usually parked the meat wagon. Anna parked beside it and went inside to find tribal police chief Luke Fisher, wearing sweatpants and boots, standing in the living room. The weary look of sleep clung to him, betraying that he'd just drifted off when he was called out of bed. Dorothy, Chris, Robbie, and Gran, looking unbalanced and apprehensive, stood gathered around.

"What the hell, Anna?" Chris stormed to the door and tore his keys from her hand.

"I was looking for Grace."

"And?" Robbie said, though it was clear she'd been unsuccessful in her search.

"Odds are she'll show up," Luke said. "Probably sooner than you'd think."

Anna thought about Erica and Amber, whereabouts unknown. Erica's father had traveled to L.A. two weeks after their disappearance to find them. He'd returned alone six days later, exhausted and overwhelmed by the city's scope, its tourists, its traffic, its noise, and all the desperate souls hoping to succeed where so many had failed.

"Has she ever taken off before?" Luke asked.

"No," Chris said.

"Well . . ." Anna muttered. All eyes darted to her.

"Anna says Grace has been sneaking out at night," Dorothy said.

"She comes and goes through the bedroom window."

"God damnit, Anna!" Chris fumed. "You just thought to bring this up now?"

Luke put a hand out to settle him down. "Teenagers do this all the time," he said.

"She was at the hotel tonight," Anna blurted. She produced the lip balm from her pocket. "I found this in one of the suites."

Luke took the lip balm. "How do you know it's hers?"

"She uses it every day."

"But how do you know this particular tube belongs to her?"

"It's hers. She must have been on the eighth floor. Fox Ballard was up there and another man too." The more Anna spoke, the more her world dissolved around her. She told them about the suspicious activity in suite 808, about who she'd seen on the eighth floor, and about the drugs she'd seen in Fox's house. Chris let more than a few choice words fly. He looked like he might strangle her on the spot. Then she had to say what she suspected about Missy Picote.

"I think I saw her in the emergency stairwell the night before her father reported her missing. She was coming down the stairs, probably from the eighth floor."

"You *think* it was her?" Luke asked.

"I didn't get a good look at her face."

"But the girl you saw . . . she was by herself? Leaving of her own free will?"

"Yes," Anna admitted. She knew exactly what Luke was getting at.

"Missy's father suspects that Missy ran off on a bender," Luke said.

"I know what Sawyer suspects."

"That doesn't mean we're not concerned about her."

"Will you at least—?"

Luke put a hand on Anna's shoulder, nodding. "I hate to ask . . . but is Grace . . ."

"Using?" Anna said. "No. Not at all."

"You're sure?"

Suddenly Anna had doubt. Could Grace be in the same grip as Missy? Could she—Anna—have missed the signs? No, she decided. Impossible.

"Get real, Luke," Chris said. "I'd know if my daughter were on drugs."

Luke's lips pulled tight and he nodded. "I'll go by the hotel to see if anyone's seen her. A recent photo would help."

Dorothy took last year's school picture from the frame on the wall.

"Will you talk to Fox?" Anna asked Luke.

"I'll pay him a visit." He took the lip balm from Anna. "It could just be a coincidence, you know?" He studied the tube, then promised to put the rest of the miniscule tribal police force on alert. "Keep your bedroom window unlocked," he said to Anna. "I wouldn't be surprised if she's home by morning. Hasn't she always returned before?"

Anna nodded. Still tense, Dorothy and Chris breathed easier, upset yet reassured by the history they'd just learned. The family followed Luke out of the house. Even Gran hobbled to the door, clutching everything in her path to maintain her balance.

"Give me a call when she shows up," Luke said as a final assurance.

Chris exhaled a heavy breath and gave Luke a half-hearted salute as Luke's truck backed off the property. Its headlights illuminated the long, dusty street. There was no one on it. No one heading home.

Day 9
12:09 p.m.

Alone at the table she usually shared with Grace and Emily, Anna picked apart the sandwich she'd packed for lunch. The two girls hadn't even glanced at her on their way past their usual seats. They'd stuck to their plan, inserting themselves at Kevin Mills's table with all of Kevin's friends.

Grace displayed her purple-painted nails—thrumming the tabletop, stroking her temples, caressing her collarbone—hoping they looked more navy than plum. She sat at the very end of the table, Emily opposite her, a strained smile on her face. She looked like a kid on her birthday being told to pose for a picture when all she wanted was to tear open the presents and dive into the cake. Anna felt sorry for her because she had little faith that Grace would get what she wanted. Kevin, his smile born of the banter between himself and his crew, didn't notice his new tablemates. No one acknowledged their presence. Nor were they bothered by it. Grace and Emily weren't welcomed, but they weren't told to leave. Anna wondered why.

Sitting alone wasn't much different than when Emily and Grace excluded Anna from their secret conversations, a barrier of empty chairs always between them. What made it worse than being ignored was what it said to others. Now everyone would know that Anna wasn't just an outsider among her peers from town but that she was deemed different among her own kind as well.

Suddenly the cafeteria's swirl of conversation seemed to be about her. The smirking lips. The pointed fingers. The guffaws. The ass of the rubber doll that had been aimed up at her face that morning left little doubt that Anna was the literal butt of everyone's jokes, their wisecracks. She shrank in her chair, wishing she could turn herself inside out. She would if she could. But even then, she'd still be red on the outside. It seemed they'd never see her any other way, leaving her with little hope that they'd change how they treated her.

Taking a deep breath, Anna let it out slow. Her paranoia passed. She was good for a laugh now and then, but she'd be a fool to think the others would waste their entire lunch hour dwelling on her. They poked fun at themselves instead, differently than when they poked fun at her. Anna had never gotten the hang of saying *fuck you* the way they said it to one another, the curse somehow strengthening their bond.

Eavesdropping on Kevin and his crew, she heard them brag about drinking and staying out late. They'd egged a car and run from the cops.

"It was crazy," they said. "Crazy, man. So fucking crazy."

Julie Long and Corrine Harris sat among them, cradling cell phones as if the devices were purebred puppies, treating them like the status symbols they were. Julie repeatedly raised and lowered the antenna, lowkey bragging. Grace eyed her with envy in between ogling Kevin.

"My dad won't stop calling," Julie moaned. "I swear I should just get rid of this thing."

"Oh my god, Marty calls every day," Corrine replied, "and he has absolutely nothing to say. Sometimes we just listen to each other breathe."

Anna shoved the bits of her sandwich back into its bag and pushed away from the table. Her eyes sought Grace's as she crossed the cafeteria, striving to signal her sister without embarrassing her. Grace's gaze, however, was glued to Kevin, leaving Anna with little choice. She sidled next to the table and took her sister by the arm.

Grace pulled away before she knew who was touching her. Her expression hardened when she saw her sister. Anna stepped back and jerked her head toward their usual spot.

"Get!" Grace snapped, as if Anna were a dog.

"You can't stay here."

"Anna, don't," Grace growled, when Corrine turned her head in their direction.

"Trust me," Anna said. "They're not your kind of people."

"What?"

"They're fake."

"I don't care."

"I don't like fake people."

A few of the others noticed Anna standing at the end of the long table. Grace's hard stare began to melt, becoming panicked as it bounced from Anna to Kevin. His head was turning. Soon he'd see Anna standing there, looking like a farmhand in a pair of her father's old overalls.

"Shit," Grace said through gritted teeth. She propelled herself up and away from the table, dragging Anna from the cafeteria to the restroom in the hall. "You'll ruin everything."

"I don't want you around them. I don't want you to act like them."

"I don't care what you want, Anna. You can't tell me who to hang around with."

"Grace, they don't even want you around. Can't you see that?"

"They do." Her voice caught in her throat. Anna almost apologized.

"Why, then?" Anna asked. "Why do they suddenly want you around?"

"They just do." Grace blinked fast. Her eyes had begun to glisten.

Anna mercifully turned away. She pulled a paper towel from the dispenser and ran it beneath the cold tap. "Guess what I found on my locker today," she said, passing the towel to her sister.

Grace exhaled a ragged breath. She pressed the towel over her eyes for a few seconds, then tossed it away. "I'm sorry," she whispered, knowing how the others tormented Anna.

"We're not one of them," Anna said, once the pain, which she attributed to desire, had drained from Grace's eyes. "They'll use you if they think you have something to give, but they'll never accept you. Don't be fooled." Anna grabbed Grace's arm again and tapped her skin. "We'll always be different in their eyes, and they'll always treat us as such. Look what they do to me."

Grace scoffed. "They don't give you shit because you're Indian, Anna. They give you shit because you . . . you're . . ."

"I'm what?"

"You're you."

Anna's stare burrowed into Grace, demanding an explanation.

"You're different, Anna. And that's not the same as saying *we're different*. It's not the color of our skin . . . not really. Not like it used to be." Grace pulled her hands through her hair, flabbergasted, frustrated. "Look at yourself, Anna. You wear Dad's old clothes. You're wearing his boots right now. They've noticed. They've all noticed. They nominated you *king*, for fuck's sake."

"That's on them," Anna said.

"It's on you," Grace insisted. "It's *because* of you. And I can't let you rub off on me anymore."

"What do you mean *anymore*?"

"Forget it." She turned toward the mirror and picked a soggy speck of paper towel from her cheek.

"Tell me," Anna badgered some more, her hand pawing at Grace's shoulder.

Grace's lips clamped tight and her cheeks filled with air. "You really wanna know?" she erupted, facing Anna head-on. "Two weeks before the start of school last year there was an orientation day for all incoming freshmen. I went with Emily. We were anxious . . . excited, a little bit scared. There were older kids there, too, juniors and seniors who showed us around campus. They helped us find our lockers and answered whatever questions we had. They all seemed pretty cool until Matt Romano, who's my age, showed up on the first day of school with something his big brother, who'd been one of our tour guides, made."

"Ryan Romano," Anna muttered. He was a senior like her. A member of the student government, he seemed like a nice enough guy, smart.

"Know what Ryan made?"

Anna shrugged.

"A list," Grace said, "ranking the freshman girls, all eighty-seven of us. Matt passed it around to his friends. Emily saw it. She was number thirty-six on the list."

"Grace . . . how could Ryan even remember all the girls—?"

"He used Matt's middle school yearbook for help. Guess what number he gave me."

"Grace, you can't let—"

"Eighty-seven," Grace said, her eyes glistening again. "Next to our names, Ryan wrote a reason for his ranking. Wanna guess what he wrote for me?"

Anna didn't want to guess. She didn't want to hear any more.

"Anna Horn's sister." Grace's voice quavered. "That's what landed me on the bottom. In last place. *Anna Horn's sister!*"

Anna felt herself flush, her flesh hot all over. She didn't say anything because she couldn't. The revelation had practically punched her in the chest.

"Do you know what that did to me? How embarrassing it was? Do you know I've *dreaded* being seen with you every day since?"

"Grace?" Anna said, short on breath, wondering if a stupid list made by someone so insignificant to her could really be responsible for the cracks in her and Grace's relationship.

"In spite of your reputation, I've managed to make friends. *Don't* ruin this for me." Grace yanked the bathroom door open and stalked away.

Anna fell against the tiled wall. She drifted down it, caught herself midway, then reclaimed her stance. It wasn't just her father's clothes, she told herself, refusing to believe that roots and ethnic traits weren't determining factors in how she was regarded.

Facing her reflection in the mirror, she saw thin eyebrows over defeated eyes, strong cheekbones, a stronger chin. Her index finger rode down the steep ridge of her nose, then quickly fell to her side when a toilet flushed and the snap of a lock echoed off the tiles.

The stall door at the end of the row swung open. A brown-haired girl wearing a suede vest over a white T-shirt emerged. Familiar yet nameless, she went straight for a sink, ignoring Anna on the way. She had to be a junior, Anna thought. The girl's narrow fingers picked at a blemish above her lip, poking it as if they could banish it beneath her skin. Anna retreated, heading for the door.

"She's acting desperate."

Anna stopped and glanced over her shoulder to confirm that the girl was talking to her.

"I'd tell her to stay away, too, if she were my little sister," the girl said. Her eyes slid toward Anna's via the bathroom mirror. "Those guys don't really like her. They just like what she does. At least that's what they've been saying."

"Who's been saying?" Anna asked, taking the bait. The rumors on campus had always been about her, not Grace.

"Homecoming?" the girl said, prodding as though she might awaken a memory within Anna. All Anna could think about was the vote and how everyone had bowed before her.

"The dance?" the girl went on. A smirk blossomed on her lips. "Well, after the dance, I mean."

"What are you talking about?"

The girl turned from the mirror, facing Anna directly. "Sorry," she said, lacking the least bit of sympathy, "I thought you knew."

The twinkle in her eyes indicated that the girl was enjoying the game. Anna took a stand in front of the bathroom door, preventing anyone from coming or going. "What?" she said again.

"You really don't know?"

Anna didn't waver.

The girl looked Anna up and down. "It's the guys," she said. Her face reddened, turning darker than Anna's. "They've been telling everyone that Grace is good with her mouth."

Worried about what Grace might see in her eyes, Anna walked home alone after school, her head half buried in the volume of Native American mythology she'd taken from Miss Shelby's trailer. Dozens of stories and illustrations filled the glossy pages. The tales came from tribal nations across the country, many sharing similarities that suggested the Native world was indeed connected by spirits throughout the land. The text contained names, phrases, themes, symbols, proverbs, and origins. It introduced mythological creatures, beliefs, rituals, and traditions while exploring how Christianity had impacted many aspects of Native life. The book had a lot to offer, including gold in the form of loopy script scrawled in the margins.

Though Miss Shelby's handwritten notes, smudged upon the glossy paper, were difficult to decipher, they sparkled like precious gems in Anna's eyes. The notes gave insight into the Takoda's ways and beliefs, even if they were little puzzles that needed piecing together. Next to the Zuni proverb, "After dark all cats are leopards," Miss Shelby had written, *Alligators and anoles.*

Anna squinted at the three words, trying to create a connection with the proverb, but her mind kept rewinding to the bathroom earlier that day. Was the rumor about Grace true? Had she done something after the dance that would haunt her? Had she been forced? Anna thought about how tenacious Grace had always been. Persistent in her pursuit of the things she wanted and slow to accept defeat, like her endless requests for a cat as a kid. Every birthday. Every Christmas. It was always the same, despite knowing her wish would go unconsidered, unheard. Grace had had to settle for a pseudo pet, a feral cat covered in gray fur except for the white around its mouth. Grace had called her Storm, both because of her color and because half her left ear had been ripped away; the jagged piece of remaining flesh had resembled a lightning bolt.

Storm would swish her ratty tail across the reservation, feasting on field mice, frogs, and grasshoppers she swatted out of the air. She needed no help feeding herself, but Grace set cans of tuna or sardines—pilfered from the kitchen cabinets—on the porch anyway, perhaps to convince herself that Storm was really hers.

Storm soaked up the sun on the Horns' front porch but showed little appreciation for the food. The raccoons would come for it after dark, a fact Grace staunchly denied. She'd pound her feet and shake her head when Dad teased that the raccoons loved her more than the ugly old cat. The sad fact was that Grace had never been able to tame Storm. She'd never even been able to pet her. The cat would come close but never close enough, maybe making Grace feel the same way Chris and Dorothy made her feel whenever their attention bounced from Anna to Robbie without pausing in the middle. Still, Grace defended Storm whenever anyone called her mangy, flea-ridden, or foul. Could the girl who'd so stubbornly and insistently made Storm hers be coerced by boys at school and then stay silent? Anna hoped not. And she hoped Grace's desperation to separate herself from her big sister hadn't been a factor at all.

The harsh scent of hot asphalt wound its way up Anna's nose as she crossed from town onto the rez. The scent, combined with the sounds of work trucks beeping and scraping against the ground, made her head ache. Approaching the work zone, she heard men calling to each other, speaking phrases that meant nothing to her.

She paused fifty feet from where the work crew was turning the dirt road into a shiny black street. The sight brought Principal Markham's words to her ears.

What can you do to change?

Change surrounded Anna. The casino, the resort, the roads, her fellow tribal members, Grace. She questioned if the changes were beneficial, or if they were merely meant to catch the eyes of others.

We all try to get noticed, Grace had said.

The casino and resort had certainly gotten the tribe noticed, but at what cost? And was it worth it? A brand-new sports car zoomed by as if in response to Anna's thoughts.

She tucked Miss Shelby's book beneath her arm and wandered into the field along the road to bypass the work crew without getting in its way. She'd have an hour before work when she got home, enough time to get ready but not enough time to smooth things over with Grace, not that she'd know what to say. For once, she hoped her little sister would be out with Emily.

Robbie was deep in the field near the house when Anna drew near, his newest toy braced against his shoulder as if the rifle were an appendage that had sprouted overnight, like the pimples that had appeared on his chin and the expanded Adam's apple that jutted from his throat. He swung the rifle from side to side and darted about the brush. Anna couldn't tell if he was aiming at imaginary squirrels, real ones, or both. Though the rifle should have made him look more grown up, the boyish zeal with which he held it in his hands made him look younger than ever.

Anna ventured closer, carefully placing her feet upon the grass so as not to alert him. She could hear him panting from twenty feet away. If any squirrels had been out there, he'd undoubtedly scared them off.

Shielding her body behind a tree, Anna watched Robbie swing the rifle in her direction. He startled and jumped back before recognizing the eyes upon him.

"Hey, Anna!" he called, and lowered the rifle. "You gotta do better than that if you wanna ambush me."

"You only saw me because I let you." She waved and carried on toward home, taking just a handful of steps before stopping and letting her backpack slide from her shoulders. She stuffed Miss Shelby's book inside, then returned to Robbie in the field.

"Let me try it," she said.

"It's not loaded. Dad says I can't shoot it when he's not around. Not yet, anyway."

Anna reached for the rifle. Robbie pulled it closer to his side. Her hand persisted.

"Come on, Anna," he said, her fingers grazing the barrel. "I don't touch your things." That was true these days, but Anna recalled the paper forest she'd constructed in elementary school, the rag dolls she and Mom had made, and the kite she'd constructed out of old plastic bags, duct tape, and Gran's yarn; all things he hadn't just touched but torn to shreds.

Anna moved her hand to the forestock and pulled. Robbie pulled back. "Anna!" He was pleading, not yelling. She could tell he wasn't trying to be nasty or mean. He sounded a lot like Grace when she'd implored Anna in the cafeteria, just before giving in and dragging Anna to the restroom. Suddenly it dawned on her that he didn't want to be seen with her either. She could only imagine his face if one of his buddies came by and saw his big, goofy sister pointing his rifle. And what if she was a better shot than he was? What would happen to his self-esteem?

"Fine, Robbie. You don't have to show me," Anna said, understanding yet slightly stung. It was the same feeling she'd felt at six when the boys had banned her from their stickball game in the field. Miss

Shelby had been there, dusting dirt from her dress following one of her story sessions by the old oak.

No girls allowed, Ty Landry, only eight at the time, had said.

Anna had looked down at herself, wondering what exactly made her and Ty so different. Their canvas sneakers were the same. So were their jeans. And his hair was almost as long as hers.

They don't see it yet. They can't, Miss Shelby had gently said.

See what?

That we're not always this or that. Sometimes we're both. There was that word again from Miss Shelby. *Both.* Anna hadn't been able to ask her about it because Miss Shelby had set off for home just then, but Miss Shelby did stop and look back before going too far. *You'd help them win the game,* she'd said, smiling.

Anna retreated from Robbie, dragging her feet through the grass.

"Don't be mad," he called after her.

"I'm not mad." She flashed a forced smile in his direction.

"Anna?" he called again.

Her feet kept moving. "Don't stay out too late," she said.

"Are they breaking up?" The question brought Anna to a standstill. Robbie ran up beside her. "They're not the same anymore. They don't treat each other the way they used to."

Anna nodded. Though no one had spoken about it, it'd been clear for some time that their parents' relationship was strained.

"What changed?" Robbie asked.

The casino, Anna wanted to say, then chastised herself for having such a stupid thought. The casino couldn't be responsible. Not really. The money it put in her parents' pockets might have opened their eyes to an option they'd never considered before, making them see that they could afford to live without each other if they could stop spending their monthly cut as soon as it came in, but it couldn't be blamed for how they treated each other.

"I don't know, Robbie. Sometimes people just change. Even if they don't mean to."

"What'll happen to us?"

Anna shrugged and took a deep breath. "We'll stick together. Like always. And maybe someday you'll show me how that thing works." She jerked her chin toward the rifle and coaxed her lips to form another smile. "Don't forget to do your homework."

"It's done."

"Sure."

"I didn't even have any."

"Squirrel!" Anna pointed at the trees over his left shoulder. Robbie spun around and ran off.

A knot formed in the pit of Anna's stomach as she neared home, where the sad ball of a human being occupied the porch steps. Grace lifted her head from her knees upon hearing Anna's footfalls along the gravel drive. She'd been chipping the purple polish from her nails. Anna stopped a few yards from the porch, still intent on avoiding Grace's eyes.

"They went to the arcade after school," Grace said in a small voice.

Anna wondered if Grace hadn't been invited to go because of her, but Grace didn't seem to be blaming Anna. The way she picked at her nails suggested that she'd come to a different conclusion. Still, the knot in Anna's stomach transformed into a pang of guilt, accompanied by curiosity Anna couldn't bring herself to voice out loud. Did Grace already know what their peers were saying at school?

A wasted breath streaming out of her, Anna walked up the steps and went inside, pausing for a second to squeeze Grace's shoulder along the way.

The breeze blew colder by the hour, making the curtains billow. Anna sat up all night by the bedroom window. The blanket around her blocked the breeze but failed to warm her inner chill.

Rustling sounded throughout the house. No one slept. No one would.

"I'm going to look for her," Chris had announced shortly after midnight. Anna felt she should be doing something as well, but what? She kept thinking about Fox and everything else that had troubled her over the past month, including the boys from school and the rumor that had gone around about Grace. It had nothing to do with suite 808, and yet she wondered if there could be a connection.

Anna groaned, mind racing. Fox. The rumor. The boys at school. Suite 808. The lip balm.

The lip balm!

Anna leapt to search Grace's things. She sent a silent prayer to the Great Spirit, hoping it'd help her find another red-and-green tube that would make her think *coincidence,* just like Chief Fisher had suggested. She sorted through the odds and ends scattered about the nightstand, the desk she and Grace shared, and atop the dresser. She sifted through the contents of the makeup bag and searched the pockets of the outfit Grace had worn the day before. She found no lip balm, no notes, no clues.

The night passed slowly, ultimately obliterated by the squawking alarm. Its abrasive caw hammered in the fact that something was wrong this time. Grace had never crept in after it went off.

Anna silenced the alarm and trudged to the bathroom, feet like bricks. No one would have forced her to school that day, but she had reason for going. She skipped breakfast and started to walk, only to be intercepted by Emily and her mom driving toward the Horn house. The jalopy pulled over and Emily's face emerged from a rolled-down window.

"Really?" she said.

"Really," Anna confirmed.

Emily's expression wilted like a cut flower beneath the scorching sun. "I thought she'd be home by now."

Anna shook her head. Emily opened the car door and scooched over on the backseat so Anna could get in. Neither said much on the way to school. Emily's mom did most of the talking between puffs of her cigarette, saying, "Never thought Grace would run away. She's too nice for that," and, "Tell your folks to hang in there. This parenting thing's tougher than eating an old boot," and the compulsory, "I'm sure she'll show up." After ruminating a bit more, Miss Karen even added, "Tell you what, Em, you'd better never pull anything like this. I'll kill you if you do." She left them at the curb in front of the school, instructing them to meet her at that very spot after the final bell.

Anna turned to Emily the instant the old car rattled away. "Tell me everything."

"I don't know where she is."

"I want to know what you talk about. All the things you say in your secret code."

Emily blew out a breath that made the wispy hairs hanging in front of her face billow up around her like spider legs. "We talk about everything."

"So you must know where she was last night."

"I already told your mom on the phone. . . . Grace said she couldn't hang out last night. She didn't say why."

"What has she said about Fox?"

"Fox?" Emily's face twisted and flushed. "She likes him. Thinks he's cute. . . ." Her eyes dropped to her feet. "He gets her drinks at the bar."

"Is Grace doing drugs?"

Emily's eyes sprang up, wide as pancakes. "No," she said. "I swear she isn't."

Anna believed her. The warning bell rang and Emily inched toward the entrance, eager to break free from Anna.

"One more thing," Anna said. "You must have heard the rumor that went around a few weeks ago?"

Emily didn't answer. She just swallowed hard.

"Is it true?" Anna asked.

Emily's clenched jaw loosened. She gave a slight nod as her lips parted, showing teeth that—for a fraction of a second—looked a little too long. The acknowledgment was a snare around Anna's heart. She clutched her chest.

"I don't think that has anything to do with this," Emily said, struggling to speak, her throat dry. She swallowed again. "She said she'd gotten over it."

"Gotten over what, exactly?"

"Disappointment, I guess. Maybe regret." Her voice slumped to a whisper. "She wants to be popular so bad. She wants to be liked. They offered her money, too."

The snare pulled tighter. Anna felt like she'd practically been kicked in the head, gut, and chest all at once. "Money?" she echoed.

"She wants that fucking cell phone so bad," Emily said, starting to cry. "I can't believe she did it. I wasn't there, or else I would have stopped her. I was with . . ." She trailed off.

Anna cupped the back of Emily's head, gentle yet firm, and brought their faces within inches of each other. "Look at me," she said.

Their eyes met.

"Would she have done it again?"

"I don't know, Anna. I don't think so."

"Could she have been with them last night?"

"She *could* have been," Emily answered quickly. "But she wasn't. Last night was the first time Kevin Mills and his friends—all his friends, not just the boys—invited us to hang with them. Like, really invited us. I thought Grace would be ecstatic, but she said she couldn't come. She didn't say why."

"Could she have been with someone else from school? Someone I don't know about?"

"I don't know. I don't think so, Anna."

"What about the hotel? Did Grace say anything about it?"

"She works there."

"Don't be dumb. Did she ever mention anything unrelated to work? Anything about the eighth floor?"

Emily's head shook in Anna's hands. "No. Nothing."

The homeroom bell prompted Anna to release her hold. The stragglers and burnouts raced to get inside. Late again. Emily backed away from Anna to catch up with the others. Anna stood at the curb for a moment more, then started down the sidewalk away from school.

"Where are you going?" Emily called.

Anna didn't answer. There was someone else she had to see.

Day 9
4:54 p.m.

The green-and-purple splotch upon the brand-new blacktop swelled as Anna approached on her way to work. Tire marks ran through the pulpy mess. Anna stood with her feet on either side of the obliterated amphibian, thinking about Grace and remembering what Miss Shelby had said about Frog. She'd spoken more fondly of him than she had of Grasshopper.

She said Frog exemplified transformation. He entered life in one form and left it in another. From egg to tadpole, to tadpole with legs, to amphibian with tail, to tailless frog, he was never the same. He began life in water, only emerging once he was his true self. He symbolized change, rebirth, and renewal, and his spirit could bring rain.

Anna stared down at the ill-fated frog. The reservation was transforming. The asphalt beneath her feet was evidence of that. And yet the very symbol of change had become a victim of it. The absurdity didn't escape her.

Ignoring the sounds of excitement floating from the casino as a floor manager snapped a Polaroid of an old woman with nicotine-stained teeth wrestling a jumbo check that blocked most of her spindly body, Anna clocked in and made her rounds, checking the storerooms and closets to make certain they were stocked.

The soap supply on the third floor was low, and the shampoo bottles were out. Anna collected the empty cardboard boxes and turned to trash them, but found Fox in the housekeeping closet doorway instead, a hand on either side of the frame, blocking her in.

"Don't do that," she said, stifling a gasp. He looked out of sorts, the top button of his shirt undone beneath his tie. Damp hair drooped against his forehead and sweat glistened on his upper lip. "Were you just outside?"

He pulled his tie a little looser. "You're doing a good job," he said.

Anna took a step back, letting the boxes fall. "It's not exactly hard."

Fox's gaze traveled down her body, then up again. His apathetic expression diminished his good looks. Chin hanging low beneath saggy undereye skin, he looked like he hadn't slept in days, and yet the wheels in his mind seemed to turn just fine. The longer he thought, the funnier Anna felt.

"I want to promote you," he finally said, glancing over his shoulder. A guest carrying a cooler, icy water sloshing with each step, passed by. Fox inched closer. He shut the door.

Anna, finding it hard to swallow within the tight confines, squeezed between two of the housekeeping carts, hands robotically rearranging the amenities and cleaning supplies. "I thought this was the promotion," she said.

"It was," he agreed. His bloodshot eyes rarely blinked. His powerful body seemed to expand.

Anna worked the lump down her throat. "What else is there?" she asked.

"The eighth floor." His voice had dropped to a whisper. Anna got the feeling that he hadn't meant for his volume to go so low. He cleared his throat and looked over his shoulder again as if he'd forgotten that he'd closed the door. "The eighth floor," he repeated, voice firmer. "I could use some help up there."

"You want me . . . ?"

"Don't act so surprised. Those rooms . . ." He trailed off, eyes clouding over, chin still hanging down.

"They're for high rollers and important guests," Anna said.

Fox's head jerked up as if he'd been startled awake. "That's right. The girls who work on the eighth are carefully chosen. Privacy is of the utmost importance."

"Of course." Anna knocked a bottle of glass cleaner from the cart with one hand and caught it with the other. "Does this mean I'm back to working weekend mornings?"

Fox shook his head. "No mornings. Never mornings. You'll still do this. You'll be on the eighth as needed. Whenever I say."

Anna nodded quickly, hoping he'd leave.

"You'll have to wear this." He took a chambermaid's coat from the hook on the door.

"But you said—"

"I'm saying this now. You don't go up there unless you're wearing this."

Anna snagged the coat from him and tossed it over the back of the cart.

"Good," he said. Reaching into his pocket, he pulled out a plastic elevator access card. "You know how this works?"

"I think so."

"Don't lose it. And don't tell anyone you have it."

"I won't."

"Promise."

Anna's face flushed.

"That card has value, Anna. No one's to go up to the eighth unless I say so. Not even you. Understand?"

"I won't say anything to anyone," she said. "And I'll only go up when you want me to."

"Good. You like your job, don't you?"

"Could be worse."

"Could be a lot worse." He consulted his watch like a man who had somewhere to be. "Here." He handed over a folded piece of paper that was torn at one end. Anna began to unfold it as he grabbed the chambermaid coat from the cart and thrust it at her again. "Quickly, Anna!" One of his big hands wrapped around hers before she could finish unfolding the paper. "Eight-oh-eight," he said. "Only that suite. Take this too." Like a magician, he made another card appear, only it didn't have a heart, club, diamond, or spade on it, just a magnetic strip that would unlock the suite.

"You want me to start up there now?" she asked.

"Quickly!" he said, shaking the coat at her.

Anna slipped her arms through the sleeves of the garment she didn't want to wear while the scents of soap, bleach, and disinfectant worked their way deeper within her. Fox wrenched open the closet door and flailed an arm until Anna was in the hall, heading for the elevator.

"Eight-oh-eight," he said again.

Anna hurried inside the glass box and pressed the button to close the doors. As they rolled shut, leaving her feeling entombed yet relieved, she saw Fox lean close to the mirror hanging in the hall, his fingers frantically combing his soggy hair into place.

Hands inexplicably shaking, Anna tapped the eighth-floor button, testing it. It felt different than the buttons above it—firmer and of higher quality, despite its identical appearance—and it remained unlit. Glancing over her shoulder in case someone might be watching through the glass, Anna inserted the access card into its special slot at the bottom of the elevator's panel. Card in place, she pressed the eighth-floor button again. It glowed this time.

Anna turned from the elevator doors while the lift ascended and slowed. The view through the glass was only slightly different than the view from the seventh floor, yet Anna felt like she was one hundred stories high. Her eyes flickered, doing a double take, when Grace and Emily appeared in the Atrium below, probably on their way to the diner for a milkshake or headed to the arcade to play pinball if they weren't just ogling boys, which—Anna suspected—was their most likely objective. Anna's impulse was to pound on the glass, to get their attention and show them where she was and what she was doing. But then she remembered her promise to Fox—not to let anyone know that she had access to the eighth—and she could only conclude that it was her silence after scrubbing vomit in the fifth-floor guestroom, in addition to her indifference regarding Chairman Ballard's private business in the conference room, that had earned her his trust.

The elevator doors rumbled open. Anna watched until Grace and Emily were out of sight, then took her first solo steps into the land of VIPs. The floor was noticeably quieter than the ones below. No TVs blared through the walls. No kids ran up and down the corridor. Fewer room doors lined the hall, spaced farther apart than those downstairs. Having overlooked the events board in the lobby the last few days, Anna wondered if any of the suites were occupied by singers, comedians, or magicians scheduled to headline the showroom attached to the casino.

She took small steps through the hall as though the hall monitor from school would suddenly appear if she broke the silence. The housekeeping closet stood in the same spot on the eighth as on the floors below. Anna slipped inside, surrounding herself with soap and towels, things that felt familiar.

She smoothed the piece of paper Fox had given her, moist with palm sweat, against a shelf and finished unfolding it. A list, like the one the chambermaids used to guide them through their daily duties, appeared. Handwritten, it included things Anna had never had to do on any of the other floors.

Take cleaning cart into room (do not leave in hall!)
Keep door <u>closed at all times</u>
Set thermostat to 68 degrees
Fill ice bucket
Empty mini bar <u>completely</u>

Why? Anna wondered. Wouldn't the guests complain if they wanted a snack or something to drink?

Close all curtains

Again, Anna was confused. She'd always been instructed to let light in.

Report to housekeeping office when complete. Remain
there until called to remake room.

Anna, chewing the tip of her thumb, reread the last item on the list until logic sank in. Fox wasn't having her prepare for an overnight guest. Half her mind told her to storm downstairs and tell Fox to find someone else to take over. This wasn't part of her job description. And the resort wasn't some seedy pay-by-the-hour motel. At least it wasn't supposed to be, though it was no secret that some tribal bigwigs often slipped up to the suites for "private business."

"It's just a job," she told herself, reasoning that whatever happened within the rooms was none of her business, and that whatever happened within an hour was the same that happened overnight, just at a quicker pace. If a couple high rollers wanted to get their rocks off then bolt, well, that's what rubber gloves were for. Besides, she'd always wanted to work in the suites.

Anna ensured the cleaning cart was stocked, gloves and all, then pushed it down the hall. Suite 808 was at the end near the emergency stairwell. Nearly as big as her entire house and a hell of a lot nicer, the magnificence of the suite blinded Anna to her duties when she turned on the light. She wheeled the cleaning cart inside and closed the door as instructed, then lowered the thermostat to 68 degrees, letting the rest of the guidelines go forgotten as she wandered deeper into the suite. The pool table's green felt delighted her fingertips. The colorful patterns at every turn, on the carpet, the wallpaper, the couches and chairs, enchanted her eyes.

Gold tassels hung from the grand spread covering the king-size bed in the bedroom. Delicate fingers played upon the duvet and then, before she knew it, Anna was sinking into the mattress, eyes closed. Cool air blew through the room's vents, seeming to cast away the stress of the day, the week, her entire existence.

Fuzzy around the edges and blank in her brain, Anna bolted upright. Panic swelled within her. Had she been drowsing on the mattress for only a moment, or had minutes ticked by? She rolled off the bed and smoothed the duvet. She closed the curtains, then ran into the main room to block out the light seeping in through the balcony doors. Racing to the mini bar—not nearly as mini as the ones in the standard guestrooms—she unloaded the contents onto the housekeeping cart. She'd just grabbed hold of the ice bucket when a loud *snap* rang out. The room lock had come undone. The door swung open.

Heart racing and panic still surging through her veins, Anna darted into the galley kitchen, out of sight from the main room. The suite's door clicked shut. Seconds of silence passed and then voices speaking in low tones met Anna's ears. One of the voices was female. Two others were male. Did one belong to Fox?

Anna hugged the ice bucket to her chest, weighing what she should do next. Announce herself? Try to sneak out? Stay put in the darkened kitchen until the suite was empty?

The voices tapered off. Another door clicked shut. The bedroom.

Anna soundlessly set the ice bucket onto the counter, then made her move. She darted into the main room, grabbed hold of the cart, and dashed toward the door, only to discover Fox standing there, his hand on the lever, about to leave.

Anna fell back, out of sight of the entryway. Her heart kicked so hard she could feel it in her neck. Why was she so afraid? she wondered. Save for taking too long, she hadn't done anything wrong.

Fox exited the suite, leaving Anna with her anxiety and whoever was behind the closed bedroom door. The suite was quiet. Too quiet. Anna's eyes bounced from the main door to that of the bedroom. She knew she should leave. She wanted to. She just had to wait until the coast was clear.

Her brain battled her feet as they crept toward the bedroom. Her ears sought sound and found none. Inch by inch, she closed in on the bedroom door, like fire, riskier the closer she got. Three feet away, she stopped, sweating. She stared, waiting, willing to accept whatever happened next. The sudden sound of water striking tile propelled her backward. She retrieved the housekeeping cart and bolted from the room, letting the door slam shut behind her, hoping the falling water would mask the sound.

"Anna!"

She yelped and fell against the door, clutching her chest. Fox stood just a few feet away, still looking out of sorts, except he now bore the expression of someone who'd been busted with something stolen stuffed down his pants.

"What were you doing in there?"

"I wasn't finished," she said. "I didn't see anything."

He grabbed her by the wrist, his grip like a brace that'd been screwed on too tight, and swung his arm as if she were a football he could lob down the hall. "Get downstairs," he said.

Anna, shaking, moved at double-speed down to the housekeeping office, where the click of the timeclock did a piss-poor job of distracting her from wondering why Fox had reacted with such rage. The phone didn't ring until twenty minutes before the end of her shift.

"Fox?" The distance between them strengthened her nerve. "What's going on up there?"

"Don't ask questions. Come back up," he said, and ended the call.

He was nowhere in sight when Anna snapped on a pair of rubber gloves and reentered the suite. The main room looked no different than it had when she'd left it. The bedroom door was open, darkness spilling out. She stepped inside and turned on the light. A feeling of disappointment set in. She couldn't say what she'd expected to find, but a minimal mess wasn't it.

The bed was ruffled, but the comforter hadn't been pulled back. A couple pillows had been knocked to the floor. Two beer bottles, one empty, the other holding dregs, sat on the nightstand next to two candy bar wrappers with half a candy bar left. A wet towel hung from the hook on the bathroom door. Another lined the floor. Unflushed piss yellowed the toilet, and a single soap wrapper occupied the bottom of the wastebasket.

Anna flushed the yellow away and replaced the towels, proceeding to scrub the shower, toilet, and sink. She made the bed, returned the ice bucket to its proper place, discarded the trash, restocked the mini bar, and reset the thermostat to 78 degrees, the determined temperature for an unoccupied room. She didn't finish until after her shift had officially ended. Tired, she would have continued working if it meant morning wouldn't come. Mornings just meant school, and school was like stepping onto a battlefield to face an army on her own.

She restocked the housekeeping cart, making it look as unused as the suite, then clocked out for the night. Fox was waiting for her by the sliding doors. Anna, beholding him through the corner of her eye, didn't get too close. She could still feel his fingertips tunneling into her skin.

"I got new leather seat covers," he said. "You still wanna walk?"

The darkness and Uncle Ray's story gave Anna reason to accept the ride. "I'll make it on my own," she said.

"Then take this."

Facing him, Anna watched his flat hand snake out of his pocket, thumb tucked under his palm. He leaned in close, putting his palm against one of hers. She didn't realize what he was doing until he moved his hand away.

"What for?" she asked, staring down at the twenty-dollar bill he'd given her.

"I overreacted earlier. I'm sorry about that. I didn't mean to. You're doing a good job," he said again. "You sure you don't want a ride?"

Anna shook her head.

"Then I'll see you tomorrow, Horn." He walked across the lot to his truck and peeled away as if the speed and his rumbling exhaust would impress her. She felt better when he was gone.

Day 12
7:27 a.m.

Breakfast dishes clattered in the sink. But they hadn't been set down or dropped—they'd been thrown. Dorothy and Chris had been at each other's throats throughout the weekend. Not in an overt way. They'd tried to keep the family from seeing, but the eye rolls, the scowls, and the distance between them was hard to miss; the discontent had been hard to miss for a while. It didn't help that Chris had come home Friday with a secondhand cross-stitch wall hanging that proclaimed, *If Momma ain't happy, ain't nobody happy.* He'd hung it over Dorothy's wall calendar, then gasped with laughter, making sure Robbie, Grace, and Anna saw.

Anna stepped into the kitchen entryway, assuming her presence would draw some heat from the flames, only to go unnoticed by her mom and dad.

"It's clean," Chris said, his eyes on the narrow counter between the refrigerator and oven. "I wiped it."

A spiral of smoke drifted up from a lit cigarette in the green glass ashtray on the stovetop. It wouldn't get smoked. Having resisted the urge to light one for the better part of six years, Dorothy had recently started burning them because she said the scent calmed her nerves. Anna sidestepped her parents and stubbed the cigarette out.

"Every morning you leave crumbs," Dorothy said. "Every morning for twenty damn years."

"I wiped the counter, Dorothy." Chris's voice was low and stern.

"I'll clean," Anna said. "I don't mind." The issue, so minor to her, spoke volumes about her parents' frustrations, the least of which had to do with crumbs on the counter. Anna didn't know all their problems, just as they didn't know all of hers. There were too many to deal with, like the weeds that sprung up around the porch. Some were stubborn. Some were thorny. Most appeared without warning.

"No," Chris said. "I wiped it. It's clean."

"Clean?" Dorothy shrieked, sounding like she'd been jabbed with a fork. Her hip knocked Chris out of the way while her index finger dotted the counter, picking up crumbs that were invisible to Anna.

Chris grunted and grabbed the dish towel from the sink. "I'll wipe it," he said.

"But you already did," Dorothy snapped. "If you already wiped it, then why wipe it again?"

"You said you see crumbs." He spoke through his teeth, straining not to yell. "If you want me to wipe it, I will."

"But you said there's no crumbs."

Chris emitted an exasperated sigh. Dorothy brushed her fingertip against her shirt.

"I just want to know which one of us you think is crazy," she said. "Either I'm seeing things, or you didn't wipe the counter in the first place. Which is it?"

Chris huffed and retreated to the living room, taking his coffee with him. "Anna, come here for a minute." Chris was bent by the door, tying his boots to his feet. "I did some legwork for you . . . some research. Here's what I want you to do before the tribal council meeting at the end of the month."

"Dad, I—"

"Make a list of the things the tribe has neglected . . . the literature, art, artifacts. Remind the council of the importance of these things and what it would mean if we lost them. Then give them a list of needs. Keep it simple, to start. You'll need space and financing. Money shouldn't be an issue. They have funds set aside for the enrichment of the tribe. I'm thinking they could set you up in the community center. It'll have to be outfitted with archival display cases. Security measures will need to be increased. You'll have to call conservators and binderies."

"Dad—"

"You'll learn as you go," he said. "Don't let any of this intimidate you. Someone's got to do it." He finished his coffee and set the mug on the table by the door, not a second before the phone chirped. He got to it ahead of Anna. "Hello? Who is this? Jackass!" he said, abruptly hanging up.

"What was that about?"

"Just a prank," he huffed. "I got one just like it last night. Probably Robbie's friends." He grabbed his wallet and keys. "See you after work."

Anna waited until she heard his car door slam, then retrieved his coffee mug so that her mother wouldn't have to. Dorothy was wiping the counter when Anna put the mug in the sink.

Day 35
11:33 p.m.
50 Hours Gone

The bedroom took on the air of a holy place. A gravesite. Dorothy set a vase of purple irises on the nightstand, close to Grace's bed. Were the flowers supposed to inspire hope?

Anna had always known there'd come a day when she and Grace would no longer occupy the same space, but it was college, backpacking through Europe, or a dream job that was supposed to separate them. Exhausted, she dropped onto her bed. The odors of the day—sweat, dirt, smoke—competed with the lingering scent of detergent clinging to the sheet. She wiped her oily face onto the linen. Maybe she'd shower tomorrow, she thought, as sleep took hold.

It didn't last long. Anna's eyes opened upon darkness that triggered panic when she perceived gasps and grunts that told her something other than Grace—something dreadful—had entered the space. Her lungs tightened. Her body tensed. Her mind raced to identify the nearest weapon at hand.

Shadows engulfed the room. The curtains fluttered from the breeze blowing in through the window, left open a crack. Anna's brain settled on the lamp; she could use it as a club if it came to that. Her heart drummed and her head throbbed, unable to make sense of the sounds that had morphed into gobbling, gulping noises. A round form lolled on Grace's bed.

The sight jolted Anna toward the wall while her hand reached for the lamp next to the vase. Fear like boiling water surged through her veins. "Dad!" she screamed for help, just a split second before realizing it was him making those unsettling sounds. Except he wasn't gobbling or gulping, he was sobbing.

On his knees at Grace's bedside, arms folded atop the mattress, Chris's head rocked from side to side upon his arms. He quieted and his head popped up at the sound of Anna's voice. His hands hurried to clean his face.

Anna's hand fell away from the lamp without turning on the light. Never had she seen her father cry, not even at Grandpa's funeral. Witnessing it filled her with shame, suggesting she'd betrayed him by waking. His sobs chipped away another piece of the world she'd known. Soon she feared everything would be foreign.

Just as Anna was about to slip away to let him have the moment and his pride, Chris's back straightened like a signpost. Anna stiffened in return, her hands desperately grabbing two fistfuls of the worn-out sheet beneath her. Was he trying to pretend he wasn't there? Should she pretend that she'd drifted back to sleep? They remained like that long enough for the shadows to shift on the wall. Long enough for Anna to think they'd be stuck in that hell forever.

"I could call her," Chris finally said, his words distorted by phlegm in his throat. "If I hadn't been so stubborn . . . if I'd bought her the cell phone when she'd asked . . . I could pick up the phone and just call her. . . ."

Anna willed herself to her father's side. Her arms wrapped around his quivering chest. She held him until he couldn't cry anymore.

"How do you do that?" he said.

"Do what?"

"Just . . . make things better."

She squeezed him tighter.

"I love you, Anna," he said, wiping his eyes against his sleeve. He kissed her forehead and put her back to bed. Anna spied something atop Grace's pillow after he left, something rectangular and small. She waited to hear the couch creak, then carefully got up to inspect it. It was the cell phone Grace had wanted. Brand-new in its box. Waiting for her return.

Day 13
9:27 a.m.

The bus's diesel breath mixed with the strong vinyl scent of its seats, half of which were already occupied by Anna's peers, laughing and playing whack-a-mole over the seatbacks with one another's heads. Anna dropped into the first available seat and scooted close to the window. Head tucked against her chest for fear of receiving a whack, her body anticipated the heavy vibrations of the bus coming to life. "Hi there, Anna," she heard, accompanied by the sensation of weight on the bench beside her.

Anna knew who it was before she turned to look. Not only was Alee Graham, who sometimes ate lunch at Anna's table, the only one in Anna's grade who had nothing to lose by talking to her, but she smelled like cat piss too, something poor Alee seemed unaware of.

"Hey, Alee," Anna said.

"Think we'll see any fish?" Alee asked.

"Only if these clowns don't scare them off."

The bus hissed and pulled away from the curb. Anna's gaze drifted up to the large rearview mirror above the driver. Her eyes zeroed in on Anthony Vaughan, admiring his flawless skin, bright lips, and straight, white teeth. He guffawed each time he swatted one of his friends in the head. The corners of his mouth cut perfect angles in his all-American face when he did.

"Whatcha looking at?" Alee asked.

Anna's eyes shifted, inadvertently meeting those of Megan Bradley, gazing into the mirror as well. "Nothing," she said. She beheld her hands, embarrassed that she'd been caught looking. Even with her heart beating against her ribs, she couldn't keep her eyes in place for long. They darted back up to the mirror and locked with Megan's. This time it was Megan who looked away first.

Anna remembered those hazel eyes well. They used to comfort her, back when she meant something to Megan. She thought about when they used to play Cat's Cradle and Miss Mary Mack on the grade school playground, their palms clapping together, moving faster and faster, their hands outpacing their chanting tongues.

It was junior high that changed things. That's when everyone suddenly got new sight and overanalyzed everything. How you cut your hair. How you combed it. If you combed it. How many pimples you had. If you were allowed to wear makeup and how much of it you wore. How you got to school. What you ate at lunch. If you bought food in the cafeteria or brought it from home in a brown paper bag. Or worse, if you still carried it in your grade school lunch box sporting cartoon characters on the side.

Anna remembered the last time she and Megan ate together, but, like the last time she'd gone out to play, been read to by her mother, or eaten a piece of Gran's pecan pie, she hadn't realized it would be the last time.

It was the first month of seventh grade. Anna had walked to Megan's house in town and then Megan's mom had driven them to the mall. Mrs. Bradley had let Megan and Anna go to the food court and whatever stores they'd wanted. She'd even hung back a dozen feet so that they could have their space, trailing them like a security guard ready to pounce at the first sign of danger.

The girls had gone into The Piercing Place, where the racks were loaded with cheap jewelry and the purchase of a pair of starter studs would garner free holes in your lobes. Megan already had her ears pierced, for longer than she could remember.

It's time, she'd said to Anna, forcing a pair of gold star-shaped studs upon her.

Anna had tossed the stars aside.

You have to, Megan had said. *All the other girls have them.* She'd shoved the studs back into Anna's hand. *Start with those. Soon you'll be able to wear some like mine.* Putting a finger behind each earlobe, she'd made her plastic neon-green hoops wiggle before picking out two new pairs in pink and yellow. Anna reracked the starter studs when Megan went to pay.

Really? Megan had said upon her return.

I didn't bring enough money. That was true; Anna hadn't brought it because she didn't have it.

Megan had rolled her eyes. The two left the mall as friends with a chill between them that neither acknowledged. When Anna called Megan later that night, after much thinking and deciding that she'd do it when she was able to scrounge up enough change to pay for the studs, Mrs. Bradley told her that Megan wasn't feeling well enough to come to the phone. She seemed just fine at school the next day, though, wearing her bright pink plastic hoops, showing them off, ignoring Anna.

The chill between them quickly became a block of ice. Megan stopped sitting next to Anna at lunch. She stopped taking Anna's calls. Stopped inviting her over. New girls—popular girls—took Anna's place in the cafeteria, in the halls, and at the mall. Megan had started to float, finding her way to the upper ranks of the middle school social structure, while Anna sank to the murky depths. Megan might have been able to keep Anna from going under for a while, but she'd shown no interest in being Anna's life preserver.

"Do you think we'll get to go in the mud?" Alee asked. "I wanna squish around in it."

"Who'd stop you?" Anna said.

"You're right." Alee clapped her hands, sending a gust of cat piss in Anna's direction.

The bus stopped and the seniors shoved one another down the steps. Anna stayed seated until it was just her and the driver, glaring at her through the rearview mirror. "Could you pretend you didn't see me?"

He shook his head and jerked a thumb toward the door. Anna reluctantly joined her classmates outside, where they'd been wrangled into a pavilion along the riverfront in the middle of town, only a few miles from school. The river that rushed before them was the same that flowed through the reservation, only it wasn't obvious by looking at it. Small shops, restaurants, and boutiques lined the nearby street. Red brick–paved pathways meandered along either side of the water where thoughtfully placed benches, small gazebos, flower boxes, and cutesy lampposts set the scene for first dates, engagement photos, and anniversary strolls. The branch of the river that flowed through town was much wider and more powerful than that which coursed across the rez.

One of the Riverfront Rangers thanked the students for volunteering their time, not knowing that few would have been there if it weren't for the service day forced upon them.

Alee jumped up and down, hands in the air, when the ranger produced the waders a select few would get to wear into the water. Overlooking her, he handed the waders to the biggest boys and tore open a box of heavy-duty garbage bags for the rest.

Bag in hand, Alee sulked away, bending to collect a flattened coffee cup, lipstick stains around its rim.

"Hey, Alee," Anna called. "This is thick plastic." She rubbed her garbage bag between her fingers. "I bet it'd keep water out."

Alee's face lit up. She looked over her shoulders until the coast was clear, then ran down the riverbank.

Anna smiled to herself and continued to pick up the bits of trash she found. A gum wrapper here, a crusty napkin there. Megan and her crew, donning their garbage bags like capes, walked ahead of Anna. One of the boys pointed at the branches of a nearby tree. A pair of red balloons was tangled near the top; one full, the other deflated and hanging down like a shriveled heart. Megan stared up at them. Her pal, Andy Wimer, threw a rock that missed both balloons and nearly pegged him in the face upon its descent.

"What the flippity fuck?" Andy, bending to retrieve the rock, said, his eyes toward the water. "Get a load of this."

Everyone turned toward the river. Alee, standing in her garbage bag, holding it up around her waist the way she would have held a burlap bag during a potato sack race, hopped through the shallows, splashing water into her face. Megan and her friends burst out laughing.

"Fucking Alee," one of them said.

"Crazy as a loon," another remarked.

Anna gritted her teeth and marched forth. She looped her bag around her belt and inserted herself into the crowd by the tree, knowing she'd get their eyes off Alee.

With a leap, she grabbed the lowest branch and pulled herself up. Aside from a few snickers, Megan and her friends fell silent. Anna could feel their eyes upon her as she navigated from limb to limb, making her way to the top. The branches bent beneath her weight, threatening to cast her to the ground. Anna held firm, her callused hands keeping a tight grip on the tree's limbs, which grew skinnier the higher she climbed. She carefully unwound the ribbon holding the balloons in place and stuck it between her teeth for the descent.

"You like that, don't you?" Andy whispered below.

"No one in the world likes that," his best friend, Curt Egeland, whispered back.

"Like a man's," Andy said.

Anna knew they were referring to what they could see from below: her backside in a pair of her father's old jeans. Andy put a hand on the back of Curt's head and pushed it toward her rear when she reached the lower branches.

"You suck!" Curt said.

"Not like her sister," Andy shot back.

The boys guffawed and ran off with the others chasing after them. Anna dropped from the tree, not bothering to scrabble down the last few feet. Megan Bradley was still standing there, left behind by her braying friends. Her gaze fixed itself to Anna's. Neither spoke. Anna just gripped the inflated balloon and squeezed until it burst.

"Megan!" someone shrieked. "Hurry before her ugly rubs off on you."

Another outburst of laughter. Another stab to the chest. Megan almost looked sorry. Almost. She dropped her gaze and ran to catch up with the rest.

Day 14
5:16 p.m.

Anna stood before the coffee maker in the housekeeping office, peering into the reflective surface near the top. She ran a finger over her right eyebrow, thinking her long eyelashes and bright eyes might be her best features. The gold flecks, like little stars, around her irises were especially unique; only she and Gran had them. She could see her parents in her reflection and bits of Grandpa too, who'd died when she was eleven. Her features weren't petite like her mom's or Grace's. She wasn't pretty like Robbie, the cut of her father's chin and wide nose saw to that. Neck too thick. Shoulders too broad. She was burly, not as robust as her dad but husky enough for others to notice. Robbie would be bigger than her; she was grateful for that at least. While she could see her family in her reflection, she couldn't entirely see herself.

You see things through all eyes, Miss Shelby had told her once, back when the tribal children were gathered around, lying flat on their backs, searching the clouds for illustrations of a story the sky spirit would tell. The boys had seen a warrior brandishing a bow. The girls had seen a snowy egret spreading its wings. Anna had seen both, and more. She'd seen the clouds, the characters, and the spirit of the Creator.

"Ugly," she whispered, still wondering what Miss Shelby had meant and what exactly everyone else saw when they looked upon her. She was thinking, too, about what the boys had said by the river. More than what they'd said about her, she pondered what they'd said about Grace. The girl in the bathroom who'd told Anna the rumor was a junior. The boys by the river were seniors. Grace was only a sophomore. Word was getting around school, and Anna didn't like it. Nor did she want to believe it.

Mouth flooded with fiery flavor from a fresh piece of cinnamon gum, she clocked in and donned the chambermaid coat Fox had left hanging from the timecard rack. She wasn't as reluctant to wear it this time.

Having taken the elevator access card from the sock in which she'd stored it, Anna rode up to the eighth floor without worrying about anyone seeing. She felt foolish for thinking that anyone would have noticed in the first place. The good thing about being invisible was that it offered a sense of security. Loneliness, too, but Anna didn't dwell on that.

She set the room the way she'd been instructed, getting in and out without dawdling this time. She was maneuvering the housekeeping cart back into the hall when Fox hustled toward her.

"Finished?"

Anna nodded. She smoothed her hands over the chambermaid coat, the cut of which strained to turn her body into something it wasn't.

"Good." Fox led her to the elevator, stopping for a few seconds on the way so that she could stow the cart in its closet. He pressed the button to call the elevator, then reached in and tapped the first-floor button when the doors rolled open. Holding a hand in front of the elevator's sensor, he said, "Straighten up in the office. I'll call later."

Anna stepped inside and watched the doors roll shut. The elevator took her down to the first floor, but when the doors swept open, she stayed put. No one was waiting to board, and after a few seconds, the doors closed again. Anna wondered who'd end up in 808. And when. And then she wondered why she was so curious. Never had she cared about who came and went when she'd cleaned the rooms on weekend mornings. But the suites, they were different. Inherently intriguing. Not to mention Fox's reaction when she'd accidentally stayed a little too long in suite 808. He'd seemed worried about what she might see. And now she couldn't cast the curiosity aside. She could stake out the Atrium, she thought, to observe the comers and goers, but she had a better chance of seeing something certain on the eighth. Before her nerves could get the best of her, she stuck the card in its slot and slapped the eighth-floor button.

Sweat prickled her skin the higher the elevator rose. "Shit," she said, sure Fox would be waiting in the hall. She swatted the seventh-floor button with hope that she could bail, but the elevator dinged and the doors slid open. Too late. She was back among the suites.

Fox wasn't there. Anna's heart skipped a beat anyway. Her shoulder blades hit the glass of the window behind her, and her chest heaved. Staying still until the elevator doors closed once more, she leapt forward and—curiosity conquering her fear—she stabbed the door-open button, reminding herself that she really wasn't doing anything wrong.

The hall outside the elevator was empty. Quiet. The housekeeping closet only thirty feet away, Anna took a deep breath, clamped her gum between her teeth, and dashed. Chambermaid coat rustling, she made it to the closet in seconds flat, wherein she shut the door and sat in a squat until her chest stopped heaving.

The disordered shelves and empty soap boxes demanded work be done within the closet, giving Anna an excuse to sidestep Fox's order. She restocked the housekeeping carts and tidied the toiletries, all the while listening for sound in the hall.

A bottle of disinfectant almost slipped through her hand when a door clicked open and then slammed shut. 808. It had to be. Fast-moving footsteps sounded in the hall. Anna braced herself. With only a split second to determine her next move, she took a deep breath and opened the closet door. She nearly collided with a woman, watery black streaks running down her face, the instant she stepped onto the corridor's vibrant carpet.

The woman, wearing a formfitting black dress, her hair up as if she'd done it for a wedding, clutched a purse in one hand and a thin wrap in the other. She whirled around upon seeing Anna and ran, rerouting herself from the elevator to the emergency stairwell.

"Are you okay?" Anna said, without thinking. It took a moment to sink in, but once the stairwell door clanged shut, Anna realized she recognized the young woman. She was the one who'd been smoking on the porch across the field from Miss Shelby's trailer.

Prompted by her thumping heart, Anna ran for the elevator, desperate to make it downstairs before Fox made the call. She was more curious than ever now.

Day 14
10:27 p.m.

The rustling leaves, the crunch of gravel, and the trembling brush along the side of the road sent shivers up Anna's spine. It was out there. Rolling toward her. She sprang forward, her pace picking up at the sound of gnashing teeth. Eyes going here, there, everywhere, all she saw was velvety blackness, like a blanket shifting in shape from something moving beneath it.

"Easy, Anna," she said, to quell her galloping heart. It wasn't just the darkness making her uneasy. It was the mystery presented by the young woman in the hall. What had upset her?

Anna had made it down to the housekeeping office after encountering the woman in time to answer Fox's call, then went right back up to restore suite 808, pretending she hadn't seen anything suspicious at all. Aside from an empty beer bottle and water droplets around the bathroom sink, suite 808 had been as clean as they come.

The porch light alleviated Anna's panic once home was in sight, but what it illuminated kept her heart rate from returning to normal. Robbie and Grace were sitting side by side on the steps, something they never did after dark on school nights.

"What's going on?" she called.

Neither answered. She saw why when she got close. Both were wearing headphones attached to their own Discmans, gifts from their parents last Christmas. The diminished sounds of aggressive drums and lightning-fast guitar licks leaked from Robbie's headphones. Grace was probably listening to the new Sheryl Crow CD she'd borrowed from Emily.

Each with a stick in one hand, Robbie and Grace scratched lines into the dirt. A crooked smile skewed Grace's lips. Robbie's brow hung low, threatening and determined. Competition turned him into something fierce. Anna reached the porch in time to see Grace scrape an X onto the ground. Robbie threw his stick down. Grace marked her triumph by drawing a line through her three successive Xs, followed by a giant V for victory. Robbie erased the tic-tac-toe grid with his foot, digging his toes deep into the dirt, then retrieved his stick and drew another. Anna waved at her siblings. Only Robbie waved back. Their parents' escalated voices carried through the windows and walls. Vibrations traveled onto the porch each time something slammed: a door, a cabinet, a drawer, a fist against a wall.

"Gran!" Anna said, voicing the first thought that came to mind upon hearing something shatter. She plowed past her siblings, only for Robbie to catch her by the ankle. He shook his head.

Anna reluctantly dropped onto the steps next to Grace. She wished she had a pair of headphones for herself. The yelling inside the house came in waves. Just when it seemed like it might be over, it ramped up again. The three of them sat out there for the better part of an hour, bathed in the yellow porch light, battling hungry mosquitos and restless moths. Grace and Robbie had the game and their music to distract them. Anna only had her thoughts.

She replayed the scene of the pretty young woman crying in the hall. Her perfectly set hair. Her messed-up mascara. Anna could only imagine what had brought on the tears. Cringing, she thought about how rough Fox had been with her the first time she'd been assigned suite 808.

One eye on Grace, she questioned if her little sister and the woman at the hotel had both gotten themselves involved in compromising situations with men. Was the rumor Anna had heard twice in the last week true? Was Grace hiding something she wasn't equipped to handle? The way she sat—head on her knees, one hand tracing Xs into the dirt—reversed her in time. If her hair had been braided, she'd have looked like her six-year-old self.

With so much tension in the air it probably wasn't the right time to address the rumor, but then again, there was no saying if the time would ever be right. Nerves on edge, Anna reached over and slid the padded earpiece from Grace's closest ear.

"What did you do after the homecoming dance?" she asked.

Grace's body stiffened. Her face grew dark. "Nothing," she said.

"You came home late."

"There was an after-party at Miguel's house."

Anna startled at the sound of something big breaking. It could have been the new TV. "There's a rumor," she said, her throat begging for water. "Kids are talking about you at school."

"Don't you think I know?" Grace moved the earpiece back into place. Anna let it sit for a few seconds, then slid it aside again.

"Is it true?"

"Shut up, Anna." Grace held the earpiece to her head this time.

Anna glanced at Robbie. He remained focused on the game, unaware that Anna had said anything or that he was winning because of her. She fought with Grace to move the earpiece out of the way, then reached over and unplugged the headphones from the Discman.

"I'll shut up if you want me to," she said, "but I'm not trying to embarrass you. I just want you to know I—"

"I know, Anna. I know. I know."

"If you were pressured—"

"I didn't do anything!" Grace growled. "Nothing happened." She yanked the headphone wire from Anna's grip and plugged it back in.

Robbie made a triumphant O. His hands and his stick flew into the air. The screen door slammed a second later when Chris stormed out of the house, blood dripping from his left hand, plopping loudly against the porch.

Anna jumped to her feet. "What happened?"

Robbie tore the headphones from his head. The screeching music continued to buzz out of them.

"Grab my keys. Start the car," Chris said to Robbie before turning to Anna. "Go get me a rag so I don't bleed all over everything."

"What'd you cut it on?" she asked.

"Just get me a rag."

Robbie's excitement erased his concern for his father's bloody hand. He pinched the car key between two fingers and hopped to the meat wagon.

"Quickly, Anna!" Chris hollered.

Anna entered the house as if it were haunted, as if something might jump out and grab her. The living room was dim. The only noise came from a radio playing oldies behind the bedsheet curtain cordoning Gran off from the battlefield Chris and Dorothy had created. Anna's heart ached for her. Her instinct was to see if Gran was all right, but Chris hollered and slammed his boot against the porch once more, propelling Anna toward the kitchen.

She had to pass the dinner table on the way. Dorothy was sitting there, staring straight ahead, her back to Anna. She was like the lone survivor in a war zone, surrounded by broken glass. The lamp lay on its side. The ashtray that had held so many of her unsmoked cigarettes was in pieces. The thick glass resembled chunks of green ice. Ash coated the tabletop and cigarette butts littered the floor.

Anna sidled next to her mother. An unlit cig dangled between Dorothy's lips. Her right thumb sat atop the spark wheel of a lighter clutched in her hand, making it *snick* again and again.

Lost for words, Anna walked carefully over the shattered glass. She gathered two wads of paper towels and dampened one beneath the tap.

"Here," she said to her father, back on the porch. The scent of a freshly lit cigarette wafted through the screen door. Grace, still holding her headphones to her ears, hadn't moved an inch, seemingly lost in her own world. Robbie sat behind the station wagon's wheel, periodically hitting the gas, making the engine rev.

"Quit it," Chris barked.

"You're not going to let him drive?" Anna asked, proceeding to dab blood from her father's hand. The cut ran deep into the thick pad of flesh beneath his left thumb. It wouldn't stop bleeding. "He doesn't have a license," she said, as though Chris didn't know, or as if it ever mattered on the rez.

"You don't have one either," Robbie shouted through the open window.

"At least I've taken driver's ed," Anna said to her dad. "Let me drive you."

"Stay with your mother." His voice dropped. "Take care of things inside."

"You mean clean up?"

Chris squeezed the towels until they were red. He grimaced and plodded down the porch steps, nearly tripping over Grace, whom he hadn't even noticed. He turned toward the porch and said, "I'm sorry, Anna," before getting in the passenger side.

Robbie put the car in reverse and planted his foot on the gas. The meat wagon rocketed backward, making a sound none of them had heard before. Chris shouted. Robbie whooped. He turned the wheel and sped down the road.

Grace still didn't move. Her gaze was off in the distant darkness,

perhaps searching for the same thing as her mother at the dinner table. Anna wavered between going in the house and staying on the
porch. A weight had settled on her that seemed to want to knock her
into the dirt with the Xs and Os, only there'd be no winning down
there for her. No one would gaze upon her, smile, and adorn her with
a V. She'd just get stomped on and erased or—worse—rolled over like
the frogs. Still, the easy thing to do would have been to let her knees
buckle, to give in and taste the dirt on her tongue, to let her parents
rip each other to shreds if that's what they wanted while the stain on
Grace's reputation continued to spread like her father's blood on the
towels. She grabbed the porch rail to keep herself from falling.

"Grace," she called, her voice a whisper, but Grace still had her
headphones on. Anna went inside to sweep up the glass.

Day 15
3:31 p.m.

Grace zoomed in and snagged the ringing phone before Anna could get a hand on it.

"Hello?" She turned toward the wall.

Anna assumed it was their father. He'd gone to stay at the hotel after getting four stitches in his hand, though Anna had hoped he'd turn to Uncle Ray to put him up for the night. It'd been six months since they last spoke, shortly after Gran's stroke. Chris had called Ray selfish and cheap. Dorothy had called him worse. Neither could understand why he refused to take Gran in. No wife, no kids, he'd seemed like the logical choice when it became clear that Gran would need additional care. Ultimately, it'd been Anna who'd determined Gran's fate by insisting she live with them, promising to help Gran with therapy and all the other tasks—bathing, dressing, and eating—she used to do on her own. If only there'd been some place other than the dining room for her to sleep.

"Stop calling here," Grace snarled into the phone, ultimately slamming the receiver onto its base.

Anna, glancing at Grace, ducked beneath the bedsheet. The phone rang again. Grace quickly silenced it. Gran was asleep in her chair. Anna woke her to move her into bed.

"No, no . . ." Gran's good hand shooed Anna away before her eyes even opened. She lifted herself, and Anna moved in close, afraid Gran would fall. Gran's limbs didn't work the way she wanted them to. It seemed that they'd forgotten their role.

"Let me," Anna said.

"No, no, no." It was one of the few words Gran could speak without slurring, each utterance more stubborn than the last. She made it to the edge of her bed and plopped down with a sigh, eyes glistening. Anna looked away. She reversed until the sheet in the doorway adorned her back.

Gran pushed herself across the bed, took a deep breath, and closed her eyes.

"How long have I lived here?" she asked.

"You don't . . . ?" Anna started, surprised that Gran couldn't remember. "Since April . . . since the stroke."

"How long am I staying?"

No one had discussed that with Gran yet. The odds of her living on her own again were slim to none. "This is home," Anna said.

Gran frowned. "She doesn't want me here," she said after a while.

"Who?"

"Your mother."

"She's frustrated," Anna said, voice low. "They're having a hard time."

"Because of me?"

Anna couldn't lie. "The stroke didn't help, but it's not you. They've been this way for a while."

"She says I've lost my marbles. I heard her. But they're still here." A crooked finger jabbed Gran's temple. "I might be a little forgetful." Her statement was nearly a question. "Am I?"

"Sometimes."

Gran cringed. "Promise me something, Anna."

"Sure."

"Never treat me the way they do." Anna thought about how her family dealt with Gran. How they used simple words and spoke in higher decibels. Dorothy and Chris seemed to forget that Gran had lived a life, that it wasn't over, and that she could hear through the bedsheet. It dawned on her, too, that Gran must be bored. Ripped from her routine, deprived of her independence.

"I promise," Anna said, recognizing that Gran still deserved her place in the family and the nation at large, which somehow affirmed that she and Grace—adrift as they might have been—deserved a place as well.

"We're more alike than you might think, Anna."

"We have the same eyes," Anna replied.

"That too," Gran said. "That too."

Day 23
9:22 p.m.

Light off, squatting behind the housekeeping carts, Anna's eyes roamed the darkness of the eighth-floor housekeeping closet, her ears searching for sound out in the hall. Fox hadn't asked her to prep suite 808 in more than a week, and now—ignoring his instructions to clean the coffee station in the housekeeping office until he summoned her to restore the room—she sat in wait of noise that would let her know when someone was leaving the suite. She didn't just want to see who'd emerge, she wanted to see how. Would someone come out crying like before?

Three minutes passed. Seven. Nine. Anna's legs burned from holding the squat. It couldn't be much longer now. She was due to clock out in thirty-eight minutes and, if the past was an indicator, she knew the guests always hit the road at least thirty minutes before the end of her shift. Crawling out from behind the carts, she groaned and lay flat against the floor, letting blood reenter her legs. Pins and needles jabbed her on the inside.

"Now or never," she whispered, wincing.

Using the doorframe, she pulled herself to her feet, then reached for a vacuum cleaner, her trembling hand bearing witness to her nerves. Having wheeled the vacuum into the hall, she plugged it in and pushed it as close to 808 as the cord would allow. No noise came from the suite.

Foot at the ready, Anna didn't stomp the power button until the elevator dinged. Cursing inside, she refrained from looking over her shoulder to see who'd arrived. She just moved the vacuum back and forth, doing her best to look busy.

The vacuum went dead. Anna stomped the power button again, knowing the plug had been pulled. A hand gripped her arm from behind and yanked her toward the housekeeping closet.

"You're supposed to be downstairs," Fox hissed, eyes bulging, nostrils glistening.

"Someone spilled glitter," she said, the most likely culprit being the washed-up pop star who'd recently spent two nights on the eighth while headlining the showroom.

Anna pulled to get away, but Fox held tight. "Some guy in two sixteen just called for shaving cream."

"I'll get it." She coughed from the cologne that coated her tongue. The musky, woodsy scent wafted off Fox like smoke from grease sizzling in a pan. Beneath the pungent odor lingered traces of something familiar and far worse, like the cat piss that clung to Alee. Anna's nose crinkled.

"I need a favor," Fox said.

Anna's eyebrows leapt up on her forehead.

"It's not really me who needs it. It's Tanya. Miss Jenny's called off tomorrow morning. Something about her kid . . . Willie, I think his name is . . . he split his nose on a bumper. Couldn't have happened at a worse time for Tanya. The hotel's packed tonight and tomorrow's Saturday, which means the girls will be working in overdrive. Tanya asked me to ask you if you could fill in for Miss Jenny. Because of her kid."

Anna nodded almost as fast as he spoke. She wasn't used to him being so talkative. If she hadn't heard him get off the elevator, she would have guessed that he'd run up all eight flights of stairs. She could feel his pulse thumping through his touch.

"I'll be here," she said, trying to pull away once more.

Fox released his clamp. "Good. Whipped cream. Two sixteen," he said, pointing toward the elevator.

"Shaving cream," Anna muttered, surmising that he just wanted her out of the way.

"Go."

Anna's feet shuffled down the hall while her gaze remained pinned to Fox. He advanced to suite 808, where he stopped outside the door, staring at it. Anna stalled at the elevator, watching and waiting until Fox's head swung in her direction, making her hop to in spite of her instincts telling her to stay.

She descended to the second floor and hurried to the housekeeping closet. Locking a complimentary can of Barbasol in a white-knuckle grip, she dashed to room 216. Silence came in reply to her knock. She waited. Knocked again. Still silence. She bent to leave the can by the door just as the lock snapped and the door swung open. Righting herself, she jabbed the can at the bleary-eyed man before her. A five o'clock shadow barely darkened his chin and cheeks.

"Hmm?" he grunted.

It took Anna a second to find her voice. "The shaving cream you called for."

He shook his head, confused. "Wasn't me. Wrong room."

Warm with embarrassment, Anna looked up and down the hall. All the other doors were shut. No one appeared in need. Fox, she decided, was a liar.

Still squeezing the can in a bloodless fist, she ran for the elevator, where she came upon two twentysomethings sharing a flask. They'd already pressed the call button for the elevator to take them down, which meant she'd have to ride with them to the Atrium before the elevator brought her back up to the eighth.

The suite will be empty by then, she thought. Bouncing on the balls of her feet, her eyes shot toward the emergency stairwell door at the opposite end of the hall. She waited until the elevator opened, just in case it was carrying anyone down from the top floor, then—finding it empty—bolted for the stairs, hoping she could scurry up six stories faster than the elevator could make its rounds.

"Bastard," Anna panted upon heaving the stairwell door open and pounding up the first flight. She was about to ascend from the third to the fourth floor when uneven footsteps sounded overhead. Certain that it must be someone descending from the eighth, she crept up the next flight, moving slowly to suppress sound, though she could do little to muffle her heavy breathing. The footfalls above landed hard against each metal step, causing them to clang. Roiled by a wave of apprehension, Anna's stomach churned, urging her to escape through the fourth-floor door. But then she reminded herself that she wasn't doing anything wrong. She was just going to look. It couldn't be Fox in the stairwell anyway, which was what really had her worried. He'd move faster and with greater weight.

Slowing even more, the footfalls became damn near painful to endure. Anna started up the next flight, only to stall and retreat to the fourth-floor landing, her free hand grasping the door lever there in case she needed to slip away.

The closer the footsteps, the greater Anna's dread. She felt danger approaching and yet her curiosity held her steady. The footsteps were just above her now, moving from the stairs to the fifth-floor landing. Anna depressed the lever, disengaging the latch. All she had to do was pull the door open to make her getaway. Keeping her eyes at an angle, she gazed up the flight of stairs before her, wondering who would round the bend on the landing above.

She noticed the legs first. Knobby knees jutted beneath the hem of a green dress. The young woman wasn't the one Anna had seen leaving suite 808 in tears. And while Anna couldn't divert her eyes, the young woman didn't notice Anna at all. Strands of greasy black hair hung like a bead curtain in front of her face, swinging with each step she took. Anna's hand fell from the door lever. Her fist loosened around the shaving cream.

The young woman stepped onto the fourth-floor landing, just a couple feet from Anna. She inched along, using the wall for support.

"Do you need . . . ?" Anna started, only to lose her voice when the woman reached around her to find the wall on the opposite side of the doorframe. They came face-to-face, and Anna noticed that the young woman wasn't a woman at all—she was a kid. The hair prevented Anna from looking into the girl's eyes, but it couldn't cover the copper cast of her skin. She was from the rez. Her height and hair made Anna think of Grace. She looked like family. But who was she? A Langdon? A Forstall? A Picote? Anna's mind raced.

"Tina?" she blurted, as the girl reached for the handrail that would help her down the fourth story flight of stairs. The girl didn't turn. She just kept going, tramping down one step after the other, clumsy and uncoordinated, the hair on the very top of her head clumped up and tangled in places, looking like it'd just been spun by a cyclone. More than Grace, she resembled Tina Peltier, but she couldn't be her. Tina had taken a job in Lafayette a year earlier and hadn't returned to the rez since.

Anna stood at the edge of the fourth-floor landing, watching, thinking, while the girl stepped onto the third-floor landing below.

"Hey!" Anna said. Still, no response. The girl flexed her fingers against the wall, using it to lead her around the bend, and then she was gone.

Anna wavered, her gaze bouncing from the flight of stairs going down to the one going up. She had two options.

Follow the girl.

See if anyone was still in suite 808.

Her feet made up her mind for her, taking the stairs two at a time up to the eighth floor, only to feel a stab in her elbow when she tried to pull the eighth-floor door open with too much force. The door would open from the inside, but from the outside it was locked. Anna should have known. As with the elevator, one needed clearance to access the eighth. She yanked the access card from her sock and inserted it into the slot beneath the lock. It worked. Chest heaving, she ran to 808 and froze outside the door. Surely someone would stop her. Fox would appear from nowhere and direct her downstairs.

But there was no one. Just silence, masking the sound of chattering teeth she heard in her head. Anna plunged the suite's keycard into the slot. The lock clicked open, and Anna cautiously stepped inside. The suite was dark. Empty. And a mess. Accompanying the usual bucket of melting ice, the disheveled bed, wet towels, and the scent of cigarette smoke on the air were overturned chairs, busted beer bottles, a splintered pool cue, and what looked like spit on the wall above the headboard in the bedroom.

Anna ventured to the housekeeping closet for supplies once her nerves had settled. She restored the suite to its original state, then descended to the office, expecting to encounter Fox somewhere along the way. She didn't see him, and so she set the can of shaving cream on his desk, where he was sure to find it.

It was after she'd clocked out, her hands robotically unbuttoning the garment she reluctantly wore, that Anna finally registered what the girl in the stairwell had been wearing. Not a dress, but a Vanda green chambermaid coat, identical to her own.

Day 24
6:40 a.m.

The alarm cawed on the nightstand between their beds. Confusion creased Grace's face when Anna rolled out from under the covers.

"I'm filling in for Miss Jenny," Anna explained through a yawn. She would have told Grace that they'd be working the same shift, but Grace hadn't come home until after Anna had fallen asleep. "Did you change the time?" She squinted at the alarm clock, which she'd set for six, to make sure she was seeing it right.

"I didn't know you'd set it," Grace said.

"Grace!" Anna leapt across the room to pull her out of bed.

"We'll make it," Grace said. "Just get dressed."

Annoyed that she'd have to start her day without a shower, Anna wondered about Grace's willingness to forgo one. Shower, hair, makeup. Those things were important to Grace, especially lately. She wondered, too, where Grace had been the night before, only able to deduce that whatever had kept Grace out all night was something she deemed more important than her looks. But what? Anna longed for the days when they used to tell each other everything. Now it was like a pane of glass had been inserted between them, making them goldfish in neighboring bowls.

As Anna fixed her hair in front of the mirror, it dawned on her that her relationship with Grace was unraveling the same way her relationship with Megan Bradley had.

"You've noticed too, haven't you?" she whispered across the room, bathed in the low light of dawn.

"Noticed what?" Grace asked.

"Me."

Grace smeared strawberry lip balm across her lips. "What's that supposed to mean?"

"You don't treat me the way you used to. You talk to Emily now instead of me. It feels like you avoid me."

Grace pushed Anna aside so that she could have the mirror. "How's that for avoiding you?"

Anna took a deep breath, held it, let it loose. "Where were you last night?"

"Out."

"Where?"

"Emily's house. We went for a milkshake at the diner, then hung out by the river."

"You were at the resort last night?"

"For, like, five minutes."

"You could've said hi."

"Didn't see you. You were working. Speaking of which . . ." Grace slipped into her chambermaid coat. While Anna wouldn't bring hers home, Grace didn't mind the coat at all. She cinched the apron tight around her waist, using it to raise the coat's hem a few inches above her knees, reminding Anna again of the girl she'd seen in the stairwell. She'd been thinking about the girl while waiting for Grace the night before, trying to determine if they'd ever worked alongside each other and how she could have overlooked her if they had. Most likely, the girl worked a different shift. But if that were the case, why had she been dressed for work at night? And why had she been stumbling down the stairs?

"Better get a move on," Grace said.

Anna brushed her teeth with fewer strokes than usual. Grace didn't touch her toothbrush. She popped a piece of her sister's cinnamon gum into her mouth instead. Still, Anna grabbed two bananas from the counter and tossed one to Grace on their way out the door. It plopped onto the porch, where it stayed.

The pair jogged along the road toward the casino and resort, Anna inhaling her breakfast, acutely aware of every absconding second. "Twenty minutes," she grumbled, tossing the banana peel into the field. "I can't believe you, Grace."

"We'll make it," she said, dabbing at the sweat already beading along her brow.

"What'd you do by the river last night?" Anna was annoyed, and she knew the question would annoy Grace as well. Grace's jaw pulled to the right.

"We were watching the sky. Looking for shooting stars."

"Shooting stars?" Anna echoed, deciding that Grace had sounded believable enough.

"There's a story about the stars, right?"

"Many," Anna said.

"Tell me one."

Still aware of the passing seconds, Anna slowed so that she could speak without running out of breath.

"Back when the great gators first allowed the Takoda people to walk on land, the Takoda elders had to make a decision about death because those who'd died hadn't experienced identical fates." The words didn't come out as smoothly as when Miss Shelby had spoken them, yet Anna's quiet, confident tone reflected their worth. "Some who'd died were permitted to return to their families, while others were sent up with the sky spirit to watch over their people at night. The tribal elders wanted all to be treated the same upon death, and so they decided that whenever someone died, the earth spirit would throw a stone into the river. If the stone floated atop the water, the deceased would get to live again. If it sank into the mud, the dead would become a star among the sky spirit, watching down upon its loved ones at night."

"Not that one, Anna," Grace said. "I know that story already. . . . The stone always sinks, ensuring that we all end up with identical fates, just like the elders wanted. Tell me a different one."

"Okay . . ." Anna said, relieved that Grace knew at least one of the old tales. "One day a girl and her friend were walking through the forest to gather wood. On their way, they saw an armadillo by a giant old tree. When they got close, the armadillo began to climb. 'Look,' said the girl to her friend, 'the armadillo has climbed to the top. It is stuck. It cannot climb down.'

"The girl and her friend tried to shake the tree, but it was too large to wobble. 'I will climb to the top and carry the armadillo down,' the girl said. She began to climb while her friend watched from below.

"'Come down,' the girl's friend called. 'You are going too high.' The girl would not come down. She reached for the highest branch, and the tree suddenly grew taller. Each time she reached for the armadillo, the tree grew higher into the sky.

"Soon, the girl was so high her friend couldn't see her at all. The girl kept reaching. The tree kept growing. The girl kept climbing. She climbed throughout the day and then it was night, and she could no longer see anything above her or below her. She felt stuck and sad because the armadillo and her friend were gone. But then the stars came into the sky around her, and they twinkled to remind her that she wasn't alone."

"What's it mean?" Grace asked. They could see the roof of the resort above the trees now. The scent of new asphalt mixed with the earthy scent of the warm autumn morning.

"Weren't you listening?"

Grace yawned.

"We all reach for something," Anna explained. "Sometimes what we long for is so out of reach that we get stuck or lost in our pursuit of it. The point is not to lose sight of what you already have because if you try too hard for things above you, you might lose sight of everything that's important."

"Oh," Grace said, and Anna wondered again if she'd been paying attention at all. Grace smacked her gum and blew a bubble. A burst of cinnamon briefly competed with the odor of the asphalt.

"Grace," Anna gasped, brought to a sudden stop at the side of the road. Grace paused and turned, her gaze aligning itself with Anna's. A narrow strip of the green and brown brush—somewhat flattened— was speckled rusty red, as if someone had just sprayed a streak of spray paint along it.

"Is it . . . blood?" Grace asked.

"What do you think—?" Anna's flesh prickled; her eyes went this way and that, scanning the swaying grass that stretched before her. But was it swaying in the wind? Or was something with weight making it move? The longer Anna stared, the more certain she became that the grass wasn't bending to the breeze. No. It was rolling, like a wave of water approaching shore. Approaching her. "What do you think it's from?" A luckless animal that had tangoed with a tire was the logical explanation, but there wasn't a carcass in sight. Still, Anna smelled death.

"Come on!" Grace yanked her sister's sleeve, pulling her away from the speckled streak. "Another dumb armadillo," she said. "I bet it didn't die . . . probably limped into the grass . . . or a coyote ate it."

Neither said anything else until after they passed through the hotel's sliding glass doors. A blast of frigid air washed over them, accompanied by a sweet, smoky aroma that weighed heavily in the corners of their eyes, slowly adjusting to the lobby's false light.

The resort was wide awake with guests ambling among the alligators, dragging on their cigarettes, eating fries from the to-go grill, and sipping bottles of beer. Anna knew that many of them had yet to sleep. Enclosed within the windowless world void of clocks and morning papers, they may not have known that the night had passed.

Anna and Grace headed for the housekeeping office. They passed the Atrium Ice Bar on the way. Fox Ballard was there, elbows on the bar's frosty slab surface, chatting to a woman seated beside him. Wearing the same clothes he'd worn the night before, unshaven and with purple bags beneath his sunken eyes, he looked like he hadn't slept and yet his mouth moved a mile a minute. The woman next to him appeared bored out of her brain, held in place by his heavy hand on top of hers.

"Grace!" Fox cried upon spotting her. He didn't acknowledge Anna with more than a sideways glance. "Shirley Temple?" He winked.

"I haven't clocked in yet," Grace said.

Fox jerked his head toward the office. "Go ahead. I'll have it ready for you when you get back."

Grace clapped her hands and twirled around, nearly skipping to the housekeeping office.

"What was that about?" Anna asked when she caught up.

"What was what?" Grace checked her hair in the reflective part of the coffee maker. "Why's it so humid in here?"

"You hang out with Fox . . . in the bar?" Anna didn't know if she was more bothered by Fox's drink offer or the wink he'd given Grace.

"You don't?" Grace said, applying her lip balm again.

"No."

"Why not? It beats wrestling bedsheets first thing in the morning."

"Wrestling bedsheets is what you were hired to do."

Grace looked at Anna as though she couldn't be serious, as though she might even be dumb. "You're for real?" she said.

"What?"

"Who works hard around here, Anna? Open your eyes. There's the easy way and there's the hard way. I learned that my first day on the job."

It was true. The resort was a money-making machine, and some tribal members treated their jobs like timeshare meetings: show up, wait out the hours, and walk away with a free gift at the end. Not everyone took their role as seriously as Anna took hers. The clock-watchers always found time to chat, and they always knew just where to lean without having to worry about someone spotting them and demanding that they get back to work. Every department, from security down to food services, was loaded with parents, children, aunts, uncles, cousins, and siblings. Some worked hard—like Anna, determined to follow her father's example, who used his proceeds from the casino to better their situation at home—but others turned the resort into an extension of their living rooms, depositing inflated paychecks on top of per capita payments for the time they spent planning Sunday supper or arguing about who hung streaked undies on the line for all to see. Few of the elites who worked in the offices behind the scenes had qualifications that would get them the same jobs elsewhere, and yet they showed up in business suits, happy to play pretend from nine to five.

Anna would've had to be deaf and blind not to notice how a good number of the other housekeepers spent the first half hour on the job sipping coffee and swapping stories. She'd shrugged it off as harmless banter before, but now she knew it was blatant disregard.

"You're not going to the bar," she said to Grace. "You can see your *friends* once your work is done."

Grace, to Anna's surprise, didn't argue. She just rolled her eyes and smacked her gum as she reached for her timecard in the rack.

Something—a small papery wad by the look of it—fell to the floor when Grace pulled her card free. Unnoticed by Grace, Anna verged on pointing it out, but Tanya came bustling in just then, words of gratitude rolling off her tongue.

"It's no problem. Sorry we're late," Anna told her, rushing to clock herself in. She hustled Grace to the third floor, where they both took hold of a housekeeping cart before busying themselves on either end of the hall.

Dog hair peppered the duvet in the first vacant room Anna entered. Her nose led her to lumps of shit beneath the bed. She reported the violation, then cleaned the next three rooms in line. Nearing Grace's end of the floor, she realized that Grace's cart hadn't moved in almost an hour. It was still parked outside the second room she was supposed to clean.

"Grace?" She tapped on the open door, then wandered in. The room was empty. The beds were stripped, their sheets balled up on the floor. Anna stormed to the French doors, threw the drapes aside, and stepped out onto the balcony. She could see down into the Atrium Ice Bar from there. Grace was on one of the stools, hunched over a glass. Fox was beside her, leaning close, his motor mouth working just inches from Grace's ear.

The sight gave Anna the sensation of being pranked again, making her feel like she'd been brought in to do the heavy lifting while the rest of them got to sit back and make plans for later that night. Her impulse was to scream from the balcony, to call Grace back to work. But if Grace didn't want to work, Anna wasn't going to force her. She went downstairs instead, where, reaching for Grace's timecard, she spotted the folded wad of paper that had fallen to the floor. Goosebumps spread over her arms when she picked up the paper, decorated with little Xs and Os along its edges, and unfolded it.

Surprise! It's me! Anna read, followed by an inked-in smiley face. *Is our secret still safe?* Another smiley face, this one with its tongue sticking out. *Keep your promise and I'll keep mine. Who's the first person you're gonna call?* Three more smileys and a few more Xs and Os stood in place of a signature. The paper trembled in Anna's hand. Her urge was to shred it, but she found herself folding it carefully along the lines instead, ultimately slipping it back into Grace's spot as she plucked Grace's timecard from the rack. Knowing that what she was about to do would light Grace's fuse and potentially drive them further apart, Anna plunged the card into the timeclock.

Day 24
5:14 p.m.

Grace rolled over to face the bedroom wall. She hadn't said a word since the scene in the housekeeping office. At first, she'd thought there'd been a mistake, that someone had accidentally clocked out with her timecard. But then Anna admitted what she'd done, prompting Grace to scream a slew of choice words—was that alcohol on her breath?—before tearing the timecard to shreds, in between pocketing the secret note and stalking out of the office. Anna later saw her venting to Fox—arms thrashing, the bead bracelet bouncing on her wrist—probably getting him to promise that she'd still get paid.

"You could have helped," Anna said from the bedroom doorway.

"It wasn't my mess."

They'd walked in on the aftermath of a food fight upon arriving home from work. Broken eggs, uncooked meat, and shattered jars of jelly and pasta sauce created abstract murals on the counters, floor, and walls. There was more broken glass, too, the dinner plates and drinking glasses this time, Chris and Dorothy conspicuously absent.

"It wasn't my mess either," Anna said, "but I cleaned it up . . . just like at work."

Grace didn't bite back with a quip. The telephone rang.

148

"Aren't you gonna get it?" Anna asked.

Grace stayed silent.

Anna retreated to catch the phone before it stopped ringing. "Hello?"

Heavy breathing met her ear. Grunting. Snickers.

"Hello?"

The line went dead a second before the meat wagon pulled up outside, stocked to the seams. Chris hauled the groceries into the house and refilled the fridge with unnecessary force, making plenty of noise as he did. Paper plates and plastic cups went into the cabinet where the ceramic and glass ones used to sit.

Gran watched her son from her wheelchair, the sheet between her room and the kitchen tacked back. When she rolled toward the counter to help unpack the bags, Chris absently grabbed the chair's push handles and stuck her in the corner of the kitchen. He didn't say anything about the fight between him and Dorothy, no apologies or excuses for what Gran must have heard on her side of the sheet.

"Hungry, Ma?" he said instead, a little too loudly. "Want something to eat?"

Gran pushed hard against the armrests and took to her feet. She limped to the counter, her strong hand grasping it for support, the other pathetically digging into the folds of her housecoat. Her fingers emerged with a rolled-up slip of paper. Hand shaking, she offered it to Chris.

"What'd you find?" he asked in the same patronizing tone. His face reddened when he took the paper and unfurled it. "Whatever you heard *her* say—"

"I'll pay my share," Gran said. "I won't be a burden anymore. It's bad enough that you and Ray don't get along because of me."

Chris shoved the check back into her pocket. "Don't worry about me and Ray." He filled her shaking hand with an apple, forcefully curling her fingers around it, then fetched the wheelchair. "Sit down. Or go back to bed."

Gran slammed the apple against the counter with surprising might, bruising its skin. "Let me live!" she hollered.

Those words resonated within Anna for the rest of the weekend. She couldn't help but wonder if Grace viewed her the same way Gran viewed Chris.

Day 26
7:51 a.m.

Rubbing her eyes until they burned, Anna felt a collision against her right ankle. Playing it cool, she yawned, pretending the shapeless genitals of the decapitated doll taped upside down to her locker didn't bother her at all. She yanked the doll's body free, ignoring the question mark on its back, while her eyes fell to the doll's head, slowly spinning at her feet.

The head had the appearance of others before it. Hair tangled in knots, eyes blacked out, a horrific scowl painted across its face. Anna blamed the bullies in her class whenever she found a doll taped to her locker, but she blamed herself whenever a head rolled down the hall. She never should have told Megan Bradley about Uncle Ray's story. She never should have said how much it scared her. Now her old fear had become one more thing the others used against her.

Let me live.

Too tired and lazy to collect the head, Anna kicked it down the hall. Giggles rang out. She tossed the body upon the heap of dolls at the bottom of her locker, then collected her books and started for class, reminding herself that another day down was another day closer to commencement.

The sight of Gran waving her good arm on the porch that afternoon rearranged the frown that had occupied Anna's face from periods one through eight. Gran looked so happy upon spying Anna and Grace in the distance, like a puppy celebrating her people's return. Though her forehead creased when she registered the sour look on Grace's face, she kept waving, and the good side of her mouth stayed twisted up in a smile.

Robbie was sitting on the steps in front of the wheelchair, the tip of his tongue clamped between his teeth, his hand sketching lines in the dirt with a stick. "I'm going to build Gran the ramp," he said, when Grace and Anna got close.

Anna surveyed the schematics. "You'll need a shallower slope. I can help."

"It's not to scale." Robbie's pride drained. He erased the design with his foot.

"It looked good, Robbie. Really."

Grace stomped into the house without acknowledging Robbie or Gran. Anna resisted the urge to go after her.

"What crawled under her skin?" Gran asked about Grace.

"I made her walk home with me." Anna had been hoping they'd be able to put the incident with the timecard behind them. Grace hadn't been ready to forgive. "I'll give her space." Anna sighed and leaned against the porch railing, facing Gran. "You got out," she said, cradling Gran's weaker hand, happy to change the subject.

"Always loved this time of year." Gran inhaled deeply through her nose. "Sometimes, when your grandfather was alive, we'd spend a night in . . . in . . ." Her eyelids clenched and her strong hand grasped a fistful of her hair. "That park where you can camp . . ."

The rumble of an approaching car cut Gran off. Anna's stomach constricted, becoming heavy with ache. Looking at the empty patch where her parents always parked, she realized she dreaded their return. The car that rolled into sight, however, didn't belong to Dorothy or Chris. Still, Anna felt ill at ease upon reading TRIBAL POLICE in big blue letters along its side; Luke Fisher, chief of the tribal police, was behind the wheel.

Gran waved again, probably expecting Luke to drive by, but he didn't. He pulled into the driveway, dust billowing behind the tires, and got out of the car.

Day 26
6:28 p.m.

The console table opposite the elevator gleamed and yet Anna couldn't remember if she'd already polished it. Unable to focus, she wiped it and then wiped it again for good measure. All she could think about was Luke Fisher pulling to a stop outside the Horn house an hour earlier.

Luke's expression had been inscrutable when he'd exited his cruiser. He'd tilted his hat to Gran, and she'd become chattier than usual, happy to have a new-old face to talk to.

Well, if it isn't the Takoda's finest, she'd said, slow and slurred. *That's one fine and official-looking vehicle you've got there, if I do say so myself. Robbie, run and get Chief Fisher something to drink.*

Luke had flexed his jaw as though he had to crack it to make it work. *That's not necessary,* he'd said.

Robbie, halfway to his feet, had dropped back onto the steps.

What can we do for you? Gran had asked.

Just making my rounds. He'd directed his words at Robbie. *There's something I could use some help with.*

Anna's stomach dropped in response. His earnest delivery had instantly put her on edge.

"Anna!" Fox waved to her from the opposite end of the hall, jarring

154

her back to the present. He was like an old pair of shoes; he looked fine from a distance but appeared more worn-out the closer he got. Eyes yellow and empty. Skin dull as if it'd been dusted with powder. Somehow, he still had a spring in his step.

"Good. Good. Good," he said, evaluating the carpet, the table, the potted plants. Something shined around his neck.

"What happened to your tie?" Anna asked.

He gripped the ornamental clasp, bearing a black stone inset in silver, beneath his chin without looking down at it. "It's a different kind of tie. A bolo." He shrugged. "I liked it. I bought it. Tanya wants you back on her shift. I told her to go scratch. She's not taking you away from me. You're mine now, Anna. All mine."

He was in his talkative way again, so unlike his real self. Anna didn't like it.

"Tanya told me what you did on Saturday morning." He laughed, then lowered his voice. "I know why you did it, but you shouldn't have. Tanya says Grace is a good worker. When she's working. . . . You know how it goes around here, don't you? Work hard. Work smart. Don't bust your ass." He dipped his hand into his pants pocket, then pulled it out and sank it into Anna's front pocket.

"What are you doing?" She put her hand where his had been as soon as it retreated. A twenty-dollar bill was inside. "What for?"

"The other night."

Anna felt sick. It was the same way she'd felt when Luke, still looking straight at Robbie on the porch, had asked, *Have you seen Melissa Picote?*

Missy, Anna had muttered under her breath.

Her father hasn't seen her since Friday afternoon, Luke had informed them, finally shifting his gaze. *It seems no one has seen her since then. I was just wondering. . . .*

Shirking off the memory, Anna asked Fox, "What about the other night?"

His eyes flicked up, indicating the eighth floor. "The money's a tip."

Anna hadn't said anything to Luke because she still wasn't sure who she'd seen in the emergency stairwell, but after Luke had said Missy Picote's name, Anna realized it could have been her tromping down the stairs on Friday night.

"I saw a young woman," she said to Fox. "A girl."

"The hotel was booked solid on Friday," he said. "I'm sure you saw a lot of girls."

"I'm not talking about a guest. She was dressed like me."

"Shana . . . Joy . . . ?" he said, referring to the others who worked the evening shift.

"Not them," Anna said. "The girl I saw was someone I'd never seen working at the hotel before."

Fox shrugged his thick shoulders. "Sorry, Anna, I don't know who you're talking about."

"Was it Melissa Picote?"

"Who?"

"Missy Picote. Sawyer and Claire's daughter."

"Sawyer." Fox laughed in a mocking way. "Did you know he voted against my uncle in the last election? He backed Abel Peltier for tribal chairman."

Anna held her gaze, waiting for an answer.

"They're separated now, aren't they? Sawyer and Claire? I heard Claire left him."

Anna nodded slowly, unsure if Claire had left Sawyer or if Sawyer had run her off. The Picotes' marriage wasn't any of Anna's business; things like that just had a way of getting around on the rez. Keeping personal business quiet was a feat. She wondered how much of her parents' troubles had already gotten around.

"I haven't seen the Picotes or their daughter in a minute," Fox said. "I'm always here."

"I guess you are. Did you know that Missy's missing?"

"Missy's missing." He chuckled. "Say that ten times fast."

"No one's seen her since Friday."

"Who told you that?"

"Luke Fisher. This afternoon. He came by my house to ask if we'd seen her. He thought Grace and I might be friends with her."

"Are you?"

Anna shook her head. "Missy's three years younger than me. A year younger than Grace. They used to play dress-up together." Anna had forgotten about the times Missy Picote had come to her house to riffle through her mother's clothes and costume jewelry with Grace. It'd only happened a few times, probably before Dorothy got fed up with the mess. Anna hadn't remembered those playdates until Grace had come onto the porch at Luke's request.

Are you all right? Luke had asked upon seeing Grace, distracted from his line of questioning by her angry eyes and the steely look on her face. Grace had nodded and yawned. Luke spoke again when it was clear that she wasn't going to give an explanation. *Do you know anything about Missy Picote?*

Grace had stalled, fidgeting with the hem of her shirt. *I heard she—*

Her father's the one who beat my boy, Gran had butted in, suddenly remembering.

What's that? Luke inquired, puzzled.

When Ray wanted to be on the council.

The tribal council election, Anna had explained. *My uncle Ray lost to Sawyer Picote.*

Luke had given Gran an insincerely sympathetic smile. *You were saying?* he prompted Grace.

I haven't seen Missy around in a while. She was supposed to start high school this year, but I guess she dropped out before she even started. I heard she's hooked on drugs. Grace shrugged.

Luke had confirmed that with a nod. *Her father says she split. We're trying to find her.*

She's probably with them.

With who?

Grace shrugged again. *Whoever she gets high with. I don't know. Sorry I can't help.* She went back into the house.

Luke hitched his pants and tilted his hat at Gran once more. *You'll let me know if you see her?*

Anna had nodded, all the while replaying the scene in the emergency stairwell in her mind. Was it Missy she'd seen? Had she been stumbling down the stairs in a chambermaid coat?

Anna's attention returned to Fox. "You're not friends with her either, are you?" she asked.

He blew air through his lips. "She's just a kid."

"Only a year younger than Grace," Anna said again.

Fox reddened. He looked down at the gold TAG Heuer watch on his wrist. "I know what you're thinking, Anna, and I don't blame you. I shouldn't have invited Grace into the bar on Saturday. I'd been up all night. I wasn't thinking. I swear it won't happen again. And just so you know, there's nothing between me and your sister. I see her around the resort. She's friendly. That's all."

Anna thought about the shaving cream. The lie. "What about Missy? Was she here before she went missing?"

Fox tapped the crystal covering the hands of his timepiece. His Adam's apple bobbed, and Anna inferred that he'd gladly accept a drink should one be offered. He'd probably take the twenty bucks back, too.

"Anna." His words came slowly. "If Missy was here on Friday, it had nothing to do with me. I was busy helping Tanya try to find someone to fill in for Miss Jenny the next morning. We couldn't find anyone, so I told her I'd ask you. If you don't believe me, talk to Tanya. All I know right now is that some kid mashed gum in the carpet on three. Take care of it, will you?"

Anna turned, partially relieved, yet still weighed down by mysteries in her mind. She paused and aimed one more question at Fox without looking at him. "Did you leave a note for Grace in the timecard rack?"

There was a pause. "I don't know what you're talking about," he said. Still, Anna suspected that the note had been penned by the same hand that had written the list he'd given her the first time she'd serviced suite 808. His heavy footsteps retreated down the hall.

Day 27
4:06 p.m.

Fog swirled low around Miss Shelby's abandoned trailer, making everything feel damp inside. The discolored carpet squished beneath Anna's feet, intensifying the commingled scent of mold and mildew hanging heavy on the air. The place was rotting; the books were slowly breaking down. They reminded Anna of the pitch for the preservation society, still sitting on the back burner. The tribal council meeting loomed only hours away, and she still didn't know what she'd say. Her mind was like her brother's boots, muddy.

Anna eased the volume she'd been studying back into its spot on its shelf. Though Miss Shelby Mire had gone to an early grave and wasn't around to care for her treasured library, Anna always brought the books back. There wasn't enough room to keep them all at home.

She squatted by the bookshelf and ran a finger along the spines of the books on the bottom. They weren't all about Native American history, traditions, and myths, but they all shed light on beliefs that had shaped the world. Together, the texts constituted a comprehensive collection consisting of stories about Norse gods and giants, Greek myths, urban legends, Catholicism, folktales from the south, mythical beasts, Islamic texts, tales of sea monsters and magical creatures,

Judaism, African American folklore, Voodoo and Hoodoo, witchcraft, the occult, spells, cryptids of North America, Japanese creatures, lore of the vampire, and the history of ghosts.

Anna's hand settled on an old text titled *The Adventures of Blind Coyote and Other American Indian Myths and Legends* collected and edited by Henry Red Elk of the Comanche Tribe. Brown and black stains inched up the yellowed and curled pages. Anna blew dust off the cover and carefully opened the book. The spine cracked. Her gaze drifted over stories about the Great Spirit, warriors, snow, red apples, and the cutting of hair as she searched for Miss Shelby's scrawl in the margins, hoping deep down to find a reference to the rolling head. The sound of tires outside drew her eyes to the window before she could find any trace of Miss Shelby on the page.

Anna held her breath, listening. A car door slammed. Another followed. The vehicle wasn't right outside Miss Shelby's trailer, but it was close enough for Anna to hear frenzied, high-pitched voices.

"—so unfair. You're so full of shit!" one of them said.

"Your room. Now!"

Anna crept to the window, feeling even more like an intruder. The young woman with big hair, the one Anna had seen crying on the eighth floor, was outside the trailer across the field. A scowling girl was with her. The girl stomped up the porch steps and stormed into the trailer, letting the screen door slam. The woman's jaw dropped as if she were about to scream, but no sound came out. She flicked her middle finger at the door, then wrangled a few well-stocked bags from the car's trunk. She lumbered up the steps and dropped the bags by the door.

"Get the groceries!" she hollered through the screen. Her narrowed eyes and furrowed brow called to mind the irritated expression Anna's mother bore when Dad got on her last nerve. The seamless curves of the woman's figure filled Anna with envy. Her hair defied gravity, and her makeup looked like it'd just been applied, dark around the eyes and bright on the lips, none of it smeared the way it'd been in the hall outside suite 808.

Anna closed the book and slipped it inside her bag. Normally she'd ensure the coast was clear before emerging from the Mire trailer, but she wanted to be noticed this time, even if the prospect made it feel like beetles were swarming in her stomach.

Anna stepped through the doorway, then descended the first step, where she stalled, waiting and watching for a reaction from the woman across the way. But the woman, heading back to the trunk, remained oblivious. Anna descended the rest of the steps and dragged her feet through the gravel on her way to the road, the sound of which finally caught the woman's attention. She glanced at Anna as she slammed the trunk shut, then dug in her purse and pulled something out.

Anna couldn't tell what it was, even when she stopped at the mouth of the woman's driveway, hoping the woman would say something.

"Hi," Anna said, before too much time had passed. It was one of the bravest things she'd ever done.

The woman plucked a cigarette and a lighter from the pack she'd pulled from her purse. Having tucked the cigarette between her lips, she rolled her thumb over the lighter's spark wheel and inhaled deeply upon touching the flame to the cigarette's tip.

"Hey," she said. Anna could relate to her defeated tone. She started down the drive. The woman didn't object.

"I'm Anna. Anna Horn. I live—"

"I know who you are. Chris's daughter?"

"Yeah." Anna waited for an introduction in return. She didn't get one.

"Haven't seen your father in a while," the woman said through a mouthful of smoke. "Guess that's a good thing."

"Yeah." Anna forced a laugh that she immediately regretted because it was so unlike her and because there hadn't been a bit of humor in the woman's voice. "How do you know my dad?"

"Everyone knows everyone around here."

Anna nodded because that was mostly true. "I don't know you," she said.

"I mind my own business." The woman took a long drag. "It's best that way. . . . Lula Broussard," she finally said, extending a hand with the shiniest red nails Anna had ever seen.

The name sparked a memory. "Joseph Broussard," Anna said, remembering the former tribal chairman who'd died two years earlier.

"My grandpa."

"Everyone loved him."

Lula shrugged. "What do you do over there?" She jerked her chin toward the Mire trailer.

Anna was tempted to twist the truth, worried that it might paint her as a bore within Lula's mind. "I go for the books," she replied, her eyes falling to her feet. "The stories."

"Stories?"

"Miss Shelby was the tribe's last singer and Legend Keeper. She knew all the old Takoda tales."

"You gonna take her place?"

There was a time when Anna believed she might, back when Miss Shelby had taken her by the chin so that they could look into each other's eyes, saying, *You're different, Anna. Unique. You could carry these stories. You could carry this tribe.* Coming from any other adult those words might have been patronizing or insincere, throwaway sentiments used to make a six-year-old feel special. But coming from Miss Shelby—so genuine, so true—they hadn't felt false at all. Anna still remembered when Dad had walked in and announced, *Miss Shelby's missing,* followed a few months later by Uncle Ray's assertion that the rolling head had eaten her. The news had smashed Anna to smithereens. Not just because she'd lost her link to the stories, but because she'd lost hope of what she might become. "I'm afraid the stories will be forgotten," she said.

Lula took another drag.

"Did you know her?" Anna asked.

"Everyone knows everyone around here," Lula said again, finally cracking a smile. Smoke streamed from between her red lips. "I didn't know her well. I was in my own world when I was a kid."

"Seems like you still are."

"You're not wrong." Lula glanced at the groceries still sitting by the door. "Noemi!" she shouted. "Get your ass out here. Shit's gonna melt."

"Your little sister?" Anna asked, trying to piece things together.

Lula smirked. "My daughter."

Lula didn't look old enough to have a child as big as Noemi.

"She's thirteen. And she's got a mouth," Lula said.

"I kinda heard."

"I guess I did too when I was her age. Just nobody cared."

"Bet she knows my brother, Robbie. He's thirteen too."

"She's obsessed with a boy named Walker." Lula rolled her eyes, her gaze settling off in the distance. She stamped her cigarette out against the porch railing, leaving a black mark next to numerous other black marks on the wood. "It's scary how similar she is to me. I try to be nothing like my ma, and yet I feel like I'm failing every day."

Anna thought about her own battle with Grace and how helpless she felt.

"Noemi!" Lula stomped against the lowest porch step. Even annoyed, she looked like she belonged on TV.

"I heard you. Jeez. Can't even pee in peace around here. Not to mention that you told me to go to my room." The screen door creaked open. Noemi leaned out, long hair falling in her face, obscuring it. She dragged the bags over the threshold into the trailer. "You can untwist your titties now." The screen door clacked shut.

"Watch it," Lula said, expending no energy to go after the girl.

"I'll get out of your hair." Anna, accustomed to tense situations, felt awkward being a part of this one because it didn't belong to her. Still, she couldn't shake the one thing that'd been on her mind since she set eyes on Lula: What had propelled her from suite 808 with tears and ruined makeup?

"What kind of books does she got over there?" Lula asked, taking a seat on the porch steps. The question came as a relief to Anna— Lula didn't want her gone just yet.

Anna took a step closer, allowing her bookbag to hang lower on her back. She practically had to dare herself to sit next to Lula, but she did, and Lula didn't turn her away.

"Anything interesting?" Lula prodded.

Anna's cheeks turned hot. Realizing she'd been silent too long, she grabbed the bag from her back and unzipped it, bringing out *The Adventures of Blind Coyote*.

"Gross," Lula said, eyeing the mold-dappled book. She refrained from touching it, choosing to crane her head over Anna's lap instead.

"Most of the books aren't specific to the Takoda Nation," Anna explained. "But sometimes there's writing in the margins." She turned the brittle pages, careful not to break them. "There!" She'd spotted Miss Shelby's scrawl. Faded, the words required Anna to bring the book within inches of her face. "'Possum cannot be trusted because he gets back up after lying down dead,'" she read.

Lula giggled. "Really? What the hell am I supposed to take from that?"

"I know it seems silly on the surface, but when you look deep, you'll see the truth within the words. The stories are true. They're valuable, too."

"I don't know about all that. I never bought into those stories. Like the one about talking alligators. Seriously?"

"Our origin story," Anna said, referring to the tale in which a red and a blue alligator allowed the Takoda people to walk on land. "At least you know it. I think my generation was the last to learn it."

"My daughter knows it," Lula said. "My brother taught it to her. He was *obsessed* with that story. Still is."

"Your brother?" Anna asked, mind searching.

"Louie. He got away from here."

"Miss him?"

Lula shrugged. "He visits every year."

Anna possessed a vague memory of Louie. He was one of the many faces at the Blue Gator Grill—once the only place on the reservation to get a burger and a beer—when Chairman Broussard held meetings there to organize the search effort for Miss Shelby after she went missing. Anna remembered those meetings well, everyone united by grief, wondering what it meant that they'd lost one of their own. "So it's just you and Noemi?"

"Just us." Lula sighed. Sudden ringing from inside her purse distracted them both. Lula pulled a cell phone from the bag and glanced at the number on the screen while Anna peered at Lula from the corner of her eye. Secretly, she wondered what made them so different. What had Lula gotten that she hadn't?

Lula held the phone until it stopped ringing. The device made her look even more like a model from a magazine. She shoved it back into her bag, then rummaged around until she found her cigarette pack again. What she took from it looked different than the cigarette she'd stubbed out. She lit it and inhaled. Smoke appeared to float out of her mouth, whereas she'd forcibly exhaled it before. The pungent scent reminded Anna of the burnouts at school.

"Want?" Lula said, offering Anna the joint.

Anna had never smoked anything before. Her instinct was to wave the joint away, but she feared that rejecting the weed would put a wedge between her and Lula. Or that Lula might just see her as square. Her fingers made the decision for her, timidly pinching the little white mystery while her tongue wet her lips.

The paper shell felt like nothing against her skin, and so Anna sucked, a little too hard. She felt the smoke more than she tasted it at first, hot and oddly grainy against the back of her throat. Her lungs tightened when she inhaled, causing her to cough so hard her head ended up between her knees, encircled by a cloud of smoke swirling like fog that'd rolled in off the river. Her hand blindly passed the joint back to Lula, and all she could think was, *I must look so ugly right now.* Lula smirked.

A lull followed Anna's coughing fit. She felt like she should go, like she didn't belong. It was the same feeling she often felt at school, surrounded by so many leering faces. Lula took another hit and blew the smoke at the sky. "It's the little things that make this life bearable," she said. "But things are getting better, aren't they?" She sounded like she was talking to herself, trying to make herself believe. "Thank god for the casino. It'll get me out of this tin can one day."

She put the joint in front of Anna's face. Red smudges stained the rolling paper. Anna glanced at Lula to make sure she wasn't goofing on her. Lula's smirk was gone.

"Do it right this time," Lula said. "It'll take some weight off your shoulders."

Anna's fingers shook upon accepting the joint.

"Your first time?" Lula asked.

Anna nodded.

"Draw the smoke slowly into your mouth and hold it there. Don't lick your lips first. It makes the paper soggy—and it's gross."

Anna blotted her lips against the back of her hand. She raised the joint and took a puff, proceeding to hold the smoke in her mouth just like Lula had said.

"Now take a deep breath. A slow one. It'll carry the smoke into your lungs."

Anna did as told. Her lungs seemed to flap, wanting her to cough. She fought off the fit by tightening every muscle in her abdomen, chest, and neck.

"Let it out smoothly," Lula said. "Smooth in, smooth out."

The smoke came out in a ribbon, smooth until the very end when Anna couldn't fight it anymore. Her shoulders heaved with each burst from her lungs.

"Feel it?" Lula asked.

Straining and striving to neither cough nor embarrass herself more than she already had, Anna nodded. *Hideous,* she thought. Her head felt like it was on a string, like a snip from a pair of scissors would send it soaring into the atmosphere.

Lula giggled again. Her laugh drew Anna in, much more welcoming than the electronic ring of the phone. "I remember my first time," she said. "Enjoy it. It'll never be that way again."

Anna drifted backward, her shoulder blades wanting to introduce themselves to the porch planks. Lula put an arm around her to push her back up. The warmth was nice, then it was gone. A cool sensation lingered in the space where Lula's arm had been.

Lula inhaled another hit. Anna strained to watch through the corner of her right eye. She had to close the left one just to keep her sight straight.

"You're not my type, Anna," Lula said, exhaling the thin, white smoke, her eyes twinkling toward the cloud-covered sun.

"What? No. I—"

"I've seen you looking at me before. From over there . . . reading your stories." Her voice had taken on a teasing lilt.

"I was just looking. . . . I'm not—" If Lula hadn't stuck the joint between Anna's lips just then, Anna would have told her that she didn't want her like that; not the way Lula was thinking. Anna was curious, though. What was it like to have a body boys ogled: one with full breasts rather than little, pointed mounds; hips that rebelled against her waist rather than continuing in a straight line down; hair, eyes, and lips done up the way TV commercials would have you believe they were supposed to be. Given the chance, Anna might have walked in Lula's skin, just for a minute, but only because she wanted to see what it was like. She suspected she wouldn't want to keep it because bodies like Lula's attracted attention Anna was ill-equipped to handle. But she couldn't help wondering. What if the sultry, sexy strutting that seemed so easy for some women fulfilled something within her? Moreover, what if possessing the fluid grace that came with being comfortable in one's own skin strengthened her self-esteem?

"I'm too old for you anyway." The lilt had vanished from Lula's voice. She sounded bitter now. "Twenty-nine," she muttered. "Thirty soon."

"Hardly old," Anna said, pinching the joint between her thumb and forefinger, refraining from smoking it. "You're not too old to talk to me."

"You think?" Lula smiled. She grabbed Anna by the chin and pulled her face toward hers. Anna resisted, leaning back. She wasn't used to being touched that way, and she had no idea what Lula was going to do next.

"You know," Lula said, pausing, her tone light and airy. "You could be pretty."

A gust of air that nearly transformed into a laugh erupted out of Anna.

"Yeah . . . with a little makeup," Lula said, turning Anna's face from one side to the other. "I could do it for you."

Faced with the offer, terror flooded Anna to the brim. She'd never worn makeup because she'd never understood it. Was it for her? Or for those who were looking at her, evaluating her? She never could shake the thought that it was no different than a mask. While she understood the desire to hide, she'd never wanted to be painted as something she wasn't.

"Just a little around your eyes and on your lips," Lula said.

Anna pulled away and tried to realign her wavy mind by shaking her head. "Shit," she said. "I have to work." She nearly burned Lula with the joint upon putting it back between Lula's fingers. Lula stubbed the thing out and put the remains into her cigarette pack. Anna stood and stumbled, feeling lost on her way down the dirt drive.

"If you change your mind—" Lula started, only to silence herself when Anna began to shake her head harder and faster. "You'll be all right," Lula said. "You should probably sit and chill."

Anna turned to face Lula. She had no intention of staying. She only wanted to ask the question still floating on the waves that had overtaken her mind.

"What were you doing on the eighth floor?"

Lula's expression was as blank as the black blouse she wore. It took a moment for the question to register, and then her eyes fell.

"That was you," she muttered, remembering. "You were looking at me . . . again."

"I work at the hotel. You were crying."

Lula dusted invisible lint from her pants. "It was nothing."

"Did Luke Fisher come by here?" Eyelids heavy, tongue thick in her mouth, Anna was still straining to keep her head from floating away. "You've heard about Missy Picote?"

Lula kept rubbing her thighs. She glanced back at the screen door.

"Missy's gone missing," Anna said. "I think I saw her at the hotel, too. She was coming down from the eighth floor . . . or at least I think she was."

Lula still didn't speak.

"Was it her?" Anna asked.

"How would I know?"

"I just thought . . ."

"I haven't seen any of the Picotes since I don't know when."

"Did Fox bring you up there?"

Air that made her bangs bob streamed from Lula's lips. She looked again at the spot where the groceries once were. "I gotta feed the kid.

Make sure she's not up to . . ." She trailed off and stood up on the porch steps. "See ya, Anna."

The screen door slapped the wood around the doorframe. Anna lingered until she heard Noemi say, "That'd better not be your new *boy*friend," from inside the trailer.

Day 28
8:12 a.m.

Musky cologne and spicy aftershave wafted off the silent man standing next to Anna on the elevator heading up to the eighth floor. An alligator from the manmade bayou lay at his feet. Still at first, the alligator began to shrink, its tail, body, and snoot retracting into its head, which gradually morphed into something much more human, covered with mud and moss, its gaping mouth full of alligator teeth. Anna jumped back but not in time to put enough distance between herself and the teeth. They sank into her left calf, tearing bloody flesh, muscle, and meat from the bone. Fading, Anna looked to the man for help.

"You're late," he said.

Anna gasped and sat up in bed. She hadn't meant to fall asleep. She'd been waiting for Grace.

"You're late," Chris said again. "It's the big goddamn day and you're late!"

"Grace," she said, casting her gaze to the opposite side of the room.

"She's gone. Emily and her mom picked her up thirty minutes ago. Jesus, Anna, you were sleeping like a log."

Anna couldn't deny it. She hadn't even heard Grace sneak in during the night. She squinted at the clock.

"Shit," she said. School was already in session. Attendance taken. "Why didn't she wake me?"

"I don't know. Just get up. Let's go."

Chris was wearing his finest work clothes and yet he wasn't at work. "You don't have to drive me," Anna said.

"Are you kidding? I'm going with."

Anna realized what day it was and where she was supposed to be precisely as her father announced it.

"The tribal council meeting, Anna. Don't tell me you forgot."

A rush of panic pulsed from Anna's chest to her limbs. She gripped the blanket and pulled it tight around her. "I'm not ready," she said, though she'd been thinking about what she might say to the council while she'd waited up for Grace. "I can't."

Chris threw his hands in the air and spun around in the doorway, halfway out of the room. "You've had a month to think about it. You're ready. You just have to talk to them. Get dressed. Let's go." He grabbed a fistful of her blanket and pulled it away, dragging it with him into the hall. "There's coffee and toast on the counter."

Anna reluctantly faced herself in the mirror. The taste of the marijuana smoke she'd inhaled with Lula the day before still lingered at the back of her throat; the smell still pervaded her nose. Perhaps it was responsible for making her sleep so heavily. Looking past her matted hair and puffy eyes, she saw her sister's bed reflected behind her. Grace never smoothed her blankets, which made it impossible to tell if the bed had been slept in. Without evidence other than the fact that she hadn't heard Grace in the night, Anna suspected that the bed had been empty through the dark hours. Grace had probably snuck into the house just in time to creep back out without Chris or Dorothy knowing.

A blast from the station wagon's horn shook Anna from her thoughts. She pulled her fingers through her hair to make it look less lifeless and flat, then opened the closet.

"I won't be there this morning," Dorothy said from the doorway. She was still in her pajamas. "I think you know why."

The scent of stale smoke clung to Dorothy's breath as well, only it was from cigarettes, not pot.

"You have to work," Anna said, stretching the truth, which was that her mother's shift didn't start until noon. "I understand."

"I'm proud of you," Dorothy said.

"Proud of what?" Anna rummaged through the closet, pushing hanger after hanger aside along the metal rod, each screeching like an upset elephant. Unsure of what she was looking for, she blindly pulled a pair of overalls from the darkness.

Dorothy stepped in and took the overalls from her, hanging them up again. "You can't wear that," she said.

"Why not?"

"You should wear something appropriate."

The words jabbed Anna. She hadn't realized it when she'd pulled the overalls from the closet, but she'd chosen them because they made her feel safe, covered, and confined. The frown on Dorothy's face deepened with each article of clothing she declined inside the closet. "The skirt you wore to Grandpa's funeral?" she asked.

"Grandpa's funeral was six years ago."

Another honk from the station wagon sounded outside. Dorothy muttered something beneath her smoky breath, then said, "I've got it." Having given up on the closet, she hurried from the room. Anna could only imagine the dreadful threads with which she'd return.

"I've only worn it once," Dorothy said. The royal blue suit jacket that she pressed against Anna's body had a notched collar and slightly extended shoulders, but still it'd be snug on Anna. It matched the pants Dorothy had in her other hand. "You can wear one of the blouses you wear to work."

Anna didn't argue because she knew it wouldn't make a difference. She didn't have the energy anyway. She dressed quickly, splashed some water on her face, and dragged her toothbrush over her tongue. Dorothy was waiting outside the bathroom, a pair of gray high heels dangling at her side.

"No," Anna said.

Dorothy put the shoes on the floor. Chris honked again. Grumbling, Anna forced her feet into the heels, at least two sizes too small.

"You look better." Dorothy picked at Anna's hair as Anna absently grabbed a piece of buttered toast from the counter on her way out.

"Quit dragging your feet," Chris hollered from the station wagon.

Anna might as well have been on stilts. She kicked the shoes into the passenger footwell and smoothed the pants over her lap when she sat down. "They're Mom's."

"I know. I paid for them," he said, claiming all the credit.

It only took two minutes to drive to the newly built community center where the tribal council held its monthly meetings. Anna clutched the slice of toast the entire time, shedding buttery crumbs onto the pristine suit. Chris stomped the brake pedal and threw the station wagon into park so roughly on arrival that Anna's nose came within inches of the windshield. He hurried inside, waving his arm like a windsock for her to follow.

Shoes in one hand, Anna tossed the toast to the birds on her way into the community center. The meeting had started, but they hadn't missed much.

The five tribal council members, along with tribal chairman Eaton Ballard, sat in a row behind a long, curved console at the front of the room. Dozens of folding chairs were stationed before them, only a quarter of which were occupied. The council members briefed the scant audience on the current state of affairs while a scribe took minutes. The meeting revolved around money, with revenue being the greatest concern, starkly different than the forgotten meetings Miss Shelby used to host out by the old oak. Anna sat next to her father and grudgingly crammed her feet back into the high heels. The council members' voices hummed like the buzz of mosquitos in her ears. She didn't care what they had to say. She could only think, *I look like a fucking clown*. No one else was wearing royal blue.

Chris nodded next to her, and then he clapped his hands so hard that she snapped out of her rumination and focused on the elected officials. Chairman Ballard sat center, taking up more space than the rest. His broad shoulders were high, not hunched, and his hands were spread far across the console rather than being clasped in front of him. His eyes were bright and his hair was slicked, his suit precisely tailored to show off the might of his fit physique. He appeared principled and powerful, a disciplined man who'd earned his tribe's trust and respect by making his fellow members feel valued and heard. He also knew the tribal constitution like the back of his hand. Anna did a double take upon noticing the brilliant blue-green stone set within sterling silver beneath his chin. A pair of black braided leather cords, silver tips dangling from their ends, hung down from the turquoise clasp. It was a bolo tie wrapped around the chairman's neck. Anna nearly gasped, thinking about Fox and how derivative he suddenly seemed. Even if he clawed his way to the tribe's upper ranks, she doubted that he'd ever look as noble as Eaton did now.

Sawyer Picote sat next to the chairman, which baffled Anna. How could he be there when his daughter wasn't? Missy had been gone for nearly five full days. Granted, Sawyer looked distracted—his chair was pushed back and his left foot, visible beneath the console, was moving a mile a minute—but still, why wasn't he out looking for her?

The rest of the tribal council members described their plans and proposals for more money-making ventures, including an RV park, a golf course, and an outdoor waterpark. Like Chris, those in the audience nodded along, their smiles growing wider the more they heard.

"Well then," council member Miss Vicky Peltier said, once they'd gone over the plans. "Shall we open the floor?"

"Just a minute, if I may," Sawyer said, his voice afflicted by phlegm. He took a drink of water and cleared his throat. "There's no reason to ignore the elephant in the room. You all know what I'm talking about. My daughter, Melissa, ran off last week. Again. She's done it before." His tongue passed over dry lips. "The truth is, she's been battling some demons lately. She's been using. Drugs. I'm sure you know that already too." He attempted to flash a good-natured smile, only to end up with a grimace. "She took a turn down a dead-end street and . . . well . . . I just hope she finds her way back. I want to say a public thank-you to Chief Fisher for all he's done this past weekend to try to find her. And to all of you as well. Your support means a lot."

"She'll come home," Miss Paula Bishop, on the edge of her seat, said. "They always do." Anna thought about Amber and Erica. Would they find their way back? Could they?

"Keep an eye out for her," Sawyer said.

Miss Vicky put a reassuring hand on his shoulder. "We'll hear the extra orders of business that have been added to the agenda."

Chris nudged Anna with an elbow. Her chest closed up like a clam. *You'll never be able to do this!* the voice in her head shouted. *You can't. You can't. You can't.*

The council called upon Clint Lavergne. On any other day, Clint could be found out on his ATV or tinkering with his truck, always wearing a shredded pair of jeans and a sweat-stained tank top. The collared shirt buttoned up to his chin and his slicked-back hair made him look like a new man. He approached the podium set in front of the folding chairs, proceeding to address the council slowly, carefully picking his words, sounding nothing like himself.

It was a gas station that Clint proposed. "What sense does it make . . . for our guests . . . to have to fill up in town? It would be much more . . . *lucrative* . . . if we owned and operated our own establishment. Everyone knows that you fill your tank before you start a trip. So why not have our guests fill up here before they . . . depart? And if we get the RV park built . . ." he said, spreading his hands to indicate the obvious. "And forget the gas for a second. That's not even where most of the revenue comes from. There's everything else we could sell . . . soda, candy, hot dogs, souvenirs . . . that's where the real money comes in. We could even sell our crafts." His confidence rose the more he spoke. "I'd be happy to run the joint. And my brother's in the beginning stages of his construction company. I'm sure we could work out a deal."

Clint's self-interest was no surprise to Anna. That was the new way things went on the rez. The council members had been nodding along as he spoke, as had the observers, including Clint's brother, who'd been nodding at double speed. The council accepted Clint's proposal along with a file folder containing the business plan he'd somehow assembled. Anna's insides fluttered at the sight of it since she hadn't shown up with more than crumbs in hand.

"This is something we've been discussing for a while," Miss Vicky said. "We'll get it done."

They called upon Noah Forstall next. "I'll make this quick. We've got people coming in from all over the south. . . . They're coming from all over the country. They get here and what's the first thing they ask? 'How far's New Orleans?'" he said, pronouncing it *Or-lee-yuns*. "'How far's the bayou?' These are places they wanna see. Well, I can show 'em. Personal tours. My boys and me'll sign 'em up and take 'em out. We'll put together trips. Give 'em a good time. They wanna see Bourbon Street and Mardi Gras and gators in the wild. I've looked into it. I'll need a few vehicles. Three or four to start. Permits, licensing, insurance. I can get it all together on my own. I just need the start-up costs covered."

"You're speaking about a personal endeavor?" Sawyer said.

"A family business for me and my boys."

"Let me get this straight," council member Jacob Langdon said. "You're talking about taking customers away from the resort? Our priority is to keep them here."

Noah rounded the podium and drew closer to the council members, his hands waving fast in a *slow down, hold up* motion. "That's why my boys and me would be taking 'em out and bringing 'em back. The guests wouldn't be leaving here to rent a room on Bourbon Street somewhere. They'd stay here."

The council members didn't look convinced. "What are you requesting?" Jacob asked.

"Seventy-five thousand for the start-up," Noah said, his voice faltering, which made Anna think he'd intended on asking for more. "I can make it work with fifty grand."

Miss Vicky extended a hand, expecting his business plan to fill it. "We'll keep the proposal in mind," she said. Her empty hand fell flat against the console.

"Just fifty thousand," Noah persisted. "I'm not asking for much."

"They don't like your idea," Edgar Forstall, grumpy as ever, said from the second row. "Next."

"Fifty thousand to start a business that'll support an entire family?" His voice rose, as did the color in his face. "Isn't that what this casino is about? Supporting tribal members? To give us a chance to rise above? Me and my boys wanna start a business. They're smart boys. They're not out getting loaded every night like other kids their age. Adam's taking business classes at Central Louisiana Community."

"The casino is in its infancy," Chairman Ballard said, stepping in. "We appreciate the novelty of your idea, but the tribe isn't funding personal loans."

"The profit wouldn't be all mine," Noah tried to explain. "This would be—"

"We'll keep the proposal in mind," Miss Vicky said again. She glanced down at the agenda in front of her. "Anna Horn."

Anna's heart kicked at the sound of her name. She suddenly needed the bathroom. Chris put a hand against her back and pushed. "You're up," he said, smiling. Miss Vicky smiled at her too.

Anna used the chair in front of her to help herself to her feet. The high heels did cruel things to her ankles. Her joints wanted to turn inward and buckle. *A newborn foal,* she thought. *A hideous royal blue foal.* She grasped the podium like a starving child grasping a loaf of bread, nearly lying on top of it. The five tribal council members and Chairman Ballard stared at her. She reminded herself that there was still time to kick off the heartless high heels and run away from the resort and the asphalt roads, to one of the remaining fields where she used to feel free. But then she thought about Frog lingering out in the field and how he would remind her of change, without which she wouldn't reach her full potential.

"Anna?" Miss Vicky said, her smile starting to wane.

Anna's anxiety spiked. She couldn't think of a thing to say, couldn't even remember why she was there. All she could think about was Grace and Fox, the hotel and Missy Picote.

"Go on," Miss Vicky goaded.

Anna cleared her throat, dry now as overcooked steak. Getting her lips to part was like separating stuck-together stickers.

"What'd you want to say?" Jacob Langdon asked.

Anna's thirsty tongue ran over her desiccated lips. *Fuck Frog,* she thought and said, "I need *fifty-one* thousand dollars."

Chris pounded the steering wheel. Twice. Three times. He winced upon hitting the new scar beneath his left thumb—stitches freshly removed—too hard. He'd kept his cool in the meeting room, smiling at fellow tribal members as they filed past on their way out, making jokes, feigning pride. *Like father, like daughter,* he'd said. *She gets it from me.* His true feelings, however, burst free as soon as he'd slammed the car door shut.

"*Damnit,* Anna, what'd you do that for?"

She couldn't talk. Mouth still dry, her unwilling tongue passed over her cracked lips, making them sting. Her heart continued to hammer her chest; the blue blazer practically pulsed each time her heart beat.

"I don't get it, Anna. I just don't get it." Chris blew a great gust of air between his lips that practically slammed against the windshield. "Did you see their faces?" His reddened, the same way Anna's had as she stood at the podium, silent, instantly ashamed of what she'd said but too stubborn and self-conscious to try to take it back. She didn't even know why she'd said it. Not really. Sure, she realized it was a way out, but from where had those words come? Why couldn't she just have said she'd changed her mind? A few of the spectators had giggled in response to the words in question, likely thinking she'd meant to make a joke, only to cover their mouths with their hands as everlasting seconds ticked by in which Anna didn't utter another word. Awkward. Uncomfortable. Anna fled to her seat the instant Miss Vicky's lips mashed tightly together, creating a straight line across her face. "How could you pull that in there?" Chris said. "You have an idea that's heads and tails above what everyone else is proposing. An idea that'll mean something to your family and this tribe."

"It's not my idea," she said. "It never was. I only asked you why the tribe doesn't have a preservation society. You turned it into this." She didn't get why it meant so much to him.

"You brought it up, which makes it your idea," he said. "But you've blown it. Don't think they're gonna give you another shot after embarrassing them like that. When did this become a joke? I went out of my way to make this happen for you, and now it's like you never cared about it at all!"

"I care about the stories," she muttered. The two-minute drive across the reservation had never felt so long. Clammy and uncomfortable air swirled within the meat wagon. Anna thought she smelled the stench of death wafting from the back.

"I'm sorry. I wasn't ready."

"Life doesn't care if you're ready," Chris said through gritted teeth. "Believe me, Anna, it's one of the toughest lessons to learn. I hope this opens your eyes."

Anna realized then why he was so invested in the idea. It was something that could reflect positively on him. While everything else—his marriage, his mother's health, his relationship with his brother, and his hold on his children—was dissolving like sugar in water, the preservation society, if successful, would grant him bragging rights. The accomplishment's glory would rub off on him, lifting him up while everything else crumbled down.

The car grumbled to a stop in front of the house. Anna looked at her father in hopes that he'd see the remorse and enlightenment in her eyes, but he didn't return her gaze. He just clutched the steering wheel, eyes straight ahead, the car still running. Anna took that as her cue to get out. She didn't turn to look at the station wagon as she ambled up the porch steps, she only listened to it back out of the drive faster than it had pulled in.

Her back to her departing father and her face inches from the closed screen door, Anna stalled, feeling like a pocket with a hole, empty. A pang of regret flared in her chest, but she couldn't go back. She'd willfully blown it. The meeting was over. Her father was already down the road, the car's tires barely audible anymore. She'd have to live with the decision she made.

The blazer slid from her shoulders, and Anna slung it over the porch railing while simultaneously stepping out of the pitiless high heels. She wasn't ready to go inside. She didn't want to explain to her mother what she'd done or why she'd done it. The bedroom window flashed in her mind. She could scale through it just like Grace during the early morning hours. But then she'd be stuck in that room, staring at Grace's messy bed, wondering where her sister went night after night.

Anna yanked the tucked blouse out of the waistband and retreated down the steps. Finishing the day at school was out of the question. So was a visit to Miss Shelby's trailer. The thought of pilfering another book after what she'd done at the meeting filled her with shame. Barefoot, she slowly walked away from the house with no destination in mind, absently counting the flat little purplish-green corpses along the way. More appeared every day.

For hours, she trekked along one of the few big roads that spanned from one side of the rez to the other, then back again, eventually finding herself sweating and standing at the far end of the expansive casino parking lot, where the natural trees ended and the opulent planted palms began. Reminded by vicious pangs that she should have had lunch hours ago and that she'd thrown her breakfast to the birds, she sat on the curb in the trees' shadows. Sounds from the road crew paving one of the reservation's streets met her ears, the grinding trucks once again calling to mind the change all around her. And when Anna's eyes traveled from the casino to the attached hotel, she found herself thinking about all the things that had weighed so heavily on her at the meeting.

The eighth floor looked no different than those below it from the outside. An attractive structure that exhibited large columns, Spanish influence, and wrought iron balconies, the hotel was the most impressive building for miles, and with more than five hundred guestrooms, it had the potential to house as many secrets.

Maybe what Fox did in suite 808 with his guests was none of her business, but with Missy Picote's whereabouts still unknown, and Amber and Erica still unaccounted for, Anna was on edge. She hoped the latter two really were in the land of movie stars and not twinkling with the sky spirit among constellations at night. And she still found it strange that Sawyer had been at the meeting, doing his duty while Missy remained missing.

Anna's eyes traveled up and down the hotel. She thought about the eight stories and the corresponding flights of stairs. She remembered how Missy—if it had been Missy—had labored to get down each step before she'd vanished. She remembered Fox's staunch denial. And how he had endeared himself to Grace.

Anna's stomach churned. What if it had been her sister shambling down the steps? She hopped up from the curb and headed toward town, thinking she would intercept Grace on her way home from school. She was too late, though. Emily's mother's car, carrying Grace and Emily in the back, zoomed past only seconds after she crossed the border between the reservation and town.

Anna kicked dirt at the old car. Roscoe's Get 'n' Go gas station stood just beyond the border. Anna went inside. She grabbed a pack of cinnamon gum and twin chocolate cupcakes with creamy filling from the racks and tossed the items on the counter atop the scratch-off lottery ticket window.

"Ten of those," she said, tapping the glass over the Lucky 7s scratchers.

"ID?" the clerk, identified as Rick by his nametag, asked. He was a year older than Anna. She used to see him at school.

Anna put cash on the counter, enough to cover the tickets, the cupcakes, and the gum.

"Gotta be eighteen for the lotto," he said, leaning over the counter to look down at her dirty feet. "Not to mention no shoes, no shirt, no service."

Anna huffed at him. She knew Rick didn't give a damn about IDs or shoes. "You sell cigarettes to your underage friends," she whispered. She'd seen him do it the last time she'd been in to buy beef jerky and a Coke. She slid the money closer to him.

"Show me something," he whispered, his eyes flicking up.

Anna's mind puzzled and then she presented her school ID when realization set in. Rick tore ten tickets from the roll. Anna nabbed them, the cupcakes, and the gum and eyed the SMILE! YOU'RE ON CAMERA sign—sporting a big yellow smiley face—affixed to the door on her way out.

Robbie was on the porch rubbing the rifle with their mother's blue blazer when Anna got home—chocolate on her breath—as though the weapon needed polishing.

"Grace inside?" she asked.

Robbie nodded without looking up from the firearm.

Gran was watching a show on the couch. Canned laughter poured through the TV's speakers. Her unamused face lit up when Anna held the lotto tickets beneath her nose. She latched on to them like an owl to a mouse, weak hand and all.

The scratchers weren't much, but Anna hoped they'd cut through the boredom and give Gran back a piece of her past, even if it was just for a short while. She'd known that Gran must have been missing her favorite vice since moving in with them. They'd found hundreds of old scratchers in Gran's house when they'd emptied it after the stroke. The tickets had been on the tables and nightstand, pressed in books, and lost between couch cushions.

"I'll get you a quarter," Anna said, though Gran had already employed her thumbnail for the job.

"Won't you look at that!" The affected side of Gran's face struggled to match the smile on the unaffected side. She held up a winner worth a dollar.

Anna left Gran to her fun. She entered the hall, which was beginning to feel like the entrance to a tomb, the bedrooms always dark or the doors always closed. She knocked on her own bedroom door, then entered without an invitation.

Grace lay beneath her blanket, head covered. Anna studied her form, trying to decide if her sister was asleep. "I blew it at the meeting," she said. "Dad's not talking to me now."

Grace stirred, the blanket remained.

"What do you think I should do?"

Grace groaned. "I'm tired."

"You were out late last night." Anna strained not to sound judgmental or upset. "Do anything fun?"

Grace grumbled something that was nothing. Anna sat at the edge of her bed. Her hands busied themselves with the clock on the nightstand, setting the alarm for the next morning.

"I guess you were with Emily?"

"Can you bother me later?"

"I have work tonight. Wanna meet for a milkshake? I'll buy." Anna hated the desperation that had slipped into her voice.

"I'm going to Emily's tonight."

"But we . . ." The desperate tone remained. Anna couldn't shake it. "We never do anything anymore."

Grace rolled over and flipped the blanket off her face. A gray hue robbed the glow from her youthful flesh. "We share a room," she said. "Isn't that enough?"

"Not really. Not when you don't come home at night."

"Shut up, Anna."

"I've never told Mom and Dad." It wasn't meant to be a threat, but it sounded like one.

"What do you want from me?"

The truth was that Anna wanted her best friend back. Could she say that, though, without Grace rolling her eyes? "I thought we could do something."

"I'm too tired." She turned toward the wall.

The words were like paper slicing through supple flesh. Anna hummed and got off the bed. "Sleep then," she said. "But tell me . . . were you with him last night?"

"Who?"

"You know who. Fox."

Grace's subsequent silence told Anna enough.

"I know you don't want me to tell you what to do. And I don't want to be Mom or Dad—"

"Emily and I were at the arcade," Grace grumbled. "He came by. It was nothing."

"What'd he want?"

"Who says he wanted anything? He played a few rounds of Down the Clown."

"Does he leave you secret notes?" The way Grace's body stiffened confirmed what Anna suspected. She so badly wanted to tell Grace to stay away from Fox, but wouldn't that drive her sister straight into his arms?

"I saw one with your timecard," Anna explained. "At least I think it was a note."

"Did you read it?"

"No," Anna lied. She reached for the doorknob. "Do me one favor," she said, stalling.

"Hmm?"

"Look at me."

Grace stayed still for a few seconds to emphasize that she wasn't Anna's dog, then propped herself on her elbows, hair in her face.

"I want you to stay away from the eighth floor. No matter what Fox says. Stay away from there."

"What?"

"Stay away from the eighth floor, Grace."

"The eighth floor?"

"Yeah. The hotel. Don't go up there, all right?"

Grace fell flat on the mattress, rubbing her eyes.

"Did you hear me? Promise me," Anna said.

"Okay, Anna."

"Say it."

"I promise."

Anna sighed. "Thanks, Grace." She lingered a moment more, still thinking about what she'd read in the note hidden behind Grace's timecard. The secret. The promise. She wanted to know what they were about, but she'd already lied and didn't want to risk driving a wider wedge between her and Grace. She left the room and pulled the door closed behind her, all the while wondering why Grace hadn't asked why she was supposed to stay away from the eighth floor. The greasy feeling in the pit of Anna's stomach suggested that Grace knew something she didn't.

Already all kinds of uncomfortable—tired, hungry, dehydrated, terrified—the toxic scent of fresh asphalt intensified Anna's headache. The road crew only had a few of the smaller dirt streets to finish paving on the rez. Soon they'd be gone, and the change would be complete.

One of the workers spotted Anna plodding along. They eyed each other for a few seconds, the same way they might evaluate a winged and toothy creature in a traveling zoo, and then he shrugged and went back to work. Anna ventured closer, attracting more eyes, some of them staring out beneath furrowed brows.

"How's the view?" one of the workers, twenty if he was a day, said. He wasn't wearing a shirt, only an orange vest over suntanned skin. His measly biceps twitched when he flexed.

"Have you seen my sister?" Anna asked. The question sounded stupid. Her desperation and exhaustion, however, held her there, hoping for help.

"How would we know?" one of the older workers, sporting a push-broom mustache, said.

Anna rubbed her temples. She didn't have a picture of Grace, and she couldn't rely on a family resemblance to help her. "She's fifteen. Black hair down to the middle of her back. Pretty. We can't find her."

The man pointed to a power line pole where someone had tacked a poster with Missy Picote's face on it, weathered now, obscuring an older poster of Amber and Erica.

Anna shook her head. "Another one."

The man's face softened, and Anna wouldn't have been surprised if he had a teenage daughter of his own. His thick mustache drooped as his head shook. "Sorry," he said. "We'll keep an eye out."

"Just tell her to come home."

"We'll do that."

Anna ambled on. Tired as ever she could remember, the last thing she wanted was to fall asleep. Not before she found Grace. Hopeful, she went by the house but didn't go inside. She just peered through the bedroom window. Grace's bed remained empty.

Walking slowly across the reservation, her barely blinking eyes searched the fields, the houses, the bridge, spending hour after hour looking for the slightest clue. Something as small as the strawberry lip balm—something she could easily miss—could be the answer she was looking for.

Her feet slowed even more when the Mire trailer came into sight later that afternoon. On any other day, she could have easily killed a dozen hours inside it, but her desire to explore the bookshelves had vanished. The stories didn't matter, not compared to finding Grace. It seemed they might never matter again. Besides, it wasn't the Mire trailer she'd come to visit. It was the one across the field.

Just after three in the afternoon, there wasn't a car in the drive. Despite the trailer's empty appearance, Anna plodded up the porch steps and knocked on the door. Receiving no answer, she settled on the stairs and gave in to a mighty yawn that stretched her parched lips as wide as her head, making the bottom one split. Salty blood smeared across the tip of her tongue when she licked it. Her head heavy, it fell into her hands atop her knees and her eyelids sagged. When she looked across the field at the Mire trailer like that, disregarding the overgrown brush crawling up its sides, she could make believe that it wasn't abandoned. She could almost see someone sitting in the front window. Someone who looked as unhappy as she felt.

Though she wouldn't have admitted it if accused, Anna slipped into a state of sleep that was neither dream-filled nor restful. Her head sprang up off her knees the instant the sound of tires grinding over gravel met her ears. The car came down the drive and stopped a few feet from the porch steps. The girl—Noemi—riding in the passenger seat broke free first. A McDonald's bag and a large cup, ice rattling, filled her hands.

"Get your bookbag!" Lula hollered from the driver's seat. Her daughter ignored her and raced up the porch steps, passing Anna without saying a word or even casting a curious glance in her direction. Noemi was only a couple years younger than Grace. She resembled her. She acted like her, too. Both girls had the air of someone who wanted to be older, someone who wanted freedoms she maybe wasn't ready for yet. Noemi stomped across the porch and hurried into the trailer.

"Anna," Lula said, hauling both her heavy handbag and her daughter's backpack from the car. "What's up?"

Anna stood, stiff from sleeping on the steps, then quickly sank back down. "My head feels heavy." For whatever reason, she couldn't just announce why she was there. Talking to Lula was different than talking to the road construction crew. Despite speaking the same language, they didn't speak the same way.

Lula cracked a smile. "I can help. Just give me . . ." She went inside with the bags, then reappeared a few minutes later wearing jeans and a sweatshirt with its neckline cut out. She sat so close to Anna that Anna could feel her heat, making her realize how chilled she was.

"Hair everywhere," Lula muttered. She picked at her cleavage with one hand, casting small clippings aside. "Do you know what it's like having itchy boobs all day?" She giggled. "Just one of the perks of being a hairdresser."

Anna laughed. It came out as a single, mortifying snort. Still, it felt good. She hadn't thought she'd be able to laugh.

Lula picked away as much hair as she could, then opened the cigarette pack wrapped within her other hand. A lighter and a joint appeared.

"If you were going to eat . . ." Anna said, remembering the Golden Arches bag.

"Just the kid," Lula said. "She likes that crap after school. Keeps her happy. We both have our vices." Lula lit the joint, took a puff, and passed it.

Anna's fingers trembled. Her heart raced. She didn't want to embarrass herself again.

"Slowly in and hold. Just for a second," Lula said.

Anna did as told and only coughed a little upon releasing the smoke. She took another puff as soon as the coughing subsided. Soon, her head began to swim.

"Better?" Lula asked.

Anna shrugged.

"Can I ask?"

"Huh?"

"What's eating you?"

Anna breathed deeply. "Grace—my sister—didn't come home last night."

"Teenagers."

"It's worse than that," Anna said, her chest suddenly tight and hot. The corners of her eyes burned. "I don't want it to be, but I think it is."

"I don't understand."

"She was at the hotel. I found her lip balm in one of the rooms."

Lula still looked confused.

"It was in suite eight-oh-eight," Anna said.

The questioning wrinkles in Lula's brow disappeared. Her eyes widened and her face slackened.

"Lip balm?" Lula said. "That doesn't mean—"

"It's hers!" Anna erupted. "I know it. I know Missy Picote was in that suite before she disappeared as well." Anna's watery mind was more certain than ever. "I saw her coming down the stairs, and no one's seen her since."

"Missy's a meth addict. Her own father admitted it."

"That fact doesn't cancel out other facts. Why do people always do that?"

"Do what?"

"Let one truth take precedence over other truths. Missy is a drug addict who was at the hotel and went missing. All those things are true, yet everyone says she's an addict like that one fact is all that matters. Like it's her own fault she's missing."

"Missy's probably strung out in some basement somewhere, wondering where, when, and how she'll get her next fix," Lula said.

Anna stewed. She didn't want to argue. She just wanted to get answers that might help her locate Grace. "Missy and Grace aren't the only two who've been in suite eight-oh-eight."

Lula took a greedy drag from the joint, averting her eyes.

"You were up there, and you were crying," Anna said.

Lula looked beaten and worried when she emitted the smoke. "That's why you came here, isn't it?" she said.

"Tell me what happened in that room. Why were you crying?"

Lula took one last puff and pinched out the joint. She started and stopped several times. "Fox . . ." she finally said. "You can't tell him I told you."

Anna made no promises. She just stared at Lula.

Lula sighed and glanced over her shoulder toward the front door. "Can we walk?"

Anna stood and, wobbling, started down the drive with Lula at her side.

"I guess it was a stupid idea from the start," Lula said, her voice a whisper. "God . . ." She ran her fingers through her hair. "Maybe I'm just fucking stupid. Or maybe I was desperate."

Anna touched the small of Lula's back, gingerly, warmly, encouraging her to go on.

"I try to save money where I can," Lula said. "I really do. I'll be damned if I'm gonna let myself end up like all the other *winners* on this reservation. But I bought the car, which was a need, not a want, and then I got Noemi new clothes for school, which set me back more than I'd planned, but what kind of mother would I be if I sent her to class in rags? Believe me, I know how cruel the kids in town can be." She fiddled with her cigarette pack, opening it, closing it, while Anna took short strides beside her, feeling like she might tip over. "With my pay at the salon and the per capita checks, I figured I'd be back where I started within a year if I stayed on track. Then boom!" The cigarettes almost fell from her hand. She shoved the pack into her pocket. "I got up one morning—late, because I'm always fucking late—and rushed into the shower, only to be blasted with ice-cold water. Talk about a wake-up call. It was the water heater. It blew. My grandpa and brother used to deal with all that shit in the house. I didn't have the slightest idea how to fix it. We were heating pots of water on the stove for two days before I bit the bullet and went into that hardware store in town . . . Putters? Potters? I don't remember what it's called."

"Patters," Anna said, listening intently, yet rapt again by Lula's shiny nails, shinier even than the cigarettes' cellophane wrapper peeking out of Lula's pocket.

"Anyway, I was standing there staring at these water tanks when Fox came up behind me with a box of lightbulbs in his hand. I hardly recognized him . . . he looks like a superhero now. I guess he saw the confusion on my face because he pointed to one of the tanks and said, 'You'll want that one for a place like yours.'

"The damn thing cost an arm and a leg. Then baldy behind the counter asked how I planned on installing it. He wanted a hundred bucks to do it himself." She huffed to emphasize her disbelief. "I was about ready to say screw it, but then Fox stepped forward and said he'd install it. He even offered to drive it out here. Thank god he did. I hadn't even thought about how I was gonna get the damn thing home."

Anna and Lula reached the end of the long drive, where Lula paused to grab the mail. She barely glanced at the envelope on top, stamped PAST DUE in bold red letters, before shoving the stack into her waistband. They turned onto the road, heading toward the Mire trailer, where they were certain no one would hear them.

"Fox installed the water heater in no time at all."

"You basically just have to connect the gas and water supply lines," Anna said.

Lula's brow crinkled. "What the hell do I know? Anyway, he was talking while he was working, saying he got this great gig at the hotel, that it was big money for little work and that he didn't even have to wake up to an alarm."

"He's the evening manager."

"Thanks to his uncle," Lula said. "He bragged while he worked about how he gets to eat dinner every night for free, in whichever of the resort's restaurants he chooses. Topped off by unlimited drinks. I wasn't impressed . . . not really, but I said something like, 'Must be nice. Wish I could make money doing nothing.' I was just making conversation, you know? Until he was done.

"But then he said, 'You could. I got a way for both of us to make easy money.' It was funny the way he said it . . . strange, I mean. Intriguing, too. Whispering, his face hidden by the water heater. I can't say I wasn't curious. And I had nothing else to do while he was . . .

connecting the supply lines?" she questioned, like she wasn't sure she'd gotten it right. "He said he had access to special rooms. Rooms like no one's ever seen before. Rooms for people with big bucks, who've done something with their lives. He said he knew a guy . . . a nobody . . . who'd pay him to use those rooms for a few hours."

"What guy?" Anna asked.

"I don't know. Fox never said his name. He told me not to ask."

"What'd he look like?"

She shrugged. "Wasn't anything special about him. Pretty tall, I guess. Not young. Not old. He had green eyes. I remember that."

The lanky man Anna had seen coming through the emergency stairwell door last night.

"The deal was . . ." Lula said, stopping. She turned away from Anna and pulled her hands through her hair. "Fuck." Her head fell back on her neck, and she exhaled toward the sky. "The deal was that this guy would pay Fox for the room and for company, and then Fox would pay me."

"Company?" Anna questioned.

"That's all it was," Lula insisted, talking faster now. "Company . . . Look, everyone knows there's hookers who hang around the casino floor, but that's not what I'm about. I swear."

Anna had seen those women around the resort. Some were from the rez. Others came from town. Blending in, they trolled the casino and bars in search of men who'd bring them up to their rooms. They stuck out like sore thumbs, though, when they left the hotel at odd hours, still dressed like the night was young.

"You agreed to hang out with a stranger for money?" Anna didn't entirely believe Lula's account, but she didn't want to insult her. She just wanted to find out what had happened inside the suite.

Lula bristled. "I didn't agree to it at first," she said, holding up her hands. "Fox came by a few times to say hi after that, and somehow we always ended up talking about the same thing."

"He pressured you."

"No," Lula insisted. "I'd been thinking about it, and I needed the money. I brought it up the last time he was here." She blew air through the left side of her mouth. "Listen, Anna, I've got a kid and a credit card that's never been paid in full. Until you've walked—"

"I'm not judging. I just want to understand. What exactly did the man want when you went into the room? Did he hurt you?"

Lula shook her head no.

"Then what was it? What happened?" Anna prodded.

Lula shook her head again. "Nothing."

"You were crying."

"He took one look at me and cursed. He said—" Her voice lowered, signaling that she didn't want to relive it. "He said I was too old. I know it sounds dumb, but hearing that . . ." She dabbed her eyes. "It hurt. I was embarrassed. I couldn't believe I'd set myself up for that." She took a moment to collect herself. "Fox still gave me money when he saw how upset I was. He's a good guy."

"Could you identify the man?" Anna, who'd hardly heard anything after Lula mentioned age, asked.

"Listen, Anna, I promised Fox I wouldn't talk about this. You can't say anything."

The pieces, however, had already begun to fall into place. "You're too old and they're too young," Anna said, trekking backward, picking up speed.

Lula leapt toward Anna and grabbed her hands. "No," she said. "It can't be. It's not what you're thinking."

Anna tore her hands away. "They're young!"

"You're jumping to conclusions, Anna, but you're wrong. Fox wouldn't do that. This was something between me and him. He's a good guy! He wouldn't do what you're thinking. You've got him all wrong. Anna!" she cried at the top of her lungs as Anna kicked up dust. "I promised I wouldn't say anything—*please*, Anna! You're making a mistake!"

Day 31
4:02 a.m.

Chris gave Anna the silent treatment through Halloween and the Friday that followed, only providing pithy answers to anything she asked. He was more focused on the big day that had finally arrived.

Only Grace was MIA when the family saw Robbie off on his first hunt, hours before the sun came up. She wasn't out with friends; she was wrapped up in bed, having refrained from sneaking through the bedroom window since the morning of the tribal council meeting. Dorothy ambled back to her room once Chris and Robbie were gone. The click of the bedroom door echoed her sigh of relief.

"Back to bed?" Anna asked Gran.

Gran shrugged.

"I'm not tired either," Anna said. She helped Gran with her strengthening exercises, then assisted her into the shower. The living room to herself, Anna sat by the window where the day's first light flooded her face, reminding her of something she hadn't pondered since before Miss Shelby's death.

You're the dawn, Anna. The balance between night and day that incorporates a little bit of both. Miss Shelby had spoken those words to

Anna during one of their final encounters, after Anna had helped Grace and Emily—five at the time, fighting over who had the prettier dolls, the bigger house, the longer hair—see that they need not rival over what they had because, when shared, their differences brought them in balance. Not to mention that their differences made playing together surprising and fun.

Contemplating Miss Shelby's words, Anna opened one of her old friend's books for the first time since the tribal council meeting. Granted, the words she read would have had greater power if they had greater reach, such as through the preservation society she'd failed to propose. Even so, Anna assigned herself the task of reading and remembering them.

She crawled back into bed after Grace woke for her Saturday shift and slept until Grace returned, looking as spent as her last paycheck.

"Tough morning?" Anna asked.

Grace slumped onto her bed. "As if you care."

"Don't be like that."

"There was shit in one of the showers," Grace grumbled.

"Wanna talk about it?"

"The shit?"

"The job."

"What's there to say about it?"

"Can we talk about us then?"

Grace took off the chambermaid coat, balled it up, and tossed it on the floor.

"I'm sorry you're mad at me," Anna said. "I wanted to apologize yesterday, but—"

"But you brought up Fox instead."

"I just—"

"It was a week ago. I'm over it, Anna." Grace sighed. "I get why you did what you did. I was pissed at you after you'd clocked me out, but

I guess I should've been pissed at myself for not doing my job . . . and for letting Tanya down. But why couldn't you have just told me to get back to work? I could've used that money."

"Would you have listened to me if I'd said that in front of Fox? You would've—"

"Whatever." Grace huffed. "It won't happen again."

"Good." Anna nodded.

"Happy now?"

Anna wished she could say yes. "That's not all I wanted to talk about."

"Now what?"

Anna steeled herself for what she was about to say. "I read the note that was with your timecard," she confessed, neither able nor wanting to keep the secret any longer. Even if it meant Grace would cut her out like gristle from a steak, she couldn't live with the lie.

Grace flinched. "God, Anna, can't you give me an *ounce* of privacy?"

"I know I shouldn't have, but . . ."

"But what?"

"I worry about you. Will you tell me what it means . . . what he wrote?" She could feel herself starting to tremble. Nerves. Uncertainty. Vulnerable to Grace's scorn.

"It's none of your business," Grace said. "And I never said *he* wrote it." She got off the bed and went to the dresser.

Anna exhaled through her nose. "I know you like him, but he . . . he's not what he seems. I wish I would have seen it from the start. I don't know what he wants from you, but the situation . . . it's not right."

"What *situation*?" she said, annoyed.

"Why's he hanging out with you?"

"Because we're friends. We have things in common."

"What do you have in common with a guy in his twenties?"

Grace pulled on a T-shirt and whipped around to face Anna. "Enough," she cried. "Just because you don't have any friends doesn't mean you get to question mine. Fox has never been anything but nice to me. And it's not because he wants something from me. We're friends. That's it. And I'm fine. Everything is fucking fine. I don't know how to make that any clearer to you. Whatever you're worried about . . . whatever you think . . . just forget it." Grace's eyes contradicted her words. Her gaze bounced from side to side, making it tough for Anna to determine what was true and what Grace wanted her to believe. "Can we please just go back to normal?"

Anna wanted that bad, but she didn't know if she and Grace were imagining the same kind of normal. "What if—?" Anna started.

"Please, Anna. You need to stop. Forget about Fox. Forget about the kids at school. Stop giving everyone a reason to rile you up."

Anna's mind muddied. "I don't even talk to the kids at school. How have I given them . . . ?"

Grace's face fell while her hands motioned up and down, referring to Anna's body as though showing off Exhibit A. Anna looked down at herself. Feet as big as her father's. Shapeless jeans that hid her form. Hips and shoulders that turned her bargain bin plaid shirt into a perfect rectangle.

"What does the way I dress have to do with what they said about you?" Anna chose her words carefully. She really didn't want to bring up the rumor. It already felt like it was long in the past.

"Like I told you before, you're a target, Anna. And you've made me one, too."

Maybe Grace was right. Maybe they ought to let it all pass. Maybe she ought to put effort into changing as well. Anna thought about Frog again, the bringer of change whose transformations came naturally. He didn't have to work the way she would.

"I'm sorry, Grace." Anna stood, then crawled onto Grace's bed, dragging Grace with her. She took Grace's hair in her hands and gently ran her fingers through the long strands.

"Anna," Grace protested.

Anna shushed her. "You're not dumb. I said what I wanted to say and now it's up to you to make your own decisions. If you ever want my advice . . ." She smiled and continued to brush Grace's hair with her fingers. It was something she used to do when they were younger, something Grace would whine for. And it was known throughout the house that only Anna was fit for the job. Any time Dorothy tried to brush and braid Grace's hair, Grace would either fall on the floor and kick or run and hide.

Grace leaned into Anna, giving in to her calming touch. Anna's hands moved slowly at first, reacquainting themselves with the task.

"No braids," Grace said, drowsy. Her eyelids drifted shut and her body slackened. She hadn't worn braids since middle school. Anna had stopped wearing braids as well, long before then, though she suspected her reason why was far different than Grace's.

Working to the right of Grace's scalp, Anna sectioned the hair and delicately weaved the simple pattern she associated with her youth. She looped the hair at the bottom of the braid into a knot, then moved her hands to the left side of Grace's head, all the while thinking she should try to remember this in case she never got to do it again. Her breathing synced with the slow and steady rise and fall of Grace's chest. Her heart swelled at the way Grace gave in to her in sleep like she never did while awake. What Anna could do without was the excessive amount of perfume wafting from Grace's skin and the scent of cigarette smoke clinging to her hair, things that spoke of Grace's secrets.

She'd just sectioned the hair into thirds when Grace yawned and jolted forward.

"Anna!" she shrieked, upon feeling the braid hanging from the right side of her head.

"I need to," Anna said, without thinking. The words just came out.

"Shit!" Grace hopped off the bed, her hair funneling through Anna's fingers. "I'm supposed to meet Emily. I said no braids!" She stationed herself in front of the mirror and fumbled with the knot. "Jesus, Anna."

"Where are you going?"

Grace got the knot free and combed a hand through her hair to loosen the braid. "Listen, Anna, I appreciate what you said, but you can focus on you now." She combed her hair with her fingers some more—the bead bracelet clacking around her right wrist—to ensure she'd obliterated the braid. "I'll see you later," she said, offering no clues as to what she and Emily had planned.

"Have fun," Anna replied, really wanting to ask if she could tag along.

Grace gathered her wallet, keys, and lip balm from the nightstand and then she was gone.

Day 33
7:48 a.m.

The cool glass of the car window warmed against Anna's cheek. A greasy, blurry blotch marred the glass when she lifted her face away. The rumble of the car could easily put her to sleep. She was tired. Grace, she figured, must be too. Anna had waited up until after two in the morning, but it wasn't until four that Grace finally crawled through the bedroom window. Anna had roused and whispered through the darkness, pleading with Grace to tell her where she'd been.

Lost track of time, was all Grace had said.

Tired or not, Grace gave no indication. She and Emily buzzed like cicadas in the backseat of Emily's mother's car. The bouncy rhythm of their coded language tickled Anna's ears. She challenged herself to decipher what the girls were saying, but by the time Emily's mom stopped in front of the school, she'd only decrypted "tonight," "phone," "wait," and possibly "sister" from Grace, followed by what sounded like "bidigitch."

A bead bracelet dangled from Emily's wrist. A carbon copy of Grace's, Anna noticed. She found herself thinking that Emily could say anything to Grace in their secret language. When Emily asked a question, Grace always gave an answer. It was a magical ability they possessed, to communicate with each other anywhere, anytime, with confidence that the message would never be criticized or condemned, knowing it could never be owned by anyone other than them.

Anna thanked Miss Karen for the ride. She wiped the smudge on the window on her way out, smearing it rather than erasing it. Emily and Grace entered the school behind Anna, acting like she wasn't with them. They laughed when she started up the stairs toward the senior hallway, making her more self-conscious than usual.

For once, she wasn't bothered by going unnoticed in class. She slumped in her seat, eyes half open, waiting for the lunch bell to ring. At the sound, she took her brown bag from her locker. The damn dolls that had amassed since the start of the semester stared up at her from the bottom. She stomped them down on her way to the cafeteria, where she found Alee Graham pouting over a library book at the table they sometimes shared.

Alee held the open book up for Anna to see. Anna nodded at the twin pages, indifferent and oblivious as to why Alee wanted her to see the typeface.

"Right at the good part," Alee said.

Anna nodded again, overlooking Alee's irritated tone. She strained to see what Grace, sitting with Emily and their group of so-called friends, was up to without overtly looking in Grace's direction.

"Why are people such jerks?" Alee asked.

"Huh?" Anna's eyebrows shot up.

"It's at the good part," Alee whined, holding the book up again. She ran a finger along the crease between the two pages. Anna noticed the thin sliver of a page that had been removed. The edge was smooth, indicating that the page had been purposefully cut rather than accidentally torn.

"Maybe the library has another copy," Anna said.

Alee shook her head. "This is the only one."

Anna spilled her lunch onto the cafeteria table, thinking she might be a book with a missing page. Whether her page was missing at the best part, she couldn't say, but there was plenty about herself she couldn't quite figure out—stuff her peers obviously couldn't quite figure out either. If only she had the page telling her what she was and who she was supposed to be.

"Maybe you can infer what happens," Anna said. "Fill in the blanks on your own." It wasn't all that different than what she did with many of the stories and scribbled notes she found in Miss Shelby's trailer. She pulled Alee's book toward her so that she could read the last line before the missing page and the first line after it. She shrugged. She wouldn't be able to figure it out without reading a few chapters first.

"Guess I'll just have to buy my own copy," Alee said. She painted ketchup onto the dry breaded chicken patty she'd purchased while Anna unwrapped the sandwich she'd brought from home. A shadow took shape on the white bread and Anna's coppery hands.

"Can we talk a minute?"

Anna found Grace standing over her, bottom lip clenched between her teeth. She shoved the sandwich back into the paper bag and pulled out the chair next to her. Grace jerked her head toward the bathroom. "Not here," she said.

Anna hopped up and away from the table. Grace moved quickly, nearly trotting toward the cafeteria exit closest to the bathrooms across the hall. Anna kept pace behind her, worrying that something was wrong. A sudden sinking feeling settled in the pit of her stomach.

"Grace?" she called. "Are you sick?"

Grace glanced over her shoulder, but it wasn't Anna she was looking at. It was Gary Cooper, who sat with Kevin Mills and Miguel Leon at Grace's lunchroom table of choice. Anna barely got a glimpse of Gary before he lunged forward, sailing toward the ground. His hands latched on to either side of her pants as he fell, yanking them down.

Anna yelped. She'd been moving so fast to keep up with Grace that her feet became ensnared by her lowered waistband; she went down just like her jeans. The cold tile of the cafeteria floor shocked her bare thighs.

Roaring laughter shook the cafeteria walls. Anna, face against the floor, wrapped her arms around her head and lay still. Her chin throbbed from slamming against the tile. Her tongue stung from her teeth sinking into it.

"I was right! I was right!" Andy Wimer, who'd come running with a pack of fruit snacks in hand, hollered as excitedly as a sweepstakes winner.

"I still can't tell," Curt Egeland, trailing Andy, said.

"What the hell?" Gary Cooper remarked, squinting at Anna's backside from a few feet away.

"Tighty-whities!" Andy said.

"Granny panties!" Curt argued.

"You owe me. I was right!"

"I don't owe you shit."

"I was right, and you know it," Andy said.

"You said boxers."

"I said briefs!"

"They're granny panties, not tighty-whities," Curt said.

Anna rolled onto her back, then reached for her waistband and flopped like a fish to pull her pants up. She crawled to the corner and stood facing the wall while her peers continued to laugh behind her. Dignity gone, she turned to face them, chin wiggling and tears stinging the corners of her eyes. She spat blood on the floor. The sight of the watery, red glob transformed her humiliation to anger, keeping her from crying.

Alee approached with Anna's bookbag hanging from one hand and her arms open, ready to cradle Anna. A cafeteria attendant walked briskly beside her. Gary Cooper scrambled to his feet and fled. Anna had no interest in confronting him. Her gaze shifted to Grace, standing a few feet away. Her expression was a mixture of horror, sorrow, and regret. She didn't speak and neither did Anna. Neither needed to. They both knew what had just happened.

Grace had set Anna up.

Day 33
1:11 p.m.

Thighs still stinging and cold from the blow they'd taken against the cafeteria tiles, Anna had hoisted her pants and run out of school, leaving her lunch on the table. The prospect of facing her classmates' stares for three more hours wasn't what led her to flee, it was that she had to distance herself from the scene, as though if it were out of sight she could convince herself that the assault hadn't happened. The fact that Grace could be so cruel, especially after they'd put a stitch or two in the tear between them over the weekend, crushed Anna. She felt flattened, like one of the frogs, as if Grace had driven an eighteen-wheeler right over her.

She walked to the bridge on the rez where the rushing river drowned out her frustrated cries. Fingers fixed to the rail, she pulled her upper body over the top of it, letting her head hang over the waves. Her distorted reflection on the water's surface made her wonder if everyone else saw her that way, as some sort of monster. And then she tried to put herself in Grace's shoes.

Grace was trying to find her way in a world where social status was everything and physical appearance spoke of one's worth. Anna understood that her little sister was trying to be part of a scene, and that fitting in required preservation of the social hierarchy, but humiliating another to fit in with fake friends was something she couldn't shrug off.

Anna spat at her reflection—her tongue still steeped with blood—and lowered herself from the rail. She remembered what she'd seen in the folds of Grace's conflicted face. Sorrow, sadness, regret. Those things spoke of Grace's virtue, even if the others couldn't see it. Anna went home to wait for her, to hear her out, to give her a chance to make things right.

"You won't believe what I just saw," Robbie said, finding Anna sitting in wait on the porch steps. He held a handful of rocks, which he flung into the field, one by one.

"What's that?" she asked, indifferent.

"They paved over a snake," he said.

Anna lifted her head from the cradle of her hands and made a questioning noise.

"The road crew covered its tail with asphalt. Its head half was wriggling to pull the rest of its body free. It's probably dead now."

"You didn't help it?"

"It was hissing. And asphalt's really hot. What was I supposed to do?"

Anna swatted him as he tossed the final rock and leapt up the porch steps. If Grace had gotten a ride with Emily, she should have arrived home before Robbie. If she'd walked, she should have been visible on the horizon by now. Anna didn't see her anywhere along the road, and so she waited on the porch, watching the sky grow dark as a storm drew near, until the clock demanded she get ready for work.

"What's up with Grace?" Robbie, spooning chocolate pudding into his mouth in front of the TV, asked when Anna went inside.

Anna shrugged, hesitant to reveal what had happened at lunch.

"She wouldn't tell me what's wrong, but I think—" he said, suddenly hopping up with a holler. A glob of pudding landed on his shirt as he flicked a spider from his elbow. Reclaiming his cool, he finished his thought. "I think someone might have been messing with Grace at school."

"When'd you see her?"

"Just now when I was checking on the pelts. They're drying good." He'd brought home three squirrels from his hunt, three shy of the braggadocious promise he'd made. He jerked his head toward the backyard. "She's hiding behind the shed."

Anna, heart thumping, tiptoed through the yard, mind racing for something to say and the right way to say it. She slowly rounded the shed where Robbie's salt-covered squirrels were drying. Grace, her back to Anna, was sitting on an old stump, her head hunched over something on her lap. Anna stalled, hoping Grace would sense her there and say something first. She didn't.

"Didn't see you get home," Anna said.

Grace startled, knocking something over. Whatever spilled from her lap sounded like rain pitter-pattering against the ground.

"Damnit, Anna," Grace said, her voice a whisper. She kept her eyes ahead, refraining from looking back at her sister.

"I was waiting for you on the porch."

"I was already home. I left school right after you." Hands shaking, she attempted to pick up some of what had fallen.

"Were you suspended?"

Grace shook her head.

"Were any of them?"

She shook her head again.

"So why'd you leave?"

"I just didn't want to be there."

"You didn't want to share the laugh?"

"I felt bad, all right?" She picked at something Anna couldn't see, then flicked a tiny bit out into the trees. "It wasn't my idea."

"That didn't stop you from—"

"I did it, Anna. I'm not denying it. I'm just . . . not happy about it either." She took a deep breath that made her quiver. "They thought it would be funny. I couldn't say no."

"Why not?"

Her shoulders went up. "I feel so lost right now."

"If you'd let me help you—"

"You can't. No one can."

"How would you know if you won't let me try?"

"Because I don't even know what would help. I thought I wanted . . ." She pulled a hand through her hair, then shook her head.

"Wanted what?"

"I don't know." Her hands wiped either side of her face, suggesting that tears had leaked out. "All I know is I'm sorry, Anna." Grace turned to face her sister, only for a second, enough for Anna to see the sincerity in her eyes. It renewed the belief Anna had always held: that the nature of a decent person is to right wrongs. "I shouldn't have done that to you."

Anna stopped herself from saying it was okay. She forgave her sister, but that didn't repair the dent in her dignity. "What's on your lap?" she asked, craning to peer past Grace's left shoulder.

"Nothing," Grace said. Her head fell lower over her thighs.

"I want to see." Anna stepped closer and stooped down to see what Grace's hands were trying to hide. It was a little loom on her lap with several lengths of string stretched across it. Small glass beads were woven between the strings, creating a pattern of flowers and hearts identical to the pattern of the bracelets Grace and Emily wore. More beads were spilled across the ground at Grace's feet. The bracelet was only half done.

"This one's for you," Grace said.

"*You* made the bracelets?" Anna's voice caught in her throat.

"Miss Karen taught me. She gave me the loom and the beads, the string and the needle."

Eyes blurry, Anna squinted at the bracelet in progress. It was beautiful, as carefully crafted as the ones Miss Karen sold, maybe better. Anna wanted it on her wrist. "I had no idea," she said, wondering how much more there was to discover about Grace.

"Doing this clears my mind," Grace said. "I'm gonna stay out here a little longer."

"Maybe we can talk later?"

Grace shrugged. "Just give me some time, all right?"

"Sure, I have to get to work anyway." Anna reached to embrace her sister, but her hand fell short of Grace's shoulder. "I'll see you later," she said.

Day 33
4:32 p.m.

Birds soaring overhead resembled black arrows against a backdrop of bruised clouds—purple and black—that darkened the sky and threatened rain. Head tilted back, Anna walked along the road on her way to work, watching the birds flying for cover and wondering if Grace was still weaving the bracelet behind the shed, perhaps staring up at the same grim clouds.

The gloomy sky—dim as a chandelier lit by just one bulb—and the chilly breeze reminded Anna of autumn nights when she was a kid, back when she and Grace would make their own candy apples with caramel their mother stirred on the stove. Their father and Uncle Ray, best buds back then, would tell scary stories after sunset. Some were a bit too real, like the one about Horace Saucier and the Takoda Vampire. But only one had filled Anna with fear that had lasted through the years.

She shivered thinking about it, especially as she heard something rolling against the fresh pavement ahead. Something rolling toward her. Her heart fluttered, then settled. It was only a car, barely visible on the horizon.

Like a black beetle on the road ahead, the distance made the car appear harmless and small. A resounding *pop* a few seconds later punted Anna's heart into overdrive once more. The beetle stopped crawling. Anna stopped walking. In the seconds that followed, she heard a car door slam, the patter of footsteps, and a male voice that said, "Well, shit."

A flashlight's beam flickered to life. Anna proceeded. It was a black Lincoln Continental on the side of the road. Anna could see the distinct hood ornament in the low light of the cloud-covered sun when she got close. She didn't recognize the car. She'd never seen it on the rez, but that didn't mean it didn't belong. New cars showed up all the time now.

The flashlight's beam moved swiftly, pegging Anna. Squinting, she made a visor of her hand and held it over her eyes. It didn't help.

"Are you just going to stare?" a man asked.

"I can't see past the light," she said.

He lowered the beam along Anna's body, illuminating her chest, her hips, her legs, then redirected it altogether. Anna's retinas burned. As the residual bright spot faded from her sight, she realized the front passenger tire had blown. The rubber sagged against the ground. She narrowed her eyes at the man.

"Who are you?"

"You don't know me."

He flashed the light into his face, reminding Anna again of the scary stories her family used to tell in the yard. Sometimes they'd pass the flashlight around and hold it beneath their chins, lighting themselves from below. The light gave the man a pointed face with peculiar shadows over his cheekbones and brows. "Evil" was an apt description for what Anna saw, but she willfully looked past the illusion and noted the man's meticulous hair, combed in a perfect part, his well-groomed mustache, and his pressed attire. He looked older than her dad, late forties. Heavy, with a shelflike belly and a flag of flesh hanging around his neck. White. Anna was certain she'd never seen him before.

"What'd you hit?" she asked. There wasn't anything in the road that would have caused the tire to blow.

"Hell if I know." He labored to his knees to inspect the tire. His right hand shined the flashlight into the dark wheel well, while his left ran over the rubber, ultimately plucking a sizable nail from between the tread. He held it in the light. "Damn. Probably picked it up in . . ." he said without finishing the thought. He flicked the nail into the grass, then got up again. "Know anyone who could help around here?"

"Who were you coming to see?"

He was silent a little too long. "The casino. Thought I'd try my luck."

"The casino's . . ." Anna pointed toward the tall trees, black in the distance.

"Must have taken a wrong turn."

"You just have to follow the signs."

"Well, it's a little late for that now."

"Do you have a spare?"

He popped the trunk and Anna went to work, first disengaging the car's air suspension system, then lifting the carpet and turning the wingnut to release the concealed spare. She hauled it out of the trunk on her own. The man stood back, staring at her as she uncovered the jack kit and slung it on the ground.

"It won't take long," she said.

He made no offer to help. He just kept brushing at the dirt clinging to his knees.

It'd been a while since Anna had changed a tire. Mark Bishop—who wasn't Indian but who had married Miss Paula and moved onto the rez—had instructed her well. Mark was a mechanic. Anna liked to watch him toil, each hand a miracle worker, giving life to rusted metal. He'd taught her all kinds of things, like how to change oil and how an engine works. "Loosen the lug nuts first," she said, mostly to remind herself.

"I know how to do it," the man said. "But I don't have a Triple A card for nothing."

"You'll need a new tire. You shouldn't drive on the spare for long."

"I know that," he snapped.

Anna slid the jack beneath the car and began to raise it. Good thing she could make do without much light, because the man didn't do her any favors with the flashlight. He was more concerned with illuminating every speck of dirt he'd gotten on his clothes. Meanwhile, the grease and grime caked on the lug nuts and tire mount transferred to Anna's fingers as she removed the flat and then hauled it into the trunk.

"Easy," the man said. He inspected the paint around the trunk to ensure she hadn't dinged it. "You like it here?" he asked, watching Anna crank the lug nuts on to secure the donut.

"In the road?" she sniped.

"What's your name?"

"Anna. Yours?"

"You're not afraid walking alone like this? Not even at night?"

Except for when she thought about the rolling head, Anna rarely felt afraid on the reservation. The unease from the story was unease she could rationalize when she stopped to think about it. In the thick of the moment, her fright-filled mind would make her see and hear a head that rolled on its own, but when she was back home—safe and sound—she could tell herself it'd only been a raccoon or an armadillo scurrying through the night. Sometimes she could even make herself believe it.

Anna lowered the car and put the jack back in its pouch. "All done," she said.

She wiped her forehead against her upper arm, barely glimpsing the piece of paper that fluttered from the man's hand to the ground. A ten-dollar bill.

"Grab it before it blows away," he said.

Anna let it lay in the dirt, refusing to snatch it like a hungry dog. She'd already been embarrassed enough for one day.

"Who were you looking for?" she asked again.

"The casino. I told you."

Anna got up and slammed the trunk since he wasn't going to do it himself. Her greasy fingerprints marred the polished surface. The smudges made her smile.

The man kicked the donut, testing it, acting like he'd done the work himself. Anna figured it was the manliest thing he could do.

"You never told me your name," she said.

"The casino's that way, is it?" He pointed precisely where Anna had pointed earlier.

"Just follow the signs."

His finger shot toward the ground. "Don't let it blow away. Rain's coming." He got in the car, turned on the headlights, and slowly performed a three-point turn after firing it up. The small spare tire gave the Lincoln a lopsided stance, like a dog limping on a busted paw.

Anna watched the taillights fade into the distance, happy she hadn't told him where she was headed despite knowing he could have given her a ride. Something about him made her cold.

Turning back toward the ten-dollar bill, Anna squinted at the dirt where it'd come to rest. The money was gone, presumably taken by the wind, which now carried the scent of something foul.

"Shit," she said, squatting to search the growth on the side of the road. She thought she saw the bill in the limited light, a different shade of green than the grass. Fingers combing the swaying blades, she screamed and fell back when something humid, like balmy breath, warmed the back of her hand. She ran to work without the ten.

Day 34
4:37 p.m.
19 Hours Gone

Lula's pleading echoed in Anna's ears as she raced to the hotel, her mind still wobbly from the pot. That didn't stop her from pursuing Fox. He should have been getting ready to start his shift, but he wasn't in the housekeeping office or killing time at any of his usual haunts. Anna wouldn't have been surprised if he'd ditched work. Still, she went floor by floor in search of him.

She found him on the fourth, nearly unnoticeable on a bed of towels in the corner of the supply closet. He looked drained, incapable of doing a damn thing, and smaller somehow. His bolo rested sloppy and loose against his wrinkled shirt, stained with sweat. The braided cords dangled down his rib cage, the one on the left hanging lower than the one on the right.

Anna knelt at his side, not the least bit afraid of him in his diminished state. She took his face between her hands.

"Don't ask questions," he mumbled.

Anna seethed. "I know what you've been up to in suite eight-oh-eight. I know all about the deal you made. Say what you want, but I know Missy Picote and my sister were up there, too. Now I need you

218

to tell me where they are." She had to mute the little voice at the back of her brain telling her she knew exactly what'd become of Missy and Grace, that they'd been mashed between serrated teeth after being sucked through wormy lips, just like Amber and Erica.

"Anna," Fox moaned, rolling onto his side to face the wall.

She squeezed his stubbly chin and wrenched his head back toward her. "Please," she started to beg, then gave herself a mental slap. Information about her sister's security wasn't something she should be begging for. She wouldn't beg again. She pushed his face against the wall, so he'd know she was serious. "Tell me everything you know."

"Told you already," he muttered, blood beginning to shine on his lower lip, which had split against the molding. "Haven't seen 'em."

Anna pushed harder against his head. Maybe it would pop, and all his secrets would come flying out. Fox's nose flattened. His body tensed. And then he morphed from a sleeping snake into one about to strike.

Anna sensed his impending reaction and recoiled, only she moved a little too slow. Fox rolled onto his back and snagged her by the wrist, his eyes spiraling, searching for her. "Go home," he said through gritted teeth.

Anna wrenched her wrist free. It felt like it might snap in his grasp. She wanted to claw his eyes out. Beat in his chest. She wanted his heart to ache as badly as hers. "I'm calling Chief Fisher," she said.

A lunatic smile wriggled across Fox's lips. "I talked to Luke last night. He said you sent him. With that fucking lip balm. I told him I don't know who it belonged to . . . I see twenty guests a day smearing that shit on their lips. They sell it by the register in the gift shop. The owner could be anywhere in the country by now. Anywhere in the world."

Grace, Anna thought. *Gone. Anywhere.*

Fox's eyes closed. He continued to smile. Blood smeared across his front teeth. "The odds of finding who that lip balm belonged to are probably the same as getting struck by lightning. Like winning the lotto."

Gran flashed in Anna's mind at the mention of the lottery. The scratchers. The gas station. The sign on the door. Anna's brain buzzed. She backed out of the closet, tripping over her big feet, and looked up at the ceiling in the hall.

"Fox," she said. "Stay here."

Anna dashed into the nearest vacant guestroom and practically fell on top of the phone. Her finger couldn't dial fast enough.

"Luke," she said, the instant he picked up. "It's Anna Horn. I'm at the hotel. I need you to get here right away."

Luke appeared in the hotel's drop-off zone a few minutes later. Anna was waiting for him just outside the sliding glass doors.

"What is it?" he said. "Did you hear from Grace?"

"There's something we have to see." She sped into the hotel, Luke at her heels.

"I came here last night like I said I would. No one saw your sister coming or going. I went by Fox's place, too. He said as far as he knows, she was never—"

"You didn't go inside Fox's house, did you?" Anna would have bet her meager life savings that Fox had kept Luke out on the stoop. She would have bet that Fox had redirected the conversation as well, after claiming no knowledge of Grace's whereabouts. "If you'd gone in, you would have seen his drugs on the coffee table. I told you he had them. I think it's meth or something he smokes."

Luke grabbed Anna by the shoulders and pulled her to face him. "It smells like you've been smoking something yourself."

Anna clamped her lips shut. She really didn't care about what she'd seen in Fox's house or what Luke thought about her. Her finger speared the air, pointing up at the Atrium's tall ceiling.

"What is it?" Luke asked.

SMILE! YOU'RE ON CAMERA.

"Security cameras. They're on every floor. You can get the footage, can't you?"

Luke stalled, staring up at the black plastic dome over the nearest security camera, thinking.

"I don't know what Fox told you, but you can't trust a word he says," Anna went on. "He's been sneaking a strange man up to the eighth floor, and he's been bringing women up there too. Girls. My sister. It's about money." The story that flowed out of her made Anna's voice tremble. Not only did she think Luke would dismiss her claims, she expected him to. Her chest heaved. Luke looked winded himself.

"Can you prove any of that?" he asked.

She pointed at the security camera again.

PART II

Day 34
5:22 p.m.
20 Hours Gone

Anna scanned the monitors in front of her, providing unceasing views into the casino, the Ice Bar, the diner, the buffet, the Atrium, hotel reception, the movie theater, and numerous other locations throughout the casino and resort.

"How do you keep track of so much footage?" Luke asked David Chapleau, head of hotel security, who'd led him and Anna into the bowels of the building, to the surveillance room where closed-circuit television operators sat before the many monitors.

"Digital multiplexers," Chapleau said. "We've got some great new technology. These things"—he placed a hand atop a long, thin box sheathed in metal—"allow us to record up to sixteen cameras at once with time-lapse and motion-detection recording. Those two features save a hell of a lot of tape."

"Is everything recorded?" Luke asked.

"Not everything. Some of the camera feeds are only monitored here by the operators. If they see something suspicious or strange, they report it."

"The hotel?" Anna questioned.

"The reception area is recorded. The corridors are monitored."

"So we can't see what happened last night—"

Chapleau was already shaking his head, dashing Anna's hope.

"—up on eight," she said.

"On eight?" His head stopped shaking. "That's the only floor we record. Because of the nature of the guests."

Anna felt like she'd just been caught from a fall. "How soon can we see it?"

"Last's night's footage? Give me a minute."

Before long, Anna sat hunched over a monitor, viewing grainy, black-and-white—almost green—footage of the long corridor she knew so well. It hardly looked like the corridor in real life, hollow, gaping, eerie. She was there in the frame.

"Motion-detection recording," Chapleau said, smiling at Anna.

She'd seen herself in photos but never on video. The person on the screen moved in ways Anna didn't associate with herself. She made the movements of her father. The movements of Robbie. The three of them shared the same wide-legged gait that made their shoulders see-saw from side to side. Were hers as wide as her father's?

"What are we looking for?"

"Can you fast-forward?" Anna said.

He did, zooming past the parts where Anna entered and exited suite 808 with the housekeeping cart, ultimately concealing herself inside the housekeeping closet, just over an hour before she'd find the lip balm beneath the bed.

"The emergency stairwell door will open twice," Anna said, recalling that she'd heard it clang open and shut two times before she'd emerged from the closet. She remembered how hellish it'd been, waiting in there for something to happen. The motion-detection camera made it so that they didn't have to wait. The stairwell door opened at 8:17 p.m., according to the timestamp in the corner of the screen. A man clutching his chest and sucking in great breaths labored through the door. He was heavy and white. A manicured mustache clung to his upper lip. Pressed pants cinched his doughy waist. Anna recognized him instantly.

"No," she gasped, thinking, *There's two.* Lula had only mentioned the lanky man. She hadn't said anything about a man like the one Anna had encountered in the road.

"Anna?" Luke questioned.

She held up a hand, telling him to wait. The man inserted a keycard and entered suite 808. Salt-and-pepper snow blurred the screen, then the stairwell door opened again, the timestamp now reading 8:21 p.m. Fox stepped forth and, holding the door open, beckoned behind himself with his hand. Anna whined at the sight of Grace, timid and uncertain, dressed in a chambermaid's coat, entering the eighth floor and then suite 808. Was that a nervous smile on her strawberry-lip-balm-slathered lips?

"Anna," Luke said again, apologetic this time. He used Chapleau's radio to order that Fox be apprehended and brought down to the basement.

"He's in the fourth-floor housekeeping closet," Anna said.

The screen flashed. Anna appeared again, looking as anxious as she'd felt upon creeping to the door of suite 808 and inserting the keycard. Fox was back in a beat, a wild bull released from the suite. He grabbed Anna by the arm and dragged her down the hall. The stairwell door opened behind them, and the lanky man materialized. Fox thumped Anna on the back of the head, gripping her hair and skull to keep her from getting more than a split-second glimpse of the man approaching suite 808. The images on the screen were far more brutal than Anna remembered.

Luke's hand landed on Anna's back. He gently grasped her shoulder and tried to redirect her from the screen so that she wouldn't have to watch Fox manhandle her into the elevator. Anna refused to look away. She now saw what she hadn't been allowed to see the night before. The lanky man entered the suite. Fox vanished through the stairwell door after he got rid of her.

"Pause it," Luke said.

"Not yet," Anna insisted.

The footage played on. The timestamp in the corner indicated that it was 9:23 p.m. when Grace, like a mouse, scurried out of the room and into the stairwell, one hand clutching a pocket. The two men followed less than three minutes later, both taking the stairs. Fox appeared shortly after that. He entered the suite, presumably to make sure it was empty and to call Anna up from the basement laundry room, and then he was gone. After the screen flashed again, Anna was back, making the discovery that a coin had been taped over the emergency stairwell door's lock plate.

Luke turned the monitor off. Anna stared at the nothingness on the screen. "I thought it was only one man in the suite," she said. After she had found Grace's lip balm in 808, she'd figured it had been Fox, then Grace she'd heard come through the stairwell door while she was hiding in the housekeeping closet, and that Grace had been joined by the lanky man after Fox had caught her—Anna—in the hall. She'd never considered that Fox had been working with more than one man. Her guts liquified at the thought of her little sister in the suite with two strange men. She needed a bathroom bad.

"Do you record the stairwells?" Luke asked Chapleau.

"They're only monitored," he said.

"Do the cameras cover the lobby? The exits?" Anna said.

Chapleau turned the monitor back on and had the footage playing in minutes flat. It showed Grace leaving—unnoticed—through the hotel's main doors roughly two minutes after exiting the suite. The lanky man left the hotel three minutes after her. The fat man Anna had encountered in the road crossed the lobby to the casino. Further footage showed that he got a drink in the bar and that Anna had run right past him in her search for Fox and Grace. She hadn't noticed him at all.

"The lots are recorded too," Chapleau said.

Soon they were watching Grace become smaller, grainier, and darker as she walked across the massive parking lot toward the trees, heading in the direction of home. She vanished from the camera's view at 9:29 p.m., not long before the lanky man hopped into his truck and drove off, license plate indiscernible. The man Anna had met in the road didn't leave the casino until 12:10 a.m. Anna had already been skull-deep in worry by then.

The breath she let out when Luke turned the monitor off left her feeling utterly empty. According to the footage, Grace was safe and on her way home just minutes before Anna found the lip balm. Though she'd seen it, she didn't believe it.

"You have to find those two men," she said.

Luke nodded, but his words weren't of any comfort. "I'd like to speak with them," he said. "Fox too. He had no right to put his hands on you the way he did. You understand, though, Anna, that nothing we've seen indicates that those men did anything wrong."

Anna's eyes were still on the screen. "Those men were with Grace. They must have been with Missy too."

"When was that?" Luke asked. "When did you see Missy Picote at the hotel?"

She thought for a moment. "Eleven days ago. October twenty-fifth."

"Do your tapes go back that far?" Luke asked Chapleau.

"Sure do," he said. "Farther than that."

Agonizing minutes passed before the week-and-a-half-old footage appeared, showing a girl who matched Missy Picote's description. The hair that hung in her face concealed her features.

"It's her," Anna said, more confident than ever.

The footage seemed to confirm that Missy Picote's last known whereabouts included suite 808, the emergency stairwell where Anna had encountered her, and the hotel parking lot. She'd disappeared through the trees just like Grace, only on legs that looked far less stable. On the screen, Anna saw the same two men who'd exited suite 808 after Grace. They left the suite after Missy as well; so did Fox.

"I've seen him on the rez," Anna said as Chapleau rewound the footage to watch it again. "The fat one. Last night . . . only hours before Grace went missing." Guilt came with the admission. She'd inadvertently helped him get to Grace.

Luke put a reassuring hand on top of hers. "Any word on Fox Ballard?" he said into the radio. Anna had never seen Luke look so severe, his eyes like lasers seeking a target.

The door behind them clicked open. The radio squealed. "Got him," a voice said.

Anna, Luke, and David Chapleau turned to find Fox with his chin against his chest, two security guards stationed behind him.

Day 34
7:07 p.m.
22 Hours Gone

Hurrying home, the old thought that had haunted Anna since she was seven came crashing back. And why shouldn't it have? If there'd ever been a night to be afraid in the dark, it was then, knowing that Missy and Grace had both disappeared after walking the same route. And what about Amber and Erica? Could they have walked this way as well? The rustle of the grass along the road. The crunch of gravel underfoot. The wind blowing past her ears and through her hair, carrying the faint scent of decay. Something, it seemed, was rolling behind her. No way would she turn around.

On-the-job training. Attempting to drown out the unsettling sounds, Anna rewound the words Fox had used to explain why Missy and Grace had been dressed as chambermaids on the eighth floor. *I was trying them out. Seeing if they had what it takes to join my team.* He'd even produced records to show that they'd been on the clock the nights they'd gone missing.

You told me Missy wasn't at the hotel, Anna had said. It was an assertion Fox ignored. *You told me and Chief Fisher that Grace hadn't been here at all!* She hadn't been able to stop herself from shaking.

Grace asked me not to tell.

Why? Luke had demanded.

Fox had shrugged. *You'll have to ask Grace.*

Luke's eyes had narrowed. *Missy and Grace are a little young to be joining your* team, *don't you think?*

Fox had shrugged again. *Anyone over the age of fourteen can legally work eighteen hours a week.*

And the men? Who are they?

Guests, Fox had said. Another shrug. The log in the lobby indicated that a certain Claude LeBlanc had reserved the suite for the nights in question, though there wasn't a phone number or a credit card for him on file.

Give it to me again, Luke had said. *Your version of things.*

Fox's story went in circles, always insisting the men were guests and the girls were employees.

Talk to Lula Broussard, Anna had said to Luke, stabbing Fox with her eyes. She hadn't left the hotel until she heard Luke say, *You're lying, Fox. Grasping. Your story will unravel, and I'll be the one pulling the string.*

The Horn house was alive with light when Anna came upon it; she could see it glowing from a quarter mile off. She saw her father, too, standing on the porch with his hands on his hips. Dorothy stood beside him, slightly withered, a few feet away. The fiery tip of her cigarette burned bright each time she took a drag.

"Damnit, Anna," Chris said, spying her silhouette. "I just got off the phone with Luke. He told me everything. You knew!" he barked.

"I didn't," she insisted. "Not everything. Not until today." She staggered into the house, her parents at her heels.

"Fox!" Chris hollered, seething, trying to hold it together. "He's got shit for brains. He's the kind of guy who uses the washrag on his ass before his face. I'd expect something stupid from him, but you, Anna? What's wrong with you?"

The words stung, but merciful silence followed, ultimately broken by Robbie when he stormed out of the house.

"We're not gonna find her in here," he said.

Dorothy ran after him. Chris did too.

Anna unintentionally locked eyes with Gran across the room. She was standing with the sheet draped over her shoulders, holding on to the wall. Her face, set like stone, contradicted the frailty of her body.

"I'm sorry," Anna said.

"I'm not angry at you."

"I don't know what to do."

Gran retreated to her bed. She patted the mattress beside her for Anna to come and sit. "Grace has changed," she said, knowing.

Anna exhaled, wishing her unease would ride away on her expelled breath. "A lot," she said.

"Is that why you didn't propose the preservation society at the tribal council meeting?"

Anna wondered how Gran knew so much. "That's part of it," she said, recalling that she'd been thinking about Grace and Fox, the hotel, and Missy Picote when Miss Vicky had summoned her to speak at the podium.

"And the other part?" Gran questioned.

"Who would care?" Anna said. "No one listens to me. You heard Chief Fisher last night. He hardly took my suspicions seriously. It's even worse at school."

"Tell me about it."

"Now isn't the time—"

"Tell me," Gran insisted.

Anna's hands passed through her hair, pulling at the scraggly bits in the back. It didn't feel right to whine about herself with Grace still gone. Gran's urging eyes, however, gave her the go-ahead. "They expect me to write beautiful prose in English, but never give me a chance to light the Bunsen burners or mix the chemicals in science.

I'm never called to solve equations on the board. They said I had to take home economics rather than woodshop. They don't let girls play baseball, basketball, or wrestle in PE. It's badminton, aerobics, and square dancing for us, as if our bones will break easier than the boys'. Was school this bad for you?"

Gran huffed. "What school?" she said. "I couldn't even go."

"Because you were a girl?"

"Because I was Indian." Silence let her words sink in. "We weren't recognized back then. No civil rights. Little government assistance. They called us names in town and banned us from the movies and diners." She labored to swallow. The pause augmented the significance of her slurred words. "Some shopkeepers would let us in if they were certain we'd buy something. And we could go to church if we stayed in the back. The reservation was all we had. It wasn't much either, not like today. I dreamed of going to school. . . . I think I would have liked it."

Hot fury flared within Anna. "Why do we bother?" she said. "Why do we try to fit in when we can just take care of ourselves?"

"It's not about fitting in, it's about finding balance. Rattlesnakes and field mice. Owls and rabbits. Alligators and deer. They're predator and prey, yet they share the same ground. Mind you that the people in town aren't predators and that we on the reservation aren't prey. You'd think we'd be able to share the same ground. You'd think it'd be easy."

It was hard for Anna not to think of her classmates as predators. "They can be so mean," she said.

Gran nodded, slowly. "You'd rather wrestle?" she asked, after a moment in thought.

Anna sucked her lips tight around her teeth and shrugged.

"You're not the only one who's fond of the tribal stories. You remind me of one from long ago." Gran held the back of her weak hand in the palm of her strong one. Her lowered eyes studied her withered fingers.

"When a boy would play as a girl or a girl would play as a boy, the child's parents would arrange a ring of dry brush out in the field. The tribal members would gather around the ring. They'd place a man's hunting bow alongside a woman's woven basket within its center. The child would then be forced through the brush, and the brush would be lit on fire.

"'Bring something out,' the child's father would call. If a boy escaped the fire with the basket, or if a girl fled the flames with the bow, then the tribe would know the child's true nature, and the child would be honored for being a perfect and unique balance of male and female, neither one nor the other, but something more—a third gender, one thought to possess two spirits instead of one. The child, it was believed, would grow to be the tribe's best protector, teacher, healer, provider, and caregiver. The child would forever be respected and revered." Gran's hands fell into her lap. "But that was long ago."

"Long ago," Anna echoed, thinking about the stories and beliefs that had been lost over time. "Do you think Miss Shelby knew that story?" she asked, recalling the perplexing things Miss Shelby had told her about seeing things through all eyes and living not as one or the other but as both.

"I'm sure of it," Gran said. She raked her fingers through Anna's hair. "She and I both saw how you played."

Anna thought about her favorite activities as a child: chasing Robbie and Grace around the yard, climbing trees, swinging from branches, crafting paper dolls, cupping tadpoles from the water with her bare hands, building bug boxes out of old cardboard and discarded mesh produce bags.

"We saw how you regarded your siblings as well," Gran said. "You've always put them first. You've never resented them."

"Why would I resent them?"

"Many firstborns do. But not you, Anna. Even now, you'd give all of yourself for Grace."

"What are you saying?"

For a moment, Gran's lips didn't part. Her eyes, so like Anna's, communicated something instead. "You need to rest," she eventually said.

"How can I sleep?"

"How can you do anything if you don't?" Her timeworn face cracked a sympathetic smile. "The others won't stop looking for her." ·

Anna reluctantly returned to her room and nearly slammed the window shut. It'd been open all day and instead of ushering Grace back in, it had removed more of her. Anna could barely smell her sister's scent over the fresh fall air that had pervaded Grace's bedsheets. Running a hand over Grace's pillow, she plucked a hair from it, then put it back. She didn't think she'd be able to rest, but sleep proved victorious, mercifully sparing her both nightmares and dreams.

Day 35
7:23 a.m.
34 Hours Gone

An insistent fist beating the bedroom door shunted Anna back to reality. "Get a move on!" her father said.

Her eyes opened upon Grace's empty bed.

"What is it?" she called, still half asleep. No amount of self-control could conceal the panic in her voice. Her chest felt as if it was flooded with acid. She raced from her room to find her dad stepping into his boots by the door, her mom already out on the porch, and Gran holding on to Robbie as he helped her from the house.

"Chief Fisher and the tribal council have called an emergency meeting," Chris said.

Anna burst outside, ready in seconds flat. The whole Horn family piled into the meat wagon. Chris's foot weighed heavily on the gas while Dorothy blew smoke out the passenger window.

The size of the crowd at the community center renewed Anna's shame, her guilt. Most of the tribal families were represented by at least two members. Lula and Noemi Broussard were noticeably absent. As was Fox Ballard, though his parents and uncle, Chairman Eaton Ballard, were in attendance. Eaton looked nearly as distressed as Sawyer Picote, who must have been wondering if something worse than meth had happened to his daughter. Sawyer came face-to-face with Chris when the Horn family hurried to the front of the room. The two men stopped stock-still, each internalizing the other's pain, worry, and fear. Exhausted eyes. Fatigued flesh. Yesterday's stubble. It was as if they were peering into the same cracked mirror. Sawyer put his right hand on Chris's left shoulder. Chris followed suit. Both men squeezed, then each pulled the other close, uniting in a wordless embrace that spoke of solidarity and hope. Chris reached out to Dorothy and drew her into the hug while Anna turned away to wipe her watery eyes.

A spread of breakfast breads, donuts, coffee, and some baskets of fresh fruit sat behind the rows of folding chairs in the meeting room. Friends, family, and neighbors milled about, helping themselves to the free breakfast, wondering why they'd been called out of bed so early on a Wednesday morning.

"I'll make this quick," Chief Fisher said, silencing the crowd. "We have two missing teenagers . . ." His jaw flexed and his eyes narrowed. "Two *more* missing teenagers," he corrected himself. "Melissa Picote and Grace Horn. And there's little to go on this time."

Anna noticed a huge stack of missing-person posters on the table next to Luke. More sat in a cardboard box on the floor. She snuck over and snagged one. Grace's class photo was printed next to Missy's, along with descriptions of each girl.

Last seen leaving the Grand Nacre Casino and Resort, it read. Grainy stills of the unnamed men who'd been at the hotel were printed at the bottom with an appeal for information about them.

"We know that Missy and Grace left the hotel on their own. Neither has been seen or heard from since. There's no doubt that both girls had contact with these two men." Luke held up one of the posters. "All four individuals were seen entering the same hotel suite—not at the same time, mind you—along with Fox Ballard." His eyes slid in the direction of Fox's parents. "Fox has had little to say so far."

Fox's parents drew closer to each other at the mention of their son's name. Chairman Ballard, face strained despite maintaining an air of composure and calm, clenched his jaw. Again his glittery bolo, fastened tight beneath his crisp collar, drew Anna's eyes, and it was then that she knew just how fake his nephew was—nothing more than a blurry reflection of the powerful and esteemed man he wanted to be—and how good Fox was at playing others for fools. She thought about Lula Broussard, so insistent that she hadn't been pressured into taking that trip up to the eighth floor, never realizing that all of Fox's friendly visits were his way of making sure she hadn't forgotten what he'd proposed. All those visits—during which he probably saw and casually referenced the PAST DUE envelopes that likely arrived in Lula's mailbox day after day, week after week—were his way of getting her to feel secure around him, his way of making her think the decision was hers to make when really he'd been steering her toward what he'd wanted all along.

"I can't say that these unnamed men are guilty of any wrongdoing at this point," Luke said. "I can't say they're innocent either. Proceed with caution if you encounter them and call me as soon as you can."

"Where's Fox now?" one of the Langdon brothers asked. "The fact that he's not here implies that he's done something wrong. What's he hiding? *Why's* he hiding?" He turned directly to Fox's father. "What'd your boy do?"

"We're not going down that road," Luke said. He stepped forward to stop Fox's father from getting out of his chair, though there was nothing he could do about the rumbling that rose from the crowd. He waved his hands from side to side as if that would cast away the conclusions floating on the air. "I contacted the sheriff in town. He's currently unwilling . . . *unable*, as he put it . . . to help. Since the girls were last seen on the reservation, their disappearance is out of the sheriff's jurisdiction, which means it's up to us to lead the search." He'd gotten a similar response from the sheriff back in July when he'd requested assistance after Amber and Erica disappeared. At nineteen, they were considered adults. They were together. There was no evidence that they'd come to any harm on or off the reservation. Considering the passage Amber's father found in her diary—*We're gonna do it one day. We really will. L.A., here we come!*—and the lies they told the night they went missing, that Amber was staying at Erica's house and that Erica was staying at Amber's, it certainly seemed that they'd abandoned their family and friends of their own free will. Too bad, so sad.

Luke had done more than just contact the sheriff about Missy and Grace, he'd taken the hotel's CCTV footage into town. If the two unnamed men had done something to harm the girls, Luke would have needed authorities from off the reservation to make the arrest since he had no ability or right to arrest a non-Indian—even for a crime committed against an Indian—on tribal land.

The complex and confusing regulations left Luke with his hands tied. Even if the CCTV footage had shown wrongdoing, Anna wouldn't have been surprised if the sheriff had turned a blind eye. It was a common occurrence across Indian country. The easy explanation was to blame it on jurisdiction, but the cold truth was it went on because too few non-Natives with the power to make a difference gave a damn. And with poverty as an insurmountable hurdle on most reservations, tribal police forces were either nonexistent, understaffed, or underfunded. Added up, reservations became easy places to get away with wrongdoing—murder included.

"My wife stayed up all night printing these posters," Luke said. "Take them with you when you go into town. Take them everywhere. Someone must have seen or heard something after Missy and Grace left the Grand Nacre's parking lot. Keep your eyes open. Search around your homes. Your yards. *Look*." He didn't say what, exactly, they should be looking for, but Anna knew. He was talking about finding bodies. "I'm working to get search-and-rescue dogs on the rez by tomorrow."

Questions were asked and hopeful words were spoken. Anna hardly heard. Grace's image on the poster hampered her. The longer she stared, the less she recognized her sister. Grace could have been any Native girl, anywhere. Anna worried that Grace's face was another that would go unnoticed, just like her little sister had always feared.

Day 35
2:18 p.m.
41 Hours Gone

In less than two days, the Horn family had morphed from an old car with a dying battery to an old car without one at all. They were broken, lost, useless. Chris paced from the living room to the porch and back like a toy train on a narrow track. Gran sat in wait by the window, her gaze endlessly shifting from the road to the nearest field to the horizon, while Dorothy busied herself with the phone, fielding nosy and sympathetic calls that came through at a breakneck pace following the meeting that morning. She spoke in a sickly monotone, saying, "Pray for us," at the end of each call.

Robbie emerged from his room with the rifle. He walked past Chris to put his grubby boots on by the door.

"You can't hunt squirrels today," Chris absently said.

"I'm not hunting squirrels." He shouldered the rifle on his way out.

"Robbie," Dorothy protested, her hand cupped over the phone's mouthpiece. She didn't get up to stop him.

Anna followed him onto the porch. She didn't try to stop him either. Though he was the youngest, Anna knew he was safer on his own than her and Grace. He was safer than every girl, even without the rifle over his shoulder.

A tribal police car came into view just as Robbie winked out of sight. It drove straight into the Horns' driveway.

"Luke asked me to come by," Officer Sam Peltier said, getting out of the car. He took his hat from his head and held it against his belly, a gesture that tricked Anna into thinking he'd come to pay his respects. "I talked to your mom about it on the phone," he said. "She told me it'd be fine."

"What would be fine?"

"I need to look at Grace's things . . . in case there's something . . ."

Anna pulled the screen door open and led him inside. Sam wasn't a big guy, but he took up most of the bedroom space, his presence wrong.

"There?" he questioned, pointing to Grace's bed.

Anna nodded.

Sam lifted the sheets and blankets, then ran his hands between the box spring and mattress, perhaps hoping he'd discover a diary with a clue inside like Amber's. Finding nothing, he dropped to the floor and reached beneath the bed. His hands moved fast, pulling out forgotten toys, stuffed animals, dust bunnies, shoes that no longer fit, worn blankets, and a shoebox full of intricately folded notes decorated with colorful zigzags, hearts, and Xs and Os on blue-lined loose-leaf paper. Anna's stomach sank.

"Are you going to read them?" she asked.

"Me or Luke."

"Could I look at them first?"

Sam hesitated, then thrust the box toward Anna. She grabbed a handful of the notes and began unfolding. What she read was what she expected. Promises. Smiley faces. References to secrets, gifts, and money; things to make Grace feel special, needed, and loved. The glaring absence at the bottom of each note spoke of how duped she was—there wasn't a signature on a single one of them. "They're from Fox," Anna said. "I'm sure he'll deny it."

Sam reached under the bed again and pulled out the loom holding Anna's unfinished bracelet, nearly three-quarters done.

"She made this?"

Anna nodded, her throat stoppered.

"It's nice." Sam pushed the loom back beneath the bed and opened a dresser drawer, prompting Anna to retreat from the house because she didn't want to watch him sift through Grace's undergarments. She walked the road from the casino to town, looking for anything suspicious along the way.

A wooden sign stood at the border.

LEAVING TAKODA INDIAN RESERVATION
PLEASE HURRY BACK

An enormous alligator, tail thrashing and its massive jaws clenching a giant pearl, was carved into the opposite side of the sign. The words GRAND NACRE CASINO AND RESORT, painted gold, were etched above the gator's prominent snout. HENI!—WELCOME! was etched below.

The road leading to the Grand Nacre had been the first one paved. Just dirt and gravel two years ago, it was blacker and smoother now than the main road in town. A wall of trees stood behind the sign and on the opposite side of the road, making the reservation seem like a secluded and secret world. Anna wondered what the townsfolk thought when they passed through the trees to visit the casino. Did they feel like they were pressing their luck in more ways than one?

She crossed to the opposite side of the road and turned back, resuming her search, which lasted through the afternoon and into the evening. The land was too vast, making her feel incredibly small, especially when she reached one of the fields where she and Grace used to play. Posters were present there, tacked to the trees along the road. Anna ran to the middle of the field and scrambled up the tallest tree she could find. She climbed as high as the branches would allow and looked out in every direction. All she saw was soft grass, more trees, and generous brush, all capable of camouflaging secrets as easily as they camouflaged rattlesnakes, wasps, and ticks.

Anna turned toward the river and came face-to-face with Grace's image once more when she passed the posts on either side of the bridge. Grace, it seemed, was both everywhere and nowhere at all. If only Anna could conjure her from her heart, her mind, or the tip of her tongue.

She hung her head over the bridge's rail, as she had when her dad helped drag the river after Miss Shelby went missing. Just about everyone on the reservation had banded together to try to find her, united by grief, frightened that one of their own—someone who'd devoted her life to the tribe and gave no indication that she'd ever want to leave it—was gone. Losing Miss Shelby had been like losing one's sense of taste or smell; life wasn't the same without her, but they'd adjusted, and in doing so they'd forgotten what she'd offered, a link to their past. No more stories. No more songs. Sometimes Anna wondered if she could bring them back, if she really could be the tribe's next singer and Legend Keeper, just like Miss Shelby had implied.

At first, the tribal elders had thought Miss Shelby might have had an accident, that she might have somehow slipped through the bridge's balusters into the water below. Dragging nets through the rushing waves, however, had been a waste of time, and time was what haunted Anna as the sunlight faded in the water's reflection. The thought of another night without Grace at home produced such pain that if Anna had slipped from the bridge, she might have let the water take her. She didn't cry, though, because crying would feel like giving up. She pushed away from the rail, leaving the water behind, and headed back toward the casino along a route she normally wouldn't take. There was little light left. Anna wasn't about to waste it.

She retraced Grace's steps through the hotel's parking lot from the sliding glass doors to the trees that separated the resort from the reservation. She'd walked the same route the night before, but she'd been too flustered and furious at Fox to consider what might have happened once Grace passed through the trees and out of the camera's view.

A well-worn path in the dirt offered passage through the pines. Anna crouched to touch it, wishing the earth spirit would grant a vision of what Grace had done after stepping foot there. The main road stretched out ahead. Turning left would lead to town. Turning right would lead to the rest of the reservation.

Limited by the diminishing daylight, Anna searched the ground. Her hopefulness made her feel foolish. Her guilt would grow, however, if she didn't try. Small bugs flew up her nostrils and buzzed in her ears. She cursed, fanning them away, starting to itch all over from phantom bites. Cars came and went to her left. Their approaching headlights swept over her as they turned down the lane to the resort. The traffic would wane overnight, but it wouldn't stop. It never did. Winners, losers, hope, and regret. The reservation saw a lot of those things, in and outside of the casino.

Anna turned toward home and squinted in response to a scuffling sound when she rounded the bend. It revitalized the worry she'd been struggling to suppress, that Grace and Missy had simply been gobbled up. Two dots of light glowed before her. Hot fear surged within her. A pair of red eyes within a ghostly visage faced her head-on, robbing her of breath until her senses returned, whereupon she realized she was looking at two taillights burning in the distance. The glint of the moon bouncing off the fresh pavement and the trunk of the car created the illusion of pallid flesh around the lights. The car wasn't moving.

Anna approached slowly, her insides tingling with curiosity and fear. Unless she scrambled through the brush, the road was the only way home. Inching forward, she soon realized that the car's engine was running and that the driver's door was open, jutting out into the road. The persistent *ding*, intent on reminding the absent driver to remove the key from the ignition, grew louder the closer Anna got. Despite the open door, the dome light was out. The interior was dark, no signs of life.

The Lincoln, Anna thought, blood running cold. It couldn't be.

Anna's mind became like a radio frequency picking up two stations at once. Noise and a whole lot of static filled her head. Desperate for Luke, Sam, or her father to come down the road, she searched for approaching headlights in the distance. It was just her and the car. The Lincoln Continental.

Run! The voice inside her head broke through the static. Logically, Anna knew the car's owner—the fat man who'd been at the hotel with Missy and Grace—could be dangerous, but she couldn't just flee from him. She couldn't let him get away.

"Hey!" she hollered. The car apparently empty, she had to assume someone was around. She thought about the tire. Maybe he hadn't replaced the spare since their last encounter. Maybe it had blown. "Where are you?" She edged along the opposite side of the road, putting space between herself and the vehicle. Her heels scraped through the grass. "Can anyone hear me?"

The tire looked fine from her vantage point. The Continental sat even, suggesting that the spare had been replaced. She ducked to peer beneath the car. Nothing but inky darkness lingered there. She crept along, eventually coming even with the open door. No one occupied the seats. She took two steps forward, pitching her upper body toward the car to look through the rear window. The backseat was empty. So was the floor.

Anna's skin prickled and started to sweat. She whirled around. If he wasn't in the car, he had to be nearby. Behind her. Beside her.

Spying on her in the dark. Her eyes strained against the blackness. Were all those pillars in the field trunks of mighty trees, or was one of them the frame of a fat man?

Anna, her gaze bouncing back and forth, continued to sidestep until the headlights, spotlighting twin flurries of dancing moths, were on her, blinding her. She looked toward home. Even at risk all alone out there, she didn't want to abandon the car. She couldn't give the man an opportunity to flee, and so she filled her lungs and imagined she was made of steel, endowing herself with just enough confidence to approach the Continental again.

She resolved to take the key and then run for help. Rounding the open door, movement drew her eyes to the red patch of taillight-lit road behind the car. Something dark and round rolled through the patch. It remained there on the road, snorting and growling beneath the bumper. Anna jumped back, heart racing. It wasn't just the rolling, round shape that caused the steel she'd imagined to melt like wax. There was something else on the road that she hadn't noticed before. Something that glistened.

Anna gasped and ran for home, leaving the key in the ignition.

Day 35
8:19 p.m.
47 Hours Gone

Anna ached for breath. Running on empty, her body threatened to throw her to the ground, to serve her up to the horror at her heels. Hopelessly telling herself that she was hearing the clack of branches knocking against each other in the wind, bugs flapping their reedy wings, or a distant car in need of a tune-up, she couldn't convince herself that gnashing teeth weren't crashing against the ground each time the rotting, rolling head revolved behind her.

She squinted at the glowing dot of the porch light when it came into sight, willing it to grow. A modicum of relief set in when she got close enough to see the meat wagon, but then the putrid thing pursuing her gained some ground. It rolled in front of her—making her skid to a stop—only to vanish within the brush along the side of the street a split second later. It circled her, thrashing the grass, stalking her like a shark hunting its prey. She clenched her eyes to block out the horror, only to instantly reopen them because being sightless increased her vulnerability. She plowed ahead, moving quickly yet planting her feet with care to minimize the sound of her steps.

The house slowly took shape before her. Just when she thought she'd make it unscathed, the hairs on the back of her neck tingled. She felt the round monstrosity behind her, like sun on her back or moisture in the air. She smelled it, too, its fetid breath and rancid skin. Whimpering, she turned, then whimpered again. It was there in the road, twelve feet back, a reaper without a scythe or hands with which to hold it. Even with the shadow of a tree hanging over the ghastly orb, Anna discerned its glistening eyes, its matted hair, the glint of its jagged teeth. She reeled toward home and made it to the porch steps— the ascent of which seemed as steep as Everest—precisely as the fiend at her feet nipped the back of her left ankle, making her scream.

Anna's fingers couldn't turn the lock fast enough upon slamming the front door closed behind her. She fell backward, sucking in greedy breaths. The doorknob jabbed her side as her sudden and startling entrance jarred a can of beer from Chris's grasp. The can bounced against the floor and spewed its contents onto the carpet and wall.

"Damnit, Anna," he said, nerves shot. His face resembled a desiccated piece of wood. Rough and cracked.

Robbie, sitting on the floor, his forehead flat against the coffee table, jolted upright. Dorothy, lying on the couch like a tube sock, shapeless and flat, took a drag that burned her cigarette down to the butt. She quickly lit another, adding to the cloud of smoke lingering over her and the phone. Gran limped from her room so fast at the sound of the slammed door that she nearly tore the sheet from its hooks.

Anna's gaze bounced from her father to Robbie, her mother, then Gran, going back and forth, back and forth. None were themselves. They were horrific impostors, soulless versions of the beings they once were. Would any of them smile again? Would they remember how to laugh? The sight of their worried faces dragged Anna's heart down to unknown depths, as if a cinder block had been tied to it. The hurt she'd been harboring since Grace went missing doubled, leaving her breathless and nearly broken by the door.

Robbie crawled to Anna and stood beside her so that she wouldn't collapse, allowing her to inspect her ankle for blood. The flesh remained intact.

"Anna?" Chris stomped to get her attention. Dorothy went right on smoking.

"The head," Anna gasped, once she'd mustered enough breath. For the first time, she wasn't embarrassed to voice her fear. She knew she wasn't mistaken. She knew what she'd seen.

Robbie wrapped an arm around her. His smell said he hadn't showered. Normally he'd laugh at her for mentioning the head, but he didn't laugh this time. She was trembling too badly for him to poke fun.

"Anna," he said, his voice so kind it intensified her pain, "it's okay. I bet it was a raccoon. You know, like all the other times."

"It chased me," she said, shaking her head. "It rolled around me. I saw its eyes."

"A raccoon chased you?" Chris moved closer.

"Not a raccoon. I stopped and looked at it. It was—"

"Damnit, Anna! Do you want to get bit? A raccoon that will chase you is a raccoon that is sick. You can bet it has rabies or distemper. If it's not scared of you, it's not right. I thought you knew that by now." He went to the window and peered out. "How close did it come to the house?"

"It rolled after me," she said, still aching on the inside and shaking on the outside. She needed Robbie to laugh at her. She needed Grace to tell her she was crazy.

"If you see it again, you come get me or your brother. We'll take care of it," Chris said.

Anna panted, hands tearing at her hair. It wasn't about the head or the raccoon or whatever it was. "There's a car!" she exclaimed.

The statement erased the agitation from Chris's expression. Dorothy peeled herself off the couch.

"Down the road," Anna said. "I saw blood."

"An accident?" Chris asked.

Anna shook her head. "Just blood." Her throat constricted, making her work even harder to get the most important part out. She struggled to swallow, eyes clenched, face askew. "It's his car. The fat man from the hotel."

Chris threw the can he'd just picked up. Foam sprayed all the way up to the ceiling. "*What?*"

"Call Luke," Anna quavered.

"Robbie!" Chris hollered, his face revitalized—if only a bit—by the revelation.

Robbie sprang from the living room, returning with the rifle in his hand a few seconds later.

"Get your boots on," Chris said.

"What are you—?" Dorothy started.

"Call Luke," Chris demanded.

Dorothy reached for the phone as Chris took Anna by the shoulders and moved her to the side of the door, treating her like a coatrack in the way. He and Robbie nearly put a hole in the porch on their way out. The meat wagon started with a rattling whoosh. Anna, head still full of static, watched her mother's lips move. Dorothy locked eyes with her and lowered the handset from her head, asking Anna for more details to give to Luke, but Anna didn't internalize a word she said. She ambled onto the porch, eyes wide, ears open, wary of the head. Chris was already speeding down the road.

"He should have taken you," Gran said, startling Anna from behind.

Dorothy appeared a moment later, car key in hand. "Let's go," she said.

Soon, the fractured Horn family stood around the abandoned car. Robbie, the butt of the rifle against the ball of his shoulder and the muzzle aimed at the Lincoln Continental, slowly circled the car as though he'd put it down if it made a sudden move. Chris got closer. He stuck his head through the open car door, refraining from touching anything inside. Flashlight in hand, he shone the beam through each window, inspecting the glass.

"Grace wasn't in here," he said. "Not against her will anyway."

"How do you know?" Dorothy asked.

Chris looked surprised to see her there. "No smudges against the glass," he said.

Unless they were cleaned, Anna thought. *Or if Grace was in the trunk.*

Luke Fisher arrived only seconds after that. Sam Peltier and the rest of the tribal police force weren't far behind. They parked their vehicles on either end of the Continental, aiming their headlights at it. Suddenly it seemed that the sun had risen on the small speck of land.

"Put that away," Luke said to Robbie.

Robbie slung the rifle onto his back. He stood with his hands on his hips, mirroring his father's moves.

"Did you open the car door?" Luke asked Chris.

"Found it that way," Chris said. "Haven't touched a thing."

Luke stuck his head into the car the same way Chris had. He took a quick look around with his own flashlight, then backed out. Anna, still skittish but comforted by the thought that the head surely wouldn't attempt to ravage them all at once, wondered what exactly he was looking for.

"Look there," Chris said. His light illuminated the glistening streak on the asphalt, dry around the edges.

"Blood," Robbie said, voice airy and hollow, the way kids talk when they've seen something astonishing.

Luke bowed to look. Sam put his arms out and ushered everyone behind the police vehicles. Anna couldn't see the blood from there. Her toes tingled at the thought that she might have stepped in it earlier. She might have tracked it into the house.

"There's quite a bit," Luke said. He traced the length of blood—splattered and spotty, not a perfect streak—with the beam of his flashlight. "Looks like it starts here." He was standing in the mouth of the open car door.

"What are you thinking?" Sam asked.

"It's not from an accident," Chris said, stepping forth again. "There's no damage to the damn car. Doesn't look like there's any blood inside it either."

"The car's not from the rez," Sam said. He took a slow walk around the Continental, stepping over the blood, illuminating every angle.

"Run the plates," Luke said.

"Sportsman's Paradise," Sam read from the bottom of the license plate, indicating it was local.

"Looks like the driver was dragged from the car," Chris said. He followed the blood trail to the edge of the asphalt, right where the brush along the side of the road began.

"*Rolled*," Anna whispered without meaning to. Rolled, not dragged. By the head. Seeking revenge. Anna wheezed when her mother suddenly grabbed her from behind. They fell into each other's arms.

"Grace?" Dorothy gasped.

Anna shook her head against her mother's chest. She felt her mom's frailty, nothing more than skin and bones in her sleeves.

"I need a cig," Dorothy said. She pulled away and pawed at her pocket.

A small crowd had gathered. Faces emerged from the shadows, attracted to the bright lights like flying termites.

Luke pulled paperwork from the glove compartment. Anna stepped beyond the invisible barrier she was supposed to stay behind. She sidled next to her father, who had rushed toward Luke to see what he'd found.

"Paul Albert," Chris read from the document in Luke's hand. "Look, there's an address there."

"It's from town," Luke said, confirming that the car was from off the rez, which most likely meant that Luke's power was limited. "Search the field," he instructed two of his men. They took their spotlights and ventured into the brush, searching for Paul Albert.

"What are you thinking?" Sam asked Luke again.

"I'll have to call this one in," Luke said.

"You think the sheriff's gonna give a damn?"

Luke nodded. "He'll care. Everyone in town will care." He flexed his jaw like he was chewing something awful, like he was about to spit. "We might not mean anything to them, but this missing man will."

Day 35
9:06 p.m.
48 Hours Gone

A search of the first fifty feet turned up nothing in the murky field. The blood trail didn't extend more than a few inches off the road. The brush beyond that wasn't disturbed at all. Luke taped off the area, promising to resume the search once the sun came up. Anna already knew they wouldn't find anything in the grass, except maybe the ten dollars she'd lost, and a mouthful of teeth.

The authorities from town arrived soon after Luke put in the call. He didn't just need their resources, he needed their power. If a crime against Paul Albert had been committed by a non-Indian on the reservation, Luke wouldn't be able to arrest or prosecute the perpetrator; a county or state officer would have to make the arrest. Even if the non-Indian had harmed a tribal member, Luke would still need a federally certified agent to step in and take control. If a tribal member harmed a non-Indian, Luke could make the arrest, but if it led to a trial, the case would go to federal court. The jurisdictional tangle made prosecuting crimes on the reservation harder than trying to start a fire with wet wood and a soggy match. So did the fact that non-tribal authorities were often too busy with their own headaches to care about what happened on tribal land.

Luke pushed air through his teeth. Anna assumed both were thinking similar thoughts. They had so little to go on. And they didn't even know if it was Paul Albert's blood in the road.

The authorities from town quickly took over, treating Luke and his crew like rookies on the job. They mimicked mastiffs with their stances, chests protruding, shoulders high, the heels of their boots slamming against the asphalt to mark each step they took.

"What kind of operation are you running here?" Sheriff Riley Barnett, a middle-aged man bearing a medium-size belly and acne scars on his cheeks, said to Luke. "It's like the wild, wild west all over again."

"Hold off on pointing fingers," Luke said. "No one knows what happened here."

"Someone knows. Someone always knows. We'll find out."

"Got ahold of *Doctor* Albert's wife," one of the officers said. "That's right. Turns out he's a doctor. His wife said he left home around seven. He was going to do some gambling."

"Didn't I say a casino here would lead to nothing but trouble?" Sheriff Barnett said to no one in particular. There'd been protests in town when construction began. People said the casino and resort would attract riffraff and squash the small-town feel they knew and loved.

Like a recruit waiting for his orders, Luke kept his mouth shut as Sheriff Barnett circled the car once more. He cocked his head at the open door. "What would make a man stop his car without pulling over, put it in park, and open the door?" Sheriff Barnett rounded the hood and stalled in the headlight beams. "Maybe he saw something in the road."

"Maybe he did," Luke said, eyeing the pristine asphalt.

"Maybe he was lured out . . . tricked by someone who saw an expensive car . . . someone who saw an opportunity to steal a fat wallet."

The sheriff walked to the side of the road and proceeded to act out his theory. "Someone flags Albert down . . . maybe pretending to be injured. Albert stops. He gets out to help. Then BAM! He's blindsided. A hit to the head. A hand in his pocket. His body hidden somewhere out there." The beam of Sherriff Barnett's flashlight played over the field. "We all know the vices your people keep . . . alcohol, drugs, gambling . . . they're not cheap."

"Every community has its problems," Luke said through gritted teeth. "But what I'm wondering, Sheriff, is why Paul Albert was driving down this road in the first place. In case you didn't notice, the casino is over there. He drove right past it."

"He must have missed the signs," Barnett said.

"He didn't miss them." Anna stepped forward. After seeing Albert on the hotel's CCTV footage, she knew he didn't even need the signs to direct him because he'd already been to the resort before.

"What do you know?" Sheriff Barnett said, dismissing her.

"I know he's been to the hotel more than once. He was there with my sister."

Luke pegged her with his gaze. "Anna?"

"Didn't my mom tell you?" Anna glanced back at Dorothy, pacing through the darkness, a cigarette glowing red between her lips. Robbie was pacing behind her.

"Tell me what?" Luke asked.

"The car. It belongs to one of the men on the security footage. The fat guy who entered suite eight-oh-eight. I thought my mom told you on the phone when she called to get you out here."

Luke pointed at the Continental. "This is the same car?" He inspected the tires.

"What's she talking about?" Sheriff Barnett asked.

"Two teenagers have gone missing in the last two weeks. That makes four since last summer," Luke said, despite having already alerted the sheriff. He'd even shown Barnett the CCTV footage.

"Yeah . . . ?"

"Grace, one of the missing girls, is Anna's sister." Luke motioned toward Anna. "Anna helped a man change a flat tire the night Grace went missing. It was the same man we saw on the security footage."

Sheriff Barnett hummed. "I guess we just put a face to the name."

"We have to find him," Luke said.

"Who found the car tonight?" Barnett asked, eyes on Anna.

"I did," she said.

"You found it just like this?"

She nodded. "In almost the exact same spot it'd been in two nights ago."

"And when you helped Albert change his tire two nights ago—"

"I didn't help him change it. I changed it. He stood there and watched."

"Were you alone when you encountered him that night?"

"Yes."

"Was he also alone?"

"Yes."

"We've got prints," one of the investigators announced. "Multiple sets." He was inspecting the Continental's trunk and bumper. Anna had little doubt that one of the sets belonged to her. She remembered the greasy marks she'd left when putting the blown tire away.

"Was he alone tonight?" Barnett went on questioning Anna.

"She didn't see him. Just the car," Luke said.

"Are you sure about that?"

"Anna?" Luke questioned.

"I was walking home and came across the car. Paul Albert wasn't here. No one was."

"Show me your hands."

Anna held them in the beam of his flashlight.

"She didn't do anything to him," Luke said.

"She has a motive," Sheriff Barnett countered.

"Having one and acting on one are very different things," Anna snapped. "But, like I said, I didn't see him tonight. I didn't have the opportunity to act."

Luke cringed at Anna's nerve. Sheriff Barnett was about to bite back when commotion erupted behind the police vehicles. Shrieks rang out above the onlookers' escalating noise. The authorities shuffled and shouted, and then a well-dressed white woman, holding a toddler in her arms, broke through the crowd. Two officers from town kept her from crossing the police tape barrier.

"Paul!" the woman screamed. "Where's my husband? What happened to him?"

Mussed blond hair fell in front of the toddler's wide, watery eyes. His stumpy teeth gnawed the knuckle in his mouth. Frightened by his mother's screaming, the strange men, and all the flashing lights, he was seconds from sobbing.

"Mrs. Albert," the sheriff said, strolling toward her. "I need you to stay calm. We're doing everything we can to locate your husband."

She saw the blood-streaked asphalt and shrieked again. "What'd they do? What did they do to him?"

The words burned. Anna knew it wasn't *they* who were responsible. She tried telling herself it couldn't have been the head from Uncle Ray's story either, yet no amount of rationalizing could erase what she'd seen roll around the back of the car shortly before she spotted the blood.

Sheriff Barnett had Mrs. Albert escorted back to her car. He wasn't done with Anna. "What was your sister doing with this man?"

"You mean, what was that man doing with my sister?"

Barnett paused for a moment, sizing Anna up. "Fair enough," he finally said.

Anna didn't want to speculate.

"Did you know your sister was with him?" the sheriff asked.

"I didn't know anything about him until we saw the security footage. But I told Grace—" Anna stopped, wondering if she was saying too much.

"Told her what?"

"I told her to stay away from suite eight-oh-eight."

"You warned her, and she didn't listen?"

Anna grew hot. "Yes," she reluctantly said.

A satisfied smile took shape across the sheriff's lips. Clearly, he thought he'd just scored a point. "Doesn't look like Dr. Albert had any warning." He flashed his light over the blood again. "Almost killed his wife to see that."

"Perhaps she'd like to know that her husband wasn't just gambling at the casino," Anna said.

Sheriff Barnett shrugged. "That won't change the facts in front of us." He stepped closer to her, and she knew he was about to hit her hard. "Let's go over this one more time. You changed Albert's tire out of the goodness of your heart. The same night—only God knows why—your sister didn't come home. Then, after you found out that Albert and your sister were in the same suite at the same time, you just happened to find his blood in the road."

"We don't know whose blood it is," Luke cut in.

"I don't think you're telling us everything," the sheriff said to Anna. "And I don't have time for lies. You need to start being honest. What really happened?"

"Back off," Chris, who'd been speculating with Sam, said. "She's not at fault here. She's just a girl."

Sheriff Barnett's eyes dipped to take in all of Anna. "Looks like a *capable* girl to me," he said. "If she can jack a car and haul a tire, she can handle a man."

"My sister's missing."

"Did you do something to Dr. Albert because of that?"

"Why is he more important than her?"

"Come on, Anna," Chris said. "You don't have to answer any more of his questions."

"No." Anna refused to go. "Chief Fisher asked you for help when Amber Bloom and Erica Landry went missing," she said to the sheriff. "He asked again when Missy Picote disappeared. And then a *third* time when we couldn't find my sister. You refused to help over and over again. And now—"

"Listen, we work with facts. I watched the security footage from your hotel. There was nothing there. Your sister took off. She made a choice. She wasn't ripped from her car in the black of night. Look over there." He pointed at Mrs. Albert, who'd gotten out of her car again, weeping into her toddler's chest. "Paul Albert has a family that deserves to know what happened to him."

"So does my sister." Anna pointed at her mother, Gran, and Robbie beyond the police tape.

The sheriff illuminated the dark streak on the asphalt. "It's not her blood on the road," he insisted.

"Maybe not, but it's her bed that's empty at night."

"You keep looking for her. That's your job. I don't know what she was doing in that hotel room or where she went after that, but if I had to bet . . . my money says she's keeping someone else's bed warm now." He paused, lips pulled tight, suggesting he knew how cruel he sounded. His eyes flashed over Chris, whose hands hung in fists, his face like stone. "She'll come back." Sheriff Barnett clicked off his flashlight and went to comfort the woman and her child.

Day 36
7:08 a.m.
58 Hours Gone

A box identical to the one that had appeared on Grace's pillow in the night sat in place of a plate in Anna's spot at the breakfast table. She knew why it was there. Her father thought she'd be safer with it.

"It's already activated and charged," he said.

Anna pushed the cell phone aside and filled the breakfast plates, quickly realizing that there was one too many. No one asked Robbie if he'd accidentally set it or if he'd meant for it to be there. The absence at the table glared. The gap where Grace usually sat was like a missing incisor in a smile.

The family ate in silence. It was the first real meal any of them had consumed since Grace's disappearance. Uncomfortable and sad, none had enough gall to voice the possibility that this was how it might be from here on out.

"It's good, Dorothy," Chris said after a while.

She thanked him with a hum.

Anna couldn't tell if it was good or not. Nothing appealed. The coffee smelled sour. The eggs were rubber between her teeth. Butter on both sides of the toast wouldn't have helped it down her dry throat any easier. She supposed the need for normalcy was what led her mother, who only pushed food from one side of her plate to the other, to make breakfast in the first place. Anna's own quest for normalcy led her back to school that morning. Not because she missed the teasing or the classes themselves, but because she'd gotten word that an all-school assembly was scheduled to encourage anyone with information about Grace's whereabouts to come forth, and she hoped it'd help.

She came face-to-face with Grace upon pulling open the high school door, the words HAVE YOU SEEN ME? printed above her sister's image. Posters hung everywhere: on office windows, vending machines, classroom chalkboards, bulletin boards, and Grace's locker. Anna felt eyes upon her, cold and unpleasant like juicy spitballs through a straw, as she walked down the hall. If her peers felt any pity or concern, they didn't express it. They only stared, harder than ever before. Bowels like liquid, she turned toward the nearest restroom. Andy Wimer and Curt Egeland emerged from the men's room right as she opened the door to the women's.

"Hey, man, that's the girls' room!" Andy said to Anna, looking to Curt for approval. They both brayed.

Anna took a step back. The restroom door closed in her face. She pushed on it once more, and again let it thump against the tip of her nose. If her bullies wanted to be right, she'd let them. What would they say then?

Sidestepping the women's washroom, Anna pushed past the boys and headed straight into unfamiliar terrain. The two were silent with disbelief until the door thudded shut, whereupon Andy said, "Holy shit!" and they both burst into hysterics.

A fluorescent bulb blinked overhead in the dim room that smelled of piss and aerosol deodorant. Anna eyed the urinals on the wall, curious yet close in appearance to the drinking fountains in the hall. She couldn't imagine using one, not without an enclosure. She couldn't imagine being that free.

Black ink doodles on the white tiles around the urinals drew Anna's eye. They depicted stick figures fucking—someone had scribbled Principal Markham's name over the figure getting rammed—and messages that read, *if u read this u r gay, Mike's mom suks!*, LOOK LEFT >>> YOU FAIL, *push harder,* and *School blows* with . . . *so does your mom* inked beneath it. A depiction of male genitalia, compulsory droplets spraying from the tip, took up a solid square foot of space. A sketch of the school with an atomic bomb falling from the sky above it blatantly communicated one student's unlikely wish. Little block letters to the left of the flush on the urinal closest to the corner lured Anna closer. She squinted at the message—FOR A GOOD TIME CALL—and mouthed the seven numbers written beneath it. She read the numbers again and again, recognizing that they were familiar but not realizing she was reading her family's home phone number until she said the numbers out loud.

The blood drained from Anna's face. She felt like she'd been whacked upside the head. The message could easily have been an assault against her, but not this time. She remembered the peculiar phone calls, the grunts and snickers on the other end of the line. This was a stab at Grace.

"Bastards," Anna said, through gritted teeth.

She pulled her boot from her foot and slammed the sole against the tile, desperate to make the numbers go away, to save her little sister from the undeserved punishment that'd been thrust upon her.

The sides of the urinal's elongated rim, speckled with piss and pubic hair, rubbed against Anna's inner thighs. The boot's sole, though, worked like an eraser against the ink.

"Holy shit," Andy, having pushed the bathroom door open, said again. Anna could only imagine what it looked like she was doing from his point of view. He ducked away. The door thumped shut. Seconds of silence followed, during which Andy surely told Curt that Anna not only wore tighty-whities but that she pissed standing up.

Anna successfully rubbed the numbers away and turned from the urinal just as Curt and Andy, like conjoined twins, poked their ugly mugs beyond the bathroom door. They looked like hyenas bearing mocking grins. Anna reached back and hit the urinal's flush. It was either that or throw her boot at them.

"Oh, Anna," Alee Graham said, bounding down the hall when Anna, dripping sweat and seeing red, finally made it to the senior wing. Alee threw her arms around Anna, and Anna tried to push her away, mostly because of the cat piss. Alee, however, held tight, and soon Anna conceded because the embrace felt true. She needed it, too.

What she saw over Alee's shoulder reignited the fire within her. She peeled Alee off like Velcro and stormed down the hall, coming up behind Russ McPhail before his buddies could tip him off. His hands moved fast, trying to tear a strip of packing tape from a roll.

Anna slammed his pencil body against her locker. The metal rattled. "What the—?" he cried, his nose squashed against the vent in the locker door. He reeled around, and Anna shoved him against the locker again. The naked doll he had crammed under his arm fell free, landing with a rubbery smack against the tile. The tape in his spidery hands got all bunched up, sticking to itself.

Snickers created a cyclone of sibilant sound around Anna. A hand landed on her shoulder, which she brusquely shrugged off, assuming it was Alee's. She pushed Russ again, making the back of his head bounce off the locker door.

"Easy, Amazon," he said.

If she had a book in her hand, she would have flattened his face with it.

"Get out of here," a voice said from behind Anna. Female. Not Alee's.

"I didn't even do anything," Russ said, tape all over his fingers.

"You got too close," the voice said.

Anna pivoted, ready to slug whomever the persistent hand belonged to as Russ, tripping on his untied shoelaces, darted down the hall.

"I'm sorry about your sister." It was Megan Bradley, nervously pulling at the flower-shaped clip in her hair. "We all are . . . really."

Anna's fist loosened. She glared, waiting for Megan to run off the same way Russ had.

"I want to help."

"Not everything's about you," Anna said, suspecting Megan had chosen that moment, right before homeroom when the hall was most crowded, so that she could attach herself to the most talked-about occurrence in school.

"I always liked Grace," Megan said.

Anna had no reason to believe that.

"I was thinking a group of us could hand out flyers at the mall. Maybe make T-shirts." Megan shrugged. "The more attention we can bring to Grace the better, right?"

"Do what you want. You always have."

Megan sighed and flicked her hair. She was on the verge of rolling her eyes and casting a glance back at her crew, consisting of girls who wore clothes they bought new despite never having worked a weekend in their lives and boys whose handwriting was all over those bathroom walls. Anna had seen Megan make those movements before. They were movements meant to degrade the other. Movements that said, "Do you see how nice I'm being? Can you believe what a bitch she is?"

Megan caught herself before her conceit took over. "Anna . . . we were such good friends," she said, voice low. "I really am sorry about Grace. I'm sorry about a lot of things. I don't even know why we stopped being friends."

"I embarrassed you."

Megan's powdered cheeks turned from pink to red. Her spangled earlobes did too. "We grew apart. It sounds stupid, I know, but we just stopped knowing each other. I don't know who you are anymore."

Anna almost said she didn't know herself either. But that wasn't true. Not anymore. The past month had changed her, and though she wasn't in full bloom yet, she knew what she was becoming. Rather, she was realizing what she'd always been, what Miss Shelby had seen in her all those years ago, the same thing Gran recognized when she told her the story about the basket and bow. "I have to go," she said, knowing that she'd just be gawked at, humiliated, patronized, or pitied if she attended the assembly, all of which would do nothing for her spirit—either of them. Having been victimized by many people in many ways, she wasn't going to let that define her. She pushed past Megan. The crowd around them parted as if she were diseased.

"Anna . . . Anna!" Megan called. Her speedy footsteps echoed Anna's. "If you need anything—"

Anna hit the brakes. Megan nearly plowed into her.

"I want my crown," Anna whispered, remembering how keen Grace had been for her to claim it. "I won it. It's mine. Get it for me."

"What about Grace?"

Anna tore the nearest missing-person poster off the wall and crumpled it in her hand. She hurried down the steps and burst through the front doors right as the homeroom bell rang.

Day 36
8:37 a.m.
59 Hours Gone

The river led Anna back to the reservation. It was a taxing journey, especially through the wooded and rocky parts along the shore, but she'd already searched the road and she'd have felt idle if she only retraced her steps. The muddy banks of the river didn't offer any clues. The relief of not finding anything balanced out the frustration of not finding anything.

Snagging a stick, Anna poked through the grass, inspecting every break in the brush and each overturned rock. When she looked up, she found herself in front of the Mire trailer, and she supposed she'd subconsciously been heading there all along.

The trailer next door appeared empty. Lula's car wasn't in the drive. It was just as well. Anna assumed Lula wouldn't want to see her, not after the way things went the last time they spoke.

She propped the stick against the Mire trailer's dilapidated steps and went inside. The odor of old things washed over her. Her eyes took in the infested couch, and she thought about the search that'd gone on for Miss Shelby ten years earlier. Anna was too young at the time to remember all the details. She recalled going to the meetings with her father, where Lula's grandpa, Chairman Joseph Broussard, told them that Miss Shelby had gone missing. She remembered how the adults had fruitlessly dragged the river and how she'd watched from the bridge, heartbroken yet morbidly wondering if Miss Shelby's entire body would be as wrinkly as her own fingertips and toes when she stayed in the tub too long. Despite the theory he'd eventually put forth—that the head had eaten her—even Uncle Ray took his canoe out on the water to search for her. He'd eventually buried her body as well. Looking at Miss Shelby's things made Anna think of everything that had been taken from the woman, and that which had been taken from them all. An uplifting spirit. A positive force. A voice.

It dawned on Anna then that she'd played a role in silencing Miss Shelby. In all the times she'd entered the trailer, she'd never entered Miss Shelby's bedroom. It seemed like such a personal space, one which Miss Shelby hadn't prepared for the outside world. But there were books in there. Anna had seen them from the doorway. They were on the dresser and the nightstand, piled up and massively disheveled, indicating that they'd been referenced often.

Venturing down the hall, Anna's body broke through a thin barrier of gossamer when she took her first steps into the room. More cobwebs covered the books on the dresser. Hesitant at first, she slid a fingertip over the book atop the stack on the nightstand. A strip of its dusty cover turned from gray to black. Unadorned by images or words, Anna understood why when she picked the book up and looked inside. It wasn't a published collection of stories or Native history like the volumes in the living room. It was a text written entirely by Miss Shelby. She'd scrawled six words on the title page: *Traditional Tales of the Takoda Tribe.*

Perhaps it was the events from the last few days that had heightened her emotions, but with Miss Shelby's book in hand, Anna began to shake. Flipping through the pages, she read the various titles—"The Origin of the Crayfish," "The Boy and the Rock," "The Thunder

Woman," "The Frog that Couldn't Hop"—and knew she'd found her holy grail. She quivered inside. Miss Shelby hadn't just been passing the Takoda's stories along like so many of the Legend Keepers before her, she'd been documenting them as well.

Anna sank toward the bed, catching herself before her jeans touched the bug-ridden mattress. Badly as she wanted to sit and read, she couldn't. Not yet. She closed the book and pressed it against her chest with one hand while the other reached for an identical book lying open, facedown, next to the bed. A pen rolled over the nightstand's edge when Anna lifted the book and turned the open pages toward herself. The page on the left was full of Miss Shelby's handwriting; the page on the right was blank. An unfinished story, an ending that would be lost forever. Anna wondered how many others had gone to the grave.

She tucked the handwritten books into her bag and left the trailer, reclaiming the stick from the porch steps on her way out. She walked along the roads that led to the far side of the reservation by the pow wow grounds and the fields beyond. It was there that she hoped to keep an accusatory eye on the one who'd yet to own up to what he'd done.

Leg up, the German shepherd mix was spraying a yellow stream onto a desiccated tree when it spotted Anna in the distance. It ran straight for her, putting its paws on her chest. She steered it aside with the stick, her eyes glued to the empty rocking chair on the front porch of the lone house at the end of the street, Fox's red pickup parked out front.

She stopped at the foot of the porch steps and glared up at the damaged screen door, hanging off its hinges. An improbable mess of beer bottles littered the porch planks. Improbable because Anna couldn't imagine anyone drinking that much.

"Fox!" she called, hoping he'd hear her from inside the house and that she sounded steadfast and strong.

Luke Fisher and Sam Peltier had questioned Fox for hours after apprehending him in the hotel, and for hours he'd stuck to his story. The hotel footage showing Missy and Grace leaving the resort, unharmed and alone, had saved him. Not even Lula's account could incriminate him. She'd spoken as highly of Fox to Sam and Luke as she had to Anna, though her version of things had shined a spotlight on Fox bright enough to make him wince. Anna wanted him to know that eyes were still on him. Luke had promised that he wouldn't stop digging. And Anna wasn't afraid to voice her suspicion.

"Come out here, Fox." She waited.

"Fine then. I'm coming up," she said when he didn't appear. Anna climbed the steps slowly, her hand tightening around the stick. She used it to move the screen door aside. Still no sound came from inside the house. The front door, its lock busted from when she'd kicked it in, hung open a crack. Hitting the knob with the stick as if shooting pool, the door swung in upon darkness.

"Fox?" her voice wavered this time. "Are you ready to confess?"

The dog's nails clicked against the porch planks behind her, shepherding her forth. Her hand blindly found a switch on the wall to the right of the door. A single bulb burning beneath a lampshade, a sweat-stained undershirt slung over it, filled the room with yellow light. The place smelled worse than Anna remembered, musty and moldy with a chemical odor that reminded her of the cleaning products she used at the hotel, except the house was far from clean.

Knuckles white around the stick, Anna stumbled over empty boxes and bags, food containers and crumpled cans. The main room and kitchen were empty. The bathroom and bedrooms, too. The dog cocked its head at her when she returned to the living room, then resumed scavenging an oily pizza box for scraps. One of Fox's dumbbells was on the floor by the door. His nametag, too.

"I won't stop searching," Anna said to the dog, wishing it would pass the message on to its master. It growled in return, but it wasn't looking at her or the pizza box anymore. Head low, lips curled, teeth bared, its muzzle was aimed at the corner, where something else seemed to be scavenging. A rumpled brown paper bag, *Southern Discount Market* printed in big orange letters on its side, rustled and twitched. Anna shrank toward the door, heart thumping, eyes locked on the black abyss beyond the bag's tattered opening, certain that something other than a hungry opossum or raccoon that'd wandered in through the broken door would roll out. She didn't wait to see what would emerge. She ran out onto the porch, and as she did, she noticed something she hadn't before. A single streak of dried blood, only about an inch and a half long and a half inch wide at its widest point, marred the light switch plate on the wall near the door. Transferred, it seemed, by someone coming or going.

Day 36
3:29 p.m.
66 Hours Gone

A yellow ribbon tied to one of the porch pillars flapped in the wind.

"Miss Paula put it there," Robbie said, from behind the screen door. Anna startled on her way up the steps. She hadn't realized it was afternoon and that he was already home from school. He took a sip from the plastic cup in his hand. "Miss Paula said yellow's the color for missing children. I didn't ask why."

Anna tossed the stick she'd been clutching over the porch railing and pushed past him into the house. Dorothy was by the phone inside, her talon-like fingers wrapped around the handset, waiting for it to ring. Chris was examining one of the missing-person posters he'd had laminated to protect against wind and rain, while Gran sat sentry by the window.

Anna, feeling empty inside, like the shed shell of a cicada, dropped onto the couch. She told them about the blood she'd seen inside Fox's house, then listened to their heavy breathing until Dorothy—cigarette between her lips and another in her hand—lifted the phone. She called Luke and told him what Anna had found.

274

"He's gonna question Fox again," she said, sounding about as life-less as Anna felt. "If he can find him."

Only the minute hand on the clock moved for a while after that until Chris, who'd been standing like a cement gargoyle, eyes growing fiercer by the second, suddenly sent a slew of posters sliding over the table and onto the floor, making Anna's heart jolt like a jackhammer against her ribs. He marched toward his wife and reached for the phone.

Dorothy ducked to the side while snagging her cigarette from the lid of a jam jar, her replacement for the old green glass ashtray. Chris grabbed the phone and punched in a number. "Luke," he barked. "You find that son of a bitch and get him to talk this instant. I want to know everything he knows, you hear me? We don't have time to sit around and wait." He paused, chest heaving. "You'd better find him. Call me!" He slammed the phone down so hard the plastic base cracked.

"Easy, Chris," Gran said.

"Don't!" Chris thrust a finger at her. A rabid dog would have been less gruff. Wild-eyed, spit leaking from the corner of his mouth, he verged on tearing Gran apart with his words. Catching himself, he collapsed onto the couch next to Anna, head in his hands. "Luke's going to drop in on Fox's parents . . . to see if Fox is there. He said he'll call back." He lifted his head and surveyed the room, much the same way Anna had. "What the hell are we doing here?" he cried. "Our little girl is missing."

"What can we do?" Dorothy said. It was what they'd all been trying to figure out for nearly three full days.

Chris's lips curled, suggesting that something terrible was going to come out. Again, nothing did. He got up and tore the cigarette from Dorothy's lips and flicked it in Robbie's drink. Dorothy scowled, but he hadn't gotten the best of her. She pulled another cigarette from her pack, lit it, and blew smoke in his face.

Chris growled. The bathroom door slammed a second after he stormed out of the living room. Robbie sniffled, staring down at the cigarette butt bobbing in his Coke. Anna, finding some strength, stood and put her arm around his shoulders. He let it remain for a few seconds, then pushed her away.

"You can come with me, Anna." He set his cup aside and readied himself by the door. "Two sets of eyes are better than one."

"Where?"

"I skipped school today to search the fields along the route Grace would have walked from the hotel to home." His voice had dropped to a whisper, presumably so that their mother wouldn't hear. "I didn't find any clues. I wanna search out by the cemetery and pow wow grounds now. Maybe by the Heaven and Hell tree, too. I know Grace probably didn't go out that way, but I don't think anyone's been over there yet. It's worth a shot."

"Why do you need the rifle if you're only looking for clues?"

"Maybe I'll come across the raccoon that chased you home last night. I'll see if I can bag it for you. You wanna come or not?"

"You go," she said, shaking her head. "Take this, too." She pulled the cell phone, identical to the one on Grace's pillow, that Chris had left for her on the table that morning from its box and powered it on. To say she didn't feel the device's magic as pixelated words—WELCOME TO WIRELESS—scrolled across the screen would have been a lie. She put the home phone number on speed dial. Luke Fisher's too.

Robbie gaped at the device. "No way, Anna. I don't need it." He gripped the rifle tight. "The phones are for you and Grace."

"Just take it." She shoved it into his free hand. "Call if you find anything."

Robbie reluctantly wrapped his fingers around the phone. His footsteps pounded down the porch steps, and then silence took charge. Anna looked from Gran to her mother, each somewhere in her own mind.

Chris barreled back into the living room holding a pill bottle in his hand. He looked around, lost, then shook an indiscernible number of pills into his mouth, smashed them between his teeth and said, "Fuck." He scratched the back of his head, popped another pill, cringed at its bitter taste, and then gathered the posters from the table and floor. The faster he tried to wrangle them, the more they slid about. "Put that shit out!" he hollered at Dorothy, now with a cigarette between her lips, one in her hand, and another sending up swirling smoke from the end table next to her. "Anna," Chris said, for no apparent reason. He set the posters by the door, then sealed himself in the bathroom again.

Dorothy reduced the cigarette between her lips to ash, which floated to the floor when she got up to throw away the cup-turned-ashtray Robbie had left behind.

Her back to Gran, Anna picked up the cigarette from the end table and, instead of snuffing it out against the bottom of the jam-jar-lid-turned-ashtray, she extinguished it against the bare flesh of her wrist. Only then did she stop shaking. Suddenly, she could breathe easier. For the moment, her heart no longer hurt. She only felt the burn.

Day 36
6:03 p.m.
69 Hours Gone

The blistered, burnt skin demanded ointment and ice. Anna, staring down at the upturned wrist resting against her thigh, let herself suffer. The fiery sting from the cigarette steered her mind away from the pain that'd plagued her since Grace went missing. If only Robbie, still searching the field, would fire a victorious shot into a rabid raccoon, she might be relieved of some of her fear as well.

Instead of a rifle report in the field, the phone rang again in the living room. Dorothy answered on the second ring. The long pause between her desultory greeting and what she said next seemed to serve as punishment for everything Anna had ever done wrong.

"Nothing?" Dorothy said. Another crumb of hope fell from Anna's diminishing loaf of optimism. Luke Fisher and his force, it seemed, had had just as much luck locating Fox as Robbie had locating the raccoon.

"Luke? It's Chris," Anna's father said, evidently taking the phone. "I want to know what that man Albert was doing on the rez. I want to know what he was doing with my daughter." He paused. "I don't care what those bastards from town say. As far as I'm concerned, the only victims here are Grace and Missy. Have they even confirmed that it was his blood in the road?" He paused again. Then groaned. "We're pretty fucking lost over here." Lost—they were like leaves on the wind, powerless against the breeze and clueless as to where they'd end up.

"He shouldn't have been on our part of the rez in the first place," Chris said. "No one should be allowed beyond the casino. We need a gate to keep people out. I've seen random cars driving around. They go to the casino, then come gawk at us like we're a fucking tourist attraction. Have you seen the disappointment on their faces when they see us in T-shirts and jeans instead of feathers and loin cloths?" Another pause. "You bet I'll take it up with the tribal council." He was silent for a while. "Is that all you can do?" A slow exhale followed the next pause. "Just . . . let me know when you find something."

The telephone's handset clacked against its broken cradle. "Luke's going to register Grace with the National Crime Information Center," Chris said to Dorothy. "He wants to get her face on the local news. I guess it's the best shot we've got."

Anna's eyes shifted from her singed skin to Grace's bed. She got up to straighten the blankets and reposition the cell phone on Grace's pillow, promising to be there when her sister laid eyes on it. It'd be the greatest day of their lives.

Lacking the power to make things right, she poked her burn and pulled the handwritten book Miss Shelby hadn't finished from her bag. She wiped the last of the dust from its cover, intensifying its moldy odor. The binding crackled when Anna opened the book and flipped through its yellow pages. She saw stories about Owl, the star spirit, the earth and the sky, the great gators, the tiny anoles, the knowing chief, the victorious wife, Brother Eagle, the sneaky bobcat, the boy who became strong, the elder canebrake, and the two sisters.

Anna's hand stopped turning pages. Her heart nearly stopped as well. Mouth as dry as the paper clenched between her fingers, she scanned the page, barely able to believe what was before her.

THE TALE OF TWO SISTERS

Long ago there was a village. In the village lived a man with his wife and two daughters. The younger daughter was no longer a child but not yet a woman. Her parents were planning a special dance to honor her passage into adulthood.

In the evening, the man said to his older daughter, "Early in the morning, go strip mulberry bark for a mulberry bark apron, but don't take your sister. She must not go."

Then the older sister said to her younger sister, "I must leave in the morning, but you cannot come with me. You must stay here." This angered the younger sister.

The older sister woke very early and set out before sunrise. She traveled north and crossed the river, walking miles to find the mulberry bark. The younger sister had also woken early and followed her sister's footsteps, despite having been forbidden to go. When she reached the spot where her sister was stripping mulberry bark, she went up to her sister and began stripping bark with her. There was a man there, and he was stripping mulberry bark too.

"I told you not to come," the older sister said.

This angered the younger sister once more, and so she stripped mulberry bark with the man instead of with her older sister. The man took the younger sister's hand and forced it on the tree. At once, she got a splinter in her finger. The younger sister cried out. The older sister pulled the splinter free and wiped the wound with leaves, but the wound continued to bleed.

"When will it stop?" the younger sister asked. "The blood keeps flowing."

Frightened, the two sisters ran back to the village. The older sister said to their father, "She got stuck with a splinter while stripping bark with a man. The blood will not stop."

"She does not listen," their father said.

This angered the younger sister a third time. She stuck the bleeding finger into her mouth. She sucked blood and spat it out. She did this all day. Still, the bleeding would not stop. And still, she was angry.

The sun began to set. The younger sister continued to suck blood from her finger. She spat it out each time until she accidentally swallowed some of the blood. It tasted sweet, which made her happy, so she sucked and swallowed some more. But soon the blood wasn't enough, so she ate her finger. It made her happy. Then she ate her hand. It made her happy too. Then she ate her other hand. Then her arms, her feet, and her legs. Then her entire body, until all that was left was her head.

The younger sister became angry again when her body was gone because there was nothing left to devour. So the younger sister, who was now just a head, rolled through the village at night in search of the man who had hurt her finger. When she found him, she devoured him. Her revenge made her happy.

And since she still wanted more, she continued to roll through the village, snarling and grinding her teeth, devouring every person she could find. When the rolling head could find no one else, it rolled home.

The older sister saw the head coming and so she ran. The head devoured its mother and its father. The older sister then dug a hole in the ground. When the head chased her, she jumped over the hole. The head could not jump. It rolled into the hole and got stuck. Scared, the older sister picked up the head and said, "Listen like a field mouse when the owl shrieks and you will see the sun in the morning." She then shook the head until it spat out her mother and her father and everyone else it had devoured. The older sister kept shaking, and soon the head spat out the younger sister's body, legs, feet, arms, hands, and fingers.

Whole once more, the younger sister realized her mistake. She promised never to disobey again. And then it was done.

Day 36
6:08 p.m.
69 Hours Gone

There it was.

That which Anna had been searching for, the very thing that had driven her into Miss Shelby's trailer after Amber and Erica went missing. A way to stop the rolling head.

Close to crying, Anna could barely read the script before her. She wiped the corners of her eyes, then read the story again, slower this time to assure herself that the words were really on the mildew-streaked paper. They relieved her, but they confused her as well. Having always believed that the rolling head belonged to the old chief, she had to wonder now if Uncle Ray's story was wrong.

Leaping from the bed, her feet crash-landed like hammers against the floor. She hopped to the bedroom door on the verge of calling out to Gran, to question her about what she'd just read, wondering, perhaps, if it was another old story Gran had heard long ago.

A gunshot sounded in the field.

"Robbie!" Anna screamed. Book in hand, she ran through the house and onto the porch, where she squinted against the setting sun in search of his frame in the field. "Robbie!" The trees hid him from view. She scurried down the driveway and out to the road. "Robbie, come home!"

He came trotting through the brush a minute later, his rifle in one hand, the cell phone Anna had forced him to take when he set off on his search in the other. Despite recognizing his gait, she hardly recognized the man he was becoming. He seemed to grow taller every day, leaner in the waist and wider in the chest.

"Did you shoot it?"

Robbie shook his head, heavy with disappointment. "I had it in my sights, I was just too far away." He shrugged. "But the shot scared it off. It's gone, Anna. Don't worry about it coming back tonight."

"Robbie . . ." Embarrassment crept in, but Anna—relieved that he hadn't hit his mark—didn't let it stop her. "Was it really a raccoon?"

Robbie's face frazzled, then settled with realization. "Seriously, Anna? Why are you still so scared of the head?"

"Why are you still scared of spiders?" she asked in return, remembering how he'd startled when one got on him.

"Spiders are real," he said. "The rolling head isn't. Uncle Ray made it up to scare you. . . . You've been imagining it all these years, turning raccoons into something you fear."

For a split second, Anna wondered if she'd let the fear live too long inside her head. Shouldn't she have outgrown it by now? Her chin wagged back and forth. "You're rationalizing," she said, knowing he was only recycling the excuse she'd used so many times over the years to keep her siblings from making fun of her whenever she came bursting through the door with distress stamped across her face. "I can rationalize your fear too. You're so much bigger than the spiders. You know you could squash them with hardly any effort, and yet you're still scared."

"Spiders are *real*," he said again, his tone final. If he wanted to laugh, he kindly kept it inside. "I'll bag that raccoon next time. You'll see." He placed a hand on her back and tried to lead her into the house. "Come on. You look tired."

"No." She settled on the porch steps. "I need to think."

"I'm gonna . . ." Robbie pointed in the direction of the pow wow grounds. "Haven't made it out there yet."

Anna waved him off. Her mind raced, connecting dots between Uncle Ray's story, Miss Shelby's version of it, and real life. Robbie could be right, she thought. Maybe the chief's head had never been out there. Maybe her imagination, stoked by childhood fear, had let her be frightened and fooled countless times by raccoons and armadillos foraging for food in the night.

Until now.

She believed Miss Shelby's stories were reflections of truth, echoes of life. And, after reading "The Tale of Two Sisters," she couldn't deny the parallels between the younger sister in the story and Grace: both had been warned, both had taken chances, both—it seemed—had suffered at the hands of men. Now Anna found herself wondering if her own sister could have morphed into the rolling head, spooling, seething, seeking revenge. Maybe it was Grace who'd gotten Paul Albert. Maybe Claude LeBlanc was next.

It came down to faith. How much stock could Anna put into a tale without feeling foolish? She had trusted Miss Shelby when it came to Grasshopper and Frog. And hadn't Miss Shelby been right about Grasshopper's carefree nature and Frog's proclivity to change? Why couldn't she be right about the two sisters too? The story's ending gave Anna hope; it filled her with guilt as well. The younger sister hadn't been happy with her older sister. Nor had Grace been happy with Anna.

"I'm sorry, Grace," Anna said to the earth, the wind, the sky, realizing that though silence had often been her best defense—even if it had been forced upon her—it hurt her too, because it robbed her of her self. "I stayed quiet too long."

Anna stood, facing the sinking sun in the sky. She could think of only one way to find out if "The Tale of Two Sisters" was really unfolding before her. She had to try. Wind howling through the field to the left of the house, she rounded the porch on her way to the yard, Miss Shelby's book tucked in the back pocket of her father's old jeans. The strong gusts blew long blades of grass and thin tree branches toward her, each reaching for her limbs. Anna remembered how she and Grace used to play tag in the yard. The long grass would get in on the fun. A jokester, it'd ensnare their ankles and pull them to the ground, then kindly apologize by catching them when they fell.

Anna also remembered how Grace had snagged her brand-new pair of purple corduroy pants on one of the trees. Grace had cried upon seeing the tear, both because she'd begged for those pants and because she was afraid Dorothy would get mad. Using brown thread because they didn't have purple, Anna had stepped in to save the cords, stitching the tear the best she could, whereupon she and Grace acted like Dorothy would never know. That was back when they used to keep secrets together, before Grace told her secrets to someone else.

Anna glanced at the drying squirrel pelts, each like a little gray slipper with a tail, as she entered the shed and reached for the round-point shovel her father used for spreading gravel in the drive. It had the heft of a heavy stone and the shaft of a baseball bat. She heaved it over her shoulder and carried it to the spot in the road where Paul Albert's car had been parked. The same spot where the rolling head had appeared. A faint trace of blood remained on the road. Anna followed it to where it ended, right by the brush of the field that had already been searched by Robbie, the tribal police, and the officers from town.

"Grace!" Anna hollered. The wind carried her voice out to the trees and back. She didn't go far into the field, just deep enough to ensure that the trees obscured the road behind her.

She took Miss Shelby's book from her pocket and read the part of the story about the hole in the ground. Certain of what she needed to do, she set the open book on a fallen log and wrapped her hands around the shovel's thick shaft. The pointed tip bit into the dirt; Anna's weight on the shovel's step drove it deeper into the earth.

She dug until the hole gaped beneath her, hungry for the head. Satisfied, she propped the shovel against a tree and put the book back into her pocket. The wind had died down, and the sun had vanished behind the trees. A faint orange glow ushered in the evening. It was the start to the kind of night they longed for on the rez: cool and quiet, except for the chirp of lazy crickets in the grass. Anna padded through the brush. A frog croaked the instant she reached the road. She looked for it on the asphalt but didn't see it there. Nervousness mixed with doubt within her, competing with hopefulness that propelled her to the middle of the road. She was eager and scared, betting on a belief most anyone would dismiss. They might have dismissed her as well, dirty, disheveled, and aimless in appearance.

She planted herself precisely where Paul Albert's Continental had been. Dusk took hold. The sky turned purple and gray, striped with white and blue. Anna eyed the faded streak of blood, almost as black as the blacktop. She stared in the direction of the hole she'd dug and visualized what she'd have to do: run until the road was invisible behind her, then leap.

Anna called to Grace. Her ears searched for the sounds the mud-and-moss-covered head would make. The sky grew darker. Anna's heart grew heavier. What would it be like when Grace returned? Would the family sink back into its old ways? Would they have a new-found appreciation for one another? Would they be capable of starting again?

The moon took its place in the sky, bathing Anna in ethereal light. She heard another croak, and this time she spotted the frog. A small lump with glistening eyes on the asphalt. Anna knelt near it and flapped her hand to shoo it out of harm's way. It acted unafraid, but Anna knew it was only trying to fool her. Body flattened, it played dead, unable to understand that Anna was trying to keep it from aligning itself with death.

"Go on." She nudged it. It clung to the ground. Stubborn. Like Grace. "You'll get squashed," she said. It wasn't just Grace and Frog who were stubborn. She was stubborn too. And stupid. She'd felt Miss Shelby's book rub against her leg when she'd bent to nudge the frog. Ink and moldy paper was all it was. How could she believe the words represented real life? A rolling head. A hole that would help make things right. A frog that wouldn't even change its mind when she tried to save its life.

The childish faith that had pumped the old tales full of power they couldn't possibly possess drained from Anna. She collapsed onto the road, chest heaving. Feeling as if she were falling, she feared she'd lost hold of the only parachute she had. All her hope was gone.

Anna lay in the road until her breath came back. The frog remained as well. She stood and bent to scoop it up. Her fingers scraped the ground, but the soft scuff of flesh she heard wasn't produced by her hand. She whipped around. There, a few dozen feet behind her, was what she sought and feared. Its small round form lolled in the moonlight, rocking from side to side in the middle of the road.

"Grace?" Anna whispered.

The form spun in a circle. Suddenly, Anna didn't know if she was crazy, stupid, or both. Her thoughts went straight to the hole. All she needed was to be chased. She stomped a foot to ensure she had the head's attention, then braced herself, ready to run. The head continued to waver, inching close to the edge of the road.

"Hey!" She stomped again. And then she realized her mistake. The head had only ever approached when she wasn't looking right at it. She turned around. Anticipation. Vulnerability. Body tingling, she waited. The head made no sound. A torturous minute ticked by. Two. Anna squinted over her shoulder. The form continued to loll. Then it began to roll.

Away from Anna.

"Shit!" Anna tripped over her feet, taking a stumbling start after the head. "Please!" she screamed.

The head moved faster than Anna, quickly increasing the distance between them as it weaved through the brush bordering the road. Anna's hammering heart threatened to detonate each time it dipped out of sight.

The head rolled past the cross street that led to the Horn house, proceeding along the river, where an osprey snatched a desperately flapping fish from the water. The pow wow grounds loomed ahead. The tribal cemetery and empty fields lay beyond that.

The evening dimmed as swirling clouds passed in front of the moon. Anna could barely see the head rolling before her. She could barely keep up. If it gained another ten feet of ground, it could easily evade her for good. Anna grunted and gasped, nearly gagging on the scent of death wafting from the head. Scant sleep and poor nutrition over the last few days had left her foggy and with little energy to spare.

She felt her frailty, yet the thought of quitting to catch her breath or to rid herself of the searing stitch in her side didn't tempt her one bit. She plowed ahead, digging deep. Even when her legs seemed like they might snap from her body, she kept pushing. Only death could stop her from following the head.

It rolled into the pow wow grounds and spun straight through the center of the dance circle. Instead of rolling toward the cemetery, as Anna thought it might, it rolled to the right, toward the vast and empty fields.

Robbie, Anna thought. Her knotted stomach might as well have been a garbage bag full of rotting meat, heavy and sick. The head rolled into the tall grass of the closest field beyond the pow wow grounds. She prayed her brother wouldn't shoot.

Throwing herself into the field, she thrashed through the wall of leaves. Branches and twigs scratched her face. Thorns tore her flesh. Like bloody tears, crimson beads streamed down her cheeks, converging at her chin.

"Grace!" she screamed. "Robbie!"

She couldn't see the head anymore. For all she knew, it could have stopped rolling. It could have been waiting for her to stumble straight into its open jaws. Arms flailing and eyes clenched against the thorns, Anna barreled through the vegetation ahead, each step more difficult than the last. The tree branches seemed to sprout bony fingers that grabbed at Anna, pulling and tearing her clothes.

Disregarding logical thought—telling her to stop, to go home and get rest that might restore her apprehensive and exhausted mind— Anna continued to push through the brush and past the trees. No longer was she struggling to keep up with the head, now she was fighting to withstand the pain of the relentless barbs and hostile branches probing every inch of her body. They hurt so much more than the lit cigarette she'd held to her wrist, making her feel better somehow.

She screeched when something she couldn't see—something that felt like teeth taking hold—ruthlessly wrenched her right ear. She clamped a hand to the side of her head, convinced the ear had been ripped away. It was still there, though, wet beneath her hand, leaking down her face. Her feet propelled her past the final wall of trees. She fell from their brutal grasp, landing in a vast and round clearing, long since ravaged by fire.

The remains of the Heaven and Hell tree, blitzed by lightning, stood before her. Its burnt trunk, wielding a few blackened, bruised branches, jutted up from the ground in the center of the clearing, crafting the illusion of a coal-black hand reaching for the sky. The ash of burnt grass and charred chunks of tree bark created a carpet all around. It crunched underfoot as Anna moved forward. Dense bushes bordered the burnt patch of land. Anna thought she was alone until she caught a split-second glimpse of the head rolling out of sight on the opposite side of the clearing.

She approached the spot where she'd seen the head vanish. The brush along the ground stopped moving. The branches above it started to shake. And then there was noise. Moaning. It sounded like—

"Robbie!" Anna shrieked.

He leapt through the trees, face branded by terror, and tumbled into the clearing. The siblings simultaneously screamed. Robbie rolled across the ash, then sprang up and grabbed Anna. His arms wrapped around her and pulled her to his chest. She could feel his pounding heart through his skin and bones.

"Don't go in there," he said, voice trembling.

"Grace!" Pulling away from her little brother, Anna pointed to the trees beyond the clearing.

Robbie clung to Anna's arm. Painfully tight. "Don't," he said, shaking all over, eyes widening at the sight of blood smeared across Anna's face. His hand was as cold as if he'd been palming a fistful of ice, and the color had drained from his flesh. The low light made it look like he'd been rubbed with ash.

"I'm g-g-gonna get Dad," he stammered.

Anna shook his hand free from her elbow. He whimpered when she moved toward the trees, and then his sprinting footsteps hammered the ground toward home, leaving Anna to pursue the head.

Passing through the trees was like walking off a plank, like entering a realm she'd never imagined. The earthy odor of ash and dirt mixed with that of something equally as earthy yet far more unsettling. Something that smelled like the head, only stronger. Anna's stomach turned. Her eyes moved slowly over the ground at her feet to the brush all around. Even in the low light, she could see streaks of red, like fire, staining the bushes and tall grass. Her stomach sank in response to the unshakable feeling that swept over her, a feeling that indicated something bad was about to happen.

Robbie hollered for Dad in the distance. His voice diminished the farther he got. Soon Anna wouldn't be able to hear him. She'd be all alone again. Wavering between venturing deeper into the brush or stepping back out into the clearing, she closed her eyes and let the moment carry her forth. There wasn't much of a choice. No matter how ill she felt, she had to take those steps deeper into the field. And she had to open her eyes.

It took a moment for Anna's vision to readjust to the moonlight. It took a little longer for her to register what she was seeing after it did. The rolling head was on the ground a few feet in front of her. Quiet eating sounds—chewing, slurping, gnawing—floated from its sallow lips and serrated teeth. A colorless eye spooled in its socket until it was aimed at Anna, the other remained fixed on the meal ahead. Anna stepped back, one hand holding her belly, the other shielding her eyes. Even with her vision obscured, she could still see the abysmal sight in her mind. It was one that would live inside her for the rest of her life.

A girl was on the ground. She had long black hair and flesh that would have been the same shade as Anna's if it hadn't been affected by death. The rolling head had hair too. Lying on her back, the girl's torso and legs were wrapped—tangled—in a bloody blanket. Her left arm was angled around her head, while her right hand and wrist were sandwiched between the earth and her back.

Anna's insides constricted. She strained not to vomit. Lurching backward, her rear met the forbidding bark of a nearby tree. She willed her hand away from her eyes. All was still. The head was gone, having left behind the fleshless fingertips of the body it'd been gnawing on.

Still hearing gnashing sounds all around and wondering if she'd been spared, Anna scanned the darkness, but rather than finding the head, her eyes landed on the body once more. Anna couldn't tell if it was Missy or Grace rotting in the dirt. The two had looked so much alike.

Anna inched forward as if on a tightwire with a fear of heights. She didn't want to erase Sawyer Picote's hope any more than she wanted to erase her own, but she had to look. The girl's head was cocked to the right, her flesh already becoming one with the earth. Ropes of hair, clotted with blood, obscured the left side of her face. Squatting, Anna whined and reached to sweep the hair aside.

Mouth agape and bone exposed at the sharpest points of her cheek and chin, the girl was a far cry from her image on the missing-person poster. Still, Anna recognized her well enough. Missy Picote.

Anna pulled her hand away slowly. She retreated from the body even slower than that. Disturbed by the carnage, it didn't feel right to leave Missy alone. Stepping backward in the direction of the clearing, her left foot caught upon a piece of cloth. She shook it free and peered down at the material. Brownish-red stains nearly covered it completely. Only a couple patches along the hem displayed the fabric's true color: Vanda green.

Glowing a few inches from the coat, Anna spotted the cell phone Robbie had dropped. She bent to pick it up, to call Luke, then stopped when she noticed a glint a few feet away. She staggered to it, squinting. The object appeared small until she realized that much of it had sunk into the bloodied grass. It was Robbie's rifle, tossed upon receiving the fright of his young life.

"Anna!" Her spine straightened. The shell of a voice sounded faint and far off. "Anna, do you hear me?" It was her father. Her feet moved toward the clearing as Gran's words about the basket and the bow echoed in her head. Her eyes bounced between the cell phone and the rifle. She bent and reached just before stepping through the blood-stained brush.

Day 36
7:29 p.m.
70 Hours Gone

Chris called to her again, still distant but drawing closer. Standing in the clearing now, Anna looked down at the rifle in her hands. She hoisted it to her shoulder and pointed it toward the sky. Mimicking the movements her baby brother always made, she set her stance, her line of sight, and her grip, prepping to fire a notifying shot. Finger on the trigger, she smelled smoke. And then she was on the ground, gasping, her breath knocked out of her.

"Why couldn't you just *stop*?" Fox seethed, appearing through the trees.

Anna had landed back among the bloody brush, the chambermaid coat, and Missy's body. Her hands like frantic crabs, they skittered over the ground around her, searching for the rifle that'd flown free when Fox sent her sailing.

"I didn't want to do this, Anna!"

The weight of his body fell on top of her. The smoke intensified, but Anna couldn't smell it, couldn't inhale. She could only taste it on her tongue and see it swirling over Fox's shoulders, turning the sky into an impenetrable black canvas.

The muscle that blanketed Anna's body left little hope that she would find her feet again. "Fox," she hiccuped, the last bit of breath escaping her. His left hand shot to her mouth, clamping down hard, freeing her right arm from the side of her body where it'd been pinned.

Her arm snaked out, hand pulling at grass and weeds, seeking leverage that might help her slip free. Her fingertips dug into the ground, curling around roots. She pulled. Her body shifted. Fox slid to her left side, crushing her arm, his left hand still braced over her lips.

The pressure of his body no longer on her chest, she drew air through her nose. His acrid breath, his stale sweat, and the smoke, the latter of which stung her eyes and throat, pervaded her. Her body reacted, battling to cough.

"I didn't want this," Fox grunted.

Anna inhaled another smoky breath through her nostrils just before he took to his knees—straddling her—and moved his right hand to her nose. He squeezed it shut, pressing his weight onto her face, driving her head down into the dirt.

Knowing she only had seconds until blackness took over forever, Anna moved her unencumbered hands all around, from her thighs to straight out at her sides, to the ground beyond her head. Her fingers never found the rifle, but they did get tangled in something that was soft in some spots and stiff in others.

She brought the chambermaid coat down on the back of Fox's neck and quickly crossed her hands over each other to grab hold of the coat's opposing ends. She pulled tight, the fabric cutting into his windpipe.

"Anna," he mouthed, and air came spilling out of him.

Neither was able to say anything more after that. It was a battle of wills. A battle of time. A battle to see who'd silence the other.

Fading—arms burning, strength waning—noise like rushing water invaded Anna's ears. She was slipping, inching ever closer to eternal darkness.

Fox's left hand tightened around Anna's mouth. His right hand, still squeezing, twisted her nose, threatening to tear it off. A battered bird dying in the dirt, Anna put all she had left into pulling the coat tight around his neck, obstructing the arteries, depriving his brain. Her eyes drifted shut, poised to never see light again. She didn't realize her lungs were filling until she felt the weight of Fox's bulk slam against her body once more. He'd collapsed, his hands falling free.

Swallowing greedy breaths, Anna rolled his body off her and pulled the chambermaid coat from his neck. She checked to see if he was breathing and was relieved to find that he was. She hadn't wanted him dead. Out cold suited her fine.

Slowly, Anna stood and surveyed her surroundings. Massive flames thrashed in the brush beyond Missy's body. Smoke swirled in her direction.

"Anna!" Her father called once more, ever closer.

She found the rifle half in and half out of the brush. She hoisted it and entered the clearing again. A car made noise along the nearest road. Brakes squealed. Doors slammed. A rush of voices—some frantic, one held forcibly steady—flooded the air.

Raising the rifle, Anna fired a shot. The voices picked up. Someone hollered. Flashes of bright light pierced through the nearby branches, creating skeletal shadows that fell at her feet.

The beams of multiple flashlights focused on Anna. She squinted, unable to see who stood before her.

"Anna?" Chris said, lowering his light. He appeared not to recognize her. Dorothy, too, wore an unfamiliar expression. Both eyed the rifle in her hands before really eyeing her. Robbie glimpsed it as well. He didn't ask for it back.

"The cell phone's on the ground," Anna said, her voice left hoarse from Fox's grip and the smoke. "Someone should call Chief Fisher."

Luke arrived in minutes flat, wearing an enlightened look upon seeing Anna with the rifle, which she used to point toward the crime scene and Fox, now writhing on the ground, rubbing his throat and making nonsensical sounds. Onlookers arrived as well, all of them whispering Missy's name.

"What about Sawyer?" Anna asked. She didn't see him among the gapers.

Luke tilted his head and looked at Chris. Chris shrugged in return.

"I'll tell him," Anna said.

"No," Luke reluctantly insisted. "I should be the one."

"Let her," Chris countered, staring at Anna with awe. "She'll know how to say it better than any of us."

Dorothy's hand caressed the side of Anna's bloody face as she walked by. Anna wanted to get out of there before they took Missy away, and before anyone started speculating about Grace. Cars passed her on the road, all of them headed toward the pow wow grounds and the fields beyond. Some of them honked. Some of them slowed. The passengers gaped through the glass at the girl with the rifle in her hands.

Day 36
8:43 p.m.
71 Hours Gone

Anna wiped her face and walked straight from the field to Sawyer Picote's house. A buttery glow leaked through the blinds of the front window. Anna didn't like what she was about to do, but there was a certain honor in doing it, one she respected the same way her father respected the process of preparing the dead for their journey from this realm to the next.

Anna rapped on the door. No response came. She rapped again.

"Round back," a muffled voice said.

Anna rounded the small house. Sawyer was sitting in an old lawn chair on the cracked pad of concrete he called his patio. He held a bottle of beer in his hand, his face pitched toward the sky. Anna propped the rifle against the house.

"Anna Horn?" Sawyer said, without looking at her. "Is that you?"

She righted a lawn chair that had collapsed against the concrete and sat next to him. His face looked tarnished up close, as if dirt and dust had stuck to the tears he'd cried.

"Phone's been singing for nearly forty-five minutes now," he said. It

299

was true. Anna could hear the endless ringing coming from inside the house. Sawyer sighed. "What do they want to tell me?"

Anna leaned her head back so that she and Sawyer were both eyeing the sky. Clouds that had blown in front of the moon were on their way out, baring heavenly jewels. Anna dropped her eyes before any of them could wink at her.

"When one of our own no longer lives, she goes with the sky spirit to watch over us at night." It wasn't just Anna's voice that hurt when she spoke those words, her heart hurt too.

Sawyer's breath rushed out of him like air from a burst balloon. He was still for a while, then began to breathe again.

"Which one shines brightest at you?" Anna asked.

Sawyer used his bottle to point. A small wave of beer splashed over the lip and landed on his lap.

"She'll always be there," Anna said.

Sawyer set the bottle down. He wiped his eyes, then reached across and took Anna's hand. She pulled him to her and wrapped him in her arms, comforting him like a mother, like a father.

Gran, sitting by the window looking out on the porch, glimpsed the rifle over Anna's shoulder. Anna was almost to the door when a pair of headlights washed over her from behind.

"Anna!" She heard the voice before she turned to see who was at the wheel. "You have to come with me."

It was Sam, frantic and frazzled, half his upper body out the driver's-side window of his tribal police car. Something slipped away at the sight of him: hope, spirit, faith—perhaps a combination of all three. Anna suspected what was coming, and so she reminded herself of what she'd just told Sawyer.

"Fox says he'll talk," Sam said, taking her by surprise. "But only if he can talk to you first."

Anna leapt from the porch and hopped in on the passenger side. She and Gran peered into each other's eyes until the darkness grew too thick between them as Sam backed down the drive.

"Did he kill her?" Anna asked.

"Couldn't get anything out of him," Sam said. "But, Anna . . . they found a second victim farther in the field."

Anna nearly left her body. Her vision blurred. Sam sounded like he was talking under water.

"It's Paul Albert. His wallet was on his body. Luke identified him with his driver's license."

Anna had Sam repeat everything he'd said. Only then was she able to breathe again.

"Luke found something folded up in Albert's pocket. We're not too sure what to think of it yet."

"What?" Anna asked.

"Luke probably wouldn't want me to say, so you're gonna have to keep it between you and me for now. . . . Albert had one of the missing-person posters on him. He knew we were looking for him."

"And the girls," Anna said.

"Real mystery we've got here," Sam muttered. "Why would a wanted man who knew we were looking for him return to the rez? And how'd he end up dead?"

"Is Luke still searching the field?" Anna asked, fearing what else he might find.

"We're not going to stop." Sam parked in front of the station. "You don't mind leaving that here?" he said, looking down at the rifle aimed up between Anna's knees. She peeled her fingers off the metal and shoved it aside, eager to get inside.

The station was small. Three desks filled the space just beyond the door, each piled high with messy stacks of paper and ruffled file folders. Sam led Anna past the desks to a door marked LOUNGE.

"We've got him in here," Sam said. He threw the door open, exposing another small space containing a refrigerator, a water cooler, and a microwave on the counter. The obstinate odors of microwavable soup, popcorn, and TV dinners wafted from inside. Fox, under the watchful eye of Dakota Deshautelle, a rookie on the job, was sitting in a plastic chair at a round table in the center of the room. A foam cup sat in front of him. Handcuffed hands held an ice pack to his neck.

His penetrating eyes found Anna's, and then he was on his feet, approaching her.

"Hold up," Sam said. He threw himself in front of Anna, who didn't waver. Fox was still brawnier than the average man—the small size of the room made him seem even larger—but he wasn't nearly as intimidating as he'd been the night Grace went missing. Anna remembered how she'd thought his arms would burst if his biceps got any bigger. Though powerfully built, he didn't look as swollen as before. She couldn't help but think that he'd melted. Face thinner, shoulders rounded and slumped, he looked a little lost, drunk, and almost as tired as Anna.

Sam escorted Fox back to his seat. "Don't get up again," he said. "Don't try to touch her." He waved Anna over and pointed to the chair across the table. Anna sat. Silence ensued. Their gazes fixed upon each other.

"Get on with it," Sam said to Fox.

"Only Anna," Fox rasped, voice hoarse.

Doubt spread across Sam's face. His hand settled on the pair of cuffs around Fox's wrists to ensure they were tight.

"We'll be all right without them," Anna said.

Sam's eyes flashed at her, evaluating the persistent handprint around her mouth and the broken blood vessels in her nose.

"Really," Anna said.

Sam reluctantly removed the cuffs. He took a step back, then another. "We'll be right outside. Don't try anything," he said to Fox. He followed Officer Deshautelle out of the lounge and closed the door behind him. The shadows of his feet lingered within the crack beneath the door.

Fox lowered the ice pack, revealing a purple fabric burn on his neck. He grabbed the foam cup and turned it, his long fingernails leaving little curved cavities in its surface. His lips were dry and cracked. Anna could smell his greasy hair and boozed-up breath across the table. He took a drink.

"Did you kill Missy?" Anna asked.

Fox lowered the cup. He gurgled at her. Literally gurgled. "You're bleeding," he said, slurring his words.

"Not from you." She wiped the side of her face against her shoulder. "Why'd you kill her?"

Noticeably intoxicated, he rubbed his red eyes and licked his split lips. His body began to tilt. "I didn't," he said, catching himself before he tumbled to the floor.

Anna glared at him, doubtful. "Grace?" she said.

"I told you. I don't know where she is." His right hand picked at his collar, pulling it away from the burn. "I know everyone thinks I do, but I don't."

"Then why'd you want to talk to me?" she said through her teeth.

He squeezed the foam cup too hard with his left hand. Water surged over the brim and through a hole made by his thumb. He flicked his hand, sending droplets of water and white bits across the table. "I used you, Anna. That means I owe you. You deserve the truth."

"Only now that you've been caught."

He shrugged. "You deserved it before this. I just didn't have the balls to sacrifice myself."

"Well, what are you waiting for?" She flicked one of the foam bits back at him. "Let's hear it."

Fox took a deep breath. His body quivered upon releasing it. It took a few attempts for him to start speaking again. His mouth had gone dry, and he had to work some spit up from deep in his throat. "It was all a mistake," he said.

Anna, sensing he was trying to shirk the blame, mulled the word over. A mistake. An error. A slipup. "Some fucking mistake," she said.

"I'm an idiot. I'm stupid. I know."

Anna wasn't interested in hearing him beat himself up for pity. Missy was dead and Grace was still out there. They mattered. He didn't. "You lied about them being at the hotel. Maybe my sister would be home right now if you hadn't. And if you really didn't kill Missy, maybe she'd be alive."

"I never thought it would lead to this. She shouldn't be—"

"But she is. Why'd you want to talk to me?"

"I don't even know where to start."

"Missy left the hotel on her own. We all saw her in the footage. How'd she end up in the field?"

More than a minute passed with Fox's eyes going this way and that, getting wetter by the second.

"Just say it," Anna said.

"Once it's out . . ." His shoulders heaved a hopeless shrug.

"Fox. You're sunk either way." She recognized his fear. It was the terror of knowing there was no going back. No second chance. It was what she feared for herself and Grace.

He dragged a finger through the spilled water on the table. He fiddled and twitched. "I'll tell you how Missy ended up in the field. But I have to tell you everything . . . from the start. . . . Last spring . . ." He sucked in air and blew out a hideous breath. "That's when it began. I was having a drink after work like I always do. At the Ice Bar. Minding my own fucking business, you know? Things were looking up for me." He almost laughed. "I finally had a job and a place of my own . . . a sense of responsibility." He continued to spread the water across the table, perhaps fearing he'd see a reflection of himself if he let the water stand. "I guess it was only a matter of time before I fucked it all up. If I'd gone home that night instead of going to the bar, maybe you wouldn't be here right now." He raised the hem of his shirt and wiped the water away. "It was a chance encounter, you know? A freak fucking thing . . . wrong place, wrong time. But I was at the bar and this guy came in and sat down and—" He took another deep breath. "I guess he was looking for someone like me."

"You're talking about Paul Albert?" Anna asked.

Fox's face puzzled. "Who?"

"Paul Albert. The fat man from the hotel. The one who was in suite eight-oh-eight with Missy and Grace. The one whose car was in the road last night."

"I never . . ." Fox said, shaking his dizzy head. "I never knew his real name."

"You worked with him and you never—"

"I didn't work with him. Not really. It was another guy. Claude LeBlanc. I think you saw him the night . . ." He didn't finish his thought, but Anna knew who he was referring to—the lanky man she'd seen step through the emergency stairwell door just before Fox wrangled her to the elevator the night Grace went missing.

"It was nothing at first," Fox said. Countless questions about Paul Albert swirled in Anna's head; still, she let Fox go on about Claude LeBlanc because she had countless questions about him as well. "We were just bullshitting at the bar," Fox said. "He talked about his wife and his kids and about how fucking miserable he was. He told me never to do that to myself, and I said I wouldn't because marriage is basically prison and who wants that?

"He asked about my tattoos and my job and life on the rez. We shot the shit. Did some shots. He asked about the women around here. He said I looked like the type who could get whatever I wanted."

For a split second, Anna would have sworn that Fox was proud.

"I might have bragged a little, but it wasn't like I—"

"Had you seen him before?" Anna cut in.

"No."

"Do you think he'd seen you?"

Fox shrugged. "Maybe." He drained the dregs from the bottom of the broken cup. Water clung to his upper lip. "Next thing I knew, he was talking about the women he got himself. He said he met them in the casino, then took them up to the hotel. He always had money. He said he was a lawyer or some shit, but who knows if that's true? I don't think so. Why would a lawyer . . ." He trailed off, blinking, his eyes begging to stay closed.

Anna nudged him with her foot.

"I don't remember if he asked about the suites or if I brought them up, but I know he joked about using them by the hour. That's . . ." He lubricated his throat. "That's when I said I could make that happen."

"He played you," Anna said.

"Huh?"

She shook her head, not wanting to help Fox shirk the blame. He may have been young, dumb, and easy to manipulate, but that didn't free him of his faults. "You made a deal?" she asked.

"We agreed that he'd pay me, and then I'd sneak him and whatever woman he was with up to one of the suites for a couple hours. It seemed like a good deal for us both. He wouldn't have to risk reserving a room whenever he wanted to fool around. He was afraid his wife would find out, and I—"

"His name was in the log at reception," Anna said.

"Fake name. I put it there." Again, pride leaked through.

"You liked it, didn't you?" Anna said. "Having a secret. It made you feel powerful. Like you're someone. Like your uncle."

Fox didn't deny it. All he said was, "Claude gave me money, too."

Anna remembered his massive TV, his gleaming watch, the drugs on his coffee table, his look-at-me truck. Status symbols. Power.

"I've never met someone so fake."

His eyes watered. "I guess I'll never get to be great." He looked off into the corner, hopeless. After a while, he shook his head and said, "Claude and I worked together through the spring. Maybe twice a month. It was going good. And then . . . The deal didn't fall apart. It just, sorta unraveled. It turned into something else. Something it wasn't supposed to be. I guess it was around July. Claude—"

"Use his real name," Anna said.

"Fuck if I know his real name. Claude started asking about the women on the rez again. He said they were enigmatic and exotic or some shit like that. He wasn't interested in the women from town . . . he said they had no appeal, no mystery. I just thought that was because he could get them on his own, but then he said he didn't want to do the shopping anymore either. That's what he called it. He wanted me to shop for him."

"Shopping?"

"Getting the women. Somehow that became my job."

"Not somehow," Anna said.

Fox blew out another fetid breath. "Fuck, Anna. I agreed to do it."

"For money. For power." She rubbed it in.

Fox hung his head. "He gave me the cash up front. I paid the women and handled the suite. All he had to do was show up. He liked it that way. The anonymity. He wanted to be invisible. It was his idea to start using the emergency stairwell instead of the elevator. He didn't even want to know the women's names."

"You used your own people."

"Fuck you, Anna. Everyone got something out of it. No one was forced."

"Were the women sober?" she asked, thinking about the increasing number of tribal members who always looked hungry, who walked around with bloodshot eyes, whose cheekbones could cut glass. They were the ones who sank instead of rising with the help of the casino. They were people like Fox himself. The only difference between them and him was that he had the good fortune of being able to call the tribal chairman "uncle." Fortune that got him his good job and access to the suites.

Fox dodged Anna's question. "It was around then that I started looking for help."

"Me," she said.

"Between my job, finding women, and cleaning up the suite . . . it was too much. And I didn't know what I was doing anyway. I can't clean for shit. I needed someone who belonged. Someone who wouldn't raise suspicion."

"Someone who'd go unnoticed and keep her mouth shut."

"I misread you," he said.

"Maybe not," she conceded. "Not at first."

"You were my best bet. You came in right around when things started falling apart. I knew the deal was going to shit. I could feel it. Something inside me, though . . . wanted to save it."

"Greed?" Anna said.

He cast his eyes down at the table. "Suddenly Claude wasn't happy with the women I was getting him. He didn't just want *regular* women anymore."

"What do you mean *regular*?"

Fox shrugged. "Women like Tanya or your mom. Women who weren't in the habit of taking money to do what he wanted them to do. *Regular* turned into *younger*. Claude said it just like that. . . . He whispered it in my ear after I introduced him to a friend from the rez. '*Younger*.'" Fox looked longingly at the mangled cup. "Not like little kids," he said, as if that made what he and LeBlanc had done any more acceptable. "Just . . . young women."

"Let me guess," Anna said, thinking about Lula Broussard. "He paid you more?"

Fox nodded. "Fuck. I know it sounds stupid, but I didn't think of it as wrong. It was a feeling, I guess. I knew I wasn't supposed to be using the suite that way—"

"The *suite*?" Anna said. "It's not about the suite."

"Everything, Anna. I knew it wasn't right, but it didn't *feel* wrong. It's fucked up. Everyone was getting something out of it. No one was forced," he said again. "It was like we were all helping each other out. Like a secret club."

"I saw Missy in the stairwell. You can't honestly say she was helped."

Another vile breath wafted Anna's way. "Missy and I were both out of our fucking minds. Same habit. Same people. I knew she needed to score, so I made her the offer. I paid her up front and even got her on the payroll at the hotel. She was happy to take the money and the chambermaid uniform and the key to the suite. She even showed up on time."

"And Paul Albert? How'd he get involved with Missy and Claude LeBlanc?"

"Who the fuck's Paul Albert?"

"The fat man. I already told you."

He grunted. "He was just a customer."

"What do you mean?"

"Claude . . . he was running some sort of business and I didn't even know it."

"You mean . . . ?" Anna said, lost for words.

"Claude didn't really want the women . . . the girls . . . for himself. He always tried out the goods, as he put it, but he was just recruiting. He was looking for girls who would work for him . . . girls he could control. I didn't know that until after he showed up with . . . what'd you say his name is?"

"Paul Albert."

"Claude told me to call the fat fuck Bob. All I know about him is that Bob paid Claude and Claude paid me. Honestly, I didn't wanna know anything else at that point. I was balls deep in something I couldn't control."

"So you sent Missy up to the suite with those two men. Then what happened?"

Fox stalled again, and Anna worried that he might change his mind about talking now that they'd arrived at what might be the most devastating part of the story. "I didn't kill her," he finally said. "It was Claude." A rush of air came out of him, nearly a sob. "She's been in the field the whole time."

Anna swallowed hard. "How'd she get there?"

"Claude followed her from the hotel. I followed him. He was so upset. Furious. I had a feeling he was going to do something, I just . . . didn't know what."

Anna thought back to the CCTV footage. Missy had shuffled through the resort's parking lot and past the trees. Claude and Fox had left only a few minutes after her, each in their own vehicles, Fox speeding to keep up. "Why'd Claude follow her?"

"Because of what she did. . . ." He rubbed his eyes again. "Like I said, Claude wanted girls he could control. Missy agreed to meet with him and the other guy . . . Bob . . . for money, but Claude couldn't control her."

Anna remembered the wreck of a girl she'd seen in the emergency stairwell. Missy had seemed pretty damn governable in her intoxicated state.

"Things didn't go the way they were supposed to," Fox said. "Missy . . . she was fucked up when she got to the hotel. High on ice. That shit can turn mice into lions. Especially when they feel threatened. I've seen it before. I wasn't in the suite with them when it happened, but I guess Missy changed her mind about what she was supposed to do there. Maybe she didn't like Bob. All I know is she went crazy. Throwing shit. Spitting. Trying to claw their eyes out."

Anna recalled the mess she'd cleaned in suite 808 after encountering Missy in the stairwell.

"Claude was pissed . . . fucking fuming," Fox said. "Humiliated too. He was worried that she was going to say something to someone. You know, about what we were doing at the hotel. I begged him not to follow her. If I'd known what he was going to do . . ."

"What did he do?"

"He hit her." Fox gasped. "She was walking along the side of the road, and he just hit her. I don't think she even saw him coming. She was so small and so light, she went down like a rag doll. Didn't even leave a dent in his truck.

"I got out of my pickup screaming. I couldn't believe he'd done it. I never should've—"

"That's already been established," Anna said, cringing through the confession.

Fox pressed his palms to his eyes, pushing his head far back on his neck. "I picked her up. She wasn't dead, only injured. Her leg . . ." He used his fingers to demonstrate how bad her leg had been broken. "The bone was through the skin. I wrapped her in a blanket from my truck. I wanted to get her help, but Claude . . . he was sure she'd rat him out after that. It didn't matter what I said. His mind was made up. If I'd gone to Luke or—"

"Don't," Anna said.

He threw his hands in the air. Tears swelled in the corners of his eyes. "What can I do?"

"Stick to the truth."

"He said we had to get rid of her," Fox continued after a moment. "Like she was a piece of trash . . . an empty cup." He crushed the battered foam cup in his hand and hurled it at the wall. Another long pause followed before he admitted his part in silencing Missy forever. "I led Claude to the field . . . through the clearing. I didn't go with him into the brush. He wrangled Missy in on his own, using my blanket like a straitjacket around her. She wouldn't stop screaming. Wouldn't stop calling me to help." Fox held his ears, suggesting he could still hear her now. "The tall grass and the bushes . . . they thrashed and thrashed and thrashed. I just wanted it to stop. The screaming and the thrashing." His hands fell from his ears. "And then it did."

"Claude was covered with blood when he came back out. 'You're as guilty as I am,' he said. Told me that if I kept quiet, he would too.

"I was afraid, Anna. Everything I did after that was because I was afr—"

"No," she said. "You don't get to do that."

"Do what?"

"Turn yourself into a victim. Just tell me what happened."

Fox rubbed his left wrist, still red from the cuff that'd been around it. "I didn't hear from Claude for over a week after that. When he called again, he said he owed Bob a *good* girl. He told me to find someone new."

"A good gi—" Anna's voice caught in her throat. "Grace," she managed, knowing Fox had started grooming her well before Claude's call.

Fox slowly nodded. He rubbed his cheeks and chin. "I can't feel my fucking face," he said.

Anna wasn't about to let him reroute her train of thought. "Why'd you choose her?"

"I liked . . ." He closed his eyes and bit the inside of his left cheek. "I *like* your sister. A lot. She's a nice girl. Fun to be around."

"She's fifteen."

"We get along, all right? I see myself in her."

Anna could see it, too. Both Fox and Grace, so consumed by what others thought of them. Both wanting to present the world with the self-images they saw in their heads. Both willing to mask, suppress, and sacrifice their true selves to become what they thought they should be.

"Besides, Grace is always around," Fox went on. "At the arcade. The diner."

"The Ice Bar," Anna said.

Fox didn't respond to that.

"My sister doesn't do drugs." Anna hated her questioning tone.

"No," Fox agreed, "but she talked about that fucking cell phone day and night. I was going to get it for her . . . as part of her pay."

"Were the men"—she winced—"happy with my sister?"

". . . Yes."

"There weren't any . . . problems?"

"No."

"Then why is she gone?"

Fox swallowed hard. "I don't know. Maybe Claude followed her too."

"Is she dead?" Holding her voice steady to ask that question required every ounce of Anna's strength.

Fox splayed his hands on the tabletop. Tears dampened his eyelashes. "I don't think so. But I don't know where she is. I'm *not* lying about that."

"You think he took her somewhere?"

"I don't know, Anna."

"How do we find him?"

Fox's shoulders heaved. "We don't. I told you, he was very careful to make himself invisible. It was his show. Everything was the way he wanted it. He has my number. I've never had his. When he wanted the suite, he'd call . . . always a blocked number . . . he wouldn't even leave messages on my answering machine. The fucker was too smart for that. I don't think he ever told me the truth about anything. Not his intentions, not his background, not even his real fucking name. I'll be damned if he's really a lawyer. And his reason for having me arrange the suite so that he wouldn't have to reserve it himself . . . because he was afraid his wife would find out. All bullshit. He wasn't afraid of anyone. Probably isn't even married. He could be anywhere. Alexandria. Lafayette. Baton Rouge. New Orleans. Believe me, Anna, I wish I knew where he was right now. I'd go knock the shit out of him and drag him back here myself."

"Claude LeBlanc," Anna muttered. Panic swelled within her. "We'll never find him." The tribal police force was too small to launch an intensive search. Without outside help, they had little hope of tracking LeBlanc down, which meant LeBlanc had little to worry about. "Paul Albert," Anna said. "The guy you knew as Bob. What happened to him?"

Fox tried to swallow. He looked like he might choke, like his own Adam's apple had lodged in his throat. "I need water." He gasped.

Anna got up and filled two cups from the water cooler. Fox drank slowly. His cup trembled in his hand.

"Claude called," Fox said, lower lip quivering. "He was in a panic. Irate. He said Bob had seen one of the posters in town with their faces on it. And even though Claude assured him that no one would be able to make out the grainy images taken from the CCTV footage, Bob said he didn't care about that. He said he cared about the missing girls. Fucked up, isn't it? He had no problem using them for his own pleasure, but as soon as he was suspected of making them disappear, he suddenly grew a fucking conscience . . . or maybe he just wanted to make sure he wouldn't be blamed. Claude said Bob was headed to the tribal police station to speak with Luke. He was going to tell Luke everything he knew about what Claude was doing at the hotel. Claude wasn't having it. He wanted Bob stopped. I was the only one who could intercept him in time."

"You killed him," Anna said, thinking about the missing-person poster Luke found on Paul Albert's body.

"I wish to God that I hadn't. Claude was so worked up that it seemed like there wasn't any other option. He said we'd both go down if Bob talked. There wasn't any time to think. I had minutes to get in my truck . . . to make up my mind. Maybe if I'd had an hour . . ." Fox cut his excuse short upon seeing the disapproval in Anna's eyes. Despite his tears, he sat straighter, the weight of his awful secret off his shoulders. "I blocked Bob in the road with my truck when I saw him coming. He had no choice but to stop." Fox swallowed hard again. "I hit him in the head when he opened his car door . . . hit him with a dumbbell. I thought one swing would be enough, but he stumbled from the car, pouring blood from a crack in his skull all the way across the road. I hit him again and that did it. I hauled him into the bed of my pickup and drove him to the field. It was so fast, so easy. Afterward . . . that's another story. I didn't sleep a single second last night, Anna."

"You don't deserve to sleep."

"When I saw you run into the field tonight, I panicked. I thought if I burned everything I might have a shot at . . ." Fox didn't finish his thought, and Anna hardly noticed. Two others, equally as important as Missy and Grace, remained on her mind.

"Amber and Erica?" she said. "They're not in L.A., are they?"

Excruciating silence took hold and then Fox wailed. He punched the tabletop so hard his knuckles bled. "They left the hotel! I *swear* they did. With money I'd given them. A lot of it. I had no reason to think that they hadn't gone to L.A. until . . . God, I still want to believe they're there."

Gone like Grace, Anna thought, pondering the one big question she had left. What was Paul Albert doing on the rez the night she'd changed his flat tire—the night Grace disappeared? He'd said he'd gotten lost and missed the signs for the casino, but that wasn't true. He'd already been to the resort the night Missy went missing. Anna remembered what her father had said to Luke on the phone earlier, that he'd seen people from town driving around the rez, gawking at tribal members and their homes. She supposed Paul Albert could have been doing just that. Maybe he'd been too early or a bit too eager, forcing him to kill time in his car before meeting Fox, LeBlanc, and Grace in suite 808. As the CCTV footage had shown, he was the first to enter the suite.

"I asked him about her," Fox said, stealing Anna from her thoughts. "When Claude called to tell me that Bob had to be stopped, I asked if Grace was all right."

"What'd he say?"

Fox's shoulders slumped even more. "He said . . ." A long pause ensued. "He said, 'Don't ask questions, Fox.' He always used to say that to me."

Anna pushed her chair backward and stood.

"I don't think she's dead, Anna," Fox said, looking up at her through bloodshot eyes. "Someone will find her."

The assurance didn't comfort her the way it might have had it come from someone else. If Grace was alive, it meant she was condemned, either rolling for revenge or being used by strange men. Neither alternative offered Anna any peace. "You hurt me," she said. "And you helped me."

"Anna?" He said her name again and again as she walked toward the door. "I told you all this because I wronged you. But that's not the only reason. I told you because I've seen your strength . . . the way you came at me the minute Grace went missing. You weren't afraid. Not one bit. You . . . you take action. You know what to do. You'll help us heal . . . maybe even me. I'm sorry, Anna."

Anna, however, wasn't sorry. Not for all of it. Knowing now what she had to do, not just for herself but the tribe at large, she closed the door behind her and found Sam leaning against the wall in the hall. "You were listening?" she asked.

"Heard every word. Come on," he said, escorting her from the station. "I'll give you a ride home." Anna went outside with him but only to collect the rifle from his car on her way to the road. She staggered into the darkness with her head tilted far back on her neck, her eyes searching the sky for a sign of Grace.

The tall metal gate standing sentry over the narrow dirt path hung open. Anna grabbed hold of the black bars and peered in at the old stones, like crooked teeth jutting out of the earth. The wind gusted against her face, urging her to turn and head back home, to see if she could finally sleep.

She'd been up all night. Fox's confession had replayed in her mind, but it wasn't just that which had filled her thoughts through the dark hours. She'd lamented the missing—Amber, Erica, Grace—while puzzling over a plan she hoped would prevent others from suffering. If she really was what Gran had implied when she'd shared the story about the basket and bow, then Anna knew it was up to her to see to it that no other Takoda woman or girl was ripped away, whether it be by someone from afar or someone who also called the reservation home—unfortunately, she knew that some predators looked all too familiar.

She didn't just want to safeguard the tribe, she owed it to Miss Shelby, whose faded memorial mural on the rear exterior wall of the Blue Gator Grill deserved a fresh coat of paint to revitalize the words—NEVER FORGOTTEN—emblazoned above her portrait. Anna couldn't let the abuse of women and girls continue. Nor could she allow the others on the reservation to forget the tragedies they'd endured, no matter how much time might pass. Remembering and remaining aware would be the first steps toward making it stop.

The wind gusted again, stronger than before. "No," she said to it, pushing forth along the dirt path. A heavyset older woman stood leaning against a cane among the graves. She waved to Anna with a feather in her hand and Anna waved back.

Noise came from the toolshed on the outskirts of the tribal cemetery: metal clanging against metal and curse-laden outbursts. Uncle Ray was inside, hunched over the open hood of a riding lawnmower that'd seen better days. Cracked and callused hands tinkered with one of its parts, while he swore beneath his breath in between outbursts. Anna called to him. He swore louder upon hitting his head on the underside of the mower's hood as he jolted upright. The impact sent vibrations through the shed that caused a rake propped against the rear of the mower to topple over.

"Anna," he said, face twisted. The scraggly beard he once proudly wore was gone, replaced by salt-and-pepper stubble that matched the gray at his temples, cropped close to his scalp. They stared at each other, awkward, neither knowing what to say. Dirt and grease shone black on his fingertips. He inadvertently smeared some of the mixture on his face upon scratching his brow.

"Didn't mean to . . ." Anna said, motioning to his head.

Ray sidled next to her in the doorway of the shed. Still skinny, a slight belly was starting to show. His dirty hands hung at his sides, and his face remained twisted. "I know I should have come by. I've been meaning to." His words came fast, betraying his unease. "I'm not good at this kind of stuff. Like with Ma . . . I can't even look at her like that."

"She's doing better," Anna said, recognizing that he used denial as a defense just as she once used silence.

Ray brushed bits of dry grass from his thighs with his knuckles. A tarnished chain still hung from his right side, keeping his wallet safe. "I've been thinking about Grace. Looking for her too." He fixated on a glob of grease clinging to his left wrist. He poked at it, spreading it, making the mess worse.

Anna stepped deeper inside the shed. "What's wrong with it?" she asked, jerking her head toward the mower.

Ray answered in no time at all. "Damn thing won't start. It's not the starter. I already tested that."

"Bad spark plug maybe," Anna said.

"Just swapped it out." He wiped his hands on a hanky he pulled from his pocket, then walked to the mower and cranked the ignition. It spluttered but didn't catch.

"Probably the carburetor," Anna said. She pushed forward, past Uncle Ray, and detached the fuel line. Having grabbed some tools, she removed the screws and the nuts that held the carburetor in place, then detached the bolt from the bowl to see inside the carb. "There's your problem," she said. It was grimy inside. "Old fuel clogs it up."

"How do you know so much?"

"Mark Bishop," she said, and searched a nearby shelf for a bottle of fuel-system cleaner. She sprayed the carburetor with it, then used a rag she found on the floor to wipe it clean. After putting the pieces back together, she signaled Ray to try the ignition. It sputtered, then caught, ultimately roaring to life.

Ray climbed into the mower's seat and rode it out of the shed. Leaving it running, he hopped down to face Anna once more. "You look like hell, kid." His voice quavered. "Do me a favor and tell your dad I'll be by soon."

"I didn't come here to talk about Grace," she said.

Ray gave a shallow nod. "You didn't come to clean my carburetor either."

"I came to see Chief Hilaire's grave."

Ray's expression became puzzled.

"I could try to find it myself." Anna peered out of the shed at the great expanse of the tribal cemetery. "But that could take hours, and I'm drained as it is."

"Is this really . . . ?" he started, then shook his head and hitched up his filthy Wranglers. "Follow me."

He led her across the well-manicured lawn, so much different than the overgrown grass in the fields and along the roadsides. The grave markers changed in appearance the deeper they ventured into the cemetery. The modern ones were rectangular and flush with the ground. The older ones struggled to stay upright. A few dozen of the markers had been erected on the same day two years earlier; not because a catastrophe had ended numerous lives at once, but because they'd been placed to honor the cemetery's oldest graves, dating back to the 1700s. Those markers didn't bear names, just simple descriptions like TAKODA WARRIOR, TAKODA WOMAN, and TAKODA MAN.

"Did you really find the unearthed graves?" Anna asked.

Ray scratched his brow again, smearing the grease he'd deposited earlier. "Jeez, Anna, that was ten years ago."

"When I was seven, you told me you found three graves that'd been dug up."

"Yeah, I did."

"You told me about the bones too."

Ray didn't say anything. He just kept on scratching.

"You said some were missing from the graves. Stolen."

"I don't remember everything I said." He chuckled. "I probably shouldn't have . . . There." He pointed at a grave a few feet ahead. The rectangular headstone protruding from the ground had just three things engraved upon it: a name, a date of birth, and a date of death. Grass covered the small swatch of earth before the headstone. All damage done to it ten years earlier had been obliterated by time.

"Were they ever found?" Anna asked.

"Huh?" Ray hung back as Anna took a few steps closer.

"The missing bones. Were they ever recovered?"

Ray shrugged. "Some of them were. I think. You'd be better off asking Luke or Sam about that."

Anna's spine tingled. She had little doubt that Chief Hilaire's remains were without a skull beneath her. She envisioned the scene the way Uncle Ray had described it when he told her what he'd found. A single track, roughly six inches wide, made by something like a tire without any tread. It'd gone around the grave and then through the cemetery, ultimately vanishing in the brush of the nearest field, never to return.

"You'd meant to scare me, right?"

"Scare you?"

"With the story you told."

He was silent, thinking.

"The chief's skull. His head!" Anna reeled around to face him, to remind him of what he'd said. "You told me it was revived when it was lifted from its grave. You said it devoured the culprit that had dug it up and that it was so full of fury after being disturbed that it kept on rolling. You said it'd devour anyone on the reservation. Anyone it wanted."

A self-conscious smirk skewed Ray's lips. "Sounds like something I'd say."

"It isn't true?"

"Anna . . . I thought you knew. You were little, but I didn't think—"

"It changed me," she said.

"I'm sorry," Ray replied after a moment.

"You don't have to be." Ray's story had frightened Anna, but it had also led her to take all the other stories so seriously. She and Miss Shelby, it seemed, found more value in the traditional tales than anyone else on the reservation. To her, they'd never just been stories. They were life. Veracity. Reflections of the world around them.

"Why are you bringing this up, Anna?"

"Where'd you hear about the rolling head?"

"I . . ." He shrugged. "I probably made it up."

"Made it up, or made it your own?"

"Anna . . ." He was confused, brushing bits of dried grass from his arms and chest this time.

"There's a story about a rolling head. An old Takoda tale. About two sisters. Did you change the story?"

Ray could undoubtedly see that she desperately wanted him to admit to altering the tale. "I guess I might have," he said. "There's so many versions of those stories, you never know—"

"She could still be on the rez," Anna said. Not a single star had winked at her on her walk home from the tribal police station the night before.

"Grace?" Ray questioned.

Anna envisioned the round form that had led her to Missy's body. "It could be her," she said, whispering, still wanting to believe.

EPILOGUE

Today there stands a nation. And in that nation there are mothers and there are daughters, there are aunts, nieces, and cousins. And always there are sisters, linked by love that knows no bounds.

In this nation there is also pain produced by an evil that came to steal its sisters away.

The older sister of one who'd been stolen promised to find her. She traveled near and far, always looking, always search-ing. "I will find you," she'd say to the elusive spirit of her younger sister. "I will search until I am old as Turtle and frail like dry grass."

Everywhere she went, she asked if her sister had been seen. Always the answer was the same, spurring her on. Hold-ing out hope, she implored the Great Spirit. She implored God. Neither led her younger sister home. She feared neither ever would.

Her younger sister and the evil that had stolen her away became like ghosts to the older sister. They haunted her in different ways, both ever present yet impossible to snare.

"Where are you?" the older sister would ask. "How are you?"

The possible answers to those questions paralyzed the older sister, they froze her heart while spawning shock and grief that settled inside her like tumors or cysts. The daily disquiet took its toll on her mind, her disposition, her sleep. But for all the harm it did to her health, it couldn't destroy her drive to make things better.

Anna looked up from her notebook, rereading the words she'd written as she walked.

Though she'd gotten herself a car after her eighteenth birthday, she still preferred to walk about the reservation. From her mother's place to her father's, to the resort and the Mire trailer, her eyes inevitably searching for something rolling around her, examining the fields as if she'd missed something the week, month, or year before, still eager to lead the head to the hole she'd dug. Only an occasional green-and-purple splotch on the shiny black asphalt could divert her gaze. Sometimes she'd find the remains of a snake or a turtle, but flattened frogs still outnumbered everything else. Sometimes she'd scrape their little bodies to the side of the road. Sometimes they were too damaged to move. Always she wondered if they were meant to be there, aligned for death.

Notebook at her side, her eyes no longer searching, Anna came upon the community center, its lot loaded with cars. The sounds of rumbling machinery came from across the way. The construction crew wasn't paving streets anymore. There was a new crew now, laying the foundation for something that just might heal the tribe.

Anna had voiced a proposal to the tribal council two months after Missy's funeral. The response was unanimous: a preservation society would serve the tribe well. What she'd proposed, though, went well beyond preserving the old stories and beliefs that had so heavily influenced tribal predecessors. Soon there'd be a museum to safeguard and exhibit old tools, pottery, clothing, European trade items, weapons, and other ancient artifacts that had been wasting away. There'd be an educational center as well, where tribal members and the public would be able to learn about the Takoda's storied past.

The preservation society and educational center, however, were only a small part of Anna's full proposal. Her vision involved more than just preserving the past; it was about protecting the present and all it possessed before anyone else was lost forever. Finally able to see herself for who she was, she'd persuaded the tribal council that the next enterprise on the rez need not be one that filled their pockets, but one that united families and mended broken hearts. Not a gas station or a waterpark, but a complex that would house the cultural and educational centers in addition to an extensive offering of healing resources. Among them would be a drug and alcohol addiction treatment center, counseling and therapy services, financial advisement, life planning, and a crisis facility. As one, the Takoda Cultural, Educational, and Resource Center would honor them all. It would be a place that would remind tourists and tribal members alike of who the Takoda people were, where they came from, and where they were headed.

Anna watched the crew work, as she had every day since the workers broke ground. Sacrificing another field had been bittersweet, but only because Anna knew that it was worth it this time. Her active role was as an advisor on the project, and she intended on being the resource center's greatest voice once construction was complete. She knew she couldn't make her Takoda brothers and sisters take advantage of the center's offerings, but she'd damn well make sure they knew the offerings were available. The tribal elders, Gran included, didn't want Anna's vision to be lost. They told her she could mend the tribe, that she could unite them in a way they hadn't been united before. Some even encouraged her to run for a seat on the tribal council during the upcoming election. She promised to give it thought in the future. Maybe she'd become the tribe's first chairwoman.

Turning away from the construction site, Anna, wearing an atypical smile, hustled to the community center's door and went inside.

Summer Langdon, who worked the front desk, looked up from the book she was reading and waved. Anna waved back, her smile spreading. The old storage room was at the end of the hall. For now it was Anna's, the preservation society's temporary home. Anna always felt a sense of purpose when she walked into that little room, which she kept at sixty-five degrees. It was a feeling far different than anything she'd ever felt darting from classroom to classroom at school.

The handwritten books she'd collected from Miss Shelby's trailer sat in acid-free boxes, protected from light and dust. The fan of a free-standing dehumidifier whirred, ensuring the humidity level never crept above 40 percent. Eventually the books would be displayed in their own climate-controlled glass cases, on display for all to see as significant relics of the Takoda's past.

Until then, the books were hers, and the tales within reminded her of what she was and what she needed to be. Defensive as Porcupine when she puts up her quills to guard against the evils of the world. Comforting as Grasshopper when he hops by to say hello. Cautious and reverent as Father Owl, who hoots to warn of danger and mourns throughout the long night for those who have suffered. A healer like Dragonfly, who follows Snake to stitch him up when he comes to harm. A disciplinarian like Mother Wolf, who snaps at her cubs. A teacher as wise as Turtle, old as the earth and nearly as round. A leader like Brother Eagle, who flies high in situations where others might fall. A fighter like Rattlesnake, who stands up to his enemies and sometimes seeks revenge. And open to change, like Frog, who lives in many forms.

The paper crown, which Grace had encouraged Anna to claim, sat askew atop the acid-free book boxes. Megan Bradley had brought it to Anna a few days after Missy's funeral, along with an apology and an offer to make amends, both of which Anna accepted as readily as she accepted the crown, understanding now that the teasing and assumptions made about her at school were vicious mistakes, misunderstandings about her by unwise adolescents who couldn't see how inimitable she was. Though that fact didn't excuse how they'd treated her, realizing it soothed her soul.

She set her notebook aside and ran two fingers along the bead bracelet tied to her wrist, something she subconsciously did ten, twenty, or one hundred times a day, then realigned the crown atop the boxes as a knock sounded against the door. Summer Langdon poked her head inside. "A package just arrived. It's for you," she said.

Anna collected the parcel and cut through the tape. She unwrapped the plaque that'd been sealed inside. "What do you think?" she asked, holding the plaque aloft, but it wasn't Summer's opinion she wanted.

Grace looked up from the interior design catalog she'd been browsing, excited to help Anna design and decorate the new complex. She squinted at the plaque, reading the words etched into the metal. "It's beautiful, Anna. It's gonna make me cry."

Scars on her face, her hands, her legs, and all the places she kept covered by clothes, Grace knew how lucky she was to be alive. And Anna knew how lucky she was to have her sister by her side. Grace had been gone for 379 long days when the unlikely call came through. Anna remembered every second of it.

Having run from the shower to get to the phone in time, she'd clung to the towel around her.

Anna? Grace had whispered, the voice of the dead.

Anna pressed the phone tight to her ear, disbelieving. *Is it really you?* she'd said.

I'm cold, Anna, Grace had cried. *I'm so cold.*

Battered and barely clothed, she'd come to on the side of a desolate road 1,1076 miles from the reservation. Pushed from a car, bloody and blindfolded, no longer of any use. She didn't know where she was or where she'd been. She only knew that she'd never been so cold. It was the first time she'd seen snow.

Chris, Dorothy, Robbie, and Anna touched down in Cleveland less than eight hours later. If their tears had been superglue, they'd still be stuck to Grace. None of them had wanted to let her go. The road to recovery was one they'd be on for months or even years to come, but it was the second chance Anna had prayed for, a chance that went against all odds.

"I feel guilty sometimes," Grace said. She was back in school but worked alongside Anna on the weekends when they weren't off at the movies or leaving tire marks on the new asphalt as Anna helped Grace learn to drive. "It doesn't seem fair, does it? That I get to be here and they don't."

"Never feel guilty for being where you belong," Anna said.

"Where I belong," Grace echoed, her eyes scanning the reservation outside the storage room's small window. She hadn't seen Amber or Erica while she'd been away, but she'd seen other girls, traded and sold, robbed of their dignity, their sovereignty, and their right to say yes or no.

Anna turned the plaque toward herself. It'd hang in the resource center once construction was complete. The words engraved upon its surface read:

For
Shelby Mire
Amber Bloom
Erica Landry
Missy Picote
and every Native woman
who hasn't made it home

Anna had nearly included Grace's name on the plaque when she'd placed the order, fearing Grace would forever be among the thousands of Native women and girls stolen from their families.

Grace dabbed her eyes and closed the catalog. "Come on," she said. "We're going to be late."

Anna grabbed her notebook, and together they walked down the hall to the large meeting room where their tribe was waiting to officially welcome Grace back home.

"You go ahead, I'll just be a minute," Anna said. There'd be music and dancing, food, and infinite hugs within the meeting room, but there was something Anna had to finish first. She waited until Grace was inside, then cracked the notebook open and pulled a pencil from the bib of her overalls. A small smile on her face, she wrote:

The return of the younger sister warmed the older sister's heart, but still it hasn't thawed. Nor will it. Not until every woman and girl—sisters that now constitute a tribe of their own, a lost nation—is back where she belongs.

Those women and girls may be gone, unvalued, and abused, but their stories won't be forgotten. Their stories will live on inside the older sister and all the others who will never stop searching.

Every morning they'll turn over another stone. Every afternoon they'll search another town. Every evening they'll ask another stranger if their loved one's photo looks familiar. And every night they'll look up at the sky with worry in their eyes, asking the same question the older sister had asked the stars while she waited, and waited.

"Do you see me?"

Author's Note

The crisis faced by the Horn family isn't one that I created—this story, rather, was created by the crisis. On September 16, 2018, I came across an article published in the *Chicago Tribune*, written by Sharon Cohen from the Associated Press. The headline: "Epidemic hits Native Americans." The subheading: "No one knows how many girls, women missing or murdered."

Cohen wrote about twenty-year-old Ashley HeavyRunner Loring, who went missing from the Blackfeet Reservation in mid-2017. Ashley's sister, Kimberly Loring, who'd been searching since day one, was quoted. "I don't want to search until I'm 80," she said. "But if I have to, I will."

Kimberly is one of thousands searching for lost loved ones. Records from the National Crime Information Center (NCIC) indicate that more than 5,200 Indigenous women and girls were missing as of 2021. The actual number of missing women and girls, however, could be much higher.

And it's not only abduction with which Indigenous women and girls are forced to contend. The NCIC also found that in some counties, Indigenous women face a murder rate that's more than ten times the national average. Other studies indicate that Native women are likely to suffer physical and sexual assault at a rate higher than—and disproportionate to—the national average.

As described in this book, complicated jurisdictional issues, along with a lack of funding and investigative resources, often play a role in why so many of these crimes get little or no attention. Bias and racism, no doubt, play a part as well.

In the earliest versions of this story, Grace didn't get to come home. I didn't think she should because I didn't think it would be fair. Gone *forever* is the reality many families face. It's the reality many are working to change.

Over the last several years, the steadfast family members—who make T-shirts, websites, and signs, and who dedicate their lives to searching, protesting, marching, and pleading in honor of their stolen sisters—have called attention to this crisis.

May 5 is now Missing or Murdered Indigenous Persons Awareness Day. Savanna's Act, signed into law in 2020, requires the U.S. Department of Justice to establish better protocols and practices to track, solve, and prevent these crimes, among other things. The Not Invisible Act, also signed in 2020, increases intergovernmental coordination by directing the Department of the Interior and the Department of Justice to establish a joint commission on violent crime within and against the Native community. And, in 2021, we saw the formation of the Missing and Murdered Unit, aimed at investigating and solving the murders of Indigenous peoples.

Clearly, this crisis widely impacts many Native nations throughout the United States (and Canada, too), and that's one reason why I chose to write about a fictional tribe. As a member of the Tunica-Biloxi Nation, I was influenced by what I've seen and experienced, but the Takoda Nation is not based on a single Native culture. Rather, it's a unification of Native stories, traditions, and beliefs. Inspiration for the rolling head, which is known to many Midwestern tribes, came from Wintu and Cheyenne legends. "The Tale of Two Sisters" was also inspired by a Wintu tale. The basket and bow ceremony comes from the Great Basin Tribes, including the Western Shoshone, the Goshute, the Ute, the Paiute, and the Washoe. The story Anna tells about the armadillo stuck in a tree is based on another Cheyenne legend. The Blackfoot Tribe's stories of Old Man and Old Woman inspired the story about death and stars in the sky, and the Takoda's origin story comes from a Tunica tale about a red and a blue alligator. The words "tamahka" and "heni" come from the Tunica as well.

Each tribe, of course, has its own history, language, and customs, and yet there's no denying that Indian Country is linked by strong—sometimes mysterious—similarities, such as spiritual beliefs, reverence for nature, and the will to remain respected and seen, things the Takoda exemplify in one way or another.

The name "Takoda," in fact, comes from the Sioux, and it means "friend to all." While I must stress that the scenarios depicted within the Takoda Tribe are not representative of every tribe's experience, I do hope that the Takoda will reinforce the interconnectedness of Native Nations while addressing challenges and injustices many tribes endure.

Among those injustices is the one faced by Two Spirits. Though the term "two spirit" was coined in 1990, Two Spirits have been recognized within hundreds of Native nations for hundreds of years. Neither male nor female, Two Spirited individuals are both and more, giving them a unique third gender status.

It's important to note that Two Spirits historically took on different responsibilities within their respective nations, though they were always honored and revered for their ability to take on and carry out the traditional roles of both men and women. From matchmaking to mediating, prognosticating, hunting, and beyond, Two Spirits were highly regarded within their tribes. Some tribes even believed that Two Spirits were born of supernatural intervention, making them shamans, healers, chiefs, and ceremonial leaders.

Condemned by colonizers—who objected to men who might have looked and acted more like women, and women who might have looked and acted more like men, and (perhaps worse in their eyes) what they perceived as same-sex relationships by Two Spirits who engaged with others of the same biological sex—Two Spirits were commonly subject to violence. They were silenced and shunned. Some still are.

While strongly associated with the LGBTQ community today (now often referred to as LGBTQ2S+), it'd be a mistake to assume that all Two Spirits identify as bisexual, gay, lesbian, or trans; their third gender doesn't indicate a sexual preference. Many Natives who identify as Two Spirit uphold the term to honor a part of history that was almost lost, while embracing freedoms of expression their ancestors were denied.

Some may wonder about Anna's sexuality. I've wondered about it, too. But to me, it never demanded more than a few lines within this story; lines that can lead you to your own conclusion, just as they've led me to mine.

Grace, Missy, Amber, Erica.

Common names representing thousands of women and girls. It's they—their names, their hopes, their dreams—who are important. I never wanted to lose sight of that. I hope you won't either. If you'd like to learn more about this issue, or if you'd like to help by getting involved, you can find a number of great resources online, including Native Hope (www.nativehope.org), the Coalition to Stop Violence Against Native Women (www.csvanw.org), MMIW USA (mmiwusa.org), and Native Women's Wilderness (www.nativewomenswilderness.org).

In the years since Ashley HeavyRunner Loring went missing, Kimberly Loring has spoken with senators, national reporters, and documentarians, gaining political traction for this critical issue by sharing her sister's story. She vowed to search until she's eighty.

She's still searching today.

Acknowledgments

My heartfelt thanks to . . .

Tanen Jones, author of *The Better Liar*, for being the first person to love this story, for choosing to mentor me (asking nothing in return), and for suggesting a specific ending. You gave so much to this book. It wouldn't be what it is without you. I'm incredibly grateful.

Amanda Orozco, for so passionately believing in this story, and for being everything and more that I need in an agent. From editing to inspiring and managing all other affairs, your talent and skill are never in doubt. I'm privileged to work with you.

Sareer Khader, for helping me see this story in a different way, for fueling ideas, and for knowing how to make good ideas great. Thanks for the brainstorming sessions, the guidance, and your brilliance as an editor. I look forward to doing it again.

The team at Berkley—including Ivan Held, Christine Ball, Jeanne-Marie Hudson, Claire Zion, Craig Burke, Jessica Plummer, Daniela Riedlova, Lauren Burnstein, Yazmine Hassan, Emily Osborne, Christine Legon, Megha Jain, Nancy Resnick, and copyeditor Courtney Vincento—for all the talent, skill, and hard work. I'm honored to be part of the Berkley family.

ACKNOWLEDGMENTS

Paolo Faso, for good vibes.

Keith Matuga, Matt Welsch, Missy Matuga, and Jenni Konstanty Coan, for *SS Beer Stain*, *X-Files* marathons, lucky numbers, and fake mustaches, but mostly for unconditional friendship.

Leo, for always talking books.

A.T., for being a constant source of support.

Dad, Lisa, and Matthew, for your love and encouragement.

Jovenae, Louie, Elliot, Danny, Miranda, Ruby, and Eric, for the greatest times, the best memories, and all the love.

Mom, for everything.

You, for reading.